Raves for the *Foreigner* series:

"Cherryh's gift for conjuring believable alien cultures is in full force here, and her characters . . . are brought to life with a sure and convincing hand." — *Publishers Weekly*

"A seriously probing, thoughtful, intelligent piece of work, with more insight in half a dozen pages than most authors manage in half a hundred." — *Kirkus*

"A large new Cherryh novel is always welcome . . . a return to the anthropological science fiction in which she has made such a name is a double pleasure . . . superlatively drawn aliens and characterization." — *Chicago Sun-Times*

"Her lucid storytelling conveys enough backstory to guide newcomers without boring longtime series followers. The characters are well drawn, and Cherryh's depiction of both human and alien cultures is riveting." — *Library Journal*

"My favorite science fiction series is C. J. Cherryh's *Foreigner* universe. Cherryh deftly balances alien psychology and human vanities in a character caught between being human and part of an alien race." — *The Denver Post*

"C. J. Cherryh's splendid *Foreigner* series remains at the top of my must-keep-up reading list after two decades." — *Locus*

"There is plenty of intrigue . . . [and] marvelous attention to detail that makes the culture of the atevi one of the most complex, multi-layered creations in science fiction. . . . The Foreigner series is about as good as it gets . . . so finely and densely wrought that you may end up dreaming of sable-skinned giants with gold eyes, and the silver spun delicacy of interstellar politics." — *SFSite*

C. J. CHERRYH

PEACEMAKER

A *Foreigner* Novel

DAW BOOKS, INC.
DONALD A. WOLLHEIM, FOUNDER
375 Hudson Street, New York, NY 10014

ELIZABETH R. WOLLHEIM
SHEILA E. GILBERT
PUBLISHERS
www.dawbooks.com

First Mass Market Printing, April 2015
1 2 3 4 5 6 7 8 9

DAW TRADEMARK REGISTERED
U.S. PAT. AND TM. OFF. AND FOREIGN COUNTRIES
—MARCA REGISTRADA
HECHO EN U.S.A.

PRINTED IN THE U.S.A.

To Jane. For the best of reasons.

Table of Contents

Prologue

By the charter of the Assassins' Guild, there are several requirements preceding a legal assassination. First comes the Filing of Intent. In this process, a Document of Intent is entered into the official state registry, stating the issue between the parties, so that there is a permanent record, sealed, ribboned, and kept in archive. Any answering document is similarly filed.

There must then be a public advisement of impending Guild Council action, and an opportunity for the Assassins' Guild Council to obtain depositions from both sides. Only after determining that there may exist adequate cause for a Filing, does the Guild Council debate the merits of the Filing, and consider the potential for remedy short of lethal action. This deliberation may, at the Council's sole discretion, entail testimony from Guild members employed by either or both sides of the debate as to whether there can be any settlement. And there may be yet another delay imposed while the Guild urges resolution short of action.

If all measures have failed to secure a legal resolution, the Filing is approved by Council vote, and there is a date set after which action is possible.

The Filing is published, and all parties are notified.

This affords an opportunity for the targeted party's bodyguard to take precautions, and a date and hour after which the complainant's bodyguard may initiate offensive action, entering whatever premises it needs to in order to reach their target.

In the case of lords or officials employing a permanent bodyguard, the bodyguard on either side will be in contact with the central Guild at all steps of the process. No advantage of information will be given to either side, but in the event an attacking or defending unit wishes to suspend action, they may contact the Guild and let the Guild mediate a solution mutually acceptable.

Generally in small cases, particularly involving property or divorce, approval is given by an office of the Council, without Council debate, but with the deposition of witnesses. Once the Filing is approved by this process, there is a time limit imposed, usually of ninety-nine days, after which all attempts to carry out an assassination must cease and the Filing is set aside.

In practice, the Guild wishes to avoid bloodshed among its own members, and Guild units may at any time ask a truce in which to advise their lord that their defense has failed and that he must cede whatever is at issue, since he and they will not otherwise survive.

The number of lords who have pressed a case against the advice of their own bodyguards is relatively small. A unit abandoning its lord or surrendering him to capture or death may be prosecuted, except if the lord has issued a false statement in the Filing or if the lord is judged to have been mentally or physically incapable of sound judgment. The latter escape clause has frequently been supported by relatives and servants.

In the case of a private citizen who has no regular bodyguard, a complainant must engage the services of the Assassins' Guild from the date of the Filing, and the case is heard by the Office of the Council. The defendant against the Filing must, on notification, either cede the case, if property or a divorce, or hire Assassins for his protection for the usual ninety-nine days—an expensive proposition for the ordinary citizen to maintain long term, hence a heavier burden of time for the complainant—but there are occasional *pro bono* Filings.

Lethal force in civil disputes is common in potential—but far less common in actuality. The Filing of Intent affords a cooling-off period, requires depositions and an official vote at some level acknowledging that a wrong exists, and it offers constant opportunities for Guild to secure a negotiated settlement.

A Filing of Intent is absolutely required before action may be taken against a person or institution, except in defense against an illicit attack. In that case, whatever force the defender can muster on the spot is legal. An attack is defined as a movement within arm's length of the defender, or the first use of a distance weapon or weapon of stealth such as poison.

It is absolutely forbidden for anyone *other* than a Guild Assassin to bring violence against a fellow citizen, except in defense of self, employer, household, clan property, or national treasure. A person who violates this law is outlawed, subject to lethal Guild action with no time limit.

In the event a person finds himself thus outlawed, he is permitted to surrender to the aiji's judgment, in consultation with the Guild.

Edward P. Wilson, Translator, ret., *The Assassins' Guild*, Emeritus Lecture Series #133, The University of Mospheira . . .

1

There were rules of operation for every guild—and in the case of the Assassins' Guild, the rules were literally a matter of life and death.

There were rules against collateral damage.

There were rules about specificity of the target. An assassination had to be announced a certain number of days in advance. And the target was limited to the individual named.

There were rules about protection of children and uninvolved parties, like neighbors, or guests.

There were rules forbidding aerial attack, explosive traps, and the use of wires where any other individual, including servants, might accidently run afoul of them.

And there were rules forbidding damage to property. An action was not supposed to happen, say, where it might damage artworks, national treasures, livestock, or a person's means of livelihood.

Well, they'd done *that,* a bit, this morning. There was bound to be complaint.

Bren Cameron closed the computer file. The last time he'd read Wilson's paper on the topic, he'd been on a plane bound across the straits to serve a new aiji in Shejidan. He'd been, in that long-ago meeting with the Secretary of State, handed his credentials, computer-printed. He'd been handed the official dictionary, containing all the words approved for him to use in communication with the atevi.

And with that, State had launched him, the youngest paidhi who'd ever held the office, as Wilson-paidhi's replacement.

He'd been excited by the appointment, scared to death of the responsibility—and completely unsure whether a novice in Wilson's job was going to survive the year—in the real sense of life and death—or even whether he might be met at the airport by some party that wasn't official, and he'd have no way on earth to know who he was really dealing with.

He'd studied the Ragi language for years. He was good at math, a requirement for the language study program. He'd qualified as a backup translator for the Department of State, intended to become one of those faceless individuals who sat in little cubicles parsing atevi publications for clues to policy and mining them for new words that *weren't* officially approved, but that ought to be known to other translators.

He'd landed at Shejidan airport on a sunny afternoon. He'd been met by two of the aiji's own black-uniformed bodyguard and escorted up into the Bujavid, the fortress on the hill that rose picturesquely above the red tiled roofs and maze-like streets of the capital. He'd been assigned living quarters, a modest suite in the servants' wing.

Then he'd been handed a small ring with three keys, and had had only enough time to toss his bag into the room before his escort had led him on a confusing route to a barren office roughly three meters by three.

The office supplies, on otherwise vacant shelves, had consisted of a packet of copying paper, a packet of fine paper, three well-used pens—computers were not part of the technology surrendered to atevi at that point—and three somewhat worn message cylinders. On that small desk had stood a bottle of ink, a bundle of reeds, a pen-rest, a shaker of sand, and a waxjack for the seals he'd create with the resized seal ring he'd worn back to the mainland. It was Wilson's ring, surrendered along with the office.

He still wore it. And used it.

He'd had no clue on that day even how to use the waxjack. Left to his own devices, he'd found the lighter beside the device, lit the wick, and discovered that its whole function was to melt white wax from a winding coil on its baroque stand and drip it—he'd hastily inserted a piece of paper to prevent a wax spatter on the brass plate below—into a small, nicely unstained white puddle on a document. One adjusted the flame to prevent the wax collecting soot.

That, indeed, was what it did. It was the finest instrument in the little office. In point of fact, it was the *only* instrument in the little office, except a penknife to sharpen reed pens—literally, to shape pens out of the little bundle of reeds, a species that grew to a natural size, of a certain toughness, and that actually made Ragi calligraphy rather easier, once one got the knack.

He'd made his first impression with his ring of office on a letter to Tabini-aiji officially reporting his presence, his satisfaction with the arrangements, and his hopes for a good relationship between atevi and humans. He'd put his rolled letter into one of the little message cylinders, the nicest. And there he'd sat—Bren Cameron, from the human enclave on the island of Mospheira, on the Earth of the atevi, the sole human allowed to set foot on the mainland—wondering how he was going to get his letter delivered.

He had become staff to Tabini-aiji, the young ruler of the Western Association, the aishidi'tat, which for complicated historical reasons amounted to the rest of the planet. The wax that would bear his seal imprint was white, like the ribbon that would tie his—at that time—very short queue.

White was the heraldic color of the paidhi-aiji—a neutral party, the translator who conveyed messages between the atevi world and the human population who'd dropped, unasked, onto their planet.

All of Mospheira lived on the tolerance of the atevi. And

the last decade or so, after a period of progress, had been a particularly anxious time—first the unexpected death of Valasi-aiji, then the rule of the aiji-regent, Ilisidi, Valasi's mother. Ilisidi had ceased meeting with Wilson-paidhi, who described negotiations with her as like talking to a stone statue.

Then Valasi's son, Tabini, had come of age, demanding the legislature elect him aiji and set aside the aiji-regent. And among his first acts in that office, Tabini had indicated to Wilson that he should go back to Mospheira and not come back.

Wilson's word for Tabini had been— *dangerous*.

Bren had had that warning. He'd read Wilson's notes.

He'd come into his office as a babe in the woods, no older in years than Tabini-aiji, and dropped into a very different life, a foreign world to which he was obliged to conform, right down to the clothes he was wearing and the ribbon that had barely enough braid to pin to.

He'd learned a lot over the years. He'd changed . . . oh, a great deal.

He sat here now on a regular train, in company with his own bodyguard, the four closest people in the world to him— towering, black-skinned, black-haired, black-uniformed. The only color about them was the deep, burning gold of their eyes.

And he loved them—*loved* them, although that had been one of the words not only missing from that early dictionary—but forever missing from the entire atevi mindset. Atevi didn't love. Everybody on Mospheira knew that. They didn't love and they didn't have friends.

But atevi had man'chi, which in the case of these four, and their Guild, meant everything. They were *his*. They'd walk through fire for him. And he loved them for it.

They, of course, still thought that love was for salads and man'chi was for people you'd die for.

That slightly mismatched feeling wasn't supposed to go both ways, either, but it did.

They'd damned near died for him this morning, and Banichi had one hand supported in a half-zipped jacket because he was too damned stubborn to wear a sling. "I can still use it," was Banichi's answer, and Banichi's partner Jago and teammates Tano and Algini simply shrugged off their unit-senior's hard-headedness as drug-induced, and watched out for him.

More than physical, that wound. Banichi had taken down a former teammate this morning—an enemy, an old relationship with a bitter history. Banichi was on painkillers and around the clock without sleep. He was finally getting a little on the train. So were his three teammates.

Banichi's team hadn't asked Banichi any deep questions on the matter, not that Bren had heard. Not even Jago had asked, and *she* happened to be Banichi's daughter—a fact it had taken Bren years to learn, and that no one within the unit ever acknowledged.

Most in this very ordinary train car were black-uniformed Guild, and most were taking the chance to catch a little sleep: Bren's own four-person bodyguard, Ilisidi's, and the elder bodyguard of Lord Tatiseigi of the Atageini—all, all had nodded off.

Ilisidi was sleeping in her own way, fully and formally dressed in many-buttoned black lace, with her cane somewhat before her and her hands on it—she at least had her eyes shut, and one was not always sure whether she really was asleep. The dowager admitted nothing about her age, but it was considerable. Lord Tatiseigi, beside her, attempted to stay awake, but he, of Ilisidi's generation, was giving way, too. The youngsters at the other end of the car—Cajeiri and his three young guests—human youngsters, all just under or over the age of ten—were all collapsed. Cajeiri's young bodyguard was cat-napping by turns, that unit stubbornly staying on duty in the presence of so many exhausted senior units.

Jase Graham, in the seat across from Bren's, was dead to the world. His two bodyguards, Kaplan and Polano, were up forward in the next car, with their five detainees, who would not be enjoying the trip in the least.

Jase was one of the four ship-captains—and another of Cajeiri's birthday guests. At least Jase had come down to the world *with* the human youngsters. But he'd actually come down, Bren was increasingly sure, because Lord Geigi, atevi master of half the space station, had gotten a briefing that had very much alarmed him.

Bren tapped computer keys with a code that had to be input, or certain stored data would vanish, and certain hidden files would, at very great inconvenience, expand and install themselves instead.

The file Bren called up now was simply titled: *For my successor: Read this.*

There were several sections to the file that came up: codes, notes on various topics, dossiers on numerous people, who to contact first and second. He double-checked that list in consideration of recent events, and of who was advantageously located at the moment, with the legislature in session. He kept the index of the collection sparse, and frequently updated. If a successor took over in a moment of crisis, that paidhi would need certain information fast. He had duplicated these essential files in Ragi and in Mosphei', since he had no idea in what language his successor might be more fluent. Both, he hoped. Both, would be good.

But there were longer sections that followed his emergency notes, because some things weren't just lists of names. Some things had to be understood in sequence ... and ideally in Ragi, from the Ragi point of view.

There was, notably, a new section he had, over recent days, rated important enough to include in the handbook.

He'd gotten a lengthy and very secret file from Lord Geigi of Kajiminda, the day before Geigi had left for the station. Geigi himself figured in the account ... in the third person. Geigi was far too modest, and far too generous, and definitely underplayed his own importance in events.

"Understand, it is not formally written. It is only a private memoir, very private, and far too blunt. I have not been discreet or courteous, nor even used the honorifics of very great people I would by no means offend. Were it to fall into any hands but yours in this state, I would resign in mortification. But some record needs to be made, by someone who knows things no one of this age will admit."

"One perfectly understands."

"You play some part in it. Please fill in anything missing. Correct my misapprehensions of human understanding: that is the important thing. And next time we meet in person, Bren-ji, I shall be very glad to receive your notes to add to mine."

Geigi had added then, somewhat diffidently, "I may someday, in my spare time, put all these notes into order. I have even thought I might write a book—though one far, far more careful of reputations and proprieties. I would hold your view of events very valuable. I know where I transgress regarding my own customs; but if I violate yours, please advise me."

It was a remarkable, a revealing narrative—scandalously blunt, by atevi standards. He profoundly trusted Geigi— and it was in an amazing amount of trust that Geigi wanted him to read it. He had taken it with him in the thought that a vacation would give him time to add the promised notes from a human perspective. And he had done a little of that writing, before the vacation had turned out to be other than a vacation.

Today . . . today definitely had not been.

But at the moment, almost as sleep-deprived as Banichi and unable to come down from the events of the morning, he wanted Geigi's comforting voice, the accent, the habitual wry understatement.

The occasional poetic bent.

His ally was safely in the heavens.

On Earth, after all the events Geigi's narrative described, things were not quite as stable.[1]

---

1. Geigi's narrative is appended: see the Table of Contents.

2

None of them were, in fact, supposed to be on this train. The train belonged to the northern districts of the aishidi'tat. It was bringing a few spare cars southward toward Shejidan. No one should be on board.

And they were *supposed* to be hosting the preliminaries for young Cajeiri's birthday party up north, in Atageini territory, at Lord Tatiseigi's Padi Valley estate, with Jase Graham and the three human children from the space station—Cajeiri's personal guests.

In uncommon haste, the aiji-dowager had swept up the entire birthday party and headed them all back to the capital. She hadn't yet notified Tabini-aiji they were coming . . . but then, their bodyguards weren't trusting outside communications channels of any sort this morning.

With a continent-spanning rail system that ran on a very precise timetable, it would have been impossible and dangerous to keep the movement of their high-priority train completely a secret from other trains on the tracks. So for the benefit of everybody who needed to know *anything*—including the Transportation authorities—this train was still running empty, its window shades down, a typical configuration for cars out of service. The story they'd given out to

Transportation was simple: a legislator in the capital had a family emergency in the north. On legislative privilege, that lord, with his staff, needed a pickup at the Bujavid station in Shejidan at mid-afternoon, and this was an already composed train that could do that handily. That was the story they had fed to Transportation: the train, composed as it was, an older train and coming from the north, could accomplish the pickup in the capital and return to the north to resume its regular operation this evening with no great disturbance to the system.

The track they were using required no routing changes, and one doubted that Transportation would do any checking of the facts behind the order ... such things happened when a lord had to attend to unexpected business. The dowager's staff had found an engine on the northern line deadheading one surplus passenger car and three empty boxcars back to a regional rail yard where normally they would have dropped off the passenger car and picked up freight. It had not been that far from Lord Tatiseigi's little rail depot at the time they had found it—an older, short-bodied train, moreover, and headed in the right direction. Perfect choice.

It was perfectly credible that a legislator in Shejidan might want to get home quickly, given the current political emergency in the north. The rail office had obliged a quiet and high-level Guild request and cleared that train from the northern line to come all the way up to the Bujavid station for that pickup—being a short-bodied train, it could do it— and they would immediately turn it around and send it back up north. One freight shipment would have to be rescheduled for a later train, but it was nothing that needed any special notice to district directors.

The train had made one very brief stop in its passage, a matter of Lord Tatiseigi's own privilege, a pause which would have attracted no great notice from the Transportation Guild, either—so they hoped. Such small stops, a request for the next passing train to delay for a small pickup, usually involved a crate or two, or even an individual letter, on a clan lord's privilege—a practice that came down from a slower, less express-minded age, that occasionally caused a small delay in traffic, but it was a lordly and district prerogative the legislature had been unable to curtail.

That old custom served them now. Their other choice would have been to bring the armored Red Train up from the Bujavid to let them travel back in style, in the aiji's personal car—and that would not only have cost precious hours, it *would* have excited notice. Armor plate was a good thing. But it was far better not to need it.

The last thing the public had known of the dowager and the foreign visitors' whereabouts was that the dowager's plane had taken the dowager and the heir, and possibly Lord Tatiseigi, off across the continental divide to the East, to await the birthday guests at her estate at Malguri . . . about as secure an estate as there was anywhere. The public knew that the space shuttle had landed earlier than anticipated, bringing down three human children who would entertain the heir preceding his official birthday in the Bujavid—and by now the public probably knew that Jase Graham, one of the four *Phoenix* captains, had accompanied the children on their flight—a perfectly understandable arrangement. Jase had spent no little time on the planet and had a previous appointment in the aiji's court. It was perfectly logical he should come down for a visit, and perfectly reasonable, too, that he and the human children would bring human security with them . . . so if *that* had been reported, it was no serious issue.

And as for where Bren-paidhi had entered the picture, the paidhi-aiji would quite logically have stayed behind the dowager's party and met that shuttle to assist the foreign guests . . . and escort them across the continent to Malguri.

If the news services had reported, however, that the foreign guests and the paidhi-aiji had not flown east at all, but had been conveyed to Lord Tatiseigi's estate at Tirnamardi, to meet the dowager and Lord Tatiseigi there, people would have said the news services had gone slightly mad. Of *course* it was a ruse, and not a very clever one. Of *course* the visiting humans and the paidhi-aiji had gone on to Malguri, most probably by plane, since the transcontinental journey by rail was brutal.

Humans—visit Tatiseigi's estate at Tirnamardi? Impossible. Lord Tatiseigi was head of the Conservative Caucus, which routinely deplored human influence and supported traditional ways against the encroachment of human technology and mores. It was barely conceivable that that elderly and conservative lord would be joining the dowager and meeting a collection of human guests at remote Malguri. Host them at his ancient estate? No.

The news services *might* have found out by now that there *was* news happening at Lord Tatiseigi's estate. Taibeni clansmen with their mecheita cavalry and with trucks and supplies, had moved into the estate's extensive grounds some days ago, while Lord Tatiseigi was still in the capital. *That* strange report might foretell another skirmish in an ancient war, since Tatiseigi's Atageini clan and the neighboring Taibeni clan had been technically at war from before the foundation of the aishidi'tat.

Mere days ago, however, in the capital, Lord Tatiseigi had signed a formal peace with the Taibeni lord by proxy. If the news services had phoned either Lord Keimi of the Taibeni or either of Lord Tatiseigi's residences, neither source would have confirmed it.

And *if* the news services had by now gotten wind of the treaty, they would still be astonished to see that Taibeni had been allowed within the ancient hedges and onto Tirnamardi's well-kept grounds. Lord Tatiseigi might have maintained two hundred years of technical unity with his *other* neighbor, the Kadagidi, while shooting at them on occasion, and vice versa, in periodic clan warfare—and one might be brought to believe that, after all this time, Lord Tatiseigi might finally have admitted the Taibeni clan to the same status as the Kadagidi, creating a framework within which business between the clans could occasionally be arranged ... but ... on the estate grounds?

Was there possibly more to it? Could there be an Atageini move in concert with Taiben, against the lately-disgraced Kadagidi?

Considering the Taibeni were blood-relatives of the aiji, signing a peace treaty with Taiben was a politic move for the Atageini, if a few centuries belated.

And the secrecy of it, or at least Tatiseigi's keeping the matter low-key? Oh, well, the Conservatives never liked to change their mind in public.

But Taibeni campfires making two columns of smoke inside the famous Tirnamardi hedges? Was *that* permitted? Had Lord Tatiseigi, who was supposed to be off across the continent at Malguri, *any* inkling there were Taibeni camping on his grounds, with mecheiti? Was there some sort of double-cross in progress?

Taibeni guards would not have let the news services disembark at the local rail station, not yesterday, not today, nor would they on any day in the foreseeable future. If any news services were ever to get to Tirnamardi, they would have to bring their equipment in from some other stop, such as the first Kadagidi station, taking a truck overland—and likely the Taibeni would stop them on that approach, too—betraying another puzzling situation, since the Taibeni were *still* technically at war with the Kadagidi, and should not be keeping track of traffic on Kadagidi land.

But perhaps the news services had not yet noticed the two—now three—Taibeni camps, despite the campfires.

Perhaps the news services had sent all their personnel buzzing around the airport in Malguri district, clear across the continent, trying to find out the truth of what was going on up at Malguri fortress—in a township without many modern conveniences, let alone good restaurants or hotels, in a town a day's flight removed from Shejidan.

This morning, however, *another* column of smoke had gone up in the green midlands, this one from Tatiseigi's neighbor, the Kadagidi estate. And since early this morning there could be no question the Kadagidi township was upset, and no more concealing the reports that the Kadagidi lands had been invaded.

Oh, there would be protests flying far and fast ... quiet, at first, but passionate. And those *would* reach the news.

By now one could assume the news services would be frantic for answers, increasingly suspecting they had been diverted off a major news event that had nothing to do with the young heir's birthday party. And by this hour, they would likely begin to get their answers ... not from the Kadagidi estate itself, which was under Taibeni occupation at the moment, but from the aggrieved household staff, who had been sent down to the Kadagidi township after being ejected from the manor house at Asien'dalun.

Within hours, that situation would surely overshadow not only the heir's birthday preparations, but the assassination of the heir's grandfather, and the impending birth of another child to the aiji in Shejidan.

The aiji-dowager and her great-grandson had been intended to carry on the birthday preparations quietly, out of the way of politics in the capital and out of reach of the news services—but, in truth, Bren now suspected, even *he* had been misled—distracted by all the preparations it had taken to set up the Malguri story and then to divert the entire birthday party to Tirnamardi. It was very possible the dowager's primary intention in setting up the Malguri story and visiting Lord Tatiseigi instead, had not been so much to deceive the news services, as to separate the Shadow Guild's two prime targets: herself—and Tabini-aiji—and get good intelligence on the Kadagidi.

Their Shadow Guild enemies, lately pressed to prove they could still reach out and commit acts of terror against the aiji's authority, had been on the move, too—but they had clearly been running behind. They'd launched a complex assassination attempt based on their estimation of where Tatiseigi would be, in their absolutely correct estimation of the effect the loss of Tatiseigi would have on the dowager's influence with the Conservatives.

As happened, the two efforts, the Shadow Guild assassination plot and the dowager's several-pronged plot to confuse her enemies, had bumped into one another ... purely by accident, the kind of accident that might befall two opponents circling one another in the dark.

Inevitable, under the circumstances, that they would collide—but one could suspect that the dowager still knew more than she was saying.

3

The curtains were not supposed to be up, because the train was supposed to be empty, so Cajeiri and his guests could not even sneak a look outside.

And it was not a rule to hedge on or cheat. Cajeiri was still only infelicitous eight, but he had the part about no cheating very clear, because people were dead this morning—nobody on their side, but a few on the other side, people who had been shooting at nand' Bren and nand' Jase; and they still had enemies loose. It had been a long night, and that was why even Guild who ordinarily would be on duty were almost all sleeping on the train. It was because they were exhausted and there might be more fighting once they got to Shejidan. It was certainly not because everybody felt safe.

Mani, Great-grandmother, had ordered a regular train to come to Tirnamardi's rail station to pick them up, and it was interesting to see what an ordinary passenger car looked like inside—brown mostly, mostly enameled metal, and the seats were not nearly as comfortable as the red car his father kept. There were sets of seats, too, with tables between; he and his guests had one such set; his bodyguards, across the aisle, had another such set. But none of the seats had cushions.

The car was not armored, either, which was another reason they had to keep the shades down.

And while mani had told him they would all just go back to the Bujavid and go upstairs and have dinner in Great-uncle Tatiseigi's apartment tonight—things were far from normal. Every promise was subject to change, and though they were trying to pretend things were normal, his three guests all knew there was trouble.

It was almost his birthday, he was almost nine, he should have had two more days at Tirnamardi, riding mecheiti and doing whatever he liked; and that had lasted about one whole day. He didn't know exactly *what* danger was out beyond those window shades—except that Kadagidi clan was definitely upset, except that Banichi was hurt and some of Great-grandmother's young men were, and except that they had the Kadagidi lord a prisoner in the next car, along with two Dojisigi Assassins, who had come to kill Great-uncle and had apparently ended up turning on the Kadagidi lord instead.

It was all about the Shadow Guild, which was scary bad news. He had so much rather it was *just* two lords fighting.

Mani had said everything was going very well—and he *almost* believed that, considering that they had apparently won, but mani had been very grim when she said it. And she had not wanted to wait for the safer, armored Red Train to travel out from the Bujavid—because speed was apparently more important than security. Or speed *was* security. The adults had not told him which. He *almost* had the feeling it was speed his great-grandmother wanted right now, not because she was running, but because she had somebody specific in her sights. She had that look she took on when she had a target. But he had no idea who that might be.

He, meanwhile, was in charge of his birthday guests, while the grown-ups did their grown-up business and laid plans and kept secrets. *He* had to explain the situation to his associates from the space station, and *he*—and his bodyguard—had to be very sure they didn't sneak a look out past the window shades. Going out to Tirnamardi they had been more relaxed and they had done a lot of looking from the bus—but on the Red Train, they had had no windows to look out once they were aboard: its walls had only fake windows. In this car, there were just woven fabric shades between them and outside, and the temptation even for him was extreme. His guests were missing a chance to look at trees and the whole world that they had come down to see.

But along the way, among those trees, there could very well be Assassins waiting to shoot at them, because, as his bodyguard had told him, trains ran on tracks, and anybody could tell the route they were going to take.

Anybody could guess, too, that the Shadow Guild was going to be very upset about what had happened to some of their people this morning.

Had they left anybody behind who would be chasing them? His bodyguard said it was possible, but the senior Guild was not telling them that.

Officially, too, everybody acted as if he was still going to have his birthday party in the Bujavid, the way they had always planned. He was not entirely sure that was still the truth. But he was at least sure that the grown-ups were doing their best to keep them all alive, and he was not a baby, to think that his party mattered on that scale, even if the whole thing did make him mad.

Very mad.

He'd understood *last* year, when they'd arrived back on the world on his birthday and they had to sneak across country . . . he hadn't been happy about it, but that was the way it had had to be.

So here they were sneaking across country this year, too. He had gotten his guests down from the space station. But their parents might not ever let them come back again, the way things were going. They might not *want* to come back, the way things were going.

Now his grandfather was dead, just north of Great-uncle's estate . . . and nobody knew why.

He was sure that if anything had happened to his parents in Shejidan, his great-grandmother and everybody else would be a great deal more upset than they were, so everything was probably all right in the Bujavid—assuming the Bujavid was really where they were going, and it was not another trick for their enemies.

And if Great-grandmother was talking about dinner plans for him and his guests—it was even possible they were going to carry on just exactly as they had at Tirnamardi, with him keeping his guests happy, while Great-grandmother and all the adults were sending out people to do things that were going to make somebody else very *un*happy.

All he and his guests had seen of the trouble so far was smoke on the horizon, and flakes of ash wafting down on the driveway at Tirnamardi. Well, that, and riders going back and forth in the night. And all of the goings-on with the Dojisigi Assassins.

It did seem odd to him that Great-uncle was not that mad at the two Dojisigi who had tried to kill him. Dojisigi clan had made trouble for everybody in the north for a hundred years at least, so they had been a problem for a long time, and the Atageini and the Dojisigi had never had any good dealings between them that he knew of.

But then so had the Dojisigi clan's neighbors, the Taisigi, been a problem just as long, and now Lord Machigi of the Taisigi was Great-grandmother's official ally.

And he did know that Dojisigi clan had had the Shadow Guild running their district for a long time, and then the regular Guild had come in and replaced the Dojisigi lord with a girl who was, his great-grandmother said, not fit to rule. So maybe Dojisigi clan as a whole had figured out that things were going to change, and wanted to ally with his great-grandmother just like Lord Machigi, before Lord Machigi got all the advantage and all the trade.

That was politics. One could just not say a thing would

never happen or that somebody would be a problem forever. He had watched all sorts of really strange changes happen, almost all of them in his eighth year.

So one had to be ready for any sort of thing to change.

The hard part was, *he* was going to have to explain to his guests the politics of what was going on, without scaring them or mentioning things that could be his great-grandmother's secrets. He was sure the fighting over on Kadagidi land was not going to be secret from the ship-folk, since Jase-aiji had been right in the middle of it. So the ship-aijiin were going to know a lot more about that situation than he could tell to anybody, since he had *not* been there.

And secondly—his three guests were not stupid, and they had seen most everything that had gone on over on Great-uncle's estate, including the ashes falling on the driveway, and the smoke beyond the hedges and the bullet holes in the bus that had taken them to meet the train.

"So are we going to meet your parents when we get there?" Artur asked him.

Gene, Irene, and red-headed Artur—his three associates from the starship where he and Great-grandmother had lived for two years ... well ... his three associates whose home was now on the space station.

His three associates who were full of questions and who did not have enough Ragi words even to ask him what was going on.

They were not used to the way atevi lived, or what it meant to be Tabini-aiji's son.

But they *did* understand politics and double-crosses. He knew that. Their own politics was trying to send all of them that had come back on the starship out to a new station over a dead planet, far away from the Earth, for a lot of really underhanded reasons, like people wanting political power and people not trusting each other. That was one thing.

And his guests by no means wanted that to happen: they

were scared to be shipped out to a lonely place where they could never come back again. So they had real reason to ignore anything bad about their visit and not mess things up.

And, he thought, they wanted to tie themselves to *him* as solidly as they could, not in a bad way, so far as he was concerned, even if it could be because they were afraid of being sent away to that other world. If they wanted favors, if they wanted *things,* that was all right. Giving them whatever they needed hardly hurt him. From his side—they were *associates. His* associates. He was who he was because he had important associates, and maybe three young people from the space station were not as important as, say, nand' Bren or Lord Geigi, but he wanted as many good connections as he could get, and they made him feel—good—when he could give them things.

That was the way things were supposed to work, was it not? Humans called associates *friends,* which was the opposite of enemy, sort of, but in a disconnected sort of way, and he was not supposed to ask about that or use that word. Even nand' Bren said it would confuse him and it could hurt him. And that it was a little early for *trust,* but that if it got to trust, it had to be true both ways.

He just knew he had to protect them and keep them happy. And since they were going back to the Bujavid, that began to mean keeping his father happy, above everything else. His father—*and* his mother.

"Will we stay with Lord Tatiseigi in Shejidan?" Irene asked, across the little table, beside Artur. "Where shall we go?"

"I don't know," he said. They were right to be worried. *He* was worried. His father could change directions very fast and his parents *might* want to talk to him, by himself, particularly to ask him what his great-grandmother was up to in all these things that had nothing to *do* with his guests— but as far as he knew, nobody had even told his parents yet that they were coming back early. "Probably we know soon. Definitely. Soon." His mother was about to have a baby, his grandfather had just been assassinated for reasons nobody had quite figured out, and his father was not going to be in a good mood if his mother was out of sorts or if Great-grandmother had created a problem. And arresting the lord of the Kadagidi could be a problem. He was not sure he wanted his guests anywhere near his parents until that all settled down.

They might stay with nand' Bren, maybe.

Except nand' Bren might not have room. Nand' Bren's apartment was the smallest on the floor.

Great-grandmother's apartment was possible. It was huge.

Everything had to solve itself soon. Even if they had just run into a life-and-death emergency about assassins and the whole world was going to be upset—his birthday was a certain date they could not move, which meant *his birthday* was going to be in the middle of whatever was going on.

If he was really going to have his birthday at all. He hardly remembered his fifth, and his seventh had happened around when they had reached Reunion, and Great-grandmother had just had a nice dinner later with his favorite things, with no celebration, not even nand' Bren, and not even her attention, since she had spent the whole time planning something. And atevi did not celebrate the unlucky numbered birthdays at all. Humans did. They were reckless about numbers. But atevi never were.

So he really had no idea how his fortunate ninth birthday would turn out, except he was supposed to get good things, and he was supposed to have a good time. So far all the things about his birthday, like his present from Great-uncle, and having his three associates down from the station, and everybody being as nice to each other as could be—that had been enough to make him look forward to the real day . . . when he might, he understood, get new privileges. Being back in the Bujavid was going to be convenient, being where he could order things to *give* his guests—but not if Great-grandmother and his father and his mother were going to be fighting so they forgot all about his birthday.

But he could not go up to the adults and talk about his problems when people were hurt and when the adults were all talking about the Shadow Guild and the Kadagidi and serious troubles. No. He was supposed to be back here with his guests, pretending everything was normal.

It felt *just* like last year, when he had had his eighth birthday. His associates had told him he should get presents. He understood now it was polite to *give* them on his birthday, at least to special people; and that the really good thing on his birthday should be how people treated him, and what he was allowed to do. He liked that idea. It would be really good if what he got was permission to go about with just his guard . . . but he had not too much hope of that, with all that was going on.

Still, there might be something new he would be allowed to do. He hoped it was good.

His privilege-gift from Great-uncle was wonderful, and was an actual present, too—a mecheita descended from Great-grandmother's famous Babsidi. And the privilege part of it was Great-uncle and mani believing he was old enough now to handle her. He had gotten that gift in front of his guests. And it had been the best day of his whole life.

Until it turned out someone had killed his grandfather, and the Kadagidi had tried to assassinate Great-uncle.

The sun sent a tantalizing shadow of something flickering across the shades.

"Don't," he said in ship-speak, as Irene glanced toward that window shade right beside her. She looked at him, a little startled, then embarrassed.

"I forgot."

"One regrets," he said in Ragi, in deliberate anger, in the most perfect court accent, "that we cannot open the shades. One regrets that we shall probably be indoors from now on. One very much regrets, nadiin-ji, that there is a *stupid* old man in the Guild."

Probably they missed half of that. He had not been thinking about simple words. He had only felt he had to say it or explode. And he was sorry now he had let his voice be sharp.

"We're fine," Gene said in ship-speak. "We're fine, Jeri-ji. We're *here*. We're on a planet. It's ordinary to you. But we've never even *seen* a planet in our whole lives. Now we've seen trees. And we've been on mecheita. And we've seen all sorts of things. Just riding the train is exciting. We're all right. We want *you* to have a good time. It's *your* birthday."

"That's right," Artur said. "Isn't it, Irene?"

"We're all fine," Irene said. "We're happy."

They were very generous. He hoped they were enjoying at least what they could see. Everything had been different for them. And there would always be rules—there had been rules about manners at Great-uncle's house, when what they all had most wanted was to remake the association they had had in the tunnels of the ship, when they had broken all the rules they ran into with no fear at all.

But it was all different, now. Here he was not Jeri-ji, the youngest of them. He was "young gentleman" and "young sir," and they were, well, his *guests,* and he was in charge of them, and he had to protect them. He had tried to explain about the Kadagidi. But they had no idea even yet what was really going on, and how bad it could get if enemies were trying to attack his father and overthrow the government again.

Last night had not upset them that badly. They had not panicked. They had not asked to go back to the spaceport or wished they were back on the space station. They said they were sorry about his grandfather—but they did not understand. They knew he was upset about his grandfather dying—but they thought it was from missing his grandfather. He thought about explaining the truth, that he was worried about whether his mother or father had ordered it, and how that would affect whether they stayed married.

But he was too embarrassed to explain *that* to them.

They could not be two years younger, and back on the ship. Then, they had all been strangers, and bored, and amused themselves by dodging the guards and doing things they were told not to do, harmless things, but forbidden things—like even seeing one another, and meeting in secret places. They were all of them older, now—smarter, more suspicious. They were all more political: that, too. *Far* more political.

And it was just a year that had passed. But so very much had gone on.

And if he understood what his guests had told him— most of the grown-ups that had let them come down to the planet had done it only in the hopes they would no longer get along, and that that would end the association for good.

He was sure that was why his parents had said yes to the idea.

He had figured that out early, without any help from anybody, the night after he had heard from his father that his associates from the ship were really going to be allowed to come.

His mother, who was really not in favor of humans at all, really, *really* hoped he and they would not get along. His mother already accused him of getting his ideas from nand' Bren, as if that was bad—his *father* asked nand' Bren's opinion on a lot of things, so was that wrong?

He thought it was not.

His father might not *quite* be planning on them falling out with each other—but with his father, *everything* was politics, and maybe his father had notions of playing politics with the ship-captains, eventually, if it did work. At very least he was sure his father was just waiting to use the association, if it worked, or end the notion, if it failed.

But he had thought entirely enough about politics for one day. He just wanted his guests to *want* to come back again.

"Are you scared?" he asked, the old question they had used to ask each other, when they had been about to do something dangerous in the ship tunnels. "Are you scared?"

"Hell, no," Gene laughed, the light-hearted old answer.

"Is it true, Gene-ji?" That was *not* the old question. *"Are* you scared? There was danger at Tirnamardi. There will be danger where I am, in Shejidan. Are you scared?"

"Are we *stupid?*" Gene asked with a little laugh. "We were scared when we got on the shuttle to come down here! Irene was so scared she threw up."

"Don't tell that!" Irene protested.

"But then she said," Gene added, " 'It's all right. I'm going!' And here she is!"

"We're all *scared,*" Artur said. "But Reunion Station was more scary. The kyo blew up half the station and we didn't know when they were coming back to blow up the rest of it. We've got Captain Jase, we've got his guards with us, we've got your great-grandmother and nand' Bren and Lord Tatiseigi, and all their bodyguards—not to *mention* your bodyguards. *They're* scary, all on their own."

Cajeiri had not quite thought of Antaro and Jegari, Lucasi and Veijico as scary, but he did think they looked impressive and official, now that they all wore black leather uniforms and carried sidearms.

"We don't know that much about what's going on," Gene said, "but it doesn't look like *you're* scared. *Are* you?"

Cajeiri gave a little laugh, and measured a tiny little space with his fingers. Old joke, among them. "This much."

They laughed out loud. All of a sudden, on this train full of trouble, they laughed the way they had used to laugh when things had gone wrong and then, for no good reason, gone right again.

It was the first time he had felt what he had been trying all along to feel about them, all the way through the visit to Great-uncle's house.

They were *his.* They were together. They were *all* feeling what he felt.

He drew a deep breath and ducked his head a little, because mani and Lord Tatiseigi would not approve of an outburst of laughter from young fools. "Shh." Most everybody was asleep, and no one used loud voices around his great-grandmother. Especially no one laughed when things were serious.

So they immediately tried to be quiet. Artur leaned his mouth against his fist and tried not to laugh. A breath escaped. Then a snort. Like a mecheita. Exactly like a mecheita. It was too much.

Cajeiri propped his elbows on their little table, joined his hands in front of his mouth and nose and tried not to make any sound at all approximating that snort. Gene and Irene were all but strangling.

They had not laughed like this since they had escaped the security sweep in the tunnels.

He was sure one of the grown-up Guild was going to come back to them and want to know what was going on.

Which only set his eyes to watering and made breathing difficult.

He tried to bring it under control. They all did. It only made it worse.

They were that tired. Nobody had gotten any sleep last night. And they laughed in little wheezes until their eyes watered.

It was a kindness when nand' Bren's two valets brought them tea and crackers. They were finally able, with moments of fracture, to quiet down, in the reverent silence of tea service.

"Sorry," Gene said, and that almost started it all over, but deep breaths and hot sweet tea restored calm, finally.

There was a small silence, the wheels thumping along the iron track, unchanging.

"I want to do everything there is to do," Irene said. "I want to see everything, taste everything, touch everything. I get dizzy sometimes, looking at the sky. But vids don't do it, Jeri-ji. You have to feel the wind. You have to smell the green. It's like hydroponics, only it's everywhere, just growing where it wants to."

"It was great," Gene said.

"It's going to *be* great," Artur said. "It *all* is. Irene's got it right. God, when Boji came climbing up that wall . . ."

"The Taibeni riding through," Gene said.

"The *storm,*" Irene said on a deep breath. "The lightning was amazing. That was just amazing!"

4

Bren poured himself another half cup of tea, timing it to the gentle rock of the rails. The clack and rumble, that sound that was bringing them closer and closer to the capital, should be soporific. His body-servants were dozing, like almost everybody else on the train. The tea, however, didn't in the least help him toward sleep.

But sleep had thus far eluded him, and he wanted warmth against a slight inner chill, and an exhaustion that, this afternoon, seemed to have no cure.

They'd *killed* people, this morning.

He'd set up the attack. He, Bren Cameron, clearly no longer working for the Mospheiran State Department, no longer *just* the aiji's translator—he'd presided over a scene of devastation.

It wasn't the first time he'd been in a firefight. But never one that so unexpectedly shook the ground, still reverberated in his bones, so out of place, so alien, in a place that never ought to have seen violence at all.

Lord Bren of Najida, it was, now. Paidhi-aiji, the aiji's mediator. Lord of the Najida Peninsula. Lord of the Heavens—Tabini had had only the vaguest idea what was above the atmosphere when he'd conferred that title, but he'd sent the paidhi-aiji up there to deal with humans and he'd wanted to make damned sure the paidhi had whatever power it took to put him in charge of whatever he could lay claim to—in Tabini's name, of course.

In one sense the title only amounted to a name, a piece of starry black ribbon on the rare occasions he chose to wear it; but in another sense it was Tabini-aiji's declaration that atevi were a permanent presence up there in space, that they meant to have a say in what went on up there, and that their representative was going to have all the respect and backing Tabini could throw behind him.

Three some years ago, that had turned out to mean Tabini's presence was going to go with humans out to deep space and back and find out whether what humans had told them about their situation as refugees was true—or not.

It had been a two-year voyage, one year out, one year back—and in their return they had brought thousands of colonists forcibly removed from their station, to be relocated on the space station above the Earth of the atevi. That was one problem.

And during their absence from the world, his, the heir's, and the aiji-dowager's—they had immediately met a bigger one: the situation back home had completely gone to hell and the government had come into the hands of Tabini's enemies.

They hadn't really *had* to right that situation at the outset: with a little encouragement, the *people* had set Tabini back in power.

Their investigation in the year since Tabini had resumed his place as aiji was only now uncovering what had *really* happened, and it hadn't been what they had first thought—what he and most people had believed as fact as late as a few weeks ago: that the coup which had driven Tabini from power for two years had involved a discontented Kadagidi lord with Marid backing, who had somehow gotten together a band of malcontent lords and their bodyguards, penetrated the aiji's security, seized the shuttles on the ground, and been able to throw the government into chaos, all because Tabini's sliding public approval had hit rock bottom.

Wrong. Completely wrong. It hadn't been in any sense public discontent with the economy—or with Tabini's governance—that had overthrown his government and set Murini in charge.

It hadn't even been Murini who'd actually plotted Tabini's overthrow.

They'd assumed it had been Murini. There had indeed been a public approval crisis, in the economic upheaval of the push to get to space.

But none of these problems had really launched the attack on Tabini.

He'd been surprised, really shocked, how bravely and in what numbers ordinary people had turned out in droves to support Tabini's return to power. Evidently, he'd thought at the time, the populace had had their fill of Murini. They'd changed their minds. They'd seen the dowager and the heir come back from space and they'd understood that humans had been telling the truth and dealing fairly with atevi, against all doomsaying opinions to the contrary.

That had brought the people out to support Tabini's return. Mostly, he'd thought then—it had been a return to normalcy the crowds had cheered for, after things under Murini had gone so massively wrong.

There'd been discontent before Tabini's fall, but no, it had *not* been lords riding a popular movement that had organized the coup.

It had not even been a small group of malcontent lords acting on their own, though one of them had been glad to take over, not understanding, himself, that he was only a figurehead.

No, it hadn't been Murini who'd done it.

He and his bodyguard had gradually understood that, and begun to look for what *was* behind the coup.

His own bodyguard and the dowager's, working together, had been pulling in intelligence very quietly, intelligence that required careful sifting—old associates making contact from retirement, giving them, as he now knew, a story completely at variance with the account they were still getting from other sources. Some individuals that they might have wanted to consult—Tabini's bodyguard—were dead, replaced twice since. And every inquiry they made had, he knew now, run up against rules of procedure—within the closely held secrecy of the Assassins, the most secretive of Guilds.

His bodyguard, and the dowager's, had protected him, protected the aiji, and protected the heir through some very dicey situations, including misinformation that had nearly gotten him killed out on the peninsula.

They'd survived that. They'd tested their channels. They'd quietly worked to ascertain who *could* be trusted ... and who, either because they were following the rules, or because they were part of the problem ... could not be relied on.

Geigi coming down to the world had been a major break. Geigi, resident on the space station during the whole interval, observing from orbit, had filled in some informational gaps; and he was sure Geigi had gotten an earful of information from his own bodyguard when he'd gone back up there.

So now Geigi had sent them the three children, a ship-captain, and two ship's security with a bagful of gear they weren't supposed to have, and in which his own bodyguard had to take rapid instruction.

It was a good thing. Their opposition, finding pieces of their organization being stripped away, was making moves of their own.

The Kadagidi setup—was major.

Done was done, now. The lid was off, or was coming off, even while this train rolled across the landscape. Those of them that opposed the Shadow Guild dared not rely on orders going only where they were intended. They could not rely on discretion. They could not trust Guild communications, or rely on any personnel whose man'chi his bodyguard or the dowager's didn't know and believe. The matter at the Kadagidi estate this morning had been Guild against Guild—they'd exposed the Shadow Guild's plot to assassinate Lord Tatiseigi. But they'd also hit right at the heart of Shadow Guild operations *inside* Assassins' Guild Headquarters.

The Shadow Guild, wounded, might think it was blind luck and an old feud that had guided the strike. It wasn't. And whatever the Shadow Guild believed, it could figure their enemies had just gotten their hands on records. Whether or not the Shadow Guild believed they'd delivered an intentional blow straight at them—it was time for the rest of the Shadow Guild operation to move. Fast.

From their own view—the Assassins' Guild might have seemed on the verge of fatal fracture, infiltrated at its highest levels, still shaken by fighting in the field against Southern Guild forces. People who guarded the aiji already felt themselves unable to rely on Guild lines of communication . . .

One assessing the aiji's chances of survival might think that the infiltration might be pervasive, and fatal.

But now they knew it was *not* that the infiltration was pervasive through the Guild, no. It was that it was that high *up*. It was not the rank and file who could no longer be trusted, and it was not a widespread disaffection within Guild ranks. It was a problem in the upper levels that had been able to set a handful of people in convenient places, that had sown a little disinformation in more than one operation—and done an immense lot of damage over a very long period of time.

Now they knew names. The dowager's bodyguard, and his own, were increasingly sure they knew names, both good and bad. And the dowager intended a fix for the problem— granted they got to Shejidan in one piece, granted they could muster the right people in the next critical hours, and granted they did *not* muster up one wrong name among the others, or bet their lives and the aiji's safety on a piece of misdirection.

They finally knew the Name behind the other names. They knew how he had worked. He was not an extraordinarily adept agent in the field, but a little old man at a desk.

His bodyguard months ago had reported the problem of tarnished names that deserved clearing—some living, some dead. A large number of senior Guild had retired two years ago, some of whom had *dereliction of duty, medically unfit,* and, in some cases, he was informed, even the word *treason* attached to their records. Some notations had landed there as a result of their resignations during Murini's investigation, some had been added as a result of Tabini's investigation into the coup and their refusal to be contacted. It had been disturbing—but credible—that persons who had never felt attached to Tabini and who were approaching retirement might just neglect to report back and go through the paperwork and the process after his return to power. Perhaps, the thought had been, these individuals had never appealed the matter or shown up in Shejidan to answer questions and have their records cleared . . . because they were just disaffected from the Guild itself, disillusioned and still angry over the handling of the whole matter.

Senior officers of the Guild had deserted in droves when Murini had taken over the government; they remained, his bodyguard had said, disaffected from current Guild leadership, opposing changes in policy. There was also old business, a lengthy list of Missing still on the Requests for Action which pertained to every Guildsman in the field: if one happened to find such a person, one was to report the location, ascertain the status if possible, request the individual to contact Guild Headquarters and fill out the paperwork—so Algini said. But there was, since Tabini's return, no urgency on that item, Algini also said, and in the feeling that there might be some faults some of these members were worried about, there was a tacit understanding that nobody was really going to carry out that order. Some junior might, if he was a fool, but otherwise that list just existed, and nobody was going to knock on a door and insist a former member report himself and accept what might be disciplinary action. Certain members had left to pursue private lives under changed names.

A message had come from two former Guild Council members, stating that, in a new age of cooperation with humans and atevi presence on the space station, the old senior leadership felt themselves at the end of their usefulness. It was a new world. Let the young ones sit in council. With marks against their names, with records tainted, who knew what was true, or which of them to trust? They were not anxious to come back to hunt down other Guild. The idea disgusted them. They disapproved of the investigation and refused to submit to a Guild inquiry.

That was the only quasi-official answer to the demands of the infamous list that the Guild referred to as the Missing and the Dead.

The stalemate still continued. Those on the list would not answer a summons or account for their movements during the coup. The list was a farce and an insult. The reconstituted records, they said, were corrupt. They would not divulge information that might reveal contacts or the location of fellow Missing.

And, no, they would not come back. And they would not ask Tabini to be included in the amnesty afforded other guilds and given on a case-by-case basis to the Assassins. They maintained the executive branch had no authority to intervene in the guilds and that the list violated that principle. It was principle.

There had been a few resignations *since* the events out at Najida. The list had grown a bit.

Angry resignations, his aishid said.

And his aishid, and the dowager's, had kept investigating . . . month after month. *Tabini's* aishid, however, couldn't. The current Guild Council refused to grant those four, who were Taibeni clan, Tabini's remote cousins, any higher rank or a security clearance, because *Tabini,* of the executive of the aishidi'tat, had ignored the Guild's recommendation for his bodyguard, and chosen his own, who were not classified as having a security clearance, or even advanced training.

It had been more than inconvenient. It had been damned dangerous . . . so much so that the aiji-dowager had finally ordered part of her own bodyguard to go into Tabini's service and back up *and train* the four Tabini had appointed. The Guild knew about the four new bodyguards: nobody had officially mentioned the *training* part of the arrangement, which was, under Guild rules, illegal.

Things had gotten that bad.

Then, even as they'd sent Geigi aloft and into safety— Algini had come to him with information that made it all make sense.

So he knew things that no outsider to the Guild was supposed to know: he knew, the dowager knew, and Lord Tatiseigi knew. Young Cajeiri also knew—at least on his level—since his bodyguard meshed with theirs, and they all were under fire, so to speak, *all* of them *and* Tabini-aiji at once . . .

Because they knew exactly where the origin of the coup was, now. It had been no conspiracy of the lords, no dissent among the people. It was within the *Assassins' Guild*. In effect, the guild that served as the law enforcement agency had fractured, and part of it had seized the government, setting it in the hands of a man who never should have held office.

The aiji-dowager and Tabini-aiji had started to correct matters by hunting down Murini; but after they'd taken down Murini, the problems had continued. They'd found themselves fighting against a splinter of the Guild they had naturally taken for Murini's die-hard supporters. But defeating the Shadow Guild in the field had turned up a simple fact: the majority of those fighting Tabini in that action had been lied to, misled, and deceived. They might not have been innocent of wrongdoing, perhaps—there were orders they never should have followed. But their attack against the aiji's forces had been under orders which turned out to have been forgeries, with *no* name that proved accurate, or that could be proven accurate.

That was when the dowager had known for certain that not everything wrong in the aishidi'tat had Murini's name on it.

The legitimate Assassins' Guild held its own secrets close as always—and, apart from its problem with disaffected senior officers refusing to debrief, or even to report in, their relations with the aiji had gone along at standoff regarding his personal bodyguard. It had seemed business as usual with the Guild.

And to this very hour *Tabini-aiji* was having to get his high-level information from his grandmother, who had the most senior team in the Guild—and *Tabini* still had to inform his own young bodyguard of what they should have been able to tell *him*.

To this hour, even a year after Tabini had regained power, they were *still* working to reconstruct what had happened the day of the coup, hour by hour, inside Guild headquarters and down their lines of communication ... trying to find out where the problems still might be entrenched.

They had gathered information, they hoped, without triggering alarms.

This much they had been able to find out, and to stamp as true and reliable.

The day of the coup, a quarter hour after the attack on Tabini's Bujavid residence, an odd gathering. . . . the lord of the Senjin Marid, the lord of little Bura clan from the west coast, the head of Tosuri clan, from the southern mountains, and four elderly Conservatives who should have known better ... had officially declared man'chi to Murini and set him in Tabini's place. It was exactly that sequence of events, that particular assemblage of individuals, and the rapid flow of information that had gotten them to the point of declaring Tabini dead, that had begun to provide their own investigation the first clues, the first chink in the monolith of non-information.

Those individuals—three scoundrels and four well-intentioned old men of the traditional persuasion—had probably all believed what they were told by a certain Assassins' Guild officer, who had gotten his information from a source who credibly denied he had given it. These seven were told, the Conservative lords all swore to it, that Tabini was dead and that a widespread conspiracy was underway, a cabal of Liberal lords that would throw the continent into chaos and expose them to whatever mischief humans up in space intended.

These gentlemen were told that they had to subscribe to the new regime quickly and publicly, and make a statement backing Murini of the Kadagidi as aiji, in order to forestall a total collapse of the government.

It had certainly been a little embarrassing to them when the announcement had turned out to be premature: Tabini was alive. But the second attack, out in forested Taiben, was supposed to have taken care of that problem within the hour. That attack cost Tabini his original bodyguard, but it failed to kill him—and no one had told the honest elderly gentlemen who had backed Murini *that* fact, either.

Where did anyone later check out the facts of an event like ... who was behind an assassination? One *naturally* asked the Assassins' Guild.

The splinter group that they had come to call the Shadow Guild—to distinguish it from the legitimate Assassins' Guild—had violated every one of those centuries-old rules of procedure and law that Wilson had written about in his essay. And down to this hour of the coup, the legitimate Guild, trying to preserve the lives of the lords who were the backbone and structure of the aishidi'tat, were still devoutly following the rulebook, as a case of—as Mospheirans would put it: if we violate the rules trying to take down the violators—what do we have left?

So at the start of it all—in those critical hours when Tabini was first supposed to have been killed in an attack on his Bujavid residence—the legitimate Assassins' Guild had mistakenly taken its orders from the conspirators.

On news that, no, Tabini was alive, then, an hour later, killed in Taiben, they had again taken orders from their superiors and from Murini—not even yet understanding the whole architecture of the problem, or realizing that among these people whose orders they trusted were the very conspirators who were hunting Tabini and Damiri.

Within three more hours, however, legitimate Guild who suspected something was seriously amiss in their own ranks had begun gathering in the shadows, not approving of the new aiji's initial orders or the conduct of the Guild as it was being run. They had evidently had particularly bad feelings about which units were being sent to search the Taibeni woods, and which were being held back.

They had had bad feelings about the recklessness with which the space shuttles and facilities on the ground were seized.

Then the units that had gone in so heavy-handedly to seize the spaceport were withdrawn in favor of more junior units who knew absolutely nothing about the technology, which made no sense to these senior officers, either.

These officers had taken even greater alarm when, that evening, assassinations were ordered without due process or proof of guilt, and senior Guild objections were not only ruled out of order—several were arrested, and their records marked for it.

The hell of it still was—the leadership of the conspiracy in that moment, even Murini himself, did not appear to have had a clear-cut program, or any particular reason for overthrowing the government, except a general discontent with the world as it had come to be and the fact that the leadership of the coup wished humans had never existed. A committee of scoundrels and confused elder lords had appointed Murini to be aiji—as a way, they said, to secure the consent of the influential and ancient Kadagidi clan to govern, and to spread a sense of legitimacy on the government. But they had not actually chosen Murini. Murini had been set before them as the choice—by a message from somewhere inside the Guild, the origin of which no one now could trace.

Murini had been, in fact, a very bad choice for the conspirators. He was a man mostly defined by his ambition, by his animosities, by his jealousies and suspicions. He'd come into office with a sense of entitlement and a set of private feuds he had immediately set about satisfying, under the illusion that he was the supreme power . . . and to make matters worse, the Shadow Guild *under* his authority hadn't questioned his orders.

The Shadow Guild *above* Murini's authority hadn't apparently seen any urgency about stopping his personal vendettas, either—except to restrain him from attacking his two neighbors in the Padi Valley, the Taibeni and Lord Tatiseigi. Attacks on those two lords most loyal to Tabini would have raised questions about Murini's motives as the defender of order and the savior of the Conservatives of the aishidi'tat: so the Guild serving Murini had kept him from that folly.

But his handlers seemed otherwise resolved to let him run his course and do in any people who argued with him.

Then once the legislature was filled with new and frightened faces, with a handful of Tabini's longtime political opponents—and once the rest of the continent was too shattered to raise a real threat—one could surmise the people really in charge would quietly do in Murini and replace the villain everyone loathed with someone a bit more—personable.

Maybe that had been the overall plan. Or maybe there had never *been* a plan. Now that one had an idea of the personality at the core of it all, one wondered if the architect of the plot, the hidden Strategist of the Shadow Guild, had had any clear idea what the outcome *could* be, with all the myriad changes that had come on the world. The Strategist, a little old clerical officer named Shishogi, had probably had an idea and a design in the beginning of his decades-long maneuvers, but one wasn't sure that it hadn't all fallen by the wayside, as the world changed and the heavens became far more complicated than a bright blue shell with obedient clockwork stars.

Shishogi of Ajuri clan, in a clerical office of the Assassins' Guild—a genius, perhaps—had started plotting and arranging to change the direction of the government forty-two years ago—and the situation he'd envisioned had long since ceased to be possible, let alone practical. *Shishogi* was not of a disposition to rule. The number of people Shishogi could trust had gradually diminished to none.

But now he couldn't dismount the beast he'd guided for so long. He couldn't emotionally accept the world as it was now. He couldn't physically recreate the world he'd been born to. And if he let go, even if he resigned at this hour—the beast he'd created would turn on him and hunt him down for what he knew, and expose all he had ever done.

What did a man like that do—when the heavens proved so much larger than his world?

Where had all that cleverness deviated off any sensible track?

Shishogi had found a few individuals he could carefully move into position. And a few more. And a few more, all people who shared his views . . . or who were closely tied to those who did. Certain people found their way to power easy. Certain others—didn't. Bit by bit, there was structure, there was a hierarchy, a chain of command that could get things done—things Shishogi approved.

This—this network—was the Shadow Guild.

Legitimate Assassins took years in training, spent long years of study of rules and law, years of weapons training, training in negotiation skills—and legitimate Guildsmen came out of that training with a sense of high honor about it all. The Guild didn't just arm a three-month recruit and shove him out to shoot an honest town magistrate in the public street because somebody ordered him to.

The Shadow Guild had taken care enough in choosing its upper echelons. It had some very skilled, very intelligent people at the top. But *all* its recruits couldn't be elite. And once the Guild tried to run the aishidi'tat, it lacked manpower. The handlers behind Murini, with a continent to rule, suddenly needed enough hands to carry out their orders. Legitimate Guild having retired and deserted the headquarters in droves, refusing to do the things the new Guild Council ordered— the Shadow Guild was suddenly in a bind. Controlling Guild Headquarters was one thing. Controlling the membership had proved something else altogether. Controlling the whole country had finally depended on misleading the membership.

And how had this shadowy splinter of the Guild proceeded, then—this old man, these officers, suddenly in charge of everything, building a structure of lies? A small group of their elite had a shared conservative philosophy. Its middle tiers weren't so theoretical—or as skilled. Perhaps in their general recruitment, they'd given a little pass to those about to fail the next level, let certain people through one higher wicket, and then told them they were making mistakes and they would take certain orders or have their deficiency made known. That was one theory that Algini held. It had yet to be proved.

Early on, for the four decades before the coup, the nascent Shadow Guild had taken very small actions, carrying on a clever and quiet agenda, exacerbating regional quarrels, objecting to any approach to humans, constantly trying to gain political ground. The Assassins' Guild, bodyguards to almost every person of note in the aishidi'tat, *knew* what went on behind closed doors.

But when a second human presence had arrived in the heavens, when Tabini had named the paidhi-aiji a lord of the aishidi'tat, claimed half the space station, and let the aiji-dowager take over operations in the heavens—that had not only scared the whole world, it had upset a long, slow agenda. Technological change had *poured* down from the heavens. There was suddenly a working agreement with the ship-humans. Atevi had become allies with the humans on Mospheira. And from very little change—change suddenly proliferated, while the world wondered what was happening up there and who really *was* in charge?

Tabini had fortified himself, anticipating opposition to his embracing human alliance: he'd set his key people into the space station, out of reach of assassination, and then sent the aiji-dowager, his heir, and the paidhi-aiji—as far as the world could conceptualize it—off the edge of the universe.

His allies had been upset.

His enemies had been alarmed.

The little old man in the Guild, seeing the world going aside from any future he had planned, had seen a need to strike now—and he'd done it, sure his people would be commanding the Assassins' Guild and they'd gain immediate control, for a complete reversal of Tabini's policy.

He'd been wrong. Not only had the middle-tier Assassins' Guild officers turned obstructionist when Murini took power, the upper echelons had organized to fight back. Other indispensable guilds had taken heart and declined to cooperate: the Scholars, the Treasurers, even Transportation had balked.

Then Murini himself had proven hard to manage.

To take over the continent, to inflict the terror they'd instilled, and to do the deeds they'd done, the Shadow Guild had had to resort, ultimately, to the three-month recruit given a photo and an entirely illegal mission.

The day the coup had moved to assassinate Tabini—a fact they all had known from early last year—the Assassins' Guild Council had been taken by surprise.

But Tabini *himself* hadn't been caught so easily—whether by accident, or a feeling of unease or the action of his very skilled bodyguard. The Assassins who had attacked

Tabini's residence had gone in flawlessly, very high-level, as Algini put it, meaning people of extreme skill, with absolutely no leaks in their operation . . . and one could, Algini had said, almost guess *which* unit.

But with all that expertise, they'd missed Tabini.

Had Tabini's bodyguard, on nothing more than a sudden bad feeling—taken him and his consort for a sudden vacation in his maternal clan territory of Taiben?

Certainly the rest of the legitimate Guild, hearing that a group in their guild's uniform had invaded the aiji's apartment and killed the aiji's servants—among them, other senior Guild members—was not going to fold its hands and hope for better news in an hour.

The legitimate Guild, realizing the aiji was the target of an assassination, and that Tabini might have escaped, had immediately launched an emergency plan to protect key people and networks and secure the government against disorder. They'd been too late to prevent the second strike against Tabini, at Taiben, but records, people, and accesses had gone unexpectedly unavailable to the conspirators—the same way, Bren thought, that his own servant staff, carpets, and furniture had been loaded onto a train and reached Najida before Murini's hangers-on could lay hands on them.

The conspirators had had far more important things than the paidhi's household furnishings vanish in those initial hours—things like the shuttle manuals; the access codes for the state archives and records; the aiji's official seal—any number of things that would have let them do more harm than they had done.

Once the legitimate Guild had begun to question the new administration's orders, very senior Guild officers had begun to retire, an hour-by-hour cascade of retirements—which the conspirators had at first mistaken for the old guard's acquiescence to a new administration. They had neglected to go after those officers and kill them. Or perhaps they'd tried—and lost a few teams.

These Guild officers, in those first few days, had needed

to find out what had happened to Tabini—but they dared not risk their search leading the enemy straight to him, either. No, the legitimate Guild's next move had been further afield, to establish contact with, of all people, the *humans,* the Mospheirans. That not-quite-high-tech linkup operation had required several men and a small boat loaded with explosives in case the navy, under the orders of the new aiji, should overhaul them.

Mospheiran authorities had been extremely glad to see them. Mospheira had stayed in close contact with the station, and the station included Geigi and the atevi community aboard the space station.

Individuals among the Missing and the Dead had linked up with Lord Geigi and set themselves at least nominally under his command.

Establishing contact with Tabini, even finding out whether he was alive—had posed a far more formidable problem. They had hesitated to invoke any network that might contact Tabini until they knew, first, that they could protect him and, secondly, that their own ranks were not infiltrated. But they had to take it on the thinnest of assurance that he was still alive.

When Tatiseigi opened his doors to Ilisidi on her return from space—Tabini knew about it almost within the hour. Tatiseigi's security and their outdated communications equipment had leaked like a sieve in those days; but one of those leaks had gone in a very good direction . . . and kept Tabini minutely aware of what was going on in the world.

In just two years of rule, Murini had set himself and his supporters on the wrong side of public opinion. From one shore of the continent to the other, ordinary citizens had been organizing in small groups, considering what they could do on their own to get rid of Murini.

And when Tabini turned up alive, with the aiji-dowager and his son appearing at his side and reporting success in the heavens, he had met widespread public support. In that rising tide, the Shadow Guild had made one attempt on

Tabini, the dowager, and Lord Tatiseigi—but they'd stopped that, with unfortunate damage to Lord Tatiseigi's grounds—and a bedroom.

And when that attack failed, when it all began to fall apart, Murini and his closest staff had run for the Marid and Murini's government had disintegrated.

In the one year since their return, Tabini and the aiji-dowager had been systematically turning over rocks left in that landscape, seeing what crept out from underneath—forgiving a few, putting some on notice, and doggedly going after the leaders. Murini had been among the first to go.

The rest had been harder. But the Shadow Guild had made truly interesting enemies in their two years in power. To firm up a deal with their allies in the *northern* Marid, they had made the mistake of targeting young Machigi, lord of the *southern* Marid, and run up against Machigi's high-level but locally-trained bodyguard.

Now Machigi, seeing the way the wind was blowing, had signed a trade agreement with Ilisidi—the first step toward an agreement with the aishidi'tat, granted only that Machigi kept his fingers off the west coast.

The Marid clan from whose territory the Shadow Guild had targeted Machigi—the Dojisigi—had now fallen to the legitimate Guild, who had lately taken the Dojisigi capital and forced the Shadow Guild out.

But not entirely. In the last month, the Shadow Guild still hiding in that mountainous province had tried an entirely new maneuver. By an order ostensibly from the legitimate Guild—they were still asking who had issued that order—they had first disarmed the best of the native Guild units, then sent them out to defend the rural areas—without returning their equipment.

That matter had only turned up last night, when the dowager had taken up two of the Dojisigi Guild who'd been thus mistreated—and made a move to rescue several hundred innocent countryfolk. Her units in the south had just last night laid hands on two of the Shadow Guild's surviving southern leadership—and what she learned had given the dowager the legal cause she needed to go against the Kadagidi in the north, this morning.

Now the Kadagidi lord, Aseida, was up ahead of them on this train, being grilled nonstop by the dowager's bodyguard—men themselves extremely short of sleep, and who had just been shot at by Shadow Guild operatives that Lord Aseida had been harboring.

Lord Aseida, who himself was no great intellect, had claimed innocence of everything. Aseida's chief bodyguard—Haikuti—had been the Shadow Guild's chief tactician, the man who for two years had ruled the aishidi'tat from the curtains behind Murini. Haikuti *might* have conducted the attacks on Tabini's residence.

The Tactician had not made many mistakes in his career. But the ones he had made had finally come home, on a red and black bus from Najida Province.

First—Haikuti having himself the disposition of an aiji, a charismatic leader whose nature would accept no authority above him—he would have done *far* better to set himself in Murini's place. There had been a point . . . with the panicked legislature agreeing to whatever Murini laid in front of them . . . when Haikuti, despite his unlordly origins, could easily have done away with Murini and seized power in his own name—except for one very important fact: Haikuti belonged to the Assassins' Guild; and anyone once a member of *that* guild was forbidden to hold any political office. Ever.

Haikuti, had he held the aijinate, would not have frittered away his power in acts of petty-minded vengeance. But, personally barred from rule, Haikuti hadn't seen fine control over Murini as his own chief problem. He was busy with other things.

Second, he was by nature a tactician, *not* a strategist, which meant he should *never* make policy decisions . . . like letting Murini issue orders.

Unfortunately, the Shadow Guild's Strategist had not always been on site to observe Murini in action—and Murini's actions on the first full day of his rule had alienated the people beyond any easy fix. It had also rung alarm bells with the legitimate Assassins' Guild and sent *them* to Mospheiran sources for better information.

From that day, the tone and character of Murini's administration was set and foredoomed, and while the Shadow Guild had begun to treat Murini as replaceable, and to ignore him in their decisions . . . the Shadow Guild had chosen to use the fear Murini's actions had created and just let it run for a year or so, while they launched technical, legal maneuvers through the legislature. The Strategist had taken the long view. The Tactician just let Murini run, to stir up enemies he could then target.

Unfortunately—the second mistake—neither had understood orbital mechanics, resources in orbit—or Lord Geigi's ability to launch satellites and soft-land equipment. They had *thought* grounding three of the shuttles would shut off the station's supply, starve them out, and that Geigi's having one shuttle aloft and in his possession was a very minor threat.

Third and final mistake, Haikuti had had a chance to run for it this morning when he had realized it was *Banichi* who was challenging him. But his own nature had led him. Haikuti had shot first. Banichi had shot true.

That had been the end of Haikuti.

The Strategist, Shishogi, Haikuti's psychological opposite—was a chess player who made his moves weeks, months, years apart, a man who *never* wanted to have his work known and who was as far as one could be from the disposition of an aiji. He had no combat skills such as Haikuti had—to take out a single target in the heart of an opposing security force.

Deal in wires, poisons, or a single accurate shot? No. The Strategist had killed with paper and ink. He was still doing it.

Papers that sent a man where he could be the right man—a decade later.

Papers that, in the instance of the Dojisigi, could undermine a province and kill units in the field.

For forty-two years, in the Office of Assignments in the Assassins' Guild, Shishogi had recommended units for short-term assignments, like the hire of a unit assigned to carry out a Filing by a private citizen, or the unit to take the defensive side of a given dispute. He had recommended long-term assignments, say, that of an Assassin to enter a unit that had lost a member, or the assignment of a high-level unit to guard a particular lord, or a house, or an institution like the Bujavid, which contained the legislature.

He had recommended, too, the assignment, temporary or permanent, of plain-clothes Assassins, who took the positions of servants—valets, cooks, doorkeepers—who served the lords, and who were supposed to be on strictly defensive assignments.

He even appointed the investigators who served the Guild Council, who *approved* the other assignments, investigators who delved into the truth or lack thereof in a Filing.

Shishogi. The Guild never released the names of its officers, but they knew that name now. One old man from Ajuri, the same minor clan as Haikuti, the same minor clan as Cajeiri's *mother*—and the same clan that Cajeiri's lately-deceased grandfather, Komaji, had ruled—until his assassination.

Shishogi was the tenth individual to have held the Office of Assignments in the entire history of the modern Guild. He had outlived his clerks and secretaries and not replaced them. His office, Algini said, was a cramped little space, massively untidy, with towering stacks of files and records. The filing system might have become a mess, but Shishogi had always been so efficient and so senior, a walking encyclopedia of personnel information, that the Council had never had a pressing reason to replace him. His antiquated, pre-computer operation had been, Algini said, a joke within the Guild.

No one was laughing, now. And one had no idea—

because Algini had not said—how many of the current Guild administration thought they owed personal favors to this man.

One had no idea what resources Shishogi might still have. There were pockets of Shadow Guild activity in the world, potentially able to carry out assassinations—last night had proven that—and there were people whose actions during Murini's rule left them very, very afraid of what Tabini's investigators might find in the records. Increasingly, honest people who had lived in fear under Murini's administration were coming forward and talking. But a few people who had things to hide were very anxious about what they knew that the Shadow Guild might want buried.

The little old man in Assignments had had the whole atevi world in his hands just a year ago.

But as of this morning, the Tactician was gone.

Now, on this train, headed back to the capital in secret, the aiji-dowager was taking direct aim at the Strategist.

5

Cajeiri waked, straightened in his seat, smoothed his coat, and saw that Jegari was awake, too, across the aisle. Nobody else was. Gene, Irene, and Artur had nodded off, Irene and Artur leaning against the wall of the car, Gene with his head on his arms on the table. Antaro, Lucasi, and Veijico were asleep, arms folded, heads down . . . one *thought* they were asleep.

The train had begun slowing down. That was a little scary . . . since that could mean all sorts of things, and they *still* could not raise the window shades to see what was outside.

"Where are we, Gari-ji?" he asked Jegari.

"One believes we are actually entering Shejidan, nandi. We should switch tracks soon."

Shejidan. He had not thought he had possibly slept that long. "Is there any news?"

"We are still running dark, nandi, not communicating with anyone, not even using the locators. We have no news."

"But we *are* still going to the Bujavid."

"One believes that we are, yes."

Others in the car were waking up, too, having felt the change in speed, and he saw no distress among the senior

Guild. The rest of his aishid woke up calmly, and had a quiet word with Jegari.

Gene lifted his head, blinked, raked his hair back. "God," Gene said in a low voice. "I'm sorry. I fell asleep."

"So did everybody for a while. Jegari thinks we are coming into the city now. We definitely should not touch the shades."

The others were stirring, Irene, then Artur, who wanted the accommodation, and got up and went to the back of the car.

"We are in the city now," Cajeiri said. "Any moment now, we will switch tracks. Rene-ji, lend me your book and I shall show you where we are."

She turned to a blank page and handed her notebook to him. He leaned forward to draw so they could see. He drew the hill of the Bujavid, and the Bujavid at the top, and he showed how the tunnel went through the hill, turning as it went.

"We will go slowly here," he said, pointing at the hill itself. "And we shall climb to the train station. And then we shall take lifts up into the Bujavid itself." There was a gap in his explanation, there, a big one, because he had no idea *where* they were going once they got into the Bujavid. But *how* to explain it did occur to him. "The Bujavid is a place like the ship. Like the station. Hallways. Passages. Quarters."

"A ship on a mountain," Gene said with a little laugh.

"A hill," he said, measuring with his fingers. "Little mountain."

"Hill," Gene said, and everybody said it.

"With passages all inside," Irene said.

"Indeed," Cajeiri said. And then he thought he should explain other things. "There are a lot of storage rooms below." He pointed on the diagram between the circle that was the train station and the Bujavid's ground floor. "Here, stairs come up to the Bujavid from the bottom of the hill, on the street outside. Everybody can go on the first level of the Bujavid—they used to have to climb all those steps, but now there's a tram from the street—a kind of train, very short track. Upper levels are restricted residency. Third level is us. Me. My parents. My great-grandmother, my great-uncle. Nand' Bren, too." He hesitated to promise them anything, when an order from his father could change every arrangement, so there was no good even thinking where they would end up, or even if they would be together. He was never to draw how the rooms in the Bujavid were laid out, anyway, his father had told him, because of security. So he just said, "I think we shall probably stay with nand' Bren." There was adult business going on and he decided his great-grandmother was likely not going to want children underfoot, hearing things they should not. He could not think his great-grandmother would send him and his guests to his father's residence—with his mother on edge, about to have the baby. It was why his father had sent him out to Tirnamardi in the first place.

Though maybe he should send Boji and his cage to his own rooms, along with his servants. Boji's cage was huge and he did not know how nand' Bren was going to deal with all of them and nand' Jase and Kaplan and Polano.

But that was a bad plan. He really did not want Boji shrieking out as he sometimes did, and disturbing his mother . . . which was why he had taken Boji with him.

He by no means wanted Boji disturbing Great-grandmother or Great-uncle, either. Nand' Bren would probably take Boji in, because nand' Bren tried to do everything he asked—but Boji was just a problem.

He had no idea what to do. His life was suddenly surrounded with problems. They were all little problems that he was supposed to be able to deal with himself, true, but they were big ones to his guests, who could not be happy locked in a room, however comfortable. The Bujavid could be miserably dull, if one were locked in a room with nothing to do.

"We shall at least have a lot of time to talk," he said,

trying to find something cheerful about their situation. "And at least we shall not have to go down to the basement if we have a security alert."

"That was interesting, though," Gene said, meaning Great-uncle's basement. "With the skeleton and all."

Great-uncle had managed a little machimi for them in his basement. There had been rows and rows of books and brown pots, and them wondering all the while if an assassin was going to come at them out of the dark. Then Great-uncle had turned out the lights and shown them the scariest things by hand-torch.

But the scary things at Tirnamardi had not just been taxidermied beasts and a skeleton—since, despite all the precautions everybody had taken, there really had turned out to be Dojisigi Assassins in the house. . . .

His guests had no idea that what was going on could get as bad as it had gotten at Najida, when there had been shells coming at the house, and assassins in the basement who had no intention of apologizing for their actions. He had killed somebody. He had killed people. He was fairly sure he had, once almost a year ago, and another man this spring that still gave him nightmares. He was not proud of it. He was not sure he should be ashamed or not, but it upset the grown-ups, who had not been able to handle it themselves. So he was not sure at all whether he had done something good or bad, or even whether he should be having nightmares about it, or not. He had not even figured how to ask mani or nand' Bren. He had not even wanted to ask his own bodyguard, who were not happy about it, because it was their job, and he had had to do it instead. He had no idea what he ought to feel, but it was nothing to talk about now, with his guests, who had already come close to a scary moment of that sort.

And he was supposed to keep all that sort of thing quiet. His guests were going back to the space station when his party was over, and he was not supposed to tell them anything detailed about the fighting, or the politics, or about the troubles grown-ups were trying to solve, or too much about which clans in the aishidi'tat were problems. Great-grandmother had said to him, privately, looking him right in the eye in a way she rarely did: "It is much more than keeping your young guests happy, Great-grandson. It is that, while we trust Jase-aiji and *his* bodyguard, and have confidence in his discretion—we are given to understand that the *parents* of your young guests represent a faction aboard the space station. *Politics* are in it. Understand that—and do *not* tell your young guests things that might upset their parents. Remember that humans do not really have man'chi, and that while you may believe you understand your guests, it is very doubtful you understand them as deeply as you may wish. We are not born equipped to understand them, and you should not bestow *any* information that may frighten them or be useful to our enemies. Let nand' Bren communicate such things to nand' Jase, where it may regard the nature of threats or danger to your father. And if your guests become distressed, refer them to nand' Bren. Do you understand me, Great-grandson? This is extremely important."

"Yes," he had said. "Yes, mani."

Politics was not his favorite word. It was, in fact, one of his most unfavorite words. Politics had his mother mad at his father, because *politics* had made his grandfather act like a fool and try to break into the apartment—and now his grandfather was dead. *Politics* had meant those scary moments in Najida's basement, with Shadow Guild bent on killing him and mani and Great-uncle.

And *politics* meant they could not raise the window shades and see the city.

Deep inside, facing the necessity of lying to his guests, he longed to throw a tantrum the like of which he had not thrown since he was, well, much younger. Doing that, however, would definitely upset his guests and raise the very questions he was not supposed to answer.

It would also annoy his great-grandmother, and draw

one of those troubled looks from nand' Bren—which were *almost* as hard to face as Great-grandmother's temper—and it would upset his great-uncle besides, who would just frown at him as if he were a stain on the carpet.

The thump of the wheels came slower and slower as the train began to climb that track he had sketched for his guests. Definitely they were entering the Bujavid tunnel now.

Bren came aware with a stiff neck, realizing he'd nodded off finally with his computer braced open in his lap, and the teacup beside his hand mostly empty—not, unfortunately, without contributing a stain to his coat, his lace cuff, and his trouser leg. Most all the Guild and the personal servants were on their feet getting hand-luggage and equipment. The train was climbing slowly, a familiar sound and motion that meant they were now in the Bujavid tunnel—and his bodyguard—including Banichi—were all on their feet, arming, preparing for arrival at the station.

He was tired and dull-witted. God, he hadn't been able to sleep at all on the train, except at the last, and now he wanted nothing more than just to shut his eyes and wake up in his own bed—but that wasn't going to happen. The next half hour or so might present more hellish problems than where they'd been, if their linking into Bujavid communications turned up trouble in the capital: they had had no word of such, but then, successful conspiracy didn't advertise its moves. They just had to hope the situation in the Bujavid was business as usual.

He put his computer away. It was a question how long the story they'd given the Transportation Guild would hold—which might tell them whether or not the Bujavid was under an active alert. The ordinary process that brought in an upbound train from the provinces was far from speedy these days. Security had grown incredibly meticulous since the coup. There would be a query. The question was how far to maintain the cover, and whether to invoke Bujavid security to secure the platform.

It was not his decision, however. The dowager's Guild senior, Cenedi, in charge of their prisoners in the next car, would make the call to tell certain people in the Bujavid station office who they *really* were—and granted the Bujavid station office was operating without problems, they would make adjustments and get reliable people into position to assure they could disembark smoothly, without, say, meeting a random work crew or other waiting passengers. Cenedi *might* have made that call as they switched onto the Bujavid spur, but if not, it would come very soon.

The operation came down, now, to *hoping* they were informing the right people, and *hoping* the Bujavid was serenely unaffected by the dust-up up in the Padi Valley. It was all riding on Cenedi's judgment.

Banichi was talking to Jago, nearby, discussing the situation. Banichi *ought* to have been lying down the entire trip. Banichi had refused, and insisted on staying armed and on active duty.

"Is everything in order?" Bren asked Tano, who was nearest him.

"Everything is in order, nandi," Tano said. "We are still not using the locators, not even our short-range communications. We shall run dark until we are in the lifts. But we are on passive reception, and our story seems to be holding up. We seem not to have roused any questions yet."

Security-wise, they were story within story within story—within story, since they were all supposed to be at the dowager's estate across the continent. It was still a little worrisome that they were arriving in the most secure building on Earth, blithely breaching their own security . . . but when they did lie, they could at least do it from inside knowledge.

Someone eventually had to advise Tabini-aiji, too, that they and his eight-year-old son were back—and Tabini would have to make a decision to let them go on hosting a collection of bright-eyed young humans, or take the youngsters himself. Natural, that a father would take custody of his own son—but the aiji-consort, who had just lost her father, was about to give birth, didn't approve of humans, and the marriage was in trouble, politically.

It was one mundane problem, in the midst of others not so mundane. But it was a large problem. They had to put the youngsters *somewhere.* Somebody had to make a decision, and it had to be one that calmed, rather than exacerbated, Tabini-aiji's domestic problems. God knew whether Tabini had told the aiji-consort the public story—or the truth about where her son had been staying.

There was at least time, in that slow climb, for everybody to get organized. "I am perfectly well-arranged, nadiin-ji," Bren said to his two valets, when they came to assist him. He needed a change of coats, at very least, but they had not packed with that in mind. "Kindly help any of the heir's guests who need assistance. We are not going to delay for precedence once the doors open. Our intention is to get off the platform as quickly as possible until we know the situation here. Help keep them in good order."

They moved immediately to do that, quietly assisting Jase to lift his duffle down, for starters, from an atevi-scale storage rack. The dowager's own servants had gone to the other end of the car, assisting with the fair lot of hand baggage the human party had with them—a significant amount of it belonging to Jase, equipment that they had not wanted to leave behind for later shipment.

Their personal wardrobes and such, two very large crates, were due to arrive with one of Lord Tatiseigi's staff and security, on another train. They had not wanted anything to delay their boarding or hold the train any longer at the local station than absolutely necessary. On the official records, that train might not even have stopped, for all he knew.

They *had*, however, transported Cajeiri's pet, Boji, a parid'ja, in an ornate, antique cage the size of a small dining set. *It*, with staff baggage, was in the car ahead of them, with Cenedi and certain of the dowager's men, with Kaplan and Polano, and all *their* gear. Boji had somewhat earned special consideration, as much of a headache as he had been last evening. The black-furred little imp, of a species fairly rare on the continent except in Taiben and the foothills of the continental divide, was noisy, escape-prone, and hard to catch, but he had been of service, and if they had had to leave Cajeiri's principal present behind in the stables, they had resolved not to leave Cajeiri's little egg-thief behind if they could possibly avoid it.

Boji *was* going to have to come up the freight elevator, however, with Cajeiri's valets, who were traveling in attendance on it. And in yet another car were certain of the dowager's bodyguard, Jase's two men, in armor, and with their gear; and the three prisoners they were bringing back with them. One almost hoped, regarding Aseida, the Kadagidi lord, now in deep difficulty with the dowager and Lord Tatiseigi, that Boji pitched one of his prolonged screaming fits. One did not, however, wish it on Cenedi—or on their other prisoners, two Dojisigi Assassins who were *also* going to have to be put somewhere. Those two honorable and sensible men did *not* deserve a bare cell in the Bujavid's detention station. Lord Aseida himself, who deserved the bleakest lodging they could find—was too sensitive a case to put into ordinary care, and one wondered what the dowager *was* going to do with the three of them.

But it was not his decision.

Bren slung his computer strap to his shoulder—Jago usually helped him with it, but Jago had her several weapons with her. They all did. There was enough firepower in this car and the next to take the entire Bujavid by storm, if that had been their intent . . . or to have defended the train, if they'd come under attack. One earnestly hoped not to have to do that.

The train ran level now, and though he'd lost track of the switches, Bren was sure he knew on what track they would arrive, and that they would face a short walk to the end of the track. He stood ready to debark. Jase did. And at the other end of the car, the youngsters surged to their feet, all gathering up their personal bags, with Bren's valet attempt-

ing to bring order to chaos. The aiji-dowager and Lord Tatiseigi alone stayed seated as the train, somewhat past the
little bump at its switching-point, came to a stop. Then Tatiseigi got up, not too obviously with the assistance of his
chief bodyguard, and gallantly offered his hand to Ilisidi,
who used the other hand for her black cane.

The movement of senior Guild outward up the aisle dis-
placed the youngsters, who crowded back into their seats,
clearing passage, but that door was not going to open until
Cenedi and their people from the car in front had deployed
on the platform and signaled them it was safe.

"Nandi." Bren gave place to Ilisidi and Lord Tatiseigi.
And to Jase, Jase happening to outrank him, at least in the
protocols of the heavens: "Just keep in front of me. Cajeiri
and the youngsters are your problem. Don't lose me. We're
all going to the same floor."

"Got it," Jase said.

The right-hand doors opened at the end of the car, and
Bren's heartbeat picked up as their company began to disembark. Ilisidi's bodyguard exited first, all business, and
quickly formed up. Then half of Tatiseigi's bodyguard.

Ilisidi and Tatiseigi went out together, the rest of Tatiseigi's bodyguard followed, and then Jase and the youngsters,
with Cajeiri and his young bodyguard. Bren exited behind
Banichi and Jago, hindmost of the principals, out into the
echoing dim chill of the station, with Tano, Algini, and his
two valets right at his back.

Down the platform, Cenedi headed toward them, from
where two of the dowager's men and Kaplan and Polano,
conspicuous in their white armor, guarded the open baggage car door. Cenedi joined the dowager, and they and the
rest of the party headed off with no delay for the baggage,
Jase's bodyguards, their prisoners, *or* the parid'ja in its cage.

They had arrived not quite in the situation Bren had envisioned: they were on track one, instead of three, which usually took provincial arrivals. Their engine faced the Red Train's
venerable engine nose to nose. So the station authority had

had the word, and shunted them over to the reserved track, saving them, and particularly the dowager and Lord Tatiseigi, a trek down the concrete platforms to the end of the line, and another exposed trek over to reach the lift columns.

That was a relief. If there was going to be a problem it should manifest now, on the short way across that concrete expanse to the lifts. Their bodyguards walked between them and the likeliest vantages for snipers, and they did not linger a moment to look about. Polano and Kaplan were going to have to rely on the dowager's men to direct them to the lifts—but they had the prisoners to bring up. Jase's guards had about enough Ragi for *go* and *stop, fire* and *hold fire,* but that was another problem, in someone else's hands. The overriding concern was getting the primary targets—the dowager and Tatiseigi—and himself and Jase and the youngsters—out of view and under cover.

They reached the bank of lifts in safety. Cenedi quickened pace slightly to reach the second lift, opened the door not by the ordinary means—but using a Guild key that not only opened the door, but took the car temporarily out of service, under a senior bodyguard's control.

That was how deeply the Guild's access was embedded in the Bujavid's systems. Units serving lords resident in the Bujavid were authorized; and to what extent their electronics could reach into systems, and whether a key like that could be locked out at a higher level, were not matters for non-Guild to know. A lord was not *used* to questioning how such things worked. A lord was *used* to trusting the people who used those accesses, and trusting that they were going to work when needed.

Today it was a great relief that it *did* work. Bren and his bodyguard boarded last, and as he turned toward the open lift door, his two valets, still outside, signaled they would wait for the next car.

The door shut. In the center of the car, next to him, were the dowager, Jase and Cajeiri, who were his height, and the youngsters, who were shorter, enclosed in a circle of Guild uniforms. Cenedi stood next to the control panel. The car immediately started to move, rising rapidly through all the many stories of warehouses and mechanicals that served the above-ground floors, not buttons available on their panel. The first number they reached was ground level, where the public had access. But nothing could stop a car under security lock. It kept rising past the second floor, slowed and stopped sedately at third level.

Home.

The doors opened. Cenedi nodded, Tano and Algini stepped out, and Bren did, into a tranquil place of antique, figured carpet runners, a broad hall with plinths and porcelains, tapestry hangings and rococo moldings, and more decorative niches and display nooks than there were doors. Luxury—and security interwoven. There were untraditional cameras that answered *only* to the residents' security, and fed images to security stations inside the four apartments. Above that figured porcelain opposite was one.

And they could finally draw an easier breath. Bren waited as the rest of the party exited.

"Are we in a house?" young Irene asked in a subdued voice.

"This is just a hallway," Cajeiri answered her quietly, and the dowager briskly tapped her cane for attention.

"Great-grandson, you and your guests will lodge with Lord Tatiseigi. You and your guests may walk easily now. We are out of danger. —Paidhi-ji, you can surely host Jase-aiji comfortably."

"Aiji-ma." Bren gave a sketch of a bow. Jase and his bodyguard he could manage easily, and Jase's company would be more than welcome.

"We are quite exhausted," the dowager said, paused for a moment, and brought her cane down smartly on a bare patch of marble floor, which sent echoes ringing. "So. We shall recover ourselves for the rest of the day. Individual staffs can see to our needs, shall they not, nandiin-ji? My grandson is aware, now, that we are here, and that a briefing will be forth-coming, such as we can arrange, but it will come from my junior bodyguard. One is certain one will come, too, from the paidhi-aiji. We shall not be offended if the paidhi-aiji should anticipate us in that matter."

"Aiji-ma," Bren said, and bowed a second time, pure re-flex, while the thought went sailing through his head that the briefing was *not* necessarily to inform Tabini on things that Tabini had rather be able to deny. There might be ac-tion coming, and the dowager might use her rest to sit and give orders that might span the continent—but whatever they did in the next few hours, the operation would *not* in-volve the aiji's very junior bodyguard. And the orders the dowager would give, involving forces here and there across the continent, *might* not be orders her grandson would hear about, until they had an outcome.

The members of her own staff that Ilisidi had stationed inside Tabini's apartment—right down to the hairdresser the aiji-consort had requested—were another matter. Doubtless someone from *that* staff would find occasion to visit the aiji-dowager's apartment in the next hour or so, bring the dowa-ger current on questions it might not be politic for the dowager to *ask* Tabini-aiji, and receive instructions about which it might not be politic to *tell* Tabini-aiji, either.

He had his own questions about the part of their opera-tion still hanging fire. And if there had been any conversation between the dowager and Lord Tatiseigi about lodging the children, he must have slept through it—but that was not a question he needed ask, now, either. He had his orders and a set of problems—Jase's lodging, and Tabini's information—in whatever order he could manage. Ilisidi held out her cane sideways, herding everyone in her own party toward the left, up-hall, and leaving Bren with his own aishid and with Jase.

"This way," he said to Jase, and, with his bodyguard, led off toward his own door, down a considerable length of or-nate and empty hallway.

6

It felt like the home stretch of a long, long race. Bren walked, aching in the knees, sighting on his own apartment's doors, midway down the stretch of hall that dead-ended at Tabini-aiji's door. He hitched the computer strap on his shoulder, putting another wrinkle in a coat that was already a disaster. Jase walked beside him.

"Quite something, this," Jase said.

"They've done extensive remodeling of this floor since the coup. Quite a lot of remodeling at the aiji's end. And mine. I now have a guest room—gift from the aiji; and you have to appreciate how precious space is, here. You and your two, you'll have room enough—*if* they don't move the parid'ja in on us. I truly hope they don't. But they well could, and one can only apologize in advance."

The hallway—this whole floor of the Bujavid—had been on its own systems since the coup, and was a complete darkness to the rest of the Bujavid. The *dowager's* men had maintained the surveillance here in their absence, and the hallway itself was a secure area, at least as secure as the dowager's own apartment. Ordinary lift cars couldn't stop here without a key. There was no likelihood of trouble.

But he didn't trust anything now, with everything that

was rattling loose. He was, he thought, on his last legs, not quite reasonable, he said to himself. Peace and quiet? That wasn't an option.

"I'm going to have to leave you on your own," he said as they neared the door. "Just ask the staff for what you want. Food. A brandy. Anything. Kaplan and Polano should be along fairly soon, but don't worry about them. The dowager's men are with them."

"Understood," Jase said.

The doors opened before they reached them. His major domo Narani and Narani's assistant Jeladi, likely alerted by Banichi or Jago via the ordinary systems, welcomed them into the foyer.

Home. Definitely. The door shut and *now* they were safe. The relaxation of tension in his bodyguard was more than palpable—he heard soft clicks as safeties went on firearms, and rattles as rifles went into a safer position for transit down narrow inner hallways. Bags of gear thumped down gently to the polished foyer floor.

And he so wished he could postpone everything, go to bed, let his aishid work on the problem, and wake up tomorrow with everything that was wrong in the world on its way to resolution.

But that wasn't the way it had to work, and his bodyguard had had enough to handle in the last two days.

Others of the servants were standing in the inner hall, and in the sitting room, which opened out onto the foyer, all ready to help them with hand baggage, coats, clothing—food, if he wanted it.

"Jase-aiji will be our guest for a number of days, Rani-ji. His aishid, Kaplan and Polano—you remember them—will be up in a moment. If not, they may need assistance. We are exhausted beyond clear thinking, and Banichi has taken a wound."

"Indeed. One regrets it," Narani said.

"Most of our baggage is delayed. There was a little difficulty at Tirnamardi. The wardrobe will come in crates. There are three human children guesting with the young gentle-man in Lord Tatiseigi's apartment." That was a bombshell, but the old man only lifted a brow, hearing it. "We shall have the honor of Jase-aiji's company; and we are not yet informed what guests the aiji-dowager will choose for her-self, but one suspects that she will keep close watch over several persons we have taken in custody, so security will be extremely close, on this floor. Komaji of Ajuri is dead, you may have heard, and we do not know by what agency. The dowager is holding Aseida of the Kadagidi under arrest, pending the aiji's decision in his case." He drew breath and said, conscious of the juxtaposition, and feeling that his own sanity was questionable: "The birthday party is, as far as we know, still on schedule."

It took a bit to astonish Narani. Or Jeladi.

"Indeed, nandi," Narani said, to news signifying a com-plete overturn of power in the Padi Valley—and Tatiseigi's sudden hospitality toward human children. "We were star-tled by your arrival, but we shall have no trouble serving at any hour, and we are well supplied in foodstuffs to assist Lord Tatiseigi's staff with the human guests. —Jase-aiji." The last was simple politeness, with a little bow—indeed, Narani knew Jase well. "We are honored."

The penultimate two of their party arrived with hand baggage, Koharu and Supani, themselves in need of rest, and the doors opened and shut again.

"Do not wait to attend me," Bren said to the pair. "Rest. Just rest. Be waited upon yourselves, nadiin-ji. You have indisputably earned it."

Reliable staff was around them, and Banichi and the rest could ordinarily head for the back hall and their own quar-ters, with staff to carry the gear, and the prospect of beds, bath, food, whatever they most wanted, not to mention information—at least as much as they dared pass about their return ... but ...

"I have one more matter to attend," Bren said. Banichi immediately gave him an attentive look—and he shook his head. "No, Nichi-ji. *You* go to bed. Rest. Jago-ji, stay with him. Be sure he does. One intends only a courtesy call next door, but one cannot say whether the aiji will have a few questions. And well he may. —Jase-ji, brandy or bed, as you choose. Tano-ji, Gini-ji. Kindly come with me."

He went back to the door. Jeladi opened it before he reached it, and he was in the hall with Tano and Algini before he realized his astonished staff had not even managed to get him into a clean coat. His clothes were in the last stage of travel-frayed and probably beyond saving. He was an utter disgrace—but if he looked disgraceful enough, Tabini's staff might just take a message. Ideally all he had to do was knock at the door, ask Tabini's staff to inform Tabini that they were back and safe, and say that he would have a full report in the morning.

Then he would take his two exhausted bodyguards home and fall on his face.

Tano knocked. Tabini-aiji's major domo opened the door.

Bren bowed, "We are back safely, nadi," he managed to say.

"Nandi," the major domo said, "please come in."

"One is far from presentable, nadi. Please offer my excuses. Assure the aiji that the young gentleman, the aiji-dowager, and the guests are all safe."

"The aiji has asked to see you in his study immediately, nandi."

Did the paidhi-aiji, the aiji's personal intermediary and diplomat, wreak havoc on a major clan and *not* explain the matter?

Possibly a message from the dowager *had* beaten him here, during the few moments he had taken in his foyer.

Or possibly the news services were already full of what had happened to the Kadagidi lord—the Kadagidi lord's servants *had* gone down to the township and their discretion was unlikely.

Absent that, they had had to let Bujavid security know they were back. And Tabini would naturally ask what in hell all the people he thought were safe and happy in Tirnamardi were doing back in the Bujavid.

Well, so—he summoned up the scraps of his fortitude, and let himself be escorted down the short hall from the foyer. He let the servant knock and open the door to Tabini's office, and he quietly tucked the tea-stained lace into his coat cuff before he entered.

Tabini-aiji was at his desk—Tabini gave him a sharp look with those pale eyes that made courtiers squirm; and Bren gave the requisite short bow.

"Aiji-ma." He offered the good news first, to ease any worry. "We are back. We are safe."

Tabini drew a deep breath. "My grandmother arrested Lord Aseida this morning and blew up his house."

"A window of his house, aiji-ma, to be exact. And it was Jase-aiji's guard who fired."

"Jase-aiji's guard."

So much they had swallowed up behind their security blackout.

"Jase-aiji accompanied the three children down, and brought two of his own bodyguard. We were all at Lord Tatiseigi's estate, enjoying his hospitality, aiji-ma, when two Dojisigi Assassins were roused out of hiding. They surrendered, and reported they had been coerced into an unFiled attempt on Lord Tatiseigi's life. Their relatives were held hostage by the Shadow Guild, and they had been sent on the last stage of their mission from the Kadagidi estate."

Tabini swung his chair to face him fully, hands clasped. "We have this documented?"

"We have the Assassins themselves, aiji-ma, who have made a full and willing report to the aiji-dowager."

A brow lifted. "Go on, nand' paidhi."

"Persons coming from the Kadagidi estate, aiji-ma, presented a lethal threat, as happened, to foreign guests and to minor children. Jase-aiji and I went this morning to that estate to make it clear to them what persons they had accidentally offended and to ask for an apology. Instead of bringing their lord to confer, Lord Aseida's bodyguard fired on us. Banichi and Jase-aiji's bodyguard returned fire. In a second incident, from an upper story, fire came at Jase-aiji and myself, and Jase-aiji's guard responded, to the ruin of a window, one regrets to say, aiji-ma. We were not the first to fire."

"Did you arrest these persons?"

"None survived, aiji-ma. We dismissed Kadagidi domestic staff to the township. None were in a position to witness the exchange on the steps."

"Is Asien'dalun left unoccupied?"

"Lord Tatiseigi's allies have possession of the premises."

"The Taibeni."

"The Taibeni, aiji-ma. We left the estate in their hands."

"We. I trust my *son* was not involved."

"No, aiji-ma. Only myself, and Jase-aiji."

"Your face."

He had forgotten he had a wound crossing his cheek. His fingers found it was swollen, and a glance sharply down revealed it had dripped blood on his coat collar. He had been obsessed by the tea stain on his cuff. It had been a *long* morning. "One apologizes for the state of dress, aiji-ma. One considered it paramount to inform you."

"Well that *someone* considered that detail," Tabini retorted. "Were there fatalities on your side?"

"None, aiji-ma." He tried to gather his scrambled thoughts. "Aiji-ma, the Shadow Guild down in the Dojisigin Marid took an entire village hostage, to force two Dojisigin Guild to carry out a mission against Lord Tatiseigi or see their relatives murdered. But seeing not only Lord Tatiseigi, but the aiji-dowager, in the presence of the young gentleman and foreign children—the Dojisigi surrendered and appealed to the aiji-dowager. The aiji-dowager freed their village last night."

"Not personally, one supposes."

That was irony. "No, aiji-ma. But not through central Guild command, one understands, which she fears may be compromised. Through her own. The action incidentally removed part of the Shadow Guild's leadership in that district."

"And my son? Participant in the goings-on at Tirnamardi?"

"At no point, aiji-ma. The young gentleman has been aware of the alarm in the house, but he was exemplary in keeping his guests from being involved, and in obeying instruction to stay in protected areas. He was quite safe and under guard when the two Assassins were taken in custody."

Tabini lifted a brow.

"I omit nothing," Bren said. "He was at no time in danger."

"But you did kindly think of us, that we should be made aware that the aishidi'tat is *missing a clan* this evening."

One could only nod quietly. And one also had to recall: "The Ajuri also lost Lord Komaji yesterday. One does not know whether you may have heard."

"Of that, we are aware. Our staff tells us *some* things. We have made adjustments."

The sarcasm and the annoyance were justified, fully.

"And *where* is my son at the moment?"

"In the Bujavid, aiji-ma. In Lord Tatiseigi's apartment. With his guests."

"Gods moderately fortunate. We are grateful our son has not stayed behind to direct the mop-up. Are we missing anything *else* you deem of interest?"

"No, aiji-ma." He drew a breath. "But one does advise the aiji that security precautions in the Bujavid should be tightened. The opposition is stirred up, not only in the Marid, but likely here in the capital."

"One would rather think they would be. Of course, we have our entire apartment staffed by my grandmother's men. One *expects* to be told something soon." There were light, quick steps in the hall. A woman's steps. From deep *inside* the apartment. Tabini's eyes darted aside and back. "One does not believe you will escape, paidhi."

A knock came at the door, and with no pause at all, Lady

Damiri swept in—a woman in her last days of pregnancy, a woman whose father had just been reported assassinated on a journey that might have taken him close to her son, at Tirnamardi, and who now, probably from security staff, found her son and company had arrived in the Bujavid and *not* told her they were coming back. "My son," she said, as Bren respectfully rose and bowed.

"Safe," he said quickly, and felt Damiri-daja's glance travel up and down his bedraggled and blood-stained self. "He is well, quite well, daja-ma. He was not with me when I acquired this. He is here in the Bujavid. He was kept far from any incident." Not quite the truth, if the opposition had had their way. "He has come back with his guests, and the ship-aiji who accompanied them—you remember Jase Graham, surely, daja-ma. Jase-aiji used the foreign weapons of his own bodyguard in his own protection and mine, and your son was at no point near the altercation with the neighbors."

"Lord Aseida is under arrest at the moment," Tabini said smoothly, never having risen from his desk. "Asien'dalun is missing a window. Our son and his guests are safely lodged with Lord Tatiseigi for the night."

Damiri greeted that astonishing information with raised eyebrows, but no greater pleasure. *She* was Cajeiri's link to Tatiseigi, who was *her* uncle. And her distaste for Lord Tatiseigi's well-known conservatism had sent *her* back to Ajuri clan. "Indeed."

"The paidhi-aiji," Tabini said, "witnessed the Kadagidi situation first-hand. He has hurried here directly to reassure us. They clearly traveled quickly and silently, to get here with no noise."

"Indeed," Bren said.

"There was an assassination attempt," Tabini said, "as we understand it, launched by the dissidents in the Dojisigin Marid, aided by the Kadagidi as a staging point, and aimed at Lord Tatiseigi."

"At my *uncle,* specifically?"

With her father just assassinated.

Her maternal great-uncle, Tatiseigi, had come under threat—with the added choice of her son and her husband's grandmother on the premises. One could see what her focus might be, in trying to parse *that* equation.

"Daja-ma," Bren ventured to say, "the mission was launched specifically at Lord Tatiseigi—set for his return, whenever it might happen. The Assassins had no fore-knowledge that he would arrive with such guests. The Assassins themselves were caught in a bind. They surrendered, confessed the situation—and we—Jase-aiji and I, went by bus to the Kadagidi estate to protest the action and receive an apology. But Lord Aseida's bodyguard did not bring Lord Aseida to the conversation. They fired on us."

"Which we are sure is not what the Kadagidi will say," Tabini muttered.

"But *we*," Bren said, "have a record of the event, aiji-ma. Jase-aiji's men recorded the action in video and sound, with every movement, every word leading up to the exchange of fire."

"Recorded." Tabini was more than interested. "Will this recording be in our hands?"

"It will be by tomorrow, aiji-ma. Jase-aiji promises it, for whatever use we wish to make of it. He can process it for our machines. One cautions—one has not seen the record yet. But so far as my memory is accurate, and Banichi says the same, Lord Aseida's Guild senior fired first."

"Haikuti," Tabini said with distaste.

"Haikuti is dead, aiji-ma. Along with two Guild units besides, and whoever fired from the window at Asien'da-lun's upper corner. We then took tactical positions in the house and grounds. My bodyguard and the aiji-dowager's prevented servants from destroying records. We arrested certain persons we believe are plain-clothes Guild, and we dismissed the rest of the domestic servants to the township, everything by Guild regulations. It *was* a legitimate Guild operation, taken in a legitimate action on my part, and their firing initiated our response."

"And where was Lord Aseida during all this?"

"Within the house, aiji-ma. He was brought out from hiding under our escort. We took him to Tirnamardi, where he asked protection of Lord Tatiseigi, who flatly refused him. In leaving Asien'dalun, we gave place to Taibeni clan who were *also* guesting on Tirnamardi estate, who were *also* offended by the operation launched from Kadagidi soil. They are holding the Kadagidi estate, in alliance with Lord Tatiseigi."

Tabini slightly pursed his lips. Tabini himself was half Taibeni. His aishid—excepting the dowager's men—was Taibeni. And this morning's turn of events now had Taibeni clan working with Taibeni clan's old enemy Tatiseigi against their other old enemy the Kadagidi. It made a very interesting turn of events.

"And Aseida?"

"Lord Aseida resides in the aiji-dowager's keeping."

"Here?"

"Yes, aiji-ma. Along with the two Dojisigi Assassins."

"On this floor?"

"I have no idea, aiji-ma. But, cooperative though the Dojisigi have been, and deeply indebted as they are to the aiji-dowager, they will surely *not* be set at liberty yet, one is quite certain of that. And one is equally sure Lord Aseida will not be. They traveled in a separate rail car and at no point has this situation been near the children."

"I leave the Dojisigi to my grandmother's discretion," Tabini muttered with a wave of his hand, "but Aseida is mine to deal with. You will remind her of that."

"Without a doubt he must be, aiji-ma, nor does one believe she would say otherwise."

"Of course not. —With a notable dearth of candidates for the Kadagidi lordship, of *course* she will not object. There will be a *firestorm* among the Conservatives, and *we* shall have to deal with the mess."

"Ajuri," Damiri said unhappily, regarding her clan, now lordless, with her father's death, "and now Kadagidi must have new lords. And there will be *more* troubles for the north."

Damiri herself was one candidate for the lordship of Ajuri. She was the very last candidate Tabini wanted in that frequently-vacated office. There was clearly subtext in the aiji-consort's uncommon statement on politics in the paidhi's hearing.

Subtext, too, in Tabini's sideways shift of the eyes, in his wife's direction.

"When shall we see our son?" Damiri asked sharply.

Angry. Yes. Damiri was angry with Tabini. Angry with her son. Angry with Ilisidi. Angry with him. Angry with her uncle. And, it was very certain, she was supremely angry at her recently-deceased father *and* whoever had killed him.

She was also the very last person on the planet the dowager wanted involved in any plan to move against the old man in Assignments—an old man who also happened to be her great-uncle.

"Daja-ma," Bren said quietly, "the youngsters are all exhausted, and very concerned about making a good impression. An alert kept them up much of the night, and they are likely headed for baths and beds now as quickly as Lord Tatiseigi's staff can settle them in. Your son is deeply concerned for your safety and your good opinion. He wishes you to know he is well. He is the only translator available for his guests at the moment, and he wishes not to disturb your peace of mind, daja-ma, by arriving here with his guests—not to mention the parid'ja."

"That *creature.*"

"Indeed, daja-ma. The parid'ja is with him. And, right or wrong in his judgment, he has wished to regroup and set himself to rights. He wishes to present himself and his guests rested, and in the most felicitous way, and he wishes not to disturb this household with the commotion of young guests."

He had averted wars. Damiri's displeasure was a harder argument. The scowl persisted for a moment, boring into him. Then:

"Tell me *this,* paidhi-aiji. *Was* my uncle *or* the dowager involved in my father's assassination?"

A reasonable question. He was ever so glad to report the negative.

"In no way or degree were they involved, daja-ma. They were aware of Lord Komaji's movement toward Lord Tatiseigi's estate — but they had given no order at all to prevent him. They were both quite shocked by the unfortunate event. I was present at deliberations and there is no question in my mind they were uncertain about his intentions. They even wondered whether your father, not knowing that the aiji-dowager or your son was present at Tirnamardi, was on his way to take refuge with Lord Tatiseigi, pending *his* return home, because of an imminent threat inside Ajuri — which the aiji-dowager believes existed. I believe *she* thinks he was indeed coming to appeal to Lord Tatiseigi. Lord Komaji and Lord Tatiseigi were not on good terms, but Lord Tatiseigi is moderate even to his enemies. We rather wonder also whether there was some particular intelligence your father meant to give Lord Tatiseigi, information that *someone* did not wish given."

"Specifically?"

God, of course she would ask that question. And he had to lie. Or at least evade. "I am not that far into the dowager's confidence, daja-ma." And back to the edge of the truth. "But one believes elements among the Kadagidi, among others, may have had a reason to fear your father's making common cause with Lord Tatiseigi against them." He glanced away, back to Tabini, an appeal for rescue.

"My grandmother will not withhold *that* information from us," Tabini said, "one is quite certain. Well-done, paidhi. Go. Rest. Have that injury treated — and deal with our guests. Keep us informed. We shall wish to see our son when he is rested."

"Aiji-ma." Another bow. A short bow to the aiji-consort.

And an escape, before the domestic discussion could start.

* * *

They reached their own door, he and Tano and Algini. And within, safely in the hands of Narani, there was finally the chance to shed the ruined coat. Bren did that, not hoping to see it again.

"The aiji has the essentials of what happened on the Kadagidi estate, and in the south," Bren told Tano and Algini before they parted company in the foyer—the two of them, in Tabini's apartment, had been standing watch with the aiji's guard, and *not* inside the office. "The aiji-consort arrived late. She asked questions regarding Lord Komaji's assassination—she is understandably angry and she wonders whether she has been told all the truth. I mentioned the Kadagidi in the context of that assassination. I did not quite lie to her, nadiin-ji, but it was a misdirection; and it was certainly an untruth, when I said I was not that deep in the dowager's affairs. The aiji clearly knows to the contrary, and probably the consort suspects it was a politic evasion and a half-answer. It was clumsy of me. I desperately need sleep, nadiin-ji."

"Sleep as you can," Algini advised him.

"Banichi?" he asked.

"He will rest," Tano said. "Jago will see to it."

With a dose of sedative, one suspected. The dowager's physician had given him several bottles of pills.

"He should *not* think his risking his health in any way serves his man'chi to *me*," he said. "One does not know how to convey that sentiment to him strongly enough. He needs several days abed."

"That will not be the case, nandi," Algini said.

Formal tone. Formal advisement. So he knew they *weren't* waiting for the second part of the dowager's plan. He had thought there would be a deal of information-gathering first.

"Then we are moving, nadiin-ji."

"Imminently," Algini said. "Banichi insists to be part of it. In plain fact, Bren-ji, he needs to be."

Damn, he thought. "One understands," he said, and the intellect understood, but the heart didn't, not at all. He'd seen Banichi go down this morning. He kept seeing it, and knew there'd been considerable blood loss. "With how much risk?"

There was no answer. They knew he knew.

"I rely on you," he said. "I rely on *all* of you. I ask that you think of your own value—to the aishidi'tat." That didn't half state it. "To me. You know that. Losing any one of you—I would be—I could continue to function in office, and I assure you I would do so, nadiin-ji, but—"

"He understands," Algini said, a rescue.

"I am not expressing myself well, Gini-ji. Do not fear I could not function in my office. But I am worried. And I value *all* of you. Extremely."

"We know. He knows. Understand, nandi—he knew that Haikuti would react to his presence. This troubles him. He knew if Haikuti did bring his lord out to parley, he would be maneuvering for position, with no regard for his lord's safety. He knew that before we left the house. Banichi moved to protect you, *and* he moved to a defensive posture to secure your legal position; but in his own judgment he put himself in that position because he wanted Haikuti stopped and he left cover because he intended to withstand Haikuti's fire to take him down definitively and legally. It served your interests and the aiji's, too, but he strongly questions which motive was foremost in his mind when he did not turn and protect you with his body. *I* say this because he will not. He is determined *not* to operate at any disadvantage now, in consideration of what he sees as a lapse of man'chi—a failure of character. We have told him we would have done the same, on the simple logic of the situation, but he considers his action, however proper, was tainted by his personal feud with Haikuti, and he is determined not to be put out of action now because of his choice. That would give Haikuti some bearing on the outcome. And he will not tolerate that thought, either."

He parsed that oblique statement for a second or two, and he understood it better than Algini might think he did. Banichi was stubbornly staying on his feet, trying to operate normally, because Banichi thought he had jumped the wrong direction under threat, in a process too fast for rational thought.

And Banichi was taking, he very much feared, a heavy dose of painkiller.

Handling luggage, for God's sake, when they'd left the train. Tano had gotten the damned equipment bag away from him and carried double when they headed for the lift. He'd marked that little transaction.

He should never have opened his mouth about his personal feelings in the situation, not with a mission pending. He was sure of that, at least. "I have nothing more to say. I am determined not to endanger the rest of you. Take care of yourselves in your own way. Do what you have to do, and please ignore my emotional foolishness, nadiin-ji. I am not expressing myself well at all this evening."

"You are not alone in your concern, nandi," Tano said. "We have tried to keep him still. And though we will benefit by his presence in the mission and his advice is clear-headed . . . we have misgivings, too."

"Then tell him—if it is useful—that I said be careful with his life, nadiin-ji."

"One will try the utmost, Bren-ji," Algini said, and with that, Tano and Algini went on down the inner hall.

He stood there. Narani and Jeladi waited, quietly, at one side. Jase had appeared in the door of the sitting room, and heard enough to make him stay there, saying nothing.

Jase wasn't linked in—but Jase knew enough to worry. He'd just heard enough to worry considerably, one was quite sure.

"Brandy," Bren said quietly, and went to join Jase in the sitting room, tea-stained shirt and trousers and all. He motioned Jase toward a chair; he took one.

"How did it go?" Jase asked.

"Well enough. The aiji is aware what happened. Not what *is* happening. And I have to sleep. *Have* to. By any means. We're going to need all our wits about us in very short order." In a surreal fog, he was aware of Jeladi moving about the buffet, quietly pouring two brandies. He didn't even want one—but he knew once his head hit the pillow, as it was, his brain would start trying to work, and no sane or useful thought was going to come of it. "The boy and his birthday have gotten lost in the transaction—at least—at least right now. At least being here—until whatever happens, happens—we can guarantee the kids' safety."

"You're not in trouble, are you?"

He took the brandy Jeladi offered, took a sip, shook his head. "Not really. Not that I anticipate. But I'll understand if policy makes an official displeasure necessary. That's also part of the job."

"Understood," Jase said, took the offered brandy, and shuddered. "Strong stuff."

"Effective," Bren said, and took his own. Unconsciousness was the objective. After two sips he didn't even taste it. "Have Kaplan and Polano made it in?"

"In," Jase said. "They're out of the armor, and glad of it."

"That video record."

"Copied. Three copies, in fact. On the train. And the record uploaded to station, should anything happen to the original down here—that's our *policy,* in a situation like this. They've given them to Jago."

"Good," he said. One worry down. At least one. He gave one critical thought to ambient security, and the effect of the brandy, and who he was talking to, and what staff was in the room: Jeladi was, like Narani, somewhat adept in ship-speak, but absolutely loyal. "I think we're going forward, soon. I can't swear to any promises we've made you or the captains. It's a situation we didn't intend to deal with until you and those kids were back aloft. But once things blew up with the Kadagidi, not to mention what's going on in the Marid, now—we have a problem. The birthday, the festivity . . .

means crowds. Means access. *And* an occasion the opposition will want to use."

"An incident, you mean."

"And we can't move the date. That's the problem. Numbers. We can't violate the numbers. The opposition didn't *mean* to trigger what they did at the Kadagidi estate, but they did. We had to answer the attack on Tatiseigi—you *don't* just let an incident like that slide. And we hurt them—we hurt them so badly that under normal circumstances they might even lie low for a year or so. But we have documents we haven't had a chance to read yet. We don't know how sensitive, or how desperate it might make them. Our enemy has one date, one public exposure, one really good chance at hurting the administration and looking powerful—there may be plans already in motion. And he has to worry what we may be able to make public—since he can't be sure what's in Haikuti's records. We have a chance to address the situation in the Guild, the only chance at this man we're likely to have; and somehow we have to prevent him hitting us first. I think my aishid is right."

"Can you maneuver this *problem* of yours into leaving Guild Headquarters? Can the aiji order him in?"

"I don't know. The aiji's not supposed to know his name. No one is. I don't know how they plan to get at him. But I think it's imperative we do it. Soon." He declined a second drink. The first was hitting hard. "I think my brain is fuzzing."

"Mine's no better," Jase said. "Whatever help I can be—"

"Appreciated," Bren said. He set his glass down, rose, went through the bow, the proper motions that weren't automatic with Jase any longer. Jase bowed, belatedly—started to lay a hand on his shoulder in passing, and stopped in midmotion, caught between cultures. "Your being here," Bren said, "is a very good thing. I only wish the kids *weren't.*"

"They're safe on this floor, though."

"They're safe on this floor. Of that, at least right now, we're sure."

7

Uncle Tatiseigi's staff had made them tea on their arrival, and his kitchen had sent out piles of little pastries while the rest of the household staff hurried as fast as they possibly could to make everything right in the guest quarters.

Cajeiri had only once ever been *in* Great-uncle's apartment—really he was twice-great-uncle, but it was too long to say, and even Mother said just "uncle." And it was no great surprise that Uncle's Bujavid apartment was so much like Tirnamardi, full of fancy vases and hangings and antiques of which one had to be very, very careful, from the chandeliers overhead to the carpets underfoot, and the lighting was gold and so dim it always looked like oil lamps. Great-uncle had invited them there in spite of his antiques, and they were all on their best manners.

He was *so* glad he was not being shunted off to his parents' apartment tonight.

The one who had to handle the surprise of their arrival and find room for them was Madam Saidin, who was the major domo for the apartment staff. Cajeiri knew her. She was a very kind, very good, very proper lady. She had taken care of nand' Bren when Great-uncle had lent his apartment to nand' Bren.

And she was just exactly the way he remembered her—graying and tall and thin and very solemn, with a little quirk of a smile when one least expected it. She was *very* good at running a staff, and seemed not at all disturbed by three human guests with a big parid'ja cage—the most unlikely combination any major domo had ever had to deal with, he was very sure. She immediately asked him very good questions, very quickly and privately—questions such as what *was* the human custom about where Irene should sleep, and did they wear nightclothes and would they be bathing together? And when he told her how they had arranged things at Tirnamardi, she gave quick, quiet orders and sent the staff into action just as if it was all the most ordinary thing in the world to have all this happen, with a very high security alert going on.

"One promises that we shall never, ever leave Boji out with just his harness," Cajeiri told her. "He got out, at Tirnamardi. That was our mistake. He chewed right through his leash and we never even saw him do it. And there was a window open."

"A light chain would prevent that happening, one would think, young gentleman," was Madam Saidin's quiet reply. "We shall see if one can be found."

A chain made ever so much more sense than that thin leather leash, once he thought of it. It was brilliant. If Madam Saidin had been in charge at Tirnamardi, Boji never would have gotten away from them . . .

But then, if Boji had not escaped, then people might have gotten killed.

Baji-naji, they had been *very* fortunate in the way that had turned out.

Only a fool would expect, however—mani had always said it—to be fortunate twice.

"A chain would be excellent, Saidin-daja. Thank you."

He gave an appreciative little bow, and off went Madam Saidin to pass a word to one of the servants who might even find such a thing somewhere in the Bujavid.

And meanwhile there began to be little sandwiches—*safe* little sandwiches, the servants assured him, because the staff had served nand' Bren and knew all about alkaloids and humans and what things humans liked.

Everything was running amazingly well. Great-uncle was *not* in evidence—perhaps he had gone off to his own suite in the apartment, well apart from the guest quarters. But someone had left the premises—Cajeiri had heard the door open and close—and it was possible that it was not a servant looking for a chain, but Great-uncle going off to talk to Great-grandmother or maybe to his father.

One thing did worry him: that right down the hall, mani, so the servants whispered, had the two Dojisigi Assassins and the Kadagidi lord lodging right in her apartment. That was no good thing for Lord Aseida: that was sure. Mani was not in a good mood with him.

But mani was not worried enough about the two Assassins, in his opinion. He was so worried he went to ask Madam Saidin what she thought, because Madam was Guild, herself, and very sneaky if she had to be.

Madam said: "One is quite certain your great-grandmother and our lord are taking proper precautions. Cease to worry, and trust your great-grandmother. If you do not worry about these things, *you* cannot worry your guests."

That was still a worrisome answer. He gave another little bow.

"Saidin-daja, I am almost nine. Please inform me. We were together on the train. We were at Tirnamardi. We understand that we must keep Boji very carefully and that we must stay in the apartment, but we also understand there is danger to my father with these people, and my great-grandmother has them in *her* apartment just down the hall, and one wishes she would just send them to the Bujavid guard."

Madam's face showed just a little frown. "Well, trust that they will not quite be lodged *in* her apartment, young gentleman. You may recall she *does* have servant passages, and a number of storerooms, some of which can be made comfortable—and quite secure. Lord Aseida is reputed only for indolence and self-indulgence: one doubts he will pose any personal threat. The two Assassins are, one understands, indebted to your great-grandmother, but one is certain they are just as securely guarded."

"Please do not keep secrets from us, nadi—my guests knew about the Assassins *and* the Kadagidi when everything was going on. Mecheiti ran past our windows and they had to clean up the bus before they would let us board."

"A distressing situation, indeed, young gentleman. One hopes to spare your guests more such sights."

She was very old. And very smart. And a bad person to lie to.

"We are not stupid, Saidin-daja, and we will not do things if we know they are dangerous to the household. Please warn us when threats are going on! My guests' man'chi is to *me*. They will not tell their parents."

She gazed down at him a moment, wise, and very senior, and nodded slowly. "Then you should know the security alert continues, young gentleman. The lord has gone to talk to your great-grandmother, and they will compose a report for your father on the matters you mention. Guards are posted at various places on this floor, including servant corridors below, and we are informed that, should any attack within the Bujavid aim at this floor, we are to bar the servant accesses and contain you and your guests in this apartment. And should any outside threat *reach* this floor, young gentleman, staff is instructed to gather you and your guests in the sitting room and take certain actions. In any alarm, please make that possible as quickly as possible. You may omit your parid'ja from the plan—he would be in no particular danger from Assassins. Only see you and your guests come immediately to the sitting room. That is what you can do. Now I have entirely violated my lord's instruction to keep this information from you. And I have given you a plan to follow. You are indeed a wise young gentleman. Please honor my confidence."

A grown-up said such a thing. It required a bow, a deep one.

"And put on a calm and pleasant face, young gentleman. You know how to do that, if your great-grandmother has been your teacher."

"Yes," he said, and managed it. "One will. One can do that."

"Excellent. You have asked for the burden, young gentleman. Now bear it. And make your great-uncle and your great-grandmother proud of you."

"Saidin-daja." One more bow, this one the formal dismissal, and he stood and watched Madam walk away, thinking . . .

But what *about* mani, and nand' Bren? What about my mother? And my *sister* that my mother has? And my father?

It was his *birthday*. It was his birthday, and they were talking about going to war again. The 'counters said everything happened because of the numbers.

But what were the numbers of his *birthday* that made these things always happen on that day?

He stood there, thinking that, and his face was not at all the face his great-grandmother would approve. He put the pleasant look back on, the way mani could, in the blink of an eye.

A pleasant face hardly helped what was inside, but it would, mani had said, give him time to think.

And he thought about what he had promised Madam, about his associates not talking to their parents, and if it was not precisely the truth, he knew now he had to make it the truth. If someone slipped, if someone said a wrong thing to the authorities in the heavens, some report that would take his associates away from him, he would still get them back, even if all the aijiin in the heavens were against them associating—even if his *father* was against it.

He had gotten them down here with all this going on.

He surely could do it twice, no matter what.

But it would be a lot easier if he could be sure his associates were careful what they said in the first place.

8

The aroma of breakfast was in the air as Bren dressed. Yesterday had not produced any regular meal, and brandy with Jase had sent him straight to bed. It didn't count as supper, not in any regard. "How is Banichi this morning?" he asked, with the intention of having breakfast sent to his bodyguards in their quarters if they were slow getting up—God knew they'd deserved it. "Is my aishid up and about?"

"They were up an hour ago, nandi, taking breakfast with Cenedi-nadi in the aiji-dowager's apartment."

"Banichi too?"

"Indeed, nandi."

The Guild did not observe such niceties as no business over food. And business did not half describe what that conversation might entail.

So he didn't invite his aishid to breakfast. He headed for the dining room alone and took his seat at a table that could seat felicitous thirteen. He was grateful that his servants, Bindanda's staff, appeared instantly to pour tea. He usually drank it without sugar, in consideration of his waistline, but he loaded in two spoonfuls, then a third, stirred it and took a sip.

Bindanda appeared in the doorway. "Nandi. Will there be any requests?"

"Whatever you have this morning, Danda-ji. Toast. Simple toast would do very nicely."

"Eggs and toast, nandi," Bindanda said.

"Excellent." He nodded to Bindanda's departing bow, took a sip. His ordinary breakfast. His staff. People were solving at least some of the problems. They were home. Home was a very good place to wake up.

Someone left or arrived at the apartment. He was not sure which. Such often happened during the course of the day, the arrival of messages, or orders from staff—but less often, when the whole floor was shut down.

Mail, likely. Letters were going to start pouring in once the Bujavid knew they were back. And though only one lift had access to the third floor when it was under lockdown, and that lift normally sat *at* the third floor, operating only by key—mail and deliveries would reach them.

Letters were going to ask questions. They were going to ask questions he could not answer. He worried about what he could say. He worried about what his aishid was doing. He ate the toast and eggs, swallowed a cup of tea, acknowledged Bindanda, who showed up for his polite appreciation . . . "Thank you very much, Danda-ji. I am fortified for the day. One cannot predict when one may be in the apartment or out. One apologizes. It depends on the aiji and the aiji-dowager, from moment to moment. I shall be in my office this morning, at least until I know differently."

"Nandi," Bindanda said with a little bow, and Bren waited only until Bindanda had gone back into his own realm before getting up, shedding the napkin, and heading for the foyer.

Message cylinders, yes, were already standing in the bowl.

Boji was upset. Cajeiri waked, rubbed his eyes, astonished for the moment at the gilt and ornate curves of the curtained bedstead, and at the vases and bric-a-braq around him and Boji's ornate filigree cage—on the one side of the bed-curtains he had left open—

Until he remembered he was in the guest bedroom in Great-uncle's apartment.

All of them were. Because they had all wanted to be together, and Irene had not wanted to be apart from every-body, Madam Saidin had put his guests in the very fine two little bedrooms a visitor's aishid was supposed to use, and his aishid had kindly volunteered to bed down in the sitting room beyond. It was a very large guest suite.

Boji, furry and long-limbed, was clinging to the bars of his cage and making his water-bottle rattle. And he had bet-ter not let out a screech in Great-uncle's apartment, at whatever hour it was.

"Hush!" he whispered. But it could not be that early in the morning: he smelled tea.

And if Great-uncle's servants had brought breakfast to the guest quarters sitting room, he and his guests ought not to oversleep and make things inconvenient for the staff. His father had dinned that into his ears even before mani had taught him it was twice true if one were a guest.

So he crawled out of bed, put on his dressing-robe, and pulled the ornate cord next to the service door. He hated to wake his servants after their hard work yesterday, but he and his guests would have to dress, if tea had arrived on the household's schedule.

And if Boji was starting to get restless, Boji had better have his egg and have his little accommodation cleaned out, or he would become inconvenient in more than one way.

He had worried about bringing Boji into Great-uncle's apartment—and he was sure he was not nearly as worried about it as Great-uncle. Great-uncle, with all the fine an-tiques in his Bujavid apartment, was surely reckoning the possibility that Boji might somehow get out of his cage again, the way he had just done in Great-uncle's house at Tirnamardi.

And it had looked for an awful moment when they had gotten off the lift as if Great-grandmother might send Boji back to his father's and mother's apartment—which *he* did not want, because his mother was already upset about his having Boji. His mother had *almost* said he could not keep him in the first place—and it was sure that Boji was going to make a racket if he was left alone and bored or hungry.

But then Great-uncle had ordered his staff to direct Boji's cage to the guest quarters of his apartment. And he had promised Great-uncle he would be triply sure there was no problem.

"Just wait," he said to Boji, and made the clicking sound that imitated Boji himself. "Be quiet. Be good. Just a little while. Hush."

The servant passage door opened quietly, and Eisi and Liedi came in, two young men a little subdued and tired from the trip. He said quietly, "One is almost certain there is a breakfast service from staff, nadiin-ji. So we should all be up. I shall be right back."

The servant passage had a little accommodation—his guests being in the two rooms within his, he had advised them last night that they should not hesitate to go through his room in any case of necessity: the bed-curtain was as good as a wall. It was a very fine arrangement, although he found the thick bed-curtains a little spooky. He had been too tired to care, last night, and whether his guests had indeed come and gone last night, he had no idea. He hurried back, now, expecting that Eisi and Liedi would have waked his guests and advised them both that there was breakfast soon to be had, and that they would have his clothes laid out ready for him.

He was not disappointed. He dressed quickly—he had to dress in the bedroom, while Irene was still in her little room, having to dress herself, and his aishid was doing the same out in the sitting room. Guild managed, that was all, having their own rules; and Jegari looked in on him, already in uniform—just a brief appearance in the doorway to tell him breakfast was indeed waiting.

Cajeiri put his coat on. Eisi knocked on one side door and the other to advise his guests they might now come and go—such had been their arrangement last night.

Gene and Artur and Irene all came out, dressed even to their coats, looking quite well put together on their own—though Irene seemed a little embarrassed in ducking back to the accommodation. Liedi meanwhile finished Cajeiri's queue and neatly tied it with a pale green ribbon—he was honoring Great-uncle's house today—and they were all in good order for breakfast.

Boji was getting restless, uttering ominous scolding sounds, as if to ask now that the household was awake, where was his breakfast? Eisi immediately went to provide him an egg, before he set up a cage-rattling racket.

Cajeiri gave a short sigh, relieved, and straightened his coat cuffs—habit, after so many breakfasts with Great-grandmother. Great-uncle's household was *absolutely* proper, and there were *so* many ways things could go wrong in a proper Bujavid apartment—but his servants and his bodyguards were doing everything absolutely right at every turn. They had come in on the train with only what they were wearing, but Uncle's night staff had gotten their clothes all clean and ready again.

And the rest of their baggage was *supposed* to catch up with them today, which would make things easier. There were crates coming by train from Tirnamardi, because they had left so fast the staff had not had time to pack. And even if he had a closet down the hall, in his own suite in his parents' apartment, he could not turn up in court clothes when his guests had none—so he could be comfortable here in Uncle's apartment, at least until the crate came. He hoped it came after supper.

Eisi and Liedi meanwhile gave a rap on the sitting room door frame and ushered them out into their sitting room. His aishid, standing at the buffet, were doubtless having breakfast themselves, but they managed to look as if they had been doing no such thing—Veijico and Lucasi were particularly good at that maneuver, and Antaro and Jegari were learning.

The suite had a beautiful little dining table, and the buffet was all laid out with fine dishes, with racks of toast and little bowls of eggs, and a large tray of morning sweet cakes, too.

They sat down, very properly. Liedi slipped an egg through the door to his partner and only one small screech from Boji escaped the bedroom. Antaro began to pour tea, all so, so smoothly, while Eisi began to serve so elegantly that Great-grandmother herself would find nothing at all to disapprove.

He was quite, quite proud of his little staff this morning. And Great-uncle's staff had provided a very fine old tea service, all wrought with gold curlicues and painted scenes. The plates were so ornate that his guests, accepting food from Eisi, kept arranging things around the painted scene in the center, as if it should never be touched.

Great-uncle was not treating them any differently from important grown-up guests. It was very good of him. And his guests were trying, too; but it was almost scary to think about, even with his guests on absolutely best behavior and all of them trying not to make mistakes—there was bound to be, somewhere in his formal birthday festivity, a state dinner, with five different sorts of crystal and all sorts of little plates and forks, with *adult* guests, all there to look at him and all the while wondering whether *he* was going do something awkward or stupid—

He hated formal dinners. And there was bound to be one.

He knew he had gotten a reputation, even before this last year. He was *sure* everybody had heard about his losing a boat at Najida and riding a mecheita across Great-uncle's just-poured pavement And it was a lot to expect of his guests, not to make a mistake with all those forks—but he could *not* embarrass his guests by correcting their table manners.

They did watch him. They did copy him. So he tried to do everything exactly right. He thought—though perhaps it was a mean-spirited thought—that his mother particularly would order the most elaborate table the world had ever seen, just to embarrass his guests in front of everybody. It was a very unhappy thought. But he had it, all the same, and he *hoped* his father would prevent any such notion, because his mother could be subtle when she was mad.

He just hoped for the sort of birthday his mother had said he had had once before, just a few gifts to him—or no gifts: he was getting too old for gifts, even if he had had the best ever, from Great-uncle and mani, and from his father, just in getting his associates here.

If they all just looked proper and used the right fork, that would make his mother happier. And she was not going to be in a calm and generous mood . . . not with her father assassinated, and her clan with no lord now, and this Haikuti person that Banichi had shot dead—he was another Ajuri. He had no idea whether his mother knew him.

Great-grandmother was tracking somebody else in Ajuri clan right now, and Great-grandmother was deadly serious, so somebody else in Ajuri was going to die. His birthday festivity was going to be a *terrible* family dinner. Mother and Great-grandmother notoriously did not get along.

It upset his stomach even thinking about it. He remembered a certain recent party when they *had* gotten together, and *he* had experimented with brandy.

But Madam Saidin had warned him to put on a pleasant expression today. That was his job.

So he did it. And talked about pleasant things instead.

There was mail. Indeed there was mail, and after everything that had happened in the last few days, it had the feeling of little time capsules—letters from before the world had turned sideways, from *before* they had two Dojisigi Assassins and the lord of the Kadagidi under lock and key in the dowager's backstairs. Bren broke seals and unrolled messages that truly, had nothing to do with current reality.

The legislature had been in session, with important bills at issue, and he hoped the tribal bill in particular would have passed. He had left Lord Dur to manage it.

But, the letter from Dur said, the upper house had not voted. The bill had been postponed because of the Ajuri assassination.

One rejoices to say the prospects are good for passage, was the word from Lord Dur. *We have two laggards arguing past issues, but events in the midlands today are demanding urgent attention. We are postponing the vote until after the young gentleman's birthday celebration, hoping that all matters can be resolved privately before the vote.*

Privately. Before the vote.

That meant one-on-one meetings and promises. Deals.

Damn. He hoped it would have sailed through without that.

Not that the next few days were going to be quieter. The last thing the world needed was for events at Asien'dalun, the Kadagidi estate, to reverberate into the debate over the tribal peoples' admission into the aishidi'tat ... which affected the voting balance. The Conservatives were going to have serious questions about the removal of a Conservative lord of very old family, no doubt about it, even if he had already been banned from court ... and the fact that the Kadagidi affair involved three prominent Conservatives and the *notoriously* liberal paidhi-aiji, not to mention involving the Taibeni and a handful of human guests, was going to create shockwaves on its own. Agitating both parties at once never helped an issue.

He had already called in political favors on the tribal peoples bill. He was going to be running low on favors, he feared, and he had already put allies at political risk. Lord Tatiseigi was going to have to help settle that one—at least on his side of the political divide.

The other messages at least proved mundane ... a day-old question on the Ajuri succession was germane, but nothing he wanted to respond to—it was nothing *Tabini-aiji* wanted to respond to, he was damned sure of that.

There were, in the stack, two questions arising from the opposite point of the compass, the always-volatile Marid—questions involving the Scholars' Guild, and the controversy over how the Marid apprenticeship system was going to combine with a proposed northern-style classroom education—neither of which were pertinent to the mess they had on their hands.

There was a letter requesting Jase-aiji's appearance before the Transportation Committee, something to do with the port, one supposed, and about as remote from current business as it was possible to be. The committee had realized, through its own sources at the shuttle port, that a ship-captain was on the planet, and they wanted to talk to him directly, probably about technical issues and regulations ... a set of technical concerns that also seemed from another universe, at the moment.

He finished the pile. He made a few notes about the birthday festivity, requesting advisement directly to him should anything unusual on that topic reach his clerical office.

And there was, yes, a query from his tailor, requesting a fitting.

God. Maybe he *should* see to that today, before anything blew up. Granted his wardrobe was stalled in transit ... it could be a good idea.

At least the tailor and the looming birthday festivity posed a distraction from darker thoughts.

But then he caught, in the tailor's note, that slight change from festivity to Festivity, the elaborate form of the word, that set his heart to beating just a little faster.

Festivity as in ... *national holiday.*

Was that an error? *National holiday?*

He rang for Narani, and when that gentleman arrived:

"Close the door. Rani-ji. Has there been a change in the aiji's plans for the birthday?"

The old man's mouth opened slightly, an expression of consternation. A deep breath. "Yes, nandi. Yesterday."

Amid all the confusion.

"One apologizes. One apologizes profoundly."

"Well, hardly a consequence to our plans," he said, but thought then— "Did the announcement come before or *after* the news from the Kadagidi estate?"

"Before, nandi. Just after breakfast."

Which meant the aiji had thought about it and changed his plans somewhat *before* yesterday morning and *before* the Kadagidi manor house had lost its local guard, its front porch, and a corner window.

One last little message lay on the desk, one of those Bujavid announcements, by the distinctive cylinder: such usually regarded public hours, a restriction within the building, or a change in the museum exhibits. He reached for it, opened it, cracked the seal, expecting to see an official announcement of the change.

Running dark since the day before yesterday evening meant that they had not been getting news. They had been in Lord Tatiseigi's television-free estate. The last word they had gotten from the outside world had been information about Lord Ajuri's assassination, a rotten enough omen for the boy's upcoming birthday, omen rotten enough to have shut down the legislature on its own, despite strong forces pushing to get the tribal bill through . . .

Now he understood Lord Dur's advisement about the suspension of the vote until after the boy's *birthday celebration,* which had seemed an odd sort of thing to send the legislature into recess. It wasn't just a birthday celebration. It was a *Festivity* that was going to shut down the city and cause a business holiday across the continent.

The memo, arrived from the Bujavid events office just this morning, said that the change in scope of the aiji's event required them to move the reception out of the

Green Hall and into the larger Audience Hall. Now the event was to be preceded, during the day, by a private dinner in the aiji's apartment and an invitation-only tour of Lord Tatiseigi's display in the Bujavid Museum—some of his fabled porcelain collection. That necessitated a museum closure on that entire day. Due to expected crowd pressure, the usual distribution of souvenir cards would be on the third landing, and not inside the Bujavid hall.

Crowd pressure wasn't the half of the reason.

"This came yesterday?" he asked.

"Yesterday, nandi." Narani gave a mortified little bow. "One is so very sorry not to have mentioned it."

"I suppose the decree was on the news. There is a *public* celebration."

"Yes, nandi."

"We were somewhat preoccupied," he said, with irony. "The matter could hardly have sat at the top of your report, Rani-ji, when we arrived as we did last night."

"You did mention the birthday, nandi. And one thought you knew," Narani said. "One *very* deeply regrets the omission."

"One is a *little* startled to hear it," he said. A national celebration was the sort of thing one did, besides the four seasonal festivals of the year, for a felicitous event, such as the launch of an important national program. There were lesser, city functions—the appointment of a lord to high office, the opening of a new public facility. These were minor, an excuse for some businesses taking a holiday, bars and restaurants doing good business . . . but nationwide?

The timing was infelicitous . . . right over the assassination of the boy's grandfather . . .

Or it was to *cover* an infelicity.

"One suspects," he said to Narani, "this is not *unrelated* to the assassination. Is there *any* word who was behind that?"

Narani answered very quietly: "Absolutely none, nandi."

He would not have said what he had just said about the timing to anyone on domestic staff *but* Narani.

"Incredible to me that the aiji would have done it," he murmured, "so close to the boy's birthday."

"One concurs, nandi."

The shift from private to public event, however—likely *did* relate to the grandfather's assassination . . . a determination *not* to have that infelicitous event overshadowing his son's fortunate ninth birthday. It was a fast decision, if that was the motive.

And depending on where one placed responsibility for the assassination, paving over it with a national festivity was either deprecating the importance of Ajuri clan, or it was fiercely deploring the event, the person that had done it, and *supporting* Ajuri clan. There was a word for it. Bajio kabisu. Overturning the odds. For the traditional-minded, for the marginally superstitious, it met adversity with a tidal wave of good omen. It overpowered a setback, in effect— wiping it out, as only a very powerful lord could do. It said: we are more than that. We cannot be affected.

This time it said, *my son* is more than this.

It put the boy in the political spotlight. In a political context.

And a slap in the face of whoever had assassinated Komaji became, by sheer chance, a slap in the face of the Kadagidi, since there was no way Tabini was going to cancel his gesture in the face of fate . . . to mourn the downfall of a much more impotant clan . . . that had happened to birth a traitor and house a problem.

Omens?

They had a boatload of omens. And there was going to be a real political to-do over the Kadagidi matter, *especially* with a boy's birthday used to plaster over it.

But Tabini was solid in public opinion since the success in the west. Unshakeable. And he was acting like it.

Well, it just took a moment to readjust one's plans.

"It requires some change," he said. "One sincerely hopes our crates from Tirnamardi arrive in good order. Whether I shall have time for the tailor—no, no, I had better not take the time. If the crates do not arrive, I shall wear the pale green—" It was a shade off from Tatiseigi's heraldry—"and lend Jase my blue suit. Those will do." A thought came to him. "One has no idea, however, how the young gentleman's guests may manage wardrobe, with or without the crates. One fully expects they *will* attend, in some capacity."

"One has not heard, nandi, but one would expect so, yes."

"One might drop that word in Madam Saidin's ear. The guests have not come prepared for such a major event. If I can assist, I shall."

"One is very sorry not to have mentioned the change earlier."

"By no means, Rani-ji. The aiji *himself* neglected to mention it last night. In retrospect, one believes he was preparing to mention it, when the consort arrived in the room—but let us not assume the aiji-dowager or Lord Tatiseigi knows this, either. Send Jeladi down the hall to advise both households. This may constitute a small emergency."

"Absolutely, nandi."

A *national* Festivity.

It had to be the shortest notice *he* had yet seen. And absolutely it was the aiji's response to the assassination of the boy's grandfather. The other . . . Tabini could not have anticipated the paidhi-aiji, of all people, would launch an attack on the Kadagidi.

But the city would manage, as most other cities and towns and villages would manage . . . well-oiled procedures that with very little to-do could close down most work for a day, bring out the licensed vendors—most of whom were carts operated by regular restaurants—and declare the city trains free of charge for the day.

Booths would blossom. The Bujavid would ordinarily open the lower floor to visitors and have all the lights on, down the grand stairs that ran down the hill—those stairs had used to be a severe trial of endurance, a test of will to reach the aiji—but nowadays a tram served, and the several landings became only another gauntlet of small colorful stands on festival days. The Bujavid Museum *was* usually open for such events. The crowds traditionally had access all the way into the lower hall, to gain the prize of official cards and ribbons for the event, whatever it was . . . the lines posing another contest of endurance.

The museum was to be closed, however. Cards would be distributed outside, on a landing.

That was uncommon. People would be disappointed in that.

It might be an ordinary security concern—counting the priceless exhibits—counting that someone *had* assassinated a clan lord in the last few days.

So if the museum was closed and there were no ribbons and banners on the steps to lure celebrants up farther than the third landing . . . they would have very few citizens disposed to come up the hill, even for the chance to catch a distant view of human children or a visiting ship-captain. That was fortunate.

"Go," he said to Narani, and added: "Advise my aishid, too. Be sure they know about the changes."

Narani left. Bren sat, rubbed his eyes and tried to figure if there was any other loose end of correspondence he needed to attend or any precautionary contact he ought to make—anything that could, for one thing, do any good for the tribal peoples bill at this point.

There was none that he could think of.

And that was the old mail. One feared to know what *today's* letters could bring.

9

A half hour later a little rap came at the door. Jago entered the office and closed the door behind her.

"Bren-ji," she said, with an I'm-on-business directness.

"News?" he asked, remembering his aishid had been in conference with Cenedi's lot. He turned his chair, expecting information from that meeting.

She stood in front of him, arms folded. "We have a plan," she said, "of sorts."

"One hears." He stood up, courtesy, where it came to his aishid. And her. "You did receive my message from Narani."

"Indeed," she said. "The change does not interfere. In fact—it may be a useful distraction."

He *thought* he was relieved to hear so. "What is our situation?"

"We have a twofold problem," Jago said. "First is safeguarding the aiji and the young gentleman from counterattack. Securing the service passages—we have done that. But this enemy may be on staff in the Bujavid, or in the Bujavid guard, or maintenance, and more—certainly for a time, and if things go wrong, permanently so—*we* will not be here to protect this floor." Jago held up a thumb. "We need to order the Bujavid guard and civilian personnel not to access this floor at all. Only Tabini-aiji can give that order. We ask that you obtain that, in the aiji's own defense." Index finger. "We need you to ask Jase-aiji to enforce that security with his guard tonight." Next finger. "We need you to ask Jase-aiji to be prepared, under the direction of the dowager or Lord Tatiseigi, to take Tabini-aiji, the young gentleman, *and* his guests down to the train station."

"The train station."

Third finger. "At need, Lord Tatiseigi's bodyguard will seize control of the Transportation Guild office in the Bujavid station long enough to commandeer a train. This is Lord Tatiseigi's part of the plan, with our modifications: it will not be the Red Train, but a freight. It will have clearance to the spaceport, and it will be defended by the dowager's own bodyguard. Once inside the spaceport perimeter, Jase-aiji will defend the spaceport, pending the shuttle's preparation to take them to the space station."

Evacuate the ruling family? God. The port, given warning, was now a defensible area—especially with Geigi in possession of the other shuttles and no few ground installations which themselves could pick up and move.

But at no time had Jago said where *he* would be during all this maneuvering. He ached to ask. Disturbing Guild in laying down instructions, however, was not a good idea. He understood the part of the plan he had heard thus far: the port was as secure an onworld position as they could achieve.

And beyond that—with Tabini and his son in orbit, inside Geigi's protection, and unassailable—their enemies would have no chance of staging another coup, no matter how extensive their plans.

With the spaceport on the continent in the aiji's control, and with an adequate landing field and service facility at Port Jackson Airport on Mospheira—loyal forces could come and go. They could take key units up to the station and send them back down again for whatever operations they wished to undertake. His aishid had talked about that before now.

Militarily—it was a good idea. The Shadow Guild would not be able to reach them. Politically—it had serious problems. They had discussed that, too.

Were they down to that?

Last finger. *"That,"* Jago said, "if things go wrong."

If things go wrong. He was vastly relieved to hear that she was laying down a contingency. And they all knew the problems with it. Doing that, lifting the aiji off the planet, would weaken the aijinate. For him to run, for him to shelter himself with humans, for him to abandon his people in a crisis and shelter behind human weapons—would say things about the world's situation, and about the relations between atevi and human . . . that they never, ever wanted to have happen.

And to *what* is this the contingency? he wanted to ask. But he waited.

Jago folded both arms. "The plan." A deep frown. "All this last year, not knowing what enemy we might face, but knowing there was at least one individual we needed to reach, we—and the dowager's aishid—have had a list of individuals who are not in good favor with the Guild Council. We are now in contact with individuals in the central district and on the west coast—and this is, for political reasons, the best idea. We should not appear to rely solely on the East."

The East—being the aiji-dowager's territory. He clearly understood the politics so far. And he suspected which "list of individuals" Jago meant. The Missing and the Dead . . . who were no longer counted loyal, or reliable.

"Member access to Guild Headquarters has been severely restricted," Jago said, "since the aiji's return to office. Ordinary Guild members no longer have routine access beyond the entry hall and the offices there. The Council Chamber is now restricted to those *on* the Council agenda—and the Council, of course, controls who gets on the agenda. The administrative hall adjacent to the Council Chamber has been declared off limits to anyone except very high ranking Guild on official Guild or state business. All these measures are new, all since the coup. They call it security. It is an inconvenience. Ordinary members have simply worked around it."

He still listened. Clearly enough—they were talking about Guild Headquarters, on the other side of the city. They needed to get inside. And it wasn't easy.

"If we assault Guild Headquarters head-on," Jago said, "and break down the doors—there will be key personnel inside that we cannot contact safely, persons who would join us if they knew what we know—but who, if they do not, will obey Council orders until the end. It will mean the loss of innocent and important people, a loss to the Guild—and assuredly the loss of records we need. If Assignments has any warning at all—those records will certainly go."

Records detailing the whole pattern of personnel assignments, Bren thought.

"You know," Jago said, "that certain of the senior Guild went underground when Murini came in. Some that were listed as dead—were not; and are not; and among them are those who operated the network to bring Tabini-aiji back. The seniormost have claimed retirement. Others have stayed dead—for the record. They have now watched the Guild purge itself once, and twice. The current Guild leadership has repeatedly ordered them back to duty, and they have not come in. This war of wills has been going on since the coup ended. Personal issues are certainly at work. These people are not in agreement with current leadership. What I am about to tell you, even the aiji has not heard—and is not to hear; but you need to know, Bren-ji."

"Whatever I should hear, Jago-ji, I shall keep even from the aiji."

"This, then. Three individuals head the current Guild Council. One of them is compliant with the other two and more a failure than a problem. The other two have a pattern of action we question. They have pushed through, with a rapidity that admits no debate, whatever the Office of

Assignments has recommended—including the recent assignment of chief officers in the Dojisigin Marid. During the trouble in the west, when we needed assistance, they were slow in moving forces, so much so that Tabini-aiji himself took the field, because his presence trumped the process of querying Guild Council. And at a critical time when the retired Guild *might* have been willing to assist the aiji's action in the south, the Guild diverted itself from assisting Tabini-aiji and us, as we had requested—and instead sent a mission to arrest the two seniormost retirees—an extended distraction that ended with one unit dead and the retirees officially outlawed. It is an outlawry without effect, since there is no other Guild in the area where they are—but it is on the books, and will justify whatever Shadow Guild can eventually reach them. The Missing *still* ignore the Council's orders. But they do not ignore us. We—Cenedi—and we—have been in contact with them since we returned from Najida, since the Council's attempt to arrest them. We sent a message yesterday morning, before we went dark, using your name, requesting a boat sent to Najida. This was code. We have had one contact since, a contact face to face, in the lower corridors, directly with us . . . with us, because they will not deal with Cenedi in this matter."

"Because he is Eastern Guild."

"Exactly so." Jago drew a deep breath. "Neutrality in disputes is the cornerstone of our guild. And there has been a cascade of events breaching that tradition: unFiled attacks on civilians, violations of code, Council refusal to bring charges in several cases, Haikuti among them. The Missing have seen the whole world change, Bren-ji. They did not approve of the space program; they fear Lord Geigi. They do not so much distrust Cenedi as they do not want the appearance of relying on the Eastern Guild. The decision they themselves made, long before the coup, to back Shishogi's quaint demands and reject computers as a human gift— they know now that was a serious mistake. They have reconstructed, with far more names than we know, what decisions set certain individuals in charge of certain offices that arranged the coup that set up Murini. And they know that Haikuti *was* involved in the attack on the aiji at Taiben, and that he remained, until yesterday, untouched and his location known—they gave us names to watch. We checked them out. We reported back information—both gave and received it. The fact that Tabini-aiji had banned the Kadagidi lord—also isolated Haikuti in safety from arrest. And the Guild has kept Haikuti's records as secret inside its files as it does any other unit's records. But the Guild in exile knew what he had done. And what information they gave us greatly troubled Algini, and troubled Banichi most of all. Tano and I—we had no idea of it. But when we went there—when we went to the Kadagidi estate—Banichi expected trouble. He and Algini expected trouble. And he did not tell you. He was held between a good idea—a chance to build a clear case against the Kadagidi—and the fact that he and Haikuti had come to blows before. He was also preserving the secrecy of our information source—and he was caught between that necessity, and the fact that even yet there was no proof, absolutely none, of what he and Algini had learned from our sources."

"Is there any doubt now?"

"None," Jago said. "None in my mind. But, Bren-ji, be warned: the people we are dealing with, the Guild in exile, are *not* people who favor humans. They are, however, and always have been, immaculately loyal to the law. And, being Guild, they have *no* reluctance to take a pragmatic approach. To restore the law, during Murini's rule, they *were* working with humans on Mospheira. They never favored Tabini-aiji *because* of his association with humans, but to restore the Guild to what it was, they will now support us and support *him.* We have their word. As of last night, we have their word. They are leaving their identities for the second time. Leaving families. Breaking off marriages. They are coming in—to take back the Guild, delve into records, and restore the law."

"What are the odds?"

"As things stand—we face a bloody confrontation with innocent members that could see the wrong side win, or at best, rob us of proof. Shishogi, if he sees himself apt to be dismissed, will destroy records. The *law* depends on proof. The Guild enforces the law. We administer the law. We support the law. And if those of us against the current Council cannot prove our case to the membership, if Tabini-aiji has to uphold us only by decree, and by the power of the aijinate—the Guild will never again *be* what we *were*. We need an authority and a legitimacy that can only come by us standing *in* the Council Chamber and proving our case, that the Council itself has broken the law."

"Can you do that?"

"Under the charter, and under current Guild rules, there are only two individuals who can enter that building and demand attention from the Council, whatever its agenda. Tabini-aiji can. The aiji-dowager can. And *she* wishes to do it. She is Eastern, however. The Guild in exile will balk at that thought."

Ilisidi?

Good God. She walked with a cane. She was fragile. Walk in there, into a fortress and demand the Assassins' Guild leadership politely resign in favor of their enemies?

Only *two* individuals could get in there. *Legally* speaking.

He suddenly knew what Jago was working toward.

"*I* can be either of those persons," he said.

"Your aishid has very reluctantly entertained that thought, Bren-ji. If *you* can get through the front doors of Guild Headquarters, officially, *we* can get in with you. If Cenedi also happens to be inside the building on the dowager's business, with a small attendance of the dowager's men ... as he can do on his own, being head of a regional Guild—and if several other units currently active happen to be there, on other business on the floor above ... we can open the building from several different points at once. Baji-naji, we can prevent the records being destroyed."

"So." He drew a deep breath. Force his way into Guild headquarters?

He'd worried a great deal, on that train ride, about his aishid eventually deciding to take on Assignments themselves—entering the Guild's headquarters, trying to penetrate the defenses of the whole rest of the Guild ... because he could not see the Assassins' Guild turning over records at anyone's asking, even Tabini's.

He'd not remotely thought they'd ask *his* help. But it made sense.

"So—" he asked. "What would we have to do, Jago-ji?"

"Pass the doors all the way to Council, while it sits in session. If it will admit us, and hear you, well and good. If not, we set ourselves in a single critical doorway, between the hallway straight ahead, which is the Council, and the hallway to the left, which leads to Assignments, and we keep that door open, preventing them from sealing the heart of the building. Likely—most likely, Bren-ji, the Council will refuse to hear you—considering the situation with Lord Aseida. *That* would actually be desirable. Outright refusal would be *quite* acceptable. Hearing you have arrived, they will view you as, if nothing else, a move by Tabini that they do not want to deal with, and that they will want to stall—especially if they get wind of any physical movement by the old Guild in the city. But should they actually let us into the Council chamber, we will be in position, and we will be armed."

"How—armed?"

"The ordinary. Indeed, Bren-ji, we have even thought of Jase-aiji's weapons. But we cannot set that precedent, and there are too many innocent people in the way. We shall have our legal sidearms. Cenedi will have no more nor less than that. And his is the more dangerous task: Assignments will know what happened in Kadagidi territory ... and if we are unlucky, Assignments and his allies in Council may know that we have been in contact with the opposition. Assignments will be particularly unhappy to see us—and Council may set up protection and issue orders to stop us at the doors. If we are lucky, they will become busy watching us and not watch Cenedi. We shall have no idea how things stand as we go in. We shall need speed, we shall need precise coordination with our other units—and all this without *any* recourse to Guild communications. We shall need the front doors opened, and, ideally, that second door opened and held open. Both are our problems. The aiji-dowager cannot do this. For one thing—their refusal of *her* would connect with a political history in the legislature that does not suit us. For another—you can move faster than she can. You are as recognizable as she is. And you are willing to take cover. We are not so certain about the dowager."

Grim joke. But he didn't have the right reflexes. He couldn't react quickly enough, nor in the right direction. He was a liability under fire. He'd proven that often enough.

Worse, they would instinctively try to protect him.

"I fear being a risk to you, Jago-ji. I am entirely willing, but I fear moving in the wrong direction. And I absolutely do not want to put you at risk protecting me."

"There are things you can learn. That you *must* learn, to do this with us. And you will definitely be wearing the vest."

Bullets hurt. *God,* they hurt. But that was nowhere in any important calculations. "Then advise me what I need to do, Jago-ji. Tell me what I need to do."

"Moving *with* us is important. We can coordinate very precisely without communications, given a known distance and a precise rate of movement. We do not wish to look as if we are counting—but we will be counting. You will practice that with me."

He nodded. He knew how that worked. "Yes."

And the rest—he would do. The stakes were that high. And it was going to be a very, very narrow window they had if they hoped to act fast enough to get at those records.

Were there people who could step into the breach and deal with the political situation if he and his aishid were shot down in a hallway?

Tabini and Geigi could.

His own brother, Toby, would connect with the Guild in exile, and with Tabini.

And never discount Ilisidi. Keeping *her* alive and safe was a priority, especially if anything happened to them. The plan could *not* entail putting her at risk.

"We are far from pleased to ask this, Bren-ji. It will be an extreme risk, and our priorities in this, you are right, cannot be to protect you. Of all units that *could* get in, we are the youngest, and our field skills, unlike some of the senior Guild, have not rusted."

"Baji-naji, Jago-ji. Our instincts in such a situation are occasionally at odds. We discovered *that* on a hillside in Malguri, and I apologize that I have not in the least reformed, though I know more than I did. I confess I am *far* happier to go in there with you than to send you in there without me. I know your feelings are quite the opposite. I can only say I *have* gotten cannier over the years."

"You cannot go armed, this time, Bren-ji. There will be detectors."

"But you can."

"We, certainly. But you, and the documents you bring to the Council, must represent the aiji, on some matter that can be proven, even if we cannot file them, to be *completely* within the aiji's rights—and completely apart from the Kadagidi matter. *There* is our proof of Council misdeed, do you understand? *That* is our issue."

"Indeed." He drew in a breath. And let it out again. "Well. Well, I shall wear the vest without a complaint on this outing. And I shall stay *with* you, Jago-ji. When shall we do this?"

"This evening," she said. "When the Guild Council meets."

This evening.

God. He was *not* mentally ready for this.

But he had to be, evidently. He had to be, to do the things that needed doing. Anything else—gave their enemies time to figure them out, or for something essential to leak, and for lives to be lost. Or the whole effort to be lost.

Tonight it was, then.

"Is Banichi going?" he asked.

"He has pills for infection, pills for pain, and a stimulant which he may be taking in excess. He has to be there—he promised the exiled Guild he would be. And," she added, "he *is* added firepower."

He understood it. He far from liked that part of it. But he understood what it was to have a member of a team down: it was like an arch missing a keystone.

"He has Algini for backup," she said. "He and Algini both know the senior units on sight, as Tano and I do not. And the plan does make sense. What more we need—you, Bren-ji, can get a document from Tabini-aiji, something with conspicuous seals and an abundance of ribbons, on a matter we might reasonably bring before the Guild."

"I shall get it," he said.

This evening, he thought. Damn.

He needed to have his valets set his court dress in good order for reasons not to do with the impending holiday. And he needed to write a few letters he hoped Narani would never have to send.

Then there was Jase.

He had to talk to Jase.

"We have a difficult day planned," was how he began, with Jase, alone, and with the inevitable pot of tea between them. But human-fashion, and because time was short, tea and discussion of business were simultaneous. "We're going into the Guild offices tonight to get our target. We're figuring how to get through the doors."

"We."

"My aishid. And I. Politically—you should not be involved in this. You should not be in the least involved."

"Damn, Bren."

That was of curious comfort, that human expression. Toby would say just about that if Toby were here. He was very glad Toby was not.

"What can I do?" Jase asked.

Toby, he thought, would ask that, too.

To that, he had an answer. "This. Guard the aiji. Guard Ilisidi. Guard Tatiseigi and the children with your weapons. With everything you've got. If you're attacked here, get a message to Geigi. Ask for help, tell him everything we know, and very likely at that point you'll *be* paidhi-aiji."

Jase took a deep breath. "You're not taking *stupid* chances, are you?"

"I have no intention of it. But my aishid is going in, for reasons they explained, so it's down to me. I'm the only official who's in any degree expendable. I can get through a certain door that needs to be opened, that otherwise would cost lives. My credentials can do it. And if the people in charge try to stop me—we've got all the legal grounds we need for what happens next. Which will either go as we hope—or not. Say that having you for backup and knowing they can't strike at our backs, so to speak, will make me a lot happier this evening. If the aiji and his household are safe— they can't win."

"Whatever I can do—yes. No question. But understand— if things blow up down here, I'm under orders from Sabin to get myself and the kids back to the spaceport."

"Exactly what we want you to do. And take Tabini-aiji, the aiji-dowager, and Lord Tatiseigi with you."

"Are they going to agree to that?"

"I'm going to arrange it at least with Tabini, and I hope he can move the other two. In whatever happens—these are the people to trust." He held up three fingers. "Those three." A fourth. "Geigi." The thumb. "My brother Toby. Any Guild working for the three. Or for Geigi. My brother's partner Barb: she understands security and secrecy, she's loyal to him and she'd carry a message, but she's a bit scattered."

"Understood."

"If you come under threat, don't waste time wondering if you should go. Go. Take everyone you can, the aiji, the aiji-dowager, Cajeiri, the guests, and anyone they insist on taking, and get down to the train station. That's the most direct route. There's a danger of someone blocking the tracks, but agents of ours are going to take control of the Transportation office in the Bujavid and try to keep that track clear for you. If at any point you are blocked, stay with the train, defend your position, and trust the dowager's people to identify anybody showing up with alternative transport. However you can, get everybody to the spaceport, shut the gates and trust no one from the outside of that fence. If for some reason you can't reach the spaceport—get to the Taibeni and the Atageini or the dowager's fortress in Malguri as a place to stay: but those are survival scenarios. The goal is, as soon as possible, get everybody up onto the station, link up with Lord Geigi, and sort it all out from there. Do *not* let the dowager or the aiji convince you to stand and fight. If you need another paidhi, consider my brother Toby. Clans that can help you: Dur, for sea transport; Taibeni, for hiding; and Atageini, for political fights. Beyond that—you do the planning."

"You're not to get yourself killed, Bren. I really want you to avoid that."

"I really intend to."

Jase drew a deep breath. "Understood. I'll do it, Bren. Me, Kaplan, and Polano—we'll do what we have to. Any help we can give you. I know Geigi's the same."

"This one, this one is something worth the risk. We're going in to rescue the law. The Assassins' Guild *is* the law, and it's had something wrong in its gut for a long, long time."

"Can you fix it?" Jase asked. Outsider's question, clear and cold and honest, and for just one beat of his heart Bren asked that question of himself.

Then he thought of his bodyguard.

"Yes," he said. "Yes, we can fix it. There's enough of us."

"Four of you," Jase objected, then, atevi-fashion: "Five."

"A little more than that. I don't know all the plan. They're still working it out. But we're going in to open those doors all the way to the inner halls and pose a serious problem to people who deserve it. And we'll fix it."

"Rely on me," Jase said. "Concentrate on yourself. *Here* will get taken care of."

There were, after that, letters and authorizations to write. In case.

To Cajeiri he wrote: *Place yourself and your guests inside Jase-aiji's protection and obey his orders without question. He will be protecting those of you in the Bujavid. I am going into this with good hope of success, but should you be reading this letter, something untoward has happened, there is a threat to you and your guests, and your great-grandmother and your father and Jase-aiji will protect you and Lord Tatiseigi by wise actions. You are an excellent young gentleman. Apply yourself to become an excellent and wise aiji, when that day comes. I am glad to take this action for your long life and success.*

To Toby: *Brother, if you've gotten this letter, things have gone wrong on the mainland and very likely I'm not on the scene any longer. Contact Geigi. Don't come to the mainland until you're sure it's safe, and until Geigi and Jase agree it's a good idea. If things I arranged went well, Tabini and the aijidowager and the heir will be on the station in safety. If not, they will be in places you can guess. Get into communication with them. Tell the President to avoid any provocation of the mainland and consult closely with Lord Geigi. Do what you can to keep the world safe. I love you, brother. And I rely on you. You don't have the command of the language I do, but you've got the understanding. I've told Jase that when he has to pass the torch, you're it. Trust Ilisidi, trust Geigi, trust Tatiseigi, Dur, and you know the rest of the names. Take good care of Cajeiri. He's the future. You and Barb—stay safe as you can.*

To Tabini: *One regrets very much, aiji-ma, that I was not able to come back. Rely on Jase-aiji and on Lord Geigi. I have arranged everything to get you and your household to safety and for you to accomplish the defeat of your enemies, the restoration of the Guilds, and the preservation of the aishidi'tat with as little loss of life as possible. I have absolute confidence in your leadership of the aishidi'tat, and I say freely that you have been the great leader that I have hoped for.*

God, he hoped that letter never had to be delivered while he was living. Tabini's ego was large enough.

Rely on my brother-of-the-same-parents, Toby. Rely on all the ship-aijiin, who view you as a very valuable and trust-worthy ally; and especially rely on Jase-aiji—he is a good ally, a human who will not change sides, and an authority with great power in the heavens. Do not, however, trust Yolanda-paidhi: she has changed.

Believe that you have earned the confidence and good will of humans and atevi alike. Rely on your grandmother and on her allies. She has always favored you and your son above all other answers for the world.

To Ilisidi:

If you are reading this at least my own part of it has not gone well. I am therefore doubly glad and honored to have replaced you in this venture, and regret only missing the actions you will take next, which I hope will be initially down the paths to safety and power that I have spent these last hours securing for you.

Rely on Jase-aiji, on Geigi, on Lord Tatiseigi, my brother Toby, and know that I have watched over you in these last hours. Thank you for many actions which you know and which I will not mention. If any of my aishid survive, take them to your service, as I also hope you will look favorably on my staff on station and my major domo and my senior staff once you return to the world.

To you and to your great-grandson I leave my estate at Najida, and I also put Najida Peninsula and its people in your care.

To Geigi:

I have undertaken a mission against enemies of the aiji.

Please take care of those closest to me, guard those I would guard, and remember me as someone who wished atevi and humans to live in peace. I have every confidence you will find a path between the ship-aijiin and the Mospheirans, between humans and atevi, and from the old ways into the new. I have complete confidence in your management of affairs in the heavens. I believe you will bring about a good solution, and I only regret that I must leave you with so much yet to do.

To Tatiseigi:

I am honored by the generous hospitality you have shown me over many years. I am particularly honored by your acts of trust and support for me personally despite our differences of degree and birth. With every year I have understood more and more why the aiji-dowager favors you so highly, and I have every confidence in her recommendations. I have asked her to care for my staff, and hope that you may assist her with that matter, as I hope you will look favorably on my people. Go with her and keep her safe. Trust Jase-aiji. He will not understand every custom, but he will do everything for your protection.

To Narani himself:

Accept my deep gratitude for your extraordinary service, your courage, and your inventiveness. I have asked the aiji-dowager to make provision for you and for senior staff, and I have bequeathed Najida to her and to her great-grandson, where you also may have a place should you wish it. I ask you see to the disposition of my clerical staff, and to the execution of my more detailed will, which you will find in the back center of my desk, under my seal. No one could have a more faithful manager than you have been, here and on the station.

It was a somewhat depressing set of notes to have to write, but curiously—it left him feeling he wanted his favorite dessert *as* lunch today, just in case; and he felt an amazing lack of stress about the idea of not having breakfast the next morning. He usually conducted his affairs in a tangled mess of this obligation and that, with overlapping scheduling, priorities jostling each other and changing by the hour—and he usually managed most of them.

But—regarding tomorrow—he discovered not one thing that he really had to do. The peripheral objectives were, for once in his career, all bundled up and handled fairly neatly.

Oh, he had things he *wanted* to do, or should do—he always had; but there was absolutely nothing weighing on his shoulders as impending catastrophe if he didn't. The people he'd written the notes to would handle everything as well as it could be handled.

Protection? Safety? He was going to be with the people who made him feel safe, come what might.

It was, contrarily, their guild he was trying to rescue, and for once he could help *them*.

They were, meanwhile, setting things up with all the skill and professional ability anyone could ask.

He was certainly not going into the situation *planning* his own demise—but there was satisfaction in the plan. Any strike at him would give Tabini and their allies plenty of moral righteousness, and the absolute right to send heads rolling, politically speaking—or literally. The assassination of his messenger to the Assassins' Guild would also justify Tabini taking to the skies and settling matters from orbit.

Disband two clans of the aishidi'tat, the Kadagidi *and* the Ajuri? That could certainly be the outcome, given the documentation *and* the witnesses the aiji-dowager now had in hand.

And in a time of major upheaval and a threat to the Guild system itself—and with Ilisidi stirring up her own factions to vengeance—Tabini might just take out two clans that had been a perpetual thorn in his side, at the same time he brought in the two tribal peoples.

The paidhi-aiji's demise under such circumstances would, politically, unify several factions, not that *he* was the favorite of several of them—but that the whole concept of the Assassins' Guild, enforcers of the law and keepers of the peace, violating its own rules to strike at a court official with the aiji's document in hand would not sit at all well with the Conservatives, the very people who were usually most opposed to the paidhi-aiji's programs. His enemies among the Conservatives were not wicked, unprincipled people—they just happened to be absolutely *wrong* about certain things. They would far rather support the rights of a dead paidhi than the live one who had so often upset the world.

And the prospect of the arch-conservatives avenging *him* . . . afforded him a very strange amusement.

He was, perhaps, a little light-headed after that spate of pre-posthumous letter-writing, but he honestly could not readily recall a time when there was so little remaining on the docket that the paidhi-aiji could reasonably be responsible for.

So. He did *not* deal with tactics. That was his aishid's business.

It was not his worry what Ilisidi was doing about the Shadow Guild in the south *or* Lord Aseida's future in the north.

He had no more now to do with entertaining Cajeiri's young guests; and he certainly didn't want to hint to the boy that there was anything so serious going on.

The one thing he did need to do right now, and urgently, was to get a meaningful document with Tabini's seal on it . . . on some issue that would *not* be what the current Guild leadership feared it was.

He encased the collection of letters in one bundle, with Narani's letter outermost, encased in a paper saying, *To open only in event of my demise. Thank you, Rani-ji.*

He tied it tightly with white ribbon. He sealed the knot with white wax, and imprinted it with the paidhi-aiji's seal.

Then he wrote one additional letter, to Tabini:

One asks, aiji-ma, that you prepare a document with conspicuous seals, empowering the paidhi-aiji, as your proxy, to bring a complaint before the Assassins' Guild Council this evening.

One asks, aiji-ma, that you complain not of the situation in the north, but that you bring to the Guild's attention the situation in the Taisigin Marid, wherein units from the capital were dismissed into the country without their weapons or equipment and where the aiji-dowager has had to intervene to restore order. One asks that you strongly question that decision and do not mention the other.

One asks further, that I be sent under your order, to deliver this document, and file it with the Guild.

He didn't seal it. He gave the first bundle to Narani, personally, saying, "Rani-ji, these letters should not be delivered unless it is likely that I am dead."

"Nandi." Narani bowed, with a rare expression of dismay.

"Which one does not intend should happen," Bren added hastily, "and if it does *not* happen, I shall certainly, and in *great* embarrassment, ask for this bundle of letters back again and destroy them. But what *must* be delivered quickly and certainly is *this* letter." He handed Narani the second letter, as yet unrolled. "Please take this letter first to my aishid and ask if this will serve their needs. Then, granted their approval of it, place the letter in my best cylinder and personally deliver it to the hands of the aiji, no other, not his major domo, not the head of his guard, and not the aiji-consort. To him alone. Await a response."

"Nandi." A deep bow, and the old man took both the bundle of letters and the letter to Tabini.

"Tell my aishid, too, I have ordered a light lunch, and a dessert," he added. "With enough for them, whether at table, or in their quarters. They may modify that request at their need. And tell my valets I shall need court dress this evening, *with* the bulletproof vest."

"Nandi," Narani said a second time, bowed, and left with the letters and his instructions.

10

Narani did not come back. Jago did. She opened the office door quietly and closed it.

"We certainly approved the letter, Bren-ji," she said. "And Narani is delivering it to the aiji." There was, unusual for Jago, a distressed pause, as if she wanted to ask something, but refrained.

"Are you wondering whether I really understand what may happen? Yes, Jago-ji. I do entirely understand. That is why I am going."

"It is still difficult," Jago said quietly, "for us deliberately to bring you into extreme danger, Bren-ji. It is *very* difficult."

"One appreciates your sentiment," Bren said. "And I *will* take instruction, Jago-ji. I only ask that you value yourselves highly as well."

"Yes," she said shortly, not happily. Then: "Cenedi *must* get out alive. Banichi and Algini *must* get out alive. You—we shall try, Tano and I."

"Jago-ji." He began to protest the priorities, and then kept quiet—just gave a nod of acceptance. "As you decide, Jago-ji." He was far from happy about any of them putting his life on a higher priority than their own, and took a deep breath, steadying down and refraining from any discussion of what was likely a recent decision. "I am following orders, in this matter."

"We hope certain units, in certain areas, will not resist us—once they understand. That will be your job, Bren-ji. We cannot advise them of our intentions in advance. If we bring in one unit on the plan—we cannot absolutely rely on their discretion with their closest ally. If we bring in another—we do not want it said that *their* lord's personal grudge was behind the action we take. If we bring in a third, others will ask why they then were left ignorant, or what motivated the choice of those so honored. Politics, Bren-ji. But I do not have to explain that to *you.*"

"No. No, that much I understand."

"If we can get out of this without firing a shot, excellent. And we rely on you—not to be stopped. If we can do that, it will be, baji-naji, a surgical operation—at least as far as the second door. That one—*we* shall finesse."

Baji-naji covered a lot of ground: personal luck and random chance. Their own importance in the cosmos and the flex and flux in the universe. If people couldn't die, the universe couldn't move. The baji-naji part in the operation—seemed to be his. And it was a big one.

Finessing the situation, in Guild parlance—meant anything it had to, with minimal force—to move what they could, any way they could, in this case, amid all the tiny threads of connection, kinship, man'chi, and regional politics that wove the Guild together, moving in to take down the Guild leadership—and clip one little frayed Ajuri thread, without disturbing what held the Guild together. Atevi politics wasn't human politics. The dividing line between personal interests, man'chi, and clan interests was not always apparent—even to the people in the middle of the situation, whose emotions might be profoundly affected by what they had to do.

And if he understood what Jago was saying, they were relying on *his* presence to jostle nerves, create hesitation ... because everybody on the planet knew the aiji's representative was the only human on the continent ... and pose their potential opponents a problem.

Posing a problem. He'd done that in the legislature, now and again.

Only the legislators, however agitated they might become, weren't armed.

"I'll—"—do my best, he had begun to say, but a rap on the door announced Narani, who bowed and said quietly, "The dowager, nandi, is sending a message."

Ilisidi had heard they had cut her out of the operation. And Ilisidi sent a message that she was sending a message?

Damn.

How had she heard? He *trusted* his staff. He *knew* who they reported to. *Him.*

He'd only sent to—

Of course—Tabini's staff. Tabini's borrowed staff. Damiri's.

He *needed* to get that document from Tabini before he faced the dowager with his explanation of what he'd done.

"Excuse me, Jago-ji." He stood up, went out into the hall and to the foyer with Jago right behind him. "My second-best coat," he said to Narani, who kept the door. With luck he *might* get out the door and headed for Tabini's apartment before a message arrived to complicate matters.

His major domo got the coat himself, and helped him on with it. He attended them, opened the front door.

No escape. The dowager's man Casimi was headed down the carpeted center of the hall toward them, and there were only two apartments at this bag end of the hall—no doubt on earth what the dowager's man intended, and they could hardly claim ignorance of the fact he was coming.

He *hoped* the oncoming message didn't include Ilisidi's order to abandon the idea or come immediately to explain the situation. He wasn't going to get shut out of the plan, and he *didn't* want a debate—not to mention defying Ilisidi to go over her head as he was about to do. That was not going to please the dowager.

There was no escape, however. He was obliged to wait

the few seconds it took Casimi to reach their door. With a backward step and a nod, he signaled Narani both to let Casimi in and to close the door on their generally empty corridor—for whatever privacy they could fold about a likely argument.

"Nandi," Casimi said, trying not to breathe quickly, "the dowager has heard you intend to go with your aishid to the Guild tonight."

"She has heard correctly, nadi," Bren said.

"She wishes you to decide otherwise."

No request to speak to him personally, nothing of the sort, indeed, simply an order he did not intend to honor. He opened his mouth to refuse.

But Jago said, at his side, "*Cenedi* is on his way here, nandi."

Cenedi. The dowager's head of security.

Was Casimi not enough?

Casimi himself looked perplexed, hearing that, and quietly stepped to the side and ducked his head, withdrawing from the question, as well he should, with his senior officer about to enter the matter.

A short knock came at the door *far* sooner than the typical walk from the dowager's door would require. Narani looked at Bren for instruction, Bren nodded, and Narani quietly opened the door.

Cenedi arrived alone, not breathing hard, and from the left, where there was only one apartment.

"Tabini-aiji is coming to call, nandi," Cenedi said, with a little nod of courtesy.

Rank topped rank.

"Indeed," he said with an outflow of breath. Was it the Kadagidi situation that brought Tabini *here* instead of calling him *there*, one could wonder—or was it the Assassins' Guild situation and the dowager's proposal to go lay siege in person?

Narani was standing by the door, ready for orders. All it took was a glance and a nod and Narani passed the matter of the door to Jago, then headed for the adjacent hall to advise staff to prepare the sitting room for a visitor.

Bren said to Casimi, with a polite nod, "One is under constraint, nadi. One by no means intends discourtesy to the dowager. Please offer my respects and say that I am required to receive the aiji's intention, whatever that may be."

"Nandi." Casimi bowed in turn and left. So there they stood, himself, Cenedi, and Jago, with Tabini inbound and their plans—

God only knew who sided with whom or what Tabini wanted in coming here. Tabini had had time to read the letter Narani had taken to his office.

So one waited for the answer.

Came quick footsteps, advancing from the inner hall of the apartment: Jeladi arrived with a little bow and took Narani's place as doorkeeper. "My apologies, nandi. Staff is heating water and arranging the sitting room for the aiji."

A committee in the foyer was no way to receive the lord of most of the world into his apartment . . . not after sending a letter that might have prompted the unprecedented visit. Bren said, quietly, "Jago-ji, advise the others," before he headed for the sitting room himself. There he settled in his own usual chair, and had the servants add chairs for the bodyguards, who would very likely be involved. Or who *might* be. He had no clue.

"You must come to the sitting room," Madam Saidin said, at the door of the guest quarters. "Your great-uncle has asked Master Kusha. You must come and be measured."

Clothes. He hated being measured. "Master Neithi already has my measurements."

Master Neithi was his mother's tailor. And he had been measured for court clothes just before he had gone out to Najida.

"Yet your great-uncle wishes to make you a gift, young gentleman, and we have no wish to involve Master Kusha in a rivalry with Master Neithi."

A rivalry. He caught that well enough. Jealousy between the tailors. The whole world was divided up in sides. At least tailors did not shoot at one another. But *anyone* could be dangerous.

"One does not wish Master Neithi to be upset, Saidin-daja."

A little bow. "That will absolutely be considered, young gentleman. This is only in consideration of your wardrobe stalled in transit, and," she added quietly, "most of all for the comfort of your guests, young gentleman, since your great-uncle feels they may be a little . . . behind the fashion. And perhaps under supplied."

If *he* was getting clothes, *they* had to get them, too, without ever saying what they had come with was too little, besides the fact that they had had to leave almost everything they owned at Great-uncle's estate. "Thank you," he said. "Yes, Saidin-daja. One understands."

"Excellent. Please bring your guests to the sitting room. There will be clothes for them."

That was a cheerful note—among so many things in his situation that were not. They had gotten up, had breakfast, just himself and his bodyguard and his guests—and they could go nowhere and they had done everything. It was getting harder and harder to turn his guests' questions to safe things. They had talked about all the pictures in the tapestries. They had inspected all the vases in the rooms they were allowed to visit. They had played cards, and he had tried not to win and not to be caught not winning.

He was glad to bring them something they would enjoy.

"Nadiin-ji," he said, "Madam says there is a surprise."

They sat around the table, with the cards neatly stacked and the game in suspension—they were trying very hard not to be bored, or worse, worried. Boji of course had set up a fuss, bounding about in his cage and chittering, sure that someone coming meant food. Boji had been in the bedroom, but since they were sitting out here in the little sitting room, of course they had had to roll Boji's cage in here so

Boji could see everything. Boji sat on his perch now with an egg in his hands—a bribe he got whenever he started to pitch a fit—staring at him with eyes as round as his guests' solemn stares . . .

But his guests' faces brightened when he said a surprise—not in the least suspecting, he thought, what that might be. They all pushed their chairs back and got up without a single question.

That was his guests on especially good behavior, with people going and coming and doors opening and closing all morning, and with not even his bodyguard permitted to go out the main doors. They knew something was going on. But a surprise? They were in completely in favor of it.

So was he.

"Eisi-ji, Liedi-ji," he said to his valets, who were trying to keep Boji quiet, "do come. Taro-ji." His bodyguards were sitting at their own table, with books open, studying things about trajectory. "We shall just be in the sitting room."

So out they went, himself, his guests, his two valets, out and down the hall to the sitting room, falling in behind Madam Saidin.

The sitting room door was open. A tall, thin man, the tailor, by his moderately more elegant dress, presided over a changed sitting room—with sample books, piles of folded clothes on several chairs; and two assistants, one male, one female, with notebooks and other such things as tailors used. There was even a sewing machine set up on its own little stand, which usually came only at a final fitting.

"Master Kusha, young gentleman," Madam Saidin said, and there were bows and courtesies—no tea. One never asked a tailor or a tutor to take tea.

"Nadi," Cajeiri said, with a proper nod. "One is grateful. Thank you."

"Honored, young gentleman, and very pleased to serve— one understands these excellent young guests and yourself have arrived without baggage, some misfortune in transport? But the major domo at the lord's estate has relayed the numbers, and we have brought a selection of the highest quality, which we can readily adjust for general wardrobe; and we shall, of course with your permission, take our own measurements for court dress. One never has too extensive a wardrobe, and we are *honored* to provide for yourself, and your guests."

Master Kusha had a long and somewhat sorrowful face, and he was not young. Rather like many of Great-uncle's staff, he was an old man, but likely, too, he was a very good tailor.

"We shall ask your guests to try on these for fit. We shall make just a few little changes—understand, nandi, simplicity, simplicity of design that needs the slightest touch of sophisticated alteration, a tuck here, a little velvet, and lace: floods of lace can make all the difference. One will be amazed, nandi, one will be amazed at the transformation we can work in these on short notice. Let us show what we can do." He waved his hand, and the assistants swept up the stacks on the chairs, ready-made clothes, coats and shirts apt for Gene, who was broad-shouldered and strong and tall, and for Artur, whose arms were almost Irene's size around; and clothes for Irene, who was tiny and the oldest at once.

"Put these on, young gentlemen and lady," Master Kusha said, "and then we shall do alterations, and I shall get my numbers for court dress, the very finest for all—will they understand at all, nandi?"

"Put them on, nadiin-ji," Cajeiri said, with a little wave of his hand. "Try. This all is yours."

They were not happy at that. Not at all. He saw it.

"Something wrong?" he asked in ship-speak.

"Talk," Gene said, setting down his stack of clothes. "A moment. Talk. Please."

He was puzzled. Distressed. He gave a nod to Master Kusha, another to Madam Saidin. "A moment, nadiin," he said. "Translation. One needs to translate for them."

"Young gentleman," Madam Saidin said, and quietly signed to Master Kusha to step back.

So they were left as alone as they could arrange. And something was direly wrong.

He should, he thought, call for tea. If he were his father. Or if they were atevi.

But neither thing was true. So he just drew them over to the farthest side of the room, and turned his back to Madam Saidin and Master Kusha and all of it, trying to muster up his ship-speak, which had gotten a little thinner than it had once been . . . that, or human words were not as suited to things on the Earth, and were just not as clear to him as they had been.

It always took a while for the lord of most of the world to do anything simple, what with staff to advise of his movements and arrangements to make. If Cenedi had blazed over here, leaving a conference with Tabini, it might have been Cenedi's briefing Tabini on the Padi Valley business yesterday that had prompted the personal visit—but given the dowager's notions of invading the Guild herself, it was much more likely this evening's business under discussion.

This evening's business—and maybe the document he had requested.

One did guess that if Tabini was coming here to discuss whatever matter Tabini wished to discuss, Tabini had certain specifics he didn't want to discuss in his own quarters—quarters which he shared with his wife, Cajeiri's mother, whose clan, Ajuri, was deeply at issue in the Padi Valley action—not to mention directly involved in their upcoming business with the Assassins' Guild.

God, he *hoped* Tabini had found no reason to doubt the aiji-consort at this point. Tabini had maintained his association with Damiri when common sense might have dictated he divorce his wife as a political and security-based precaution—an action which, with Damiri no more than a week from giving birth, had its own problems. Tabini couldn't divorce Damiri at this point. He surely wouldn't set up a conflict with her.

Tabini *had* thrown out all Damiri's staff a number of days ago, so that now all the senior security in Tabini's apartment were the dowager's people ... hence the dowager's very good grasp of what was going on in the world.

Discuss the imminent assassination of a Guild officer who happened to be Damiri's relative?

He'd personally rather not have that discussion in Damiri's hearing, either.

And probably that was exactly Tabini's reasoning in coming here to talk. He *hoped* that was all that was going on ... but there were ungodly many possibilities in the political landscape.

Tano and Algini arrived in the sitting room, with Banichi and Jago following. Banichi was not moving briskly today, and Banichi would *not* keep the arm rigidly bandaged. The hand stayed tucked inside the jacket. Bren just acknowledged Banichi with a particular nod—not arguing with him, not with life and death matters afoot.

There were, thankfully almost immediately, the quiet set of sounds that heralded an arrival at the front door. Not one man, but maybe two or three, Bren thought, by what he heard. So Tabini had not brought his full security detail with him, maybe not even his own aishid—unprecedented as the visit itself, if that was the case.

Servants hurried about last-moment preparations. Narani opened the door, showing Tabini into the sitting room *with* Cenedi, and with Cenedi's frequent partner Nawari in attendance, not on the aiji-dowager, but on Tabini. Again— *that* had never happened.

Protocol dictated the paidhi rise, bow, offer a seat.

"Aiji-ma. One is honored."

"Sit," Tabini said, with an all-inclusive sweep of his hand—Bren, Cenedi, Nawari, Bren's own bodyguard, everybody but the servants. It was an order, and Tabini was deadly serious.

"Tea," Tabini said. Nothing of business was appropriate until they had had a cup, ritually delivered; and moods like

Tabini's current one were precisely the reason for the custom.

"Nadiin-ji?" Cajeiri said, and made it a question. His guests looked very uncomfortable.

"I *told* you," Irene whispered to Gene and Artur. "We just have to *do* things. Don't make a problem."

Gene and Artur did not even look at her. Or at him. Gene just drew a heavy breath.

"What?" Cajeiri asked. *"What?"*

But Gene and Artur said nothing, and still looked at the floor.

They were upset. That was clear. And it seemed to be about the clothes. "Children's clothes look bad?" he asked. It was all that would fit them. "Master Kusha makes them right."

"That's not it," Gene said.

"What?" he repeated, and then thought they might not understand the situation he could only explain in Ragi. "Nadiin-ji, our baggage may come tonight. Maybe not. And those are all country clothes. This is the *Bujavid,* nadiin-ji. You need better. You were always going to need better."

"Whose credits?" Gene asked.

Whose credits?

Then he understood. For an instant he saw the ship corridors again, where humans had to have a card to get a sandwich or a drink, where everything in all their lives had been measured so closely, and you were allowed so much and more could not be had, because you had to work on the ship to earn a larger share.

None of the station-folk had been able to work, and all the share they had had even for food was what the ship allotted for them, measured out by how old you were and whether you were a boy or a girl and how tall you were—all of it calculated by a set of numbers atevi never had to calculate. If they were hungry on a particular day, they still could not get more. The station-folk had been really unhappy on the ship, which had been worse than the station. And sometimes people had been hungry.

Not his associates. Never his associates. He had brought them sweets from mani's kitchen. Sausages. And bread.

He remembered. For an instant they were there in the tunnels again. "This is not the ship," he said to his guests, and made a wide gesture at everything, the sitting room, the whole world, if he could have thought of the ship-speak words. "My uncle. My guests. No numbers here. You need the clothes."

"What can we say?" Gene said. "It's *your* birthday, Jeri-ji. We brought you *presents.* But *nothing* like this."

"Presents." Reunioners had come onto the ship with almost nothing, and it was painful to think how little they still must have, starting with nothing on a station where very few could earn extra.

But if they were his people, they had every *right* to match him, well, as far as lords could—because they *were* his. It was a matter of pride, and the way everybody would look at them. They could not wear their clothing: the old people would be scandalized—but he could not quite tell them they would embarrass him.

If he were a grown-up, he would be sure they *could* match him in exactly the right degree. But he was just eight. And it was very good of Great-uncle and mani to step in to fix things. It was only right that they did, because he was *theirs,* and it was their pride involved if *his* people looked wrong or rude.

But clearly it was not right, in his guests' opinion. And one part of him hurt, as if they were pushing his gift rudely away, as if they were not wanting to be here today, and were upset and embarrassed.

But he was sure they really *did* want to be here. They were modest, and grateful, and always polite to him. That would not have changed in a handful of minutes. So he was the one at fault: he had to explain it in a way that would not embarrass them.

He shrugged, gave a second little shrug, and resorted to one of those stupid things they had used to say on the ship, when they were completely out of answers. "Atevi stuff. Atevi stuff."

"Human stuff," Gene said, the right answer and gave an answering and unhappy little shrug.

"Here!" he said, pointing at the floor underfoot. "You are here!" He wanted to say so much else to them, so very much else . . . but if there had been words they could understand to make it all work, he would not be atevi and they would not be human. And they just stood there, both unhappy, which was unbearable.

"Gene," Irene said, trying to calm things down. "Just listen to him."

But Gene just went on frowning, and it was not right, and nothing could make it right. Gene was the one who always measured shares of the food he brought, so they were exactly right. *Exactly* right, not a crumb off equal — because it mattered to Gene.

And here they were, measuring again, only there was no way for it ever to come out even.

Fair, Gene would say. And it was one of the strongest things about Gene. He always was . . . fair. But sometimes you had to argue with him. And sometimes it was as if he knew Gene best of all of them.

"Hey," he said, that word that meant *listen,* and he laid a hand on his chest, the way he had done when they had first met in the ship corridors, almost the first children he had ever seen. And they'd stared at each other. He said, solemnly, as he'd said then: "Cajeiri. I'm Cajeiri."

Usually it was Irene that understood language things first, but not this time. "Gene!" Gene said staunchly, with the same solemn gesture. And Gene swept a gesture at Irene and Artur. "Irene. Artur. Human."

"Ateva," he said. It was their first meeting all over again. "No change!"

"No change," Gene said. "No change, us."

"Friends," Cajeiri said in ship-speak, right across the room from Madam Saidin and Master Kusha and his own valets and everybody. "And," he said in Ragi, "I can give *you* gifts for *my* birthday, if I want! Adults do. So I can. This is how atevi do. Yes?"

Gene gave a nervous smile. They all did, and touched hands the way ship-humans did, then laughed.

"Friends," Artur said, and Irene, who followed the rules most of the time, said, "We're not supposed to say that, you know."

"We still can," Cajeiri said, and added somberly, because it was always true: "until we grow up."

11

The tea service went around at its own deliberate pace, deliberately drunk, during which the mind had ample opportunity to race, and there was *no* light conversation, only a meditative pause.

"How is my son," was Tabini's belated question, "in *your* view, paidhi?"

"Very well, aiji-ma," Bren said. "I have inquired. He continues as unaffected and as uninvolved as we can manage."

"A wonder in itself," Tabini said darkly. He set his teacup down quietly on the side table. Bren set his down scarcely touched. So with all of them, immediately.

"You and your aishid intend to enter Assassins' Guild Headquarters," Tabini said, "bearing an order of mine, with the intent to enter it in Council records. You intend to provide access for an assassination of the consort's elder kinsman and the forcible seizure of Guild records."

"Yes, aiji-ma. One hopes you will lend your seal to such a document."

"One understands that this is not conceived as a suicide mission."

"One hopes it will not be, aiji-ma."

"We have also had it suggested," Tabini said grimly, "that

this document—with many and conspicuous seals—be an official inquiry into the *Dojisigi* situation—for official purposes."

Bren gave a single nod. "The Guild Council will likely be dealing with the Kadagidi matter, aiji-ma. One believes the Dojisigi matter will be unexpected."

"To throw the *Assassins' Guild* off its balance?" Tabini asked with the arch of a brow, and just then Cenedi put a finger to his left ear, atop that discreet earpiece, frowning as he did so.

"The aiji-dowager," Cenedi said, "is on her way."

"Gods less fortunate!" Tabini hissed, and cast a look at Cenedi, but Cenedi's face remained impassive. One doubted that Cenedi or Nawari, apparently having been in conference with Tabini, had yet had time to break the news to Ilisidi that the paidhi-aiji was going on this venture and *she* was not. But there were a number of the dowager's staff serving in Tabini's apartment, who might have found a way to know about the request for the document, and who *might* have relayed the information. There was a broad choice.

"I declined the aiji-dowager's request to come to her for a conference not half an hour ago," Bren said quietly, not going so far as a complete denial of responsibility, "since I was about to come to speak to you, aiji-ma. Then Cenedi intervened with the news that you were coming to visit *me.*"

"Oh, we have no question," Tabini said. "We do not ask. We do not need to ask how my grandmother keeps herself informed, granted her staff is *our* staff." A deep breath. "Nand' paidhi, this mission is *your* request?"

"One certainly cannot permit the aiji-dowager to undertake it herself, aiji-ma."

Tabini gave a short, sharp laugh. "One cannot permit! If you are able to deny my grandmother *anything* she has set her mind to do, paidhi-ji, you surpass my skills." And soberly: "I am *not* willing to lose you, paidhi. Bear that in mind. Do *not* decide to protect your aishid. I know you. *Do not do it!*"

He could *feel* his bodyguard seconding that order.

"One will be cautious, aiji-ma."

"Cautious! Caution has nothing to do with your decision to take this on." A deep breath. "But you are right: you are the *logical* one to undertake this. There is no combination of Guild force more effective that we can bring within those doors, than the combination in this room. And I do understand your strategy—having this document regard the Dojisigi matter. Clever. I shall write your document—it will take me far less than an hour—and set the seals of various departments on it. But I hope the cleverness of your choice of documents will *not* have to come into play. To that end, and in that spirit— Take this." He pulled off the massive seal ring he wore on his third finger, and proffered it.

No human in history had ever borne *that* object.

Bren rose. One did not ask even Banichi to handle that seal. He took it personally, and bowed, deeply. "Aiji-ma."

"This seal I need *not* affix. I send it with you. If they refuse *that* at the doors, they will be in violation of their own charter, and on that refusal alone, I can bring the legislature against them—but one fears any delay will give them time to destroy documents, and one does not even mention the threat to you. One hopes this will get you all out unscathed."

"One is grateful, aiji-ma." Bren settled back into his chair, and slipped the ring on. It was too large even for his index finger. He had to close his hand on it. "But should something happen—you will have every legal grounds the legislature could ask." He held up the fist with the ring. "This will not see disrespect."

"We assure the aiji," Banichi said, "if they disrespect your authority, those doors still will open tonight."

"Besides the Office of Assignments," Cenedi said quietly, "be it known, aiji-ma, nand' paidhi, that we have two problems within the Guild Council, and one more presiding whose qualifications to preside over Council are questionable. Those three will need to resign. We shall make that clear." Cenedi, standing near the door, walked closer and into Tabini's convenient view. "The names of the problems, aiji-ma: the one you know. Ditema of the Paigeni."

"Him. Good riddance."

"Add Segita of the Remiandi."

"We do not know him."

"They are both senior. They came in after the coup. They have conservative views which are, themselves, not in question; but their support of the Office of Assignments has repeatedly, since your return, blunted all attempts to insist that Assignments should operate under normal rules and create an orderly and modern filing system. One interpretation is that they have felt a certain sympathy for a long-lived institution of the Guild, and they have *innocently* made it easier for Assignments to misbehave. Another interpretation is less forgiving. Their age and rank have completely overawed the less qualified members that currently fill out the rest of the body, and no one stands up to these two voices. They have pressed the matter of non-returning Guild. We, on the other hand have appealed to certain retired members to come back to active duty, and they *have* agreed to do so. This would include eight of the old Council . . ."

"*Not* Daimano," Tabini said.

"She *would* be in that number," Cenedi said. "She is, in fact, critical to the plan, aiji-ma. If you support her return, three others will come, among them two other very elder Guild members that we most need in the governing seats. You know who."

"Gods less fortunate," Tabini muttered.

"Daimano is an able administrator. And whatever else she ever was, she is no ally of Murini."

Tabini gave a wave of his hand. "We do not interfere in Guild politics. If the Guild elects her—may she live long and do as she pleases. Not that I offer *any* speculation at all on the Council's composition, nor shall ever officially remember these names."

"I shall relay that, aiji-ma," Cenedi said.

"Key to the old Guild, you say."

"She stood by you during Murini's regime, aiji-ma. She, in fact, directed the entire eastern network, when Prijado died."

"Then we owe her gratitude for that, though one is certain it was reluctant. We shall owe her for *this,* if she can bring order."

"Order," Cenedi said dryly, "is certainly one thing that will result from her administration."

"Not to mention needing a decade of hearings to get a simple document issued. Forests are in danger, considering the paper consumption with this woman in office."

"We shall argue for computers in Assignments and Records, aiji-ma. We have had ample example of pen and ink filing systems. She *wants* to take the Assignments post for a year, at least, to supervise its operation, and to have the records under her hand."

"Gods less fortunate. So be —"

There was a distant sharp report, the impact of brass on ancient stone, right outside the apartment. And a subsequent rap at the outer door.

"She is here," Cenedi said, *not* regarding the woman under current discussion. Cenedi drew a deep breath, and added: "Aiji-ma, regarding the Guild Council, and Daimano, we shall deal with the difficulties."

"Let her in, paidhi," Tabini said, and Bren nodded to Banichi, who said something inaudible, short-range.

The outer door had already opened, and one could hear the advancing tap of the dowager's brass-capped cane on terrazzo and on the foyer carpet as she passed the door. With that came the footsteps of her attendant bodyguard.

"The aiji is in the sitting room with nand' Bren," Bren heard Jeladi say, out in the foyer, and heard the arrival head their way with scarcely a pause. Tap. Tap. Tap.

Jeladi opened the door and stood out of the way.

"Well!" Ilisidi said, arriving in the room with two of her indefinite number of bodyguards—staff hastened to move in a suitable chair appropriately angled, beside Tabini, and two more, beyond hers. *"Well!"*

She sat down, upright, with the cane in hand beside the chair arm. It was Casimi and his partner Seimaji who had escorted her in. Seimaji moved quietly to take a chair at her right hand, while Cenedi and Nawari stayed where they sat, somewhat facing her.

"The document!" she said sharply, with a wave of her left hand.

Casimi, not yet seated, proffered to Tabini the rolled parchment he carried, a large one with abundant red and black ribbons attached. Nawari rose and took it, serving as Tabini's staff for the moment.

"That is," Ilisidi said, "for your use, Grandson, *if* you are still in process of formulating a cause to take before the Guild Council."

Tabini shot out a hand. Nawari passed it to him, and Tabini scanned the parchment, frowning.

"The paidhi-aiji has wanted a document about the southern situation."

"Read on. It covers that matter. Abundantly."

"What have you *done* with the two Dojisigi?" Tabini asked, reading on.

"Why, fed them, housed them, like any good host. I have requested them to stay politely to quarters and answer any questions we may have at any hour. Meanwhile, since the day before yesterday midnight we have liberated a Marid village from scoundrels, defused a bomb, dislodged a traitor from a lordship, taken down a Shadow Guild leader in the Marid, and brought your son safely home. What else should we do?" Ilisidi waggled her fingers, and Casimi produced a second ribboned and sealed parchment from inside his jacket. "This deposition, to be placed in evidence at the appropriate time, is signed, and witnessed. You may find it interesting reading—a detailed account of the actions of the Guild officers in charge of the Dojisigin Marid, how the local Guild were disarmed, how they were kept under arrest, then released and sent out as protection for their respective villages, units split apart, and most of all, sent into problem districts without so much as sidearms. These two were split from the other team of their unit, whose whereabouts we do not know even to this hour, nor what orders they may have been given, nor what hostages may be at stake. These two in our custody have asked permission to go south to find their partners. We have denied that, but we have warned Lord Machigi . . . who is one likely target of any second Dojisigi-based operation, and we have personally requested him to negotiate a bloodless surrender of the partners of these men should they come into his territory. We will urge Machigi to make a public statement of what happened in the Dojisigin Marid once our operation tonight goes forward."

"I have no criticism of the plan," Tabini said, passing the documents to Cenedi. "Well done, honored Grandmother."

Everything was amazingly amicable. Bren almost began to relax.

"It is, however, an underhanded business," Ilisidi said, her long fingers extending, then clamping like a vise on the head of the cane she had beside her, "an *underhanded business,* Grandson, first to thrust off on your ailing grandmother a flight of human children, asking me to extend *my* security to guard the East *and* the north, with *precious* little assistance—"

"*I sent you the Taibeni!*" Tabini retorted, voice rising. "What more do you want? My house guard? No? Of course not! They are already *yours!*"

"Aijiin-ma," Bren said quietly, unheard.

"I have my *own* bodyguard fully extended," Ilisidi retorted, "watching your residence, guarding Lord Aseida and two Dojisigi Assassins, *and* assisting Lord Tatiseigi, who has *gallantly* opened a household filled with delicate antiquities to host *your* son—"

"*Your* great-grandson, who has had as much of your rearing as mine! And he is *Lord Tatiseigi's* own grand-nephew! If the lad with *your* teaching cannot manage the situation—"

"And three human guests who cannot even perceive a warning!"

"*You* were supervising him when he routinely ran the halls of the ship unguarded, held clandestine meetings with the offspring of prisoners who had all but started a war in the heavens, a population who had to be forcibly removed from that place, and who to this day present a problem on the station! If you had prevented his association with these children in the first place, we would not have human guests in the middle of this crisis!"

"And you would not have a son well-acquainted with factions and powers in the heavens as well as the aishidi'tat! The boy has become an asset to the aishidi'tat, educated in all the politics that may foreseeably affect us! The boy has influence and alliances many a lord of the aishidi'tat would covet! Do you wish to pass *blame* for this situation? I shall not hesitate to claim responsibility for it!"

"His attachment is inconvenient, at the moment!"

"When is it ever convenient? Your years and mine pass at one speed—but the boy? His years race toward a new age, *his* age, in which *he* will face decisions without the benefit of *your father's* bad example—"

"Do not call upon my father for an example! And while we are praising the efficacy of your teaching, my *father* was all your handiwork!"

"Back away from that brink, grandson! My *son* had *his* father for an example! He had flatterers at his ear whom *his father* allowed in court! And he had the same damnable, wilful temper! I have no idea where you acquired it, if not from your grandfather! It passes in the blood, I suspect, and is *none* of mine!"

"*You* have no temper? *Ha!*"

"Aijiin-ma!" Bren said. "One would treasure the thought

of unanimity in an undertaking, unanimity, and harmonious good wishes."

"See?" Ilisidi said. "*Harmony*. There is a word for you, Grandson. Can we manage *harmony*, in the few hours before the paidhi undertakes a great risk in our names?"

Tabini's nostrils flared. His scowl did not much diminish, but his voice was quieter. "We have been informed of as much as we wish to know, and we greatly mourn our lost aishid at this moment. These young men who serve us now have all the will and courage one could ask, but have not yet acquired the skills or the rank to undertake a challenge to the Guild. And the risk we run in this operation is life and death, nothing less, not alone for the paidhi-aiji."

"Not for him alone," Ilisidi said. "But we have a plan."

"We are *sure* you have a plan," Tabini said, "and that we are about to hear it."

"We have unexpected assets," Ilisidi said, "which will not, perhaps, surprise our enemies, since the events at Asien'dalun, but arms which will protect these foreign guests, *and* your son, and the rest of us while these things are underway, and in any attempt at a second coup. Bren-paidhi, do you concur? More to the point, does *he?*"

Jase. Jase, who had surfaced only briefly this morning to confer with him, and who had graciously informed Narani he and his bodyguard would rest and allow the household to rest—unless the young gentleman needed them. And who had already taken the responsibility the dowager asked.

"Jase-aiji does concur," Bren said. "He understands the risk, and I already have his promise. No hostile operation can reach this floor with his bodyguard in place. One cannot swear to the safety of the entire building, but the safety of the persons on this floor—yes, aijiin-ma. This Jase-aiji has told me: he *can* contact the station without going through the Messengers' Guild, and if Lord Geigi were advised that you, aijiin-ma, or the young gentleman, his guests, or the spaceport itself were threatened with any harm, we all know Lord Geigi has the means and the will to act. Lord Geigi has, nand' Jase informs me, considerably fortified the spaceport in this last year. And should any violence overtake you, aiji-ma, Jase-aiji would immediately move to your defense. It would be a very foolish act to attack here in the Bujavid."

"A foolish act, or an entirely desperate one," Tabini said. "And should they have any such notions and find themselves countered, they may well become desperate."

"Jase-aiji's weapons can defend you. More, he will get you and the aiji-dowager and your son to safety at the port ... should there be need." He saw Tabini take in a breath. "Please accept this idea, aiji-ma. Preserve *yourself.* We cannot have these bandits in charge again. The aishidi'tat cannot suffer this again. Rely on Jase-aiji. You will be constantly *in* the network, and in charge of it, at all points. Communication between the station and the ground will not depend on any system they can possibly cut off, and you can rely on Geigi to carry out your orders."

"We have discussed the resources of the heavens. We have discussed it with Lord Geigi. I have prepared orders, honored Grandmother, which will—just as a formality, since we believe you could bully your way through on any day you chose—put the Bujavid guard and the transport station *and* the spaceport under your control—should anything befall me."

Ilisidi raised an eyebrow and nodded somberly. "Then we should accept those orders. On the other hand, if we are not permitted to be foolish, neither are you, grandson. The paidhi's plan involves, one takes it, *reaching* the spaceport."

"My own plan consists in not replicating the mistakes of the last incident," Tabini said. "Reaching the spaceport, yes. And *holding* it. *And* its communications."

Getting off the planet, Bren thought, but he had no intention of arguing with Tabini at this stage. If Tabini just agreed to get that far—with Jase—they had everything they needed. "One is grateful for your agreement," he said.

"We shall not be caught by surprise, paidhi," Tabini said. "And *you* are not to die."

Bren inclined his head. "One will do one's best, aiji-ma."

"Give us back the Guild," Tabini said. "Give us *that* one resource, and this firestorm over the Kadagidi and the Ajuri will evaporate in the morning sunlight."

The legislature was in session. The enemy's rumors about the Kadagidi situation would have traveled. One could only imagine.

Would it all evaporate? He was less sure.

"They can stew," Ilisidi said with a wave of her jeweled fingers. "Would we had shot that fool Aseida outright."

"Would that someone had, long since," Tabini said, and set his hands on his knees, preparatory to rising. "However, honored Grandmother, you will decline to dine with your guests this evening. You will attend *my* table tonight, so Cenedi informs me."

His own aishid's plan. Guard the aiji. Get their problems into one defensible spot. The aiji's apartment lacked the servant passages that made other apartments a security sieve. Get them all into the aiji's premises and set Jase and Jase's guard to hold it—while they provoked all hell to break loose.

Ilisidi arched a brow. "Dinner, is it?"

"The party will include the young gentleman, his host, his guests, and the ship-aiji, so we are already informed. The paidhi-aiji is invited, of course, as a courtesy, but we understand he has a prior engagement. Now we know what that engagement is."

"Aiji-ma." Bren gave a little, seated bow, then rose as the others rose, and bowed a second time. Tabini had agreed. *Jago* had prompted him to ask what he had asked of Jase. *Cenedi* had argued out what they needed from Tabini. Their bodyguards had nudged the pieces into place.

Now the dowager had agreed.

It was done. Arranged. And the action was underway.

In that moment of realization Bren had a little twinge of

panic—a sense of mortality. Fear—maybe, at how very fast things were moving. But he refused to entertain it: there was no time for second thoughts. He bowed, saw his guests to the foyer, and watched Tabini depart.

He felt, then, the dowager's hand on his arm. It closed with startling force. "Do not lose," Ilisidi said, and walked out.

"I have one fancy coat," Jase said, "for the formal party. Should I wear that to the aiji's dinner?"

"God. No. You can't wear it to both. Borrow one of mine," Bren said. "My staff will see to it. Brown, blue, or green?"

"Blue." Jase's own formal uniform was blue. "Moral reinforcement."

"Your bodyguard will be in armor all evening, until God knows when, maybe into morning. Sorry for them. Staff *will* see they get fed."

"No question they'll be in armor," Jase said, "and all of us will be hoping like hell we won't need it. They'll appreciate the food. Especially the pickle, apparently."

"God, humans that *like* the pickle."

"They seem to."

"Amazing. Enjoy your dinner this evening. *Watch* the exchanges between Ilisidi and Damiri—the dowager's going to be on a hair trigger. Damiri's going to be operating with a sure knowledge something's going on and I'm not sure anybody's telling her anything. She's going to be upset. Cajeiri's going to be nervous. Most of all keep all the youngsters low key and don't let them get scared."

Jase exhaled a short breath. "I'll be hoping to hold dinner down."

"Calm. Easy. It'll all work. That link to Geigi . . . if you can assure me that's going to be infallible and available from inside the Bujavid, I'll be a *lot* happier this evening."

"I won't tell you how. But, yes, rely on it."

*   *   *

It was court dress for the paidhi-aiji, no less, the best, a leather briefcase to hold the relevant documents with their wax seals and trailing ribbons, and, this time, *no* small pistol in his pocket. Bulletproof vests or the like were standard with the Guild itself—it was no problem, Jago told him, for him to take that precaution. But a firearm on his person was not in the plan. Innocence. Absolute innocence was what he had to maintain. There were detectors near the door.

He was nervous as he dressed. He tried not to be. He had to sit or stand while his valets worked, and he found himself disposed to glance about, thinking—I might not be back here again. He caught himself on that one—bore down instead on recalling the image of Assassins' Guild Headquarters, and the floor plan his bodyguard had drawn for him, where the guards would be; and what they had to do in this or that case.

A rail spur ran through the cobbled plaza around which the various guilds clustered. It was an antique line, a track used these days for six regular trains from the old station, four freight runs for the uptown shops and a twice-daily local for office workers in the district. The area saw mostly van and small bus traffic, few pedestrians, except Guild members going to a few local restaurants or to the two sheltered stops, since there were no other businesses nor residences in the area.

They would have someone in place to shunt the train off onto that spur, and that would get them into the plaza.

That part had to work. The train would reach a certain point—and stop, not at a boarding point.

There were sixty-one paces from a certain lamp post to the steps of the Assassins' Guild, seven shallow steps up to the doors that had to open, and beyond that, three taller steps up to a hall that held all the administrative offices which ordinary non-Guild might ever have reason to visit—prospective clients might have business there; witnesses called in particular cases might give depositions there.

Each of those nine offices had a door and small foyer,

each outer door being half hammered glass, the inner generally a full panel of the same.

Each office also had a service entry in the rear, onto a hidden corridor. Those could pose a problem.

Each office was staffed with lightly armed Guild clerical personnel, but they were visited, occasionally, by regular Guild on business, who might pose a more serious threat.

The hall reached a guarded door at the end, a single door that divided the public from the one other Guild section that was ever available to outsiders—the Guild Council.

There was, slight problem, a hall intersecting the left of that door, a short side hallway of six offices, which came to a dead end at the wall masking the service corridor.

That guarded door at the end of the public-access hall opened onto a wider area with a jog to the left, a short continuation of the main hall, and the double doors of the Guild Council chamber at its end. Those double doors were guarded whenever the Council was in session. To the right of anyone coming into that broad quasi-foyer was a wall with a bench, and to the left was a wooden door that stayed locked: that was the administrative corridor, where even high-ranking visitors did not go, and that was Cenedi's problem.

The Council Chamber, those guarded double doors in that offset stub of the main hallway, that was their target—as far as they could get toward it . . . or *into* it if everything worked well.

Arrangements, contingencies, branching instructions, if this, then that, meeting points, timing, nooks in the public hall that might afford protection at some angles if they were stalled and under attack . . . nooks that were no decorative accident, but designed with defense in mind, equally apt to be used by those attacking them: there was one angle, which the guards at the second, single door, commanded, that had a vantage on all three of those spots. . . .

He had never been so deeply involved in the details of a technical operation. They'd taken a space station with less worry.

And he only knew *their* part of it. Cenedi would be in that administrative hallway next to the Council chamber, conducting the dowager's business. Cenedi was the one of them able to get close to the Office of Assignments. Cenedi had the seniority to start with minor business at some minor office in the administrative section and get into that critical hallway on his own ... they hoped.

And somewhere involved in all this were other persons who were, Jago had said, *in* the city, and keeping a very low profile. That group had heavier arms. They would be moving, somehow, somewhere. Jago hadn't said and he hadn't asked.

But once that contingent arrived—he could figure that part for himself—that outer hallway wasn't a good place to be. Court dress was going to stand out like a beacon wherever he was, as if a fair-haired human didn't, on his own. In a certain sense that fair hair and light skin was a protection: honest Guildsmen would try not to shoot a court official ... but the Shadow Guild, granted that Assignments had his own agents inside Guild Headquarters, would definitely aim at him above all others. And *that* part he really didn't want to think about in detail. Not at all.

Cajeiri was in the good coat he had traveled in. Everybody was dressed as best they could, scrubbed and anxious, in such ready-made clothes as Master Kusha had left with Great-uncle's staff, with an assistant's instructions to shorten a sleeve or let out a seam or add a little lace: Master Kusha had left the material for that, too. And it was not the fine brocade of their festivity dress, which Master Kusha had taken away with him, but they were presentably fashionable and the clothes were pressed and clean, which was as good as they could manage until Master Kusha sent back the others—because their baggage had *not* come in yet, and they had a formal family supper to attend.

Irene was the only one whose hair could manage an almost proper queue—but what ribbon the guests should wear had been a question for Madam Saidin, who had lent her one of her own, a quiet brown that was not of any particular house, and on Irene's pale hair and Artur's red, and against Gene's dark brown, it stood out like a bright color.

His aishid was likewise lacking their best uniforms; but their black leather was polished, the best they could do. Everybody was the best they could manage, and his guests' clothing was finer than his own, at least in terms of appearances, but Jegari had said that he would go to his suite the instant they were in his father's apartment, and bring him his best coat from his own bedroom closet . . . so he would go in to dinner with a proper respect and keep his mother happy.

Madam had told them the time to be in the sitting room, and it *was* time. Antaro opened the door and they all went in good order—he had worked out how they should go, being an extreme infelicity of eight—he had Liedi and Eisi go with his guests, to make a fivesome of them, and those two would have dinner with his father's staff.

So they numbered ten when they went into the sitting room; and Great-uncle, who still looked very splendid despite the missing baggage, waited for them with his bodyguard.

"Nephew," Great-uncle said, giving him a look that clearly noted the traveling coat.

"I shall change coats, Great-uncle, once we arrive."

"Very good," Great-uncle said, nodding approval. "Well done, nephew, that you think of such things."

He felt very pleased, hearing that. He hoped his mother and father thought as well of him.

There was a knock at the front door, and he heard it open. He heard the strange machine-noises of Jase-aiji's bodyguards' armor, a presence which he had not expected: Kaplan and Polano had never gone about in armor on the ship, but he supposed that, like the Assassins' Guild, they must have rules about what equipment they used in what sort of place.

Jase left his bodyguard out in the foyer and came into the sitting room, escorted by Madam Saidin—he was wearing court dress, and he bowed to Great-uncle, and to him and his guests. Jase-aiji seemed very pleased with what he saw.

"Nandi," he said to Great-uncle. "We will wait just a moment. One wished to allow time for any last-moment difficulty, but," he said with a glance at the guests, "one sees everyone in very good order."

"We understand," Great-uncle said, which was a little strange for Great-uncle to say. Were they going to stop and take tea and wait?

Were his mother and father having an argument? Was that what the waiting was about?

But Great-uncle simply stayed standing, as if he knew the wait would not be that long, and engaged Jase-aiji in a discussion of the arrangements for the festivity—where Jase-aiji's men were evidently going to provide some of the security.

That would be odd—Jase-aiji's guards, in armor, at his birthday, by Great-uncle's arrangement, and it would certainly get attention—the way he could hear their little movements out in the foyer—just now and again, because they could just stand and stand and stand, like statues, and one forgot they were alive—until they moved.

People were going to talk about that, he thought. They were very scary when they stood like that. And inside they were just Kaplan and Polano, who were not always mannerly, but always friendly and cheerful: he felt very comfortable with them when they were not in armor.

Definitely they were going to be a sensation at his festivity.

"Nadiin-ji," Bren said to the household. Most of his servant staff had gathered in the foyer to see them off. There was no keeping the secret now that the paidhi-aiji and his bodyguard were not going to the aiji's party this evening, that

they were about to do something in support of the aiji-
dowager's staff—and that even this safe hallway might become dangerous.

The domestic staff's job was to keep the apartment's front
door shut and keep out of the servant passages—to lock
them, in fact; and—an instruction he had given to Narani
alone, but that Narani would give once they left—they were
to watch those locked doors of the servants' passages, which
led down to the second floor and its resources. Those doors
were solid, and once they were locked, there were alarms at
a certain point; and if any alarm went off, they were to gather
quickly in the foyer, abandon the apartment, and go next
door to the aiji's apartment, to warn the aiji's staff.

"Narani will be in charge of house security until we return," he said. "Narani-nadi will give specific orders after we
have left. I rely on you."

There were solemn nods. Bindanda was the other staff
member in charge during a crisis, not well-known to be
Guild, which was the way Bindanda wanted it. And Bindanda had his own instructions regarding arming a deadly
installation in the servants' hallway access—if an alarm
went off. One hoped no such thing would happen.

As for the rest of the staff—for the honest young countryfolk from Najida, mere boys and girls, youthful faces solemn with concern, and for his oldest servants as well, one
had the strongest temptation to say something quite
maudlin—

Which would only scare the young people, worry them
and raise questions one by no means wanted to answer.

At this point, briefcase in hand, on the verge of leaving
his own safe foyer, Bren found himself as superstitious as
the most devout 'counter, and he was determined not to
give way to it.

So he just said to the servants who had gathered, "Baji-
naji, nadiin-ji. Take good care of my guests."

"We shall, nandi," Narani said, and at a nod from Banichi, opened the front door.

Tano and Algini went out first—with sidearms, ordinary equipment. They might have been going on a social visit. They walked briskly down the corridor to a point that happened to coincide with a fine old porcelain figure on a stand. They stopped there.

It was time. The clockwork gears began to move.

Bren exited the apartment with Banichi and Jago, similarly armed, on his left and his right. Narani took a stance outside the open door, keeping watch in the direction where the hall ended, at Tabini's apartment, which could not reasonably be expected to threaten them, but it was the rule— one security element watched one way, one watched another. Bren walked at a brisk pace, with his two senior bodyguards. Tano and Algini moved on ahead to the lifts. Tano used his key and opened the car kept waiting at the third floor during their lockdown, no delay at all. Narani meanwhile would be closing and locking the apartment door, not to answer it for anyone except the company in Tabini's apartment.

They entered with Algini, Tano withdrew the security key, stepped inside just as the door shut, reinserted the key in the console.

Three key-punches destined them for the train station, and the car descended in express mode, a rapidity that thumped a little air shock between levels.

They were launched. From here on out, everything was programmed, interlinked. Unstoppable. Locators on wrists, that usually flickered with microdots of green and red and gold, were quite, quite dead. So was voice communication. They were again, as the Guild expression was, running dark.

It all became next steps now, step after step after step. At this point he was no longer in charge; Banichi was; and he had no doubt that Banichi was clear-headed—that Banichi knew exactly what he was doing, how far he would have to push himself, and why he was doing it. Tabini had said it: they were one of two extant units that had the rank to lead and do what needed doing. That had been set in stone from the beginning.

So he had to be where he was, had to go where they were going to go, had to stay with his bodyguard step by step, keep up with their strides and read their cues, right into the heart of a guild whose purpose was to eliminate threats.

It was, on the one hand, insane. It was not going to work. It was on the other hand, necessary, and if it didn't work, well, essential as he thought he was to the universe—if they didn't succeed, he had arranged—rather cleverly, he thought—another set of clockwork gears to move, and other things would happen, things that didn't need him and his team to survive.

Jase-aiji's white-armored bodyguard went first into the hall, a very strange and scary sight; and there was nobody else out—not at mani's door, not at nand' Bren's. Cajeiri walked with his guests and *his* bodyguard, behind Great-uncle and Jase-aiji, with Eisi and Liedi tucked in behind—and all of them inside the formation of Great-uncle's bodyguard. They walked as far as mani's door, and stopped, with Kaplan and Polano standing frozen for the moment, no twitch, nothing that looked alive. Great-uncle's senior bodyguard knocked, and mani's major domo opened the door. Two of mani's young men came out into the corridor, and then mani herself, in black lace sparkling with rubies, real ones. Great-uncle bowed and she joined them with her guard, too. *She* would not have been standing in her foyer waiting. Word would have passed that they were on their way, Cajeiri was sure.

And Cenedi was not with her. Neither was Nawari, who almost always was, if Cenedi was not. That was odd. They had to be somewhere about. Perhaps they were already in Father's apartment.

They walked on down, mani and Great-uncle exchanging pleasant words. They were going to stop at nand' Bren's apartment, Cajeiri guessed.

But he was wrong. They just walked past that door.

So maybe nand' Bren had gone early, too, to talk to Father. They kept walking, with the steady machine-sound of

Jase's guard, and the tap of mani's cane, to his father's apartment, at the end. That door opened just before they reached it, to let them in.

Jase-aiji's two guards took up a stance on either side of that door, and froze there, out in the corridor. Mani and Great-uncle and Jase-aiji went in, and Cajeiri did, keeping his guests close.

Father's major domo was there to welcome them, with his staff, and mani and Great-uncle were prepared to go on to the dining room . . . but with a word to the major domo, Jegari dived off with Eisi and Liedi. Cajeiri lingered, waiting with his guests, hoping not to create a fuss.

"One is changing coats, nadi," he said quietly to his father's major domo, and received an understanding nod.

And because things felt odd, and because Jase-aiji had never once mentioned nand' Bren, "Is nand' Bren here?"

There was a slight hesitation, amid all the movement of bodyguards sorting themselves out and mani and nand' Jase and Great-uncle going to the dining room.

"No, young gentleman, he is not. He is not expected, this evening."

That was odd.

"Is Cenedi here?"

"No, young gentleman."

"Indeed." He stood there until Eisi came hurrying back with a change of coats. He shed his plain one and put on the better coat, letting Eisi help him with the collar and his queue and ribbon—and all the while mani and Great-uncle were conversing with Father's staff, and with their bodyguards, he was thinking, Something is wrong. Something is very wrong. Has Banichi gotten worse?

He escaped Eisi's hands, however, and, with his guests, overtook the grown-ups right in the doorway of the dining room.

"Mani," he said as quietly as he could. "Nand' Bren—"

Mani gave him the *face* sign. Just that. *Face.* Be pleasant. And she was not going to answer.

Now he *knew* something was wrong, and it involved nand' Bren, and maybe Banichi.

But where were Cenedi and Nawari, who were always with her?

His heart was beating hard. And he had to put on a pleasant expression and smile and talk to his parents and everybody else as if nothing at all was wrong.

Which was a lie. He was sure it was.

12

It was the Red Train waiting at the siding. The oldest locomotive in service, the aiji's own, sat lazily puffing steam and ready to roll, only three cars—two baggage cars and the passenger car, its standard formation for the aiji's use. It was a formation everyone in the city knew: the antique black engine, bright brass embellishing its driving wheels, bright brass side-rail, and red paneling along its flanks. The door of the last car, the aiji's own, stood open for them, old-fashioned gold lamplight from inside casting a distorted rectangle on the concrete platform. Guildsmen stood at that open door, the dowager's men, who, as they approached, gave crisp, respectful nods and stood back to let them board.

Banichi and Jago went first up the atevi-scale steps. Jago immediately turned to give Bren a hand up, and, absent witnesses, Tano gave him an easy if unceremonious boost from behind.

Tano and Algini came right behind them, and slid the door shut before Bren so much as turned to look back.

In nearly the same moment the engine started moving, puffing as it went, a machine more in time with oil lamps than electricity, relic of a time when rail had been the fastest way to the coast. The red car had well-padded seats at the rear, a small bar stocked with crystal and linens, luxuries from a gilt and velvet age. One noted—there was even ice in the bucket.

There was leisure in their plan now, time enough to settle in the comfortable seats at the rear and try not to let nerves get to the fore. No train, modern or ancient, could run races down the curving tunnels of the Bujavid hill. The train went at its usual pace on this section of the track, and they sat, not speaking, just doing a short equipment-check. There was one flurry of green lights from Banichi's hitherto dead locator, and Banichi said: "Everything is on time" as it went black again.

Bren drew even breaths, tried to keep his mind entirely centered in the moment, and counted the turns that brought them down the hill.

Cajeiri sat at table in his nearly-best, in a more splendid company than they had had at Tirnamardi. The servants had had to get a cushion so Irene would be tall enough at table; but overall, looking across the table, they all three looked very fine, though very solemn, and almost too quiet. Cajeiri tried his best to be cheerful and even make them smile— but it was doubly hard, because his heart was still thumping away, reminding him that somewhere something was wrong, and people important to him were in some kind of danger.

Father's major domo had sorted them out—Cajeiri was very glad he had not had to think about that at all, because he had far too much going on in his head. Great-uncle was opposite Great-grandmother, next to his parents' vacant places, which insulated him from his mother—he was very glad of that, and nand' Jase was across from Great-grandmother, and then Artur and Irene were across from him; Gene was next to him, far more comfortable company.

Even if the servants had taken all the extra pieces out of the table and moved everything up close, it was a very big dining hall. It swallowed them—and his guests were always a little uneasy in big rooms. *We keep looking for a hand-hold,* Gene had said once at Tirnamardi; and they had all laughed about it . . . as if the Earth could make a sudden stop.

But right now the feeling in his stomach made him wonder if it could.

Staff had set out the formal-dinner glassware, the state silver, the best plates. The service was a great honor to his guests. But it made it harder for them to pick the right fork. "Which comes first?" Gene whispered, and Cajeiri touched the little one above the plate, then made the *attention* sign they used, and signaled just a comforting, *Watch me.*

Then the bell rang, and the door opened, and his mother and father came in.

Everybody but Great-grandmother had to get up. Cajeiri stood up and bowed, and looked up to see his mother, who was wearing Great-uncle's green and white, looking straight at his guests, and not smiling. She did smile at Great-uncle and him and Great-grandmother. And maybe at Jase-aiji: he was not certain—he was giving a very deep nod, and another to his father, who was solemn and sharp-eyed this evening.

His father swept a glance over everybody, the way he did when he was presiding over strangers.

And something was definitely going on. His father was preoccupied. Cajeiri saw it the second before his father smiled and nodded and welcomed everyone as if nothing were wrong at all.

Where is nand' Bren? he wanted to ask out loud, but somehow—he thought—there was so much going on, there had been so many movements one should not ask about—shades not to be lifted, questions not to ask—that he swallowed that question and sat down quietly with his guests, hoping that whatever it was would turn out all right.

The train picked up a little speed as it emerged from the tunnel. Tano used the train's internal communication, at the other end of the car, to talk to the engineer.

"The switches are set," Jago said, cited the time to the half-minute, and Banichi quietly nodded.

Two critical switchpoints, one that shunted them from the Bujavid track to the eastern track, which the Red Train used occasionally; and another, down by the canal, that would shunt them onto the ancient line that ran down to the freight yards and warehouses, and up to the ancient heart of the city.

The Red Train, in Bren's own memory, had never taken the eastern route, let alone switched onto the central city track, and it was far from inconspicuous. People who saw that train might think that Tabini himself, one of his family, or a very high official, was on the move. They would ask themselves whether they had heard that the aiji would be traveling—and they would think, no, there had been no such advisement on the news; and with the heir's suddenly-public birthday Festivity imminent, it was hardly likely Tabini himself would be traveling.

A high official, likely.

And what, they might wonder, was the Red Train doing on *this* track, headed east on a track usually carrying freight? Might it be headed for the old southern route, for the *Marid?*

Not likely.

Would it take the northern end of the old route, up to the Padi Valley, to the Kadagidi township? There *had* been trouble up there.

Both those routes were feasible—until they reached the next switchpoint.

If the operation had leaked in advance, the first indication of trouble might come with that switch *not* sending them onto the old freight depot spur. Bren sat waiting, as aware as the rest of them where they were on the track—and aware of the story they'd handed the Transportation Guild, who, unlike the public, *knew* where trains were going—or had to be convinced they did.

Tatiseigi's men and the dowager's had moved into the

Bujavid office of the Transportation Guild with an order from the aiji-dowager. The Red Train was to shunt over to the old mid-city spur for a pickup at the freight yard—artworks for Lord Tatiseigi's special exhibit in the Bujavid Museum *for* the Festivity. The fact that there actually *were* large crates from Lord Tatiseigi's estate in the system waiting for the regular freight pickup after midnight . . . was useful. The fact that the large crates contained all their spare wardrobe from Tirnamardi, the things they had not had time to pack, was nothing the dowager's men needed to explain to the operators in the Transportation Guild offices.

Perfectly reasonable that the Red Train should move to bring in crates of priceless artwork. Unusual. But reasonable. That part of the operation was the dowager's own plan, and one they had readily adopted into their own.

The train had reached a straight stretch of track, and the car rocked and wheels thumped at a fair speed. Bren had studied the map. His own mental math and the straightaway run told him they were beside the old industrial canal, and right along the last-built perimeter of the Old City. They were coming up on their second switchpoint, *if* the men that were supposed to have gotten there had in fact done their job.

If they didn't make the switch—if they didn't, then there was a major deviation in the plan. Then, in fact—the mission changed.

Slow, slow . . . slow again. Tano and Algini quietly got up, went to the intercom at the other end of the car, and waited there.

What would they do—if the switch didn't happen?

Stop the train and deal with the situation?

Nobody had told him that part.

A little jolt and jostle then, and the train gently bumped onto the other track, slowly making a fairly sharp old-fashioned turn due south.

Bren let go a breath.

Likely so did the engineer, the fireman, and the brakeman, the personnel that ran the Red Train—all three on the aiji's staff, elderly gentlemen, veteran railroaders in what amounted to a mostly retired lifestyle, brave gentlemen, occasional witnesses to history; and once or twice under fire. *They* had survived the coup—they had simply boarded another train and ridden off to the north coast, unable to rescue their beloved old engine, so it had served that scoundrel Murini for a time. But it, and they, were back where they belonged. The crew might not know the extent of the mission this time, but they had orders that had nothing to do with the freight yard: to take an unaccustomed route, stall the venerable engine at a certain prearranged point in front of the Assassins' Guild Headquarters, and hold fast no matter what happened . . .

A mechanical breakdown was what they would radio to Transportation Headquarters, which was, ironically, just two streets over from the Assassins' Guild.

It was a slow progress now. There were no windows in the red car, but they would be passing the very edge of the Old City, the mazy heart of Shejidan, defined by its walled neighborhoods and narrow, cobbled streets. This was the oldest track in the system—and that was another reason the Red Train, while a novelty here, was a logical choice—being of the same vintage as the handful of city engines. The sleek modern transcontinental cars that ran out of the main Shejidan rail station could not navigate the Bujavid tunnels, and while the gauge was the same, the longer cars could not manage the curves of the trans-city route. Older, shorter cars and smaller engines served the Bujavid and plied the city's warehouse to market runs with the same equipment as they had used a century ago, cycling round and round the loop that encircled the city's ancient center, like blood pumping from a heart to the body and back again. Older trains served the less populous districts of the continent at the sort of speed that *let* a provincial lord stop a train for a mail or freight pickup—which was why their incoming crates from Tirnamardi had arrived at the city freight depot. And the vintage city trains picked up mail, they picked up fruit and vegetables, flour and oil and wine, and transported them to warehouses for local pickup, or to the express line for transcontinental shipment. They occasionally stopped and quickly offloaded a stack of crates onto the public sidewalk, for one of the larger shops. They picked up passengers, usually from designated stops, but would now and again let themselves be flagged to allow a random boarding. The system halted, oh, for long enough to get a stalled van off the tracks. It halted to allow a spate of pedestrian traffic to cross up in the hotel district. Or for a large unscheduled mail pickup.

But the whole city rail was about to come to a cold, prolonged halt. The situation would be reported, after a few moments, for safety's sake, and it would be up to the dowager's men to guarantee the Transportation office up in the Bujavid did not rush crews to reach the train at fault . . . but that it did stop traffic.

"We are still on time," Jago said quietly. Banichi sat staring into space, counting, in that process that knew to the second where they were, where Cenedi was, and where their support was. Banichi signaled. Locators went *on*.

Bren sat still, avoiding any distraction whatsoever: silence was the rule, while his bodyguard thought, watched, counted. He had the all-important briefcase between his feet. He had his vest. He *didn't* want to take another hit. The last one he'd taken was enough.

But shooting was not the order of the day. Finesse had to prevent that, as long as possible, and finesse needed that briefcase, and the very heavy seal ring he wore. Needed those things, and steady nerves.

Slower still. Straight. Now he was very sure where they were, on the track that ran right through the middle of the broadest cobbled plaza in Shejidan . . . the old muster ground, which the Guilds had claimed as the last available land in the heart of old Shejidan, back when the aishidi'tat was organizing and the Guilds were becoming the institution they were now.

Slow, slow, slow ... until the train stopped, exhaled, and sat there.

Banichi and Jago got up. Bren picked up his briefcase and stood up, letting Banichi and Jago get to the fore. He walked behind them to the end of the car where the door was, where Tano and Algini were waiting. There they waited just a handful of seconds.

From now on, Banichi led, Banichi set the pace, and it was going to be precise, once they reached a certain street lamp on the plaza. From that point, it was sixty-one paces to the steps, seven steps up to the doors, and beyond that—

Banichi gave a hand signal. Algini opened the door and stepped out into the twilight, not at the usual platform height. Algini landed on his feet below, Tano did, and the two of them immediately pulled spring pins that released three more filigree brass steps.

Banichi descended. Jago did. Bren took the tall steps down and used Jago's offered hand to steady him as he dropped to the cobbles.

The car was sitting close *by* the lamp post in question, in front of the featureless black of the Assassins' Guild Headquarters ... a building as modern-looking as anything one might expect over on Mospheira. Its design made it a block, slits for windows, black stone with inset doors, with none of the baroque whimsy that put a lively frieze of an ancient open-air market around the Merchants' Guild, or a staid and respectable set of statues to the Scholars' Guild that sat next to it. The Assassins' Guild just looked ... unapproachable, its doors, as black as the rest of it, set deep in a relatively narrow approach. Wooden doors, Banichi had told him. Ironwood. It took something to breach that material.

But those outer doors should not routinely be locked. Banichi had said that, too. They were not *supposed* to be locked. They *could* be. The inner door definitely would be.

They reached the lamp post. He thought Banichi might pause there, if they were somehow off their time—but Banichi and Jago kept going. It was his job to stay with them, and Tano's and Algini's to stay with him. It was a pace he could match if he pushed himself. Banichi said speed mattered. But it couldn't look forced to any observer, just deliberate.

Sixty-one paces. They crossed the cobblestone plaza on a sharp diagonal, crossed the scarcely-defined street, and the modern paved sidewalk that skirted the Guild's frontage.

Seven steps up to the iron-bound doors, which might or might not open.

At the last moment Banichi touched something on his locator bracelet and Jago pounded once with her fist on the dark double doors.

There was a hesitation. Then a latch clicked and the left-hand door, where they were not, swung outward—a defensive sort of door, not the common inward-swinging sort. Guards in Guild uniform confronted them.

"The paidhi-aiji," Banichi said, "speaking *for* Tabini-aiji."

Bren did not bow. He held up his hand, palm inward, with the seal-ring outward.

The unit maintained official form—the two centermost stepped to the side, clearing their path without a word of discussion.

They were in.

Bren went with Banichi and Jago in front of him and Tano and Algini behind. It was the tail end of a warm day at their backs. The foyer swallowed them up in shadow and cool air, and three steps up led to a hallway of black stone, where converted gas lamps, now electric, gave off a gold and inadequate light beside individual office doors. Antiquity was the motif here. Deliberate antiquity, shadow, and tradition.

Hammered-glass windows in the dark-varnished doors. Black stone outside . . . and that glass in those doors was, Bren thought, all but whimsical—a show of openness, even of casual vulnerabiiity . . . in the fifteen offices that dealt with outsiders to the Guild.

These outer offices had nothing to do with Tabini-aiji's order. A business wanting a guard for a shipment, yes. Someone with legal paperwork to file. A small complaint between neighbors. A request for a certificate or seal. It *was* the national judicial system, where it regarded inter-clan disputes.

The aiji's business had no place in this hall, which led past the nine offices of the main hall toward an ornate carved door, and at the left, a corner, with six more offices in a hall to the left, just as described.

Two guards at their backs, down those three steps to the double-doored entry. *Four* guards at a single massive wooden door, this time.

"The aiji's representative," Banichi said, and a second time Bren held up his hand with the ring.

This time it was no automatic opening of the door. "Seeking whom, paidhi-aiji?"

"The aiji sends to the Guildmaster, nadi, understanding the Guild Council is in session this evening."

There was no immediate argument about it. Guild queried Guild, communicating somewhere beyond those doors.

Bren waited, his bodyguard standing still about him. It was thus far going like clockwork. Neither of these outer units should have the authority to stop them.

"The paidhi-aiji," the senior said, in that communication, not in code, "bearing the aiji's seal ring, a briefcase, and with his own bodyguard."

There was a delay. The senior stayed disengaged from them, staring across the hall at his counterpart in the second unit. There might have been a lengthy answer, or a delay for consultation. And there might yet be a demand to open the briefcase.

The senior shot a sudden glance toward Bren. "Nand' paidhi, the Council is in session on another matter. You are requested to wait here."

"Here?" Indignantly. They needed to be *through* that second set of doors. Bren held up his fist, with Tabini's ring in evidence, and put shock in his voice. "*This*, nadi, does not wait in the public hall!" With the other hand, he held forward the briefcase. "*Nor* does the aiji's address to the Guild Council! If the Council is in session, so be it! *This* goes through!"

"Nand' paidhi." The senior gave a little nod to that argument and renewed his address to the other side of the door. "The paidhi has the aiji's seal ring, nadi. He strongly objects."

There was another small delay. Nobody moved. There was an eerie quiet—both in their vicinity, and from all those little offices up and down the two halls that met here. What was going on back at the outer doors, at any door along that hallway, Bren could not tell. One could hear the slightest sound, somewhere. Atevi ears—likely heard far more than that, possibly even the sound of the transmission.

Or movements within the offices.

Were they expected? Was the place in lockdown? What was behind all those office doors?

Banichi and the others stood absolutely still, and Bren refused to twitch—as still as his own bodyguard. He could do it. He'd prepared himself to do it, and lean on their reflexes, not his own. The click of the door lock in front of them echoed like a rifle shot.

And that door, that single, massive wooden door, opened on brighter light, with four more guards the other side of it, at an identical intersection of hallways—again, a blank wall on the right, an ornate carved door, however, closing off the hall of offices on the left. A short jog over, and a short hallway, beyond these guards, led to barely visible closed doors, also guarded by a unit of four.

That was the Council Chamber, down that stub of a hall. The left-hand hall—that was Guild Administration. And at the other end of it sat the Office of Assignments.

Exactly as arranged, Bren stopped . . . not quite inside, as

Banichi and Jago encountered the guards. He was *in* the doorway. So were Tano and Algini, just behind him, beside that thick outward-opening single door. The guards in front of them posed an obstacle, wanting to look them over. There were still the six guards in the outer hall, at their backs—and four automatic rifles, not just sidearms, to judge by the two men visible, guarded the Council doors ahead.

He was causing a small problem. The outer four guards could not shut the door, and were mildly unhappy about it, the inside guards were trying to move them on without a fuss—

Fuss—was a lord's job.

He shot up his fist, with the ring in clear evidence. *"This,* nadiin, is the aiji's presence, and my case contains his explicit orders. Tabini-aiji sends to the Guildmaster, demanding urgent attention, and he will not be pleased to be stalled or given excuses about agendas. Advise the Guildmaster! There is no delay about this!"

"The Guildmaster is in Council, paidhi-aiji," the senior nearest said in a quiet, urgent voice, "and the Council is in session. We will send word into the chamber and we will take you to his office to wait. He will see you and receive the orders there."

Double or nothing. Bren pitched his voice low, where only the immediate four might hear him—for what good it did, if electronics was sending voices elsewhere. "I, speaking for the aiji, ask you now, nadiin, *where is your man'chi?* Is it to the Guildmaster, or to the aishidi'tat? They are *not* one and the same. Is it to the Guildmaster, or to the Guild? They are *not* one and the same."

"Paidhi, this is neither here nor there. We are not refusing the aiji's request. Even the aiji—"

He kept his voice down. "You are *betrayed* by the Guild leadership, nadiin. Stand down *now!* This is the aiji's order! Obey it!"

Faces were no longer disciplined or impassive. Eyes darted in alarm, one to the other, and, to the side, Banichi had just deftly bumped the door frame, and inserted a little wad of expanding plastic in the latch-hole.

"Close the doors!" the inside senior said, and suddenly they were facing four rifles, from the Council doorway.

"Retired Guild is returning," Banichi said. "The Missing and the Dead are returning, at the aiji's order and in his service. Will you shoot, and then face them? Assist us. Or stand down."

"Banichi," one said to the senior in a low voice. "That is Banichi." And the unit senior inside said, "Nadi, we are under orders. Retreat. Retreat now. Quickly."

Bren didn't turn his head to see. The four behind them were Tano's and Algini's problem. The four immediately in front of them were trying to persuade them to retreat.

"He will *not* retreat," Bren said. "Nor will this!" He held the ring in view.

"The *aiji's* orders," Banichi said quietly. "If your man'chi is *not* to the Shadow Guild, *separate* yourself from the Guildmaster, or stand in opposition. The Council leadership has committed treason."

A bell began to ring. Hall overhead lights began to flash. The offices, Bren was thinking. If those offices back there were occupied . . . but the back accesses down that hall were in *Cenedi's* territory.

"Shut down your equipment," Banichi said to the units confronting them. "All of you. Now. Take the aiji's orders, Daimano's, Cenedi's . . . and mine." It wasn't working. Not in the four in the background. *"Paidhi!"* Banichi said.

His job. He was ready for it, on Banichi's wounded side— he spun around Banichi as Jago did the same with Algini. A flashbang sailed past him into the inner hall and blew as Tano hurled the massive door shut. It rebounded under rifle fire from the Council door guards—and opened again, splinters flying, everything in terrible slow motion.

Turn and duck when I call you, Banichi had told him, forewarning him about splinters, and something still caught him in the back of the head, so brain-jarring he was unaware of completing his turn to the door: he went down beside Banichi, leaning on him for an instant. Tano bumped into him and Banichi, getting into cover, as the door edge passed them on its next rebound — Tano had drawn his side-arm, covering the left-hand hall. The outer four door guards were down — lying over against the wall beside Jago and Algini as automatic fire over their heads continued to hammer the splintering door. The outbound volley and Jago and Algini's move had likely thrown the outside guards to their present position a little down the corridor wall, pressed tight to avoid the fire that had the door swinging insanely open and shut under the shots and the rebound. Fire inside lagged — and Jago flung another flashbang skittering in on the polished floor. God, Bren thought — hope the guards inside weren't equipped with worse to throw back.

The guards down by the front door were Banichi's to watch, those two men, and all those office doors. But those guards were gone, vanished, likely *into* the offices. Bren moved over against the wall in the side hall and stayed quiet — while from the Council hallway bursts of automatic fire shredded the door and made retreat back down the outside hall impossible. One of the door guards had been hit. His comrades worked to stop the blood and treat the wound, under Jago's implacable aim.

They were in possession of the doorway and the outer halls — and trapped there, with Tano aiming a pistol down the length of the short hall, Banichi watching the long hall, Jago with three problems and a wounded man at extremely close range, and Algini covering the door from an angle, to be sure nobody came at them from inside. The guards inside the Council hallway weren't coming out — the four they had talked to close at hand had disappeared, somewhere out of the line of fire — and the four Council Chamber guards had progressively shredded the door, which, thanks to Banichi's small plastic plug, hadn't closed *or* locked, and made it a very bad idea for anybody to exit into the hallway. Right now there was a lull in fire. There was just the bell making an insane racket, and glass from ricochets into office doors and overhead lights lying all down the hall.

"Young fools," Banichi remarked in a low voice. "They have finally come to their senses, waiting for orders, waiting for us to move. They are over-excited. Seniors will use gas, if they can reach the stores. That will be a problem."

The service corridor communicating with all those offices was the weakness in their position. Defenders were *bound* to come at them via the offices, and when that happened, they were in trouble, be it gas or grenades. It was a cold stone floor, a cold wait—good company, Bren said to himself. He just had to do what his aishid needed him to do, keep quiet, keep out of the way, and not distract them.

Suddenly the wall at Bren's back thumped, strongly—it made his heart jump; made his ears react. But then he thought: Cenedi. That intersecting administrative hallway, the other side of the wall. Something had just blown up. Cenedi *might* be giving the opposition worries from the other direction.

He snatched a glance at Banichi's locator bracelet. Dead black. No signals at the moment. And nobody had moved, only shifted position a little, tense, waiting. The alarm bell kept up its deafening monotone ringing and the lights kept flashing.

Then the floor thumped under them, and a shock rolled in from the doors down the hall. The massive outside doors flew back, counter to their mountings, one upright, one of them askew and hanging, then falling in an echoing crash.

That wasn't defense. It was *inbound*. Bren flattened himself to the wall with Banichi and Tano, as far from the inner door frame as they could get. Smoke obscured the street end of the hall, smoke and sunset-colored daylight, and two, three, *five* moving shadows in that smoky light. Three solid figures appeared out of it, flinging open office doors, and more shadows arrived up those three steps from the foyer, pouring into the hall from outside, opening office doors one after another, treading broken glass underfoot.

Secondary passages, secondary passages all over the place, in every office, in the Council chamber. It was the Assassins' Guild. Of *course* there were secondary passages. Every building in the aishidi'tat had back passages. . . .

A burst of fire came out the ruined Council-area door, and a concentrated volley came back, right past the door frame. No more fire came out.

A flood of bodies occupied the hall, shadows moving fast in the smoke. Bren put his hand down on the stone floor, thinking if that was their side inbound, it might be time to get up and have it clear who they were—and his hand slipped.

He wrenched halfway about to get a look at Banichi, saw his face in the flashing lights of the alarm system. Banichi was sitting upright, but not doing so well, and it was blood slicking the floor. A lot of it.

"Damn it." Bren got to his knees, ignoring the rush of bodies past them as he tried to get Banichi's coat open. "Tano-ji! He's bleeding!"

"Likely a broken stitch," Banichi said faintly, above the continuing din of the bell. "One is just a little light-headed. Stay *down*, Bren-ji. Tano, turn on the bracelet."

Tano did that. Banichi's locator started flashing, communicating who they were, *where* they were.

Bren had a handkerchief—a gentleman carried such things. He put it, still folded, inside Banichi's jacket, under Banichi's arm, and felt heat and soaked cloth. "Press on that, Nichi-ji. Do not move the arm. Just keep pressure on it."

"One hesitates to remark," Banichi said, as another flashbang went off somewhere behind the wall and gunfire broke out, "one hesitates to remark that you are contributing no little blood, Bren-ji."

His scalp stung when he thought about it. Adrenaline had been holding off an ill-timed headache, and he felt dizzy when he shifted about, which seemed likely from too much desk-sitting.

"That arm must not move," Tano said to Banichi. *"Must*

not, Nichi-ji, do you hear? Do not try to get up yet." Tano was securing his own communications earpiece, which had fallen out, and voices were coming through it, fainter than the bell and the firing and shouting going on in the adjacent hall. There was more than the smell of gunpowder. There was smoke in the air—smoke the source of which they couldn't see, as yet, but this had the smell of woodsmoke. Something was afire.

Tano didn't move from where he was. Algini and Jago were on their feet, but not crossing that open doorway, just watching, with guns in hand, Jago still keeping the guard unit with the wounded partner quiet and out of the way. Bren knelt there with his body-armor between Banichi and whatever traffic passed them ... not of much use, but at least he could keep an eye on Banichi, be sure he was conscious, and be ready to get up and invoke Tabini's name if any problems rebounded in their direction.

Gunfire, acute for a moment, had tapered off. And the bell stopped ringing and the lights that had survived the barrage stopped flashing. In that sudden, absolute silence, Bren felt the world quite distant and himself gone shaky, whether from contributing to the bloody puddle on the floor or from a sustained expectation of dying—he was not sure.

Tano got to his feet and spoke to someone on com. Bren stayed tucked low, one knee under him, the briefcase right by him, one hand on Banichi's arm. He wished he had a medical kit with him ... but that briefcase could have no illicit weapons, offer no signs to anyone who would examine it that it was *anything* other than a paidhi's proper business. That briefcase was their justification and their protection— that briefcase, and himself, bearing the aiji's ring, the legal equivalent of Tabini's presence.

For some few minutes that eerie semi-silence in the halls went on. Across the perilous gap of the shattered doorway, Jago and Algini maintained their watch in two directions. Tano remained standing, watching that side hall, but things were much quieter. The trapped guard unit had stayed very still, concentrating on their own wounded, and now and again exchanging quiet words with Jago. Then quietly she got up, and under her armed watch, that unit laid their weapons on the floor, got up, lifted their wounded partner to his feet, and went on through that shattered doorway, apparently to seek medical help inside.

Dare we move? Bren wondered. But he noted flashes from Jago's bracelet, across the hall; and from Tano's and Banichi's, near at hand, and Algini and Tano were listening to something.

"We have secured the Council chamber," Tano said.

"Up," Banichi murmured then. "We are not done here. Bren-ji. The papers. The Council."

That was the plan. The papers—ultimately—had to be proven for what they were. The justification for their action had to be laid down in official record.

"Can you?" he asked. "Banichi? You could stay here with Tano and Jago. Algini and I can go."

"Half this blood is yours," Banichi said, and drew a knee up and put his other hand down. "I can walk."

"Stubborn," Jago said. "Stubborn, unit-senior."

"Let us have this done," Banichi said. "Let us see this happen. *Up,* Bren-ji. Tano. Lend a hand."

Bren stood up, watched uneasily as Tano gently assisted Banichi to his feet, providing most of the effort. For a moment Bren thought, *He can't do it,* and Banichi leaned against the wall, light-headed. But Banichi shook them off then, obstinate and setting his own two feet. Algini joined them. Lights sparked on bracelets.

"Briefcase, Bren-ji," Banichi said, leaning against the wall, and Bren bent quickly and picked it up—feeling a little dizziness in that move; and the knee and shin of his trousers were dark and soaked. Banichi was right. Between himself and Banichi, they were a bloody mess.

They were in sole possession of the outer hall, except a guard the incoming forces had set at the ruined front door. Shouted orders reverberated from inner halls.

The splintered door beside them had long since stopped swinging, jammed in a way that had provided protection for Jago and Algini. Jago stood in that doorway now, pistol in both hands, got a look in one direction, nodded to somebody unseen, and a man walked into their hallway: Nawari, who frowned in concern at the sight of them.

"Nand' paidhi," Nawari said with a little nod.

"The office," Banichi asked immediately. "The problem."

"Settled," Nawari said. "There was some burning. An incendiary. *He* is dead, apparently a suicide, considerably burned, but recognizable. The records—suffered, but were not destroyed. And we intercepted one man with several notebooks from that office."

So Shishogi was dead, unable to be questioned. But notebooks, removed under such circumstances . . . that might be a very fortunate find.

"One expected such a device," Banichi said. "The bill?"

"Two of ours out of action," Nawari said, "counting yourself. Two of the resistance dead, three, counting the target. Fourteen in the building wounded, one hundred forty-seven voluntarily standing down pending a resolution. Sixteen under arrest, undergoing sorting now, testimony to be taken: they are suspect. A new Council is about to meet to declare a quorum, record the change, and close the meeting. Yourself, nadi-ji, and especially the paidhi-aiji . . . are needed there as soon as possible."

Banichi said, "Bren-ji."

The aiji's documents. The justification. The legalities. "One is ready," Bren said. "Banichi, if you can do this—then you are to have that seen to. Immediately."

"Agreed," Banichi said. Bren found his aishid around him—his head was beginning to throb with his heartbeat now, the buzz in his ears seeming louder than some voices, and he was beginning to feel a little sick at his stomach— the stress of the moment, he said to himself. He had to get through this, just a few more minutes, to get Banichi the help he needed, to get the whole business settled.

They walked with Nawari into the foyer on the other side of that splintered door, an area overhung with gray smoke, splinters from the door, dust-filmed puddles of water, and an amazing number of brass casings lying about— not to mention the leaking skein of gray fire hoses deployed through the open door of the left-hand hall. That one door, amid all the chaos, was relatively untouched.

The Office of Assignments—Cenedi's target—lay in that direction. But their own business was straight ahead, down the blood-spattered stub of a corridor to the open Council chamber. They just had to get to the heart of that chamber, just had to stand up that long.

Bar the paidhi-aiji, carrying no weapon but the aiji's ring and bringing a briefcase with *nothing* but the aiji's and the aiji-dowager's legitimate demands for an investigation? That was actionable.

Shoot at him? Wound his aishid? That was a shot fired at Tabini-aiji.

They *had* the bastards. They had them, legally. He just had to drive the last nail in. Had to stay on his feet. They all five had to hope there wasn't some holdout, somewhere— but self-protection wasn't their business any longer. Nawari opened the doors, gave orders to those guarding them. They entered the chamber, walked down the descending aisle, past tiers of desks, where a gathering of Guild, some with wounds, all heavily armed, filled the space around the long desk that dominated the speaker's well.

Their entry held universal attention from below—eyes tracking him and his aishid, and their progress down the steps and levels that split the chamber's seating.

The long desk at the bottom belonged, one understood, to the Guildmaster and his two aides. The less conspicuous desk to the side, obscured by the crowd, belonged to the recording secretary.

Thirty-three seats in the chamber, all counted— twenty-nine councillors if all the seats were filled. Three at the long desk. And the recorder.

He and his aishid reached the bottom of the aisle, and as they did, the armed gathering at the bottom of the well began to flow upward into the tiers of desks, spreading out to fill those places. A senior woman slipped her rifle from her shoulder and laid it on the long desk, at the right-hand seat of the three. A man, completely gray-haired, sat down in the central seat, and laid a pistol in front of him, and leaned another, a rifle, against the desk, sat in the leftmost seat, at which point the woman—likely Daimano—sat down.

Which of these was taking the office of Guildmaster was uncertain. The leadership changed seating at whim, Jago had forewarned him, when outsiders were present; and under the circumstances, one was not sure that even all the Guildsmen taking the Council seats were themselves sure who was setting himself in charge.

But the retired and the Missing and the Dead, as Jago called them, were claiming their places in the chamber, some resuming old seats—more of them taking seats to which they had elected themselves, a complete change of the Council as it had been constituted this last year. The recorder's seat was still vacant as the man at center declared for silence in the room, and a last few took their places.

An old man, completely gray-haired, took the seat of the recording secretary, a last scrape of wood on stone as that chair moved into place, a thump and a riffle of pages as he opened the massive book that had apparently rested there safely shut during the tumult outside.

There was a distinct smell of smoke in the air here, too. There was still shouting back and forth outside the chamber, until the outer door definitively shut and muffled what was going on up on the main floor.

"Nand' paidhi," the man centermost said.

"Nadi." Bren bowed deeply to him, and to the two flanking him, no formality omitted. He shifted the briefcase to the other hand. "I speak as paidhi-aiji, for Tabini-aiji, with his ring." His voice was undependable, hoarse from the smoke and the dryness. He held out the bloodied ring as steadily as he could, tried quietly to clear his throat, resisting the impulse to wipe the gold clean. Dignity, he said to himself. Calm. As if he *did* rule the aishidi'tat.

Happy with humans? They were not. His aishid had warned him they were bringing back a cadre of old leadership that opposed humans and all they brought with them — a leadership that might wish that he had been a casualty, leaving them to settle things without him.

"In the aiji's name, bearing his orders, with his seal—his request for an investigation of orders given in the Dojisigin Marid; bearing also, in the aiji's name, corroborating documents from the aiji-dowager."

"Enter the documents, paidhi-aiji!"

"Nadi!" he said, the proper response, and with another bow, and leaving his aishid standing, he went aside to the recorder's table, set his briefcase on that desk—and found his fingers stuck together about the bloody handle, his cufflace on that wrist absolutely matted, both his hands too filthy to do more than open the two latches to show the ornately ribboned and sealed documents inside. "Recorder," he said, "if you will kindly assist me."

The recorder rose, carefully took the documents in clean hands, entirely emptying the case, and set them, unstained, on the desk. Using an old-fashioned glass pen and inkwell from a recess within the desk, the recorder wrote in his book, and carefully printed a number on the first corner of each document and signed beneath each.

Then he rose and bowed. "Paidhi-aiji," he said, with an unexpected fervor. "The Guild is in receipt of the aiji's orders."

"Nadi," Bren said with gratitude. The shakes wanted to attack him now and he called up reserves, determined not to delay attention to Banichi by falling on his face. He walked back to his aishid and faced the Guildmaster's desk for a statement of a sort he had done often enough in the aiji's court.

"The nature of the aiji's business," the Guildmaster said, "paidhi-aiji, a summation."

"Tabini-aiji requests, with these documents, under his seal, an investigation into orders given in the Dojisigin Marid—regarding a situation in which local Guild were disarmed, their units separated, and put into the field without equipment." Deep breath. "The second document, for the Guild's attention, from the aiji-dowager, under her seal: the deposition of two Dojisigin Guild whose village was threatened with destruction if they refused to carry out an un-Filed assassination of a northern lord."

"To which these documents pertain, nandi."

"To which these documents pertain, nadi."

"The Council will recess for three hours. We will reconvene to hear the documents read. Is there dissent?"

There was silence in the chamber.

"Done!" the Guildmaster said. "The Council enters recess."

Finished.

Bren bowed slightly, the Guildmaster nodded, and Bren wanted only to get himself and his aishid back to safe ground. But suddenly Tano was supporting all of Banichi's weight.

He immediately added his own help, for what help it was. Algini did. Banichi was out, dead weight, his skin gone an unhealthy color in the dim lighting of the chamber; and it took Algini and Tano both to hold him up.

"Help him!" Bren said, turning to the Guildmaster, to the chamber at large. "*Help* him!"

People moved. The Guildmaster called for a medic in a voice that carried, and doors at the side of the well banged open on a lower hallway.

"He thought he'd broken a stitch," Bren said. "Get a compression on that."

They let Banichi down on the edge of the first riser. Tano worked to get the jacket off. The handkerchief he'd lent was soaked. Tano put his hand on the wound, pressed hard, maintaining pressure. A call for a medic rang out down the inner hall.

The world was out of balance, sounds going surreal. It couldn't happen. They couldn't lose him. Tano and Algini both were doing their best to stop the bleeding, needing room. Shoved aside, Bren could find nothing to do with his hands, nothing to do at all that was not already being done. It seemed forever, a time measured only in the pounding of his own heart; but then a racket at the door on their level brought a new group into the chamber, one of them a gray-haired woman and two men with a bloodstained gurney.

That team moved in, taking over, talking rapid-fire to Tano, Jago standing uncertainly near. Algini shifted next to Bren and said in a low voice, "There is a medical facility. Surgeons are already there. He will get the best they can manage, on a priority."

When or how he had no inkling. "Yes," he said. He watched them, with Tano never releasing his hold, lift Banichi up onto the sheeted conveyance, saw them—thank God— hoist a drip bag and clean an area for a transfusion, no wait-ing about it, even while they were taking him away through the doors. Tano went with Banichi. Algini stayed. Jago did.

And just as that group passed the back-passage doors, Cenedi turned up at the chamber doors, and came hurrying down the steps to reach them.

"One heard the call," Cenedi said. "Nand' paidhi, nand' Siegi started from the Merchants' Guild before the call went out. He should be here by now."

Siegi. The dowager's own physician had attached himself to Cenedi's mission, and the Merchants' Guild was right next door. Thank God, Bren thought. Siegi had done the first surgery. He would instantly have an idea what he was dealing with.

"Are *you* injured, nand' paidhi?"

"No," Bren said. He had a damnable headache. He re-membered why, but it was nowhere near as serious. He didn't want to touch it to find out differently. "I shall not put myself in the way, nadiin-ji, but I am not going back to the Bujavid until Banichi goes with us. One is very grateful— very grateful—to the Guild and to nand' Siegi. Express that for us."

Cenedi listened solemnly, nodded, and went and spoke to the Guild authorities.

"You speak as the aiji," Algini cautioned him in a low voice. "They *will* obey your orders absolutely."

That shook his confidence. He cast a look at Algini, and at Jago, and felt the warm weight of that gold ring on his hand, a trust and a burden. "I should not," he said. "I should not become an inconvenience in this business, nor offend the Council. But I *want* to go down where Banichi is."

"It is a small room, Bren-ji," Algini said. "A very small room. Let the surgeons work."

There was so much blood. It was caked on his hands, sticking his fingers together, beginning to powder as a fine red dust.

And all around the halls outside were sounds of movement, of things happening he no longer understood. The Guild was taking account, dealing with its own wounded, of whom Banichi was only one . . .

But Banichi was *his*. His team. If anybody deserved to survive this, Banichi, who'd done everything to avoid bloodletting in the halls . . . to open the doors and hold position, distracting the whole Guild for a few critical minutes while the heavy-armed Guild of which they were the vanguard, arrived outside and got through the front doors the hard way . . .

Banichi had held the security doors open all the way to the heart of the Guild with nothing but a little wad of plastic—and a junior guard unit had panicked and damaged that door seconds before Cenedi started another action in the administrative wing.

He drew a deep, shuddering breath as Cenedi came back to them. "The objective," he said to Cenedi. "How did we fare?"

"Shishogi is dead. The office was firebombed. We are sure we lost some records. But the fire suppression system functioned, incidentally preserving his body, and particularly certain books across which he had fallen. The shelves fell, preserving others. We have sealed that office. Experts will go through the records."

"One heard of other notebooks . . ."

". . . which we intercepted. Yes. Perhaps it was intended we intercept it. Or it may be real. We shall look into that item very carefully." Cenedi acknowledged Algini's presence with a nod. "Gini-ji, we have secured the entire hall, and we are mapping the last hours of function of that office, going back to yesterday dawn."

Algini gave a single nod. Yesterday. When they had taken out Haikuti and come back to Shejidan. The hours between had been one long chain of movement and planning.

And now—

Now it had succeeded—

But it wasn't over. They were far, far from done with the mop-up.

"Where were they?" he asked Jago, when Cenedi had gone. "The returning Guild. Where were they? Over in the Merchants' Guild?"

"A few were," Jago said. "*We* brought the heavy-armed contingent, those that could not move inconspicuously."

We brought them.

Damn. The baggage cars that always attended the Red Train. They'd not come alone. The moment they'd cleared the doors, *that* group, observing from the train, had started their own countdown.

He let go a long breath. Two baggage cars. And a wad of plastic. And a team he desperately wanted to get back in one piece. He wanted everything finished, wrapped up, a success—but it wasn't, yet. It wouldn't be, until he could take Banichi with him. Banichi himself, he had no doubt, would tell him go, get everybody back to the Bujavid—do not be a fool, Bren-ji—but Banichi wasn't in charge right now.

That ring, that heavy, heavy ring, said that he could do as he pleased. And he was being human, and probably his obstinacy was upsetting his bodyguard, even obstructing the Council—but they'd said, hadn't they, a three hour recess?

He trusted Algini and Jago not to let him be a total fool. And they stayed by him, tired, bloody, standing, then sitting on the edge of the lowest riser. Any coming or going around that open door through which Banichi had gone drew the same quick, tense glances, two atevi, one human.

It might be different reasons in the nervous systems. But what they fervently wanted right now was unquestionably the same thing.

13

No one had spilled anything—except Artur had bumped his water glass and nearly overset it. Artur had gone bright pink, and murmured, quite correctly, perfectly memorized, "One regrets, nand' aijiin, nandi."

"Indeed," mani had said, and the grown-ups had nodded, and everything had settled again.

So had Cajeiri's heart—as servants went on setting out the next course. It took Artur quite a while to change colors back to normal. Madam Saidin's foresight had taught his guests that phrase—with the correct honorific for the circumstance, over which no few atevi might stumble in confusion. Irene had joked somewhat grimly that she had to memorize it perfectly, because she was sure to do something wrong. But it turned out Artur was the one; and Cajeiri caught his eye across the table and signaled approval, once and slightly, more a blink than a nod. Artur made an unhappy face back, just an acknowledgment—one had to know their secret signs to spot it.

There was a fruit ice, to finish. Everyone was happy with that. Throughout, they had hardly spoken a word, except Artur, and except Gene, once, to ask what a dish was: a servant had assured him it was safe, and the servant was right.

The grown-ups had talked about the weather—actually—talked about the weather. It had been that gruesome. Nobody was at ease. Nobody mentioned nand' Bren, not once. Cenedi and Nawari should have been attending Great-grandmother, to hand her the cane when dinner was done, and to move her chair, and to do all those things. They were all stuck at the dinner table, in that huge room, with nothing to do, as if the air was afire and no one could mention it.

That was why, he thought, there had been no delay in serving dinner. That was why they had no more than gotten to the apartment before they were sent in to table, and why there had not been that long a delay, either, before his father and mother had come in.

The grown-ups knew *what* was going on; Cajeiri was sure of it. The rest of them knew *something* was going on. They all were wound tight as springs. Everything was. The servants were walking very quietly. Nobody but poor Artur had even clinked a glass, and that had sounded like a bell.

Now at last his father finished his glass of wine, and signaled the attending servant not to refill it. That was everyone's signal that dinner was over.

"Shall we go for brandy?" his father asked.

There was quiet agreement, everyone rising, and Cajeiri got up. His guests did—servants moved to assist his guests in moving the chairs, though Gene managed—Cajeiri gave it only a little push to help it move straight back. So they all four gathered, with Antaro and Jegari, who had stood along the wall with the other senior bodyguards, and who now attended their lords: Lucasi and Veijico were out in the hall, where they ought to find out things—but he doubted they were learning any more out there.

What's going on? Cajeiri wanted to ask Jase-aiji, when they came near, going out into the sitting room. He could ask it in ship-speak, and nobody but his guests would know what he asked.

But he feared to break the peace, such as it was, that kept

questions out of the conversation and kept everybody polite. He went in with his guests, and as his mother and his father sat down—his mother, like them, to be served a light fruit juice and his father and everybody else receiving a brandy glass. His father asked politely whether his youngest guests had enjoyed their dinner.

There was crashing silence. It was an unscheduled question, one Madam Saidin had not prepared them to answer.

Then Irene said, in her soft voice, with only a little lisp, "Dinner was very good, nand' aiji. One is very grateful."

"Yes," Gene and Artur said, both nodding deeply.

"Excellent," his father said, and Cajeiri resumed breathing—there had been no mistake, no infelicity. He was *not* superstitious. Mani said superstitious folk were fools. But it felt as if any mistake they made could bring everything crashing down, everything balanced like a precarious stack of china. People he relied on were not here. They were about to go far off the polite phrases they had memorized for the occasion, and with nand' Bren not here to fill up the gaps.

His father went on to ask Lord Tatiseigi about his art exhibit down in the public museum—and they talked about which pieces were there, and then wandered off into talking about Lord Geigi's collection out in the west, and the effort to retrieve a piece that Lord Geigi's nephew had sold.

Mani said that she was tracking it—and they went off about that, then stopped to explain the matter to Jase-aiji.

There was not a word about the Dojisigi or Lord Aseida.

There was not a word about what had gone on at Tirnamardi.

They just talked on and on. Jase-aiji had hardly said a word all evening, and he had had hardly a word from his parents, either—not "We were worried," nor anything of the sort—which, considering they had come in from a situation with Assassins, and had sneaked into the Bujavid, seemed another considerable lack of questions. It was as if nothing had happened at all.

Then, after they had worn that matter out, his mother asked, almost the first word she had uttered, "Your guests, son of mine—they are all older than you, are they not?"

"Yes, honored Mother."

He waited, wondering whether she was going to make some observation about that point, but she looked elsewhere, and meanwhile Great-grandmother had called one of her bodyguards forward and asked a question he could not hear. The young man seemed to say no, or something like no.

It was more than weird. It was getting scary.

He took a deep, deep breath then and asked, very calmly, very quietly, "Have we had any security alerts tonight, honored Father?"

"Nothing our guests should worry about," his father said.

And almost as he said it, all the bodyguards twitched at once, and Jegari checked his locator bracelet.

Father's chief bodyguard moved first, and went to his father, bent close to his ear and said something, no one else moving, *everybody* else watching.

His father asked a question, and got an answer that Cajeiri could almost hear, it was so quiet.

His father nodded then, and drew a deep breath. "Guild transmission has resumed," he said. "Cenedi has just reported the mission is a success."

"Excellent," mani said, and Lord Tatiseigi and Jase-aiji all breathed at once.

"May one know?" Cajeiri asked, but mani was talking to his father and all he could do was try to overhear, because it was grown-up business, and he had the feeling it was very, very important.

There was something going on with the Assassins' Guild. He caught that much. Some signal had hit everybody's ear at once. His father asked whether documents had been filed, and his bodyguard said they had been.

It could be that his father had just Filed Intent on someone, but he heard no names, and his mother just looked upset. His father put his hand on hers and leaned over and talked just into her ear a moment. She nodded and seemed in better spirits then . . . so at least it was not something between *them*.

It was Assassins' Guild business, he was absolutely sure of that. Some sort of papers were filed and something had upset his mother until his father reassured her.

He knew far more than his three young guests were supposed to know—that there was a little old man in offices in Guild Headquarters, who was behind a good deal of all their troubles, and that man's name, Shishogi, was a name he was not supposed to mention. Shishogi was another of *his* relatives, and his mother's relative, and Shishogi *might* have been involved in Grandfather being killed.

Had Cenedi possibly done something about Shishogi?

And where was nand' Bren tonight? Maybe nand' Bren's bodyguard was helping Cenedi.

He wondered if his guests were understanding enough to make their own guesses.

And he would have to tell them, once he found out, but he did not expect that his father was going to say anything definite in front of them.

"Is there word from Bren-paidhi, nandiin?" Jase-aiji asked then.

"Well. He is well," was the answer.

Well was very good news.

But why did his father have to assure Jase-aiji that nand' Bren was well? Had nand' Bren anything to do with Shishogi, if that had been what was going on?

Maybe it had been some other problem.

At least the grown-ups were relaxing. Father called for another round of brandy and fruit juice, and the bodyguards, from stiffly watchful, had moved together, opened the door to the hall, and were conferring in their own way, passing information which Cajeiri desperately wished he could hear.

"What's going on?" came a whisper from Gene.

"The Guild," he whispered back, in Ragi, and then in

ship-speak, quietly, so his mother would not hear: "Our big problem, maybe. Fixed, maybe. Not sure."

Gene passed that on to Irene and Artur, heads together, and his mother was, at the moment, talking to his father, so they went unnoticed.

Whatever had happened, the Guild meeting at the door broke up, and bodyguards went back on duty, with no different expressions. That was all they could know, because nobody was going to say anything to his guests. Antaro and Jegari had moved over to the door and had not moved back to the far side of the room.

But he had no wish to have his father officially notice that his very junior bodyguard knew anything about his father's business. He so wanted to call them over as everybody else had and ask what was going on, but he decided not to attract grown-up attention. He would find out when the dinner was officially over and they all could go back—

He *hoped* they could all go back to Uncle Tatiseigi's. He *hoped* not to be moved back here to his father's apartment, if there happened to be any thought of that, now that whatever emergency had been in question seemed settled. He had no inclination to attract any sort of reconsideration from the grown-ups.

Clearly mani and Great-uncle were not going to leave yet. They were all going to sit here and drink brandy and fruit juice, probably until there was some sort of all-clear. He had experienced security alerts often enough in his life that he knew how that went.

So he had another glass of fruit juice himself, and distracted his guests with a little running side conversation about how the conspirators during the coup had shot up his father's apartment and how, when they had come back to Shejidan, they had had to live with mani until workmen could completely redo the apartment—cutting off any access to the servants' passages on the floor below, and moving walls around, swallowing up one apartment that had been across the hall and shortening the hallway outside . . .

It was a stupid topic, but it was the only distraction he could think of with examples he had at hand. His guests were polite, and listened politely, while their attention kept flicking off toward the adults, who were having their own discussion, once bringing mani's and father's bodyguards back in for another conference.

The old man in the little office.

That was in *Guild Headquarters*.

They sat in the well of the Council Chamber while the whole building echoed with movement, and now and again to heavy thumps, possibly the clearing of barricades, or dealing with one of the ruined doors.

Bren and Jago and Algini sat, shared a cold drink of water that one of Cenedi's men had provided—and waited. Nand' Siegi had long since arrived with his own medical team. They had that comforting word. And very likely there would be triage. Banichi would get care—but there would be some sort of priorities established. And questions would only add to the problems.

At very long last Tano came in from the lower corridor, and immediately nodded reassurance as he shut that door. Tano joined them—cleaner than they were, wearing just his uniform tee, and with face and hands well-scrubbed. "He's done well," Tano said. "The bleeding is stopped. Nand' Siegi found the source, which was exactly what Banichi himself said. He is out of danger, nand' Siegi assures us, granted he stays quiet. His color is improving. It is up to us to assure he follows nand' Siegi's orders, takes his medicine—and he is to have *no more* of the stimulant he was taking."

The knot in Bren's stomach had begun to unwind itself. When Jago asked, "Impairment?" and Tano answered, *"If he follows orders, no impairment that exercise cannot mend,"* then all the tension went, so that he leaned against the railing behind him.

That was a mistake. His head hit the rail above and sent a flash of light and pain through his skull. But it didn't matter. "He will follow orders," he said calmly. "He will. God. What a night."

All around him were locator bracelets functioning normally. The halls reverberated with confident strides . . .

And the aiji's personal train was sitting out there midtracks, blocking the normal mail train and all the freight deliveries that should be going uptown.

He had washed his own hands and face in a small lavatory adjacent. But his coat and his trousers were caked with blood that was drying at the edges, making it necessary to watch where he sat. His head throbbed. He didn't care. Now it was all right. Everything was entirely all right. He found his hands shaking.

"Sit down, Tano-ji. Rest for a bit."

"I have been sitting, nandi. I have to go back down to restrain my unreasonable unit-senior when he wakes up."

"We probably should move that train," Bren said. "If it would be all right to move him onto it."

"I believe it should be," Tano said. "We can likely move him aboard, as he is, with very little problem."

"We should not have the paidhi-aiji outside the building without sufficient guard," Algini said. "Jago-ji, go up and advise Cenedi we shall need escort, at this point, to return us to the Bujavid."

"Yes," she said.

"Pending approval from nand' Siegi," Bren said. "We will do nothing against Banichi's health."

"Yes," Tano said, and left again.

Father set down his brandy glass, which was the signal for everyone to take notice. "We have had a very good evening," Father said, "and the aiji-consort needs her rest. Certainly our son and his guests need theirs." A nod, to which Cajeiri nodded politely, sitting on the edge of his seat—and hoping for a word with Jase-aiji once they got to the hall.

"We have had a very great success," Father said, "an excellent dinner, excellent guests—" More nods. "Nod," Cajeiri said, and his guests took the cue and bowed.

"So," his father said, "let us bid our guests good night and good rest, and to our son, a special good night. We are *very* glad you are back safely in the Bujavid, and we welcome your guests."

"Honored Father." A second, half-bow, as best one could, while seated.

His parents got up. Everyone did. His father's bodyguards opened the doors, and the senior guests went out into the foyer. So did his mother and father, which they ordinarily would not do, but his father was in an extraordinarily good mood, one could tell it, and exchanged a word of thanks to Jase-aiji, who had had one of his two bodyguards evidently standing in the foyer all evening. Cajeiri gave a little signal to his guests and led them out quietly, so they all stood in a row, waiting to go out with everybody else.

"Nand' aijiin, nandi," Irene said, then, in a breath of a space, and he suddenly knew Irene was going to say something—Cajeiri held his breath as all the grown-ups looked at his guests as if the hall table had just spoken. "We wish to thank the aiji and his household for his hospitality. We are greatly honored."

There was a little astonished silence. Then his father nodded politely, and his mother—Cajeiri took in a breath—asked: "What is your *name*, child?"

"Irene, nandi. My name is Irene."

"Come." His mother beckoned Irene closer, and closer, and closer. "You are also older than my son, are you not, nadi?"

"Yes, nandi." Again, and properly, a little bow. His mother reached out toward Irene—not to touch, but her hand lingered close.

"Oldest of all your associates, in fact."

"Yes, nandi."

"So small. You are so very small." His mother drew her

hand and rested it above the baby, and it was a curiously gentle move, as if his mother were on the verge of deep distress. "I shall have a daughter soon. I look forward to it. Have you enjoyed your stay, Irene-nadi?"

"Have you enjoyed your visit?" Cajeiri rephrased it, feeling as if the whole business could explode at any minute. But his mother seemed quite gentle in her manner, very restrained, looking for something.

"Yes, nandi. Very much, thank you."

"A mannerly child. And your associates? Gene? And Artur?"

"Yes," Gene said, and bowed. "Yes, nandi."

"Artur, nandi," Artur said, doing the same.

"So." His mother nodded, and looked at him, and looked at Irene. "Your family approves your being here?"

"The aiji-consort asks," Jase-aiji translated to ship-speak, while Cajeiri was trying to think of the words. "—Does your mother approve your being here?"

Irene looked at him, and hesitated, and it was not a simple answer. *Nothing* about Irene's mother was a simple answer.

"Yes, nandi," Irene said cheerfully, with no hint of a shadow in the answer.

"Good," his mother said. "Good that your mother was consulted."

"Honored wife," Tabini said, "we should let our guests go to their beds, should we not?"

"Indeed." She turned a slow glance toward mani, toward Great-uncle, and lastly toward Cajeiri. "Well done," she said to him, "well done, son of mine."

Well done? He could not recall *ever* hearing that from her. Scarcely even from his father.

"Good night, honored Grandmother, nandi," his father said. Great-uncle and mani took their leave, sweeping Cajeiri and his guests toward the hall. Cajeiri looked back, from the hall, and nand' Jase was still talking to his father. Jase's single bodyguard walked out into the hall and stopped again, like a statue. Two of his father's guard came and stood there, too.

When he looked all the way down the hall, he saw another white statue down at the far end, by Great-uncle's apartment, with two black-uniformed Guild standing beside him. So that was where Jase-aiji's *other* bodyguard had been all evening.

That was scary.

Jase-aiji came out behind them; and the one bodyguard went with them and the other began walking toward them from the far end of the hall. Jase-aiji walked as far as nand' Bren's apartment and stopped and wished them all good night. That door opened and Jase-aiji went in, but the bodyguard who had been with them just froze where he was, still standing guard in the hall. The other one had stopped by Great-uncle's door, likewise frozen.

And Great-uncle and mani just kept walking toward mani's apartment.

Were they all just supposed to go home now and go to bed, as if nothing unusual was going on?

Mani and her bodyguard stopped at her apartment—with never a word, except, from one of mani's bodyguards, "Cenedi reports everything quiet, aiji-ma. Nand' Bren is returning."

From where? Cajeiri desperately wanted to know.

But mani went in, and he and his guests and Great-uncle and their bodyguard just walked on.

"Great-uncle." Cajeiri had no hope of an answer, but he tried. "May one ask?"

"Everything is very well," Great-uncle said, and added: "The Assassins' Guild has just changed leadership, young lord. The guards are precautionary, since there may still be individuals at liberty in the city. But one rather supposes the Guild will sort out its own *very* quickly. This is a former administration of the Guild, and they will set things to rights as we have not seen in at *least* three years."

He was in awe. Great-uncle had never been so forthcoming, as if he were *someone*, instead of a child. "Great-uncle," he said very respectfully. "One hears. One is grateful to know."

"Do your guests understand?" Great-uncle asked. "One rather thinks they know something has been amiss."

"I shall tell them," he said. "They are worried. But I shall explain, Great-uncle, so they will understand."

"Indeed," Great-uncle said, and they arrived at their own door, which Madam Saidin opened for them.

Will Kapian and Polano stand there all night? he wondered. Perhaps they would.

But things were going to be set to rights, Great-uncle had said.

And the Guild that protected everything had changed leadership—

And what about the old man who had caused everybody so much trouble?

Was their enemy in the Guild now gone?

He wanted to know. It seemed major things had gone on and nand' Bren was somewhere in it, and so, he guessed, was Cenedi. The whole world had been in some kind of quiet commotion tonight—and how much he and his guests had been at risk in it, he was not sure, except that they were still being taken care of and kept safe and he had most of all to keep from scaring his guests—and most of all, their parents.

Maybe the world was really going to change. Things set right, Great-uncle said, and he could not quite imagine that. People could always turn up hunting them—and clearly nobody was taking chances in this hall, tonight.

But nand' Bren was coming back, and Cenedi was reporting in, so he decided, as Great-uncle's doors closed behind them—that he really could tell his guests everything was all right.

The Red Train was back in its berth, no longer blocking rail traffic. Mail was moving again. Freight deliveries were happening. Day-shift employees were finally able to take trains home, those who had not given up and walked. Night-shift employees could get to work in the city.

But the councils of other guilds in all those other buildings—Transportation, the Merchants, the Scholars, were reportedly in emergency session, trying to inform themselves what had just gone on in the Assassins' Guild.

Nobody of a certain rank was getting much sleep to-night.

Neither, Bren reflected, was the paidhi-aiji or anybody around him. They reached the apartment, bringing Banichi with them, medical gear and all, bound for the comfort and safety of the security station in the depths of the apartment.

Jase's men were still on watch out in the hall, with Guild beside them to watch with ordinary atevi senses—and with the ability to recognize anybody who had reasonable business on the floor. Jase had made it back to the apartment before him, exchanged court clothes for a night robe—and met them coming in.

"Good God," was Jase's comment, seeing their bedraggled condition, and Banichi, on the gurney they had borrowed, with the ongoing transfusion: "How bad?"

"It could have been far worse," Bren said. "Nand' Siegi's patched him up again—he's to stay quiet." His voice was breaking up . . . too much smoke, likely. "How did it go with the dinner?"

"Very well, actually. Better than you had . . . clearly. Can I do anything?"

"We're just good for rest, letting Banichi just rest and stay quiet. Maybe a cold drink. A sandwich." He said the latter as Narani stood by, awaiting instructions, and the delivery of his ruined coat. He shed it—shed the stained vest and even the shirt. It was an impropriety in the foyer, but they were not standing on ceremony, and their garments were shedding a powder of dried blood, too filthy even to let into the bedroom. "Forgive me," he said, "Rani-ji, I think everything I have on is beyond rescue. I shall shed the rest in the hall. I shall try not to touch the furniture. One believes the crates with our wardrobe will arrive tonight, or tomorrow."

"I shall draw a bath, nandi."

"Draw it for my aishid. For me, the shower will do very well." Jago had done a field repair on the rip in his scalp—loosed a few hairs about the cut and knotted them together, closing the wound, and Tano had poured astringent on it. That had hurt so badly he had all but passed out—quietly, however, with dignity. He had managed that, at least, a nice, graceful slump that had not ended on the Council Chamber floor only because Algini had held him up. His aishid had wanted nand' Siegi to have a look at the patch job before they left—but he was sure it was, despite their worries, enough for tonight. He had his own little pharmacopeia in a dresser drawer, including an antibiotic he could take. He dreaded the thought even of trying to shower the blood off his hair, but he had to: it was a mess. And he was sure Jago's repair would hold.

"My aishid," he said to Narani. "They should have—whatever they want. *Anything* they want, nadi-ji." He changed languages, for Jase. "We did what we went in to do. The old man's dead . . . he tried to take out the records, but we've got most of them. The returnees have control of the Guild. They're going to be sorting the rank and file for problems, and we've probably got a few running for the hills by any means they can find. But the new ones, the ones that've come into the Guild during the last three years, are reporting in from all over the aishidi'tat, asking for instructions, realizing there's been a change of policy. There's a good feeling in the wind. The younger ones have got to be confused, but apparently the reputations of those taking charge carry respect. The Missing and the Dead, as Jago calls them, have just risen up and taken over." His voice cracked. "And we're going to see a Guild we haven't seen since we left the planet. Which is good. Very good. They'll argue with Tabini. But at least they won't undermine him.

And there won't be anybody conducting intermittent sabotage from Assignments."

"Go get that shower," Jase urged him. "Go sit down. If there's anything I can do—let me know."

"Thanks," Bren said, and headed down the corridor toward his bedroom, and the chance to shed the rest of his clothes in some decency.

But sleep? He didn't think so.

"Has he waked?" he asked Tano, who had, with Jago, sat by Banichi the while.

Banichi's eyes opened a slit, a glimmer of gold.

"He *is* awake," Banichi answered for himself.

"Good," Bren said, and sat down on the chair Tano snagged into convenient proximity for him. "How are you doing, Nichi-ji?"

"One sincerely regrets the distraction in the Council chamber," Banichi murmured faintly. "And the general inconvenience to the operation."

"We did it, understand. We took down the target."

"So one hears," Banichi said. "Cenedi has come back?"

"Cenedi is on his way back to the Bujavid," Tano said. "The Council is in session, probably at this moment. Other guilds are meeting to hear the reports. They are not waiting for morning."

"The city is quiet, however."

"The city is *entirely* quiet," Jago said from her spot in the corner. "The city trains are running again. The city will only notice the mail is a little late tomorrow."

"One believes," Banichi said, "the rumors will be out and about."

"One believes they will outrun the mail delivery," Tano said. "The aiji will make an official statement to the news services at dawn. The legislators are being advised, some sooner than others."

Those who employed bodyguards, notably lords and administrators all over the continent, would have been waked out of sleep by their bodyguards, giving them critical news from the capital. Viewed from the outside, the Bujavid's high windows probably showed an uncommon number of lights in the small hours tonight—the sort of thing that, in itself, would have the tea shops abuzz in the morning, if they had not had the stalled train for a topic. And a number of people would be both up late and rising early—not quite panicked, but definitely seeking information ... which that Guild of all Guilds might not release, except to say that the leadership of the Guild was now the former leadership, with the former policies. One could almost predict the wording.

The damage within the Assassins' Guild had been very limited—only three deaths in the whole operation, the target being one, and the other two, Algini said, died firing at a senior Guild officer who had identified himself.

Finesse. Banichi's plan had gained entry into the heart of the building for the returning Guild. Cenedi's had been the action in the administrative wing while the initial distraction was going on. And both had come off as well as they could have hoped.

"Juniors who have come up during the last three years," Algini remarked, "will be finding out that the rules on the books and the rules in operation are now one and the same."

"That may come as a great shock to some," Banichi murmured, and moved one foot to the edge of the bed.

"No," Bren said. "No, put that foot back, nadi. You are *not* to move, you are not to sit up, you are not to shift that arm, and you are not to take any more of those pills you have been taking."

"The arm is taped," Banichi said, "and I am well enough."

Bren held up his fist—with the aiji's ring glinting gold in the light. "This says you take nand' Siegi's orders. Do you hear?"

"One hears," Banichi said. "However—"

"No," Bren said. "You have your com unit. You have

your locator. You may move your other arm, but you are not to lift your head, let alone sit up. When nand' Siegi says so, then you may get up."

Banichi frowned at him.

"I am quite serious," Bren said, rising. "It is the middle of the night, the household is hoping for sleep, and there is no good worrying over details out of our reach. If the leadership you left in the Guild cannot lead after all this, we are all in dire difficulty, but one does not believe that will be a problem. We are certain they have some notion what to do next. So sleep. Well *done,* Nichi-ji. *Very* well done."

"Nandi," Banichi said faintly.

"So stay in bed," Jago said, and reached for a glass of what was probably ice water. "Have a sip."

"One cannot drink lying flat," Banichi objected.

Bren left the argument, however it might come out, and made his way down the hall barefoot. His head hurt—it didn't precisely ache; or maybe it did. His scalp certainly hurt. The repair held, however. And he was exhausted. Sleep—he was still not sure was possible. He didn't think he'd sleep for the next week, his nerves were wound so tight.

But unconsciousness, in the safety of his own bed—he might manage that for a few hours.

There were so many things in motion, so much going on, still, that had to be tracked—over which the Guild did *not* preside. But Banichi was safe. Everybody was back, or on the way back.

He reached his room, not without the attention of his valets, who waited there.

There was one more piece of business, he thought, closing his fist—the heavy ring, washed clean now, tended to slide and turn and he would not take it off, not for an instant. He could not send it back by courier, even his most trusted staff.

But he could not rouse Tabini-aiji out of bed, either. The matter seemed at an impasse, something he could not resolve.

His valets saw him to bed. He sat on the edge of the mattress, looked at the ring in the dim light, thinking ... so many things yet to do, so many things so long stalled by the situation they'd just, please God, *finally* set in order, the last piece of what they'd needed to set right before the world would be back in the sane order they'd left when they'd gone off to space.

Better. They no longer had the Human Heritage Party to cause trouble on the other side of the strait.

And the man who'd been trying to run atevi politics on this side of the strait, from a decades-old web of his own design—was dead, tonight. The web would still exist. But the Guild leaders now back in power had every reason to want it eradicated—so it had stopped being *his* business. The Guild itself would take care of its own problem.

His problems centered now around Tabini's problems, and the dowager's. If they could now get certain legislators to move on those—and get those critical bills passed ...

And get lords appointed in Ajuri and the Kadagidi territory who weren't working against the aiji ...

He became aware that he had not dismissed his two valets. They were still standing there, staring at him with concern.

"I shall return this in the morning," he said of the ring. "Kindly tell Narani, nadiin-ji, that I have to do that in the morning, before anything else."

Koharu and Supani said they would relay that message, and he simply put himself into bed face down, so his head would not bleed on the clean, starched pillow casing.

It was so good. It was so very good for everyone to be alive, and for them all to be home.

"One has finally heard," Veijico said, "officially, what has happened—at least what Guild Headquarters is saying happened."

They were all in night-robes—they had been trying to sleep when Veijico and Lucasi had slipped into the guest suite, so sleep was no longer in question. Antaro and Jegari had gotten up to ask what Veijico and Lucasi had learned. Cajeiri had heard that, and he could not stay abed: he had gotten up and asked them to tell him—

But they had gotten nowhere with that explanation, before Gene and Artur had come out of their room and asked what was going on, and then Irene had come out—so there they were, all of them, wrapped in over-sized adult robes, shivering in the lateness of the hour and the spookiness of the whole situation.

"There were a lot of Guild officers who had never come back to Shejidan since the Troubles," Veijico said. "Your father and your great-grandmother brought them back tonight. The Guildmaster that has been in charge since your father came back to office is overthrown, the Director of Assignments is dead—"

"They got him!" Cajeiri said.

"They did, nandi. We are not supposed to name names of anybody. But that person is gone. And the people who have been high up in the Council have stepped down. Except two who are under arrest. The old officers have come back and they are in charge."

"This is good," Cajeiri said for his guests. "A good thing has happened."

"But we are not supposed to say anything more than that," Lucasi said, "because the Guild does not discuss its business."

"But you are happy about it," Cajeiri said.

"We believe it *is* good," Lucasi said, "because of who went to change it."

"Nand' Bren and Cenedi-nadi."

"Yes," Veijico said. "They did."

"And they all are back."

"Now they are, nandi. Banichi is injured. He is home and doing well. Cenedi-nadi, Nawari, all the ones from your great-grandmother's aishid, are all back and accounted for. We are under a continuing alert: there are a few individuals the Guild is actively hunting tonight, a few who were not in the building tonight, and some who may have gotten out and run or gone into hiding. We—being where we are, and assigned under the former leadership—one is certain all four of us will be up for review, nandi, regarding our assignment with you. Our man'chi will be questioned. We hope we shall not be removed."

"What is she saying?" Artur asked—it was not the sort of conversation they had ever had, on the ship, and there were words Cajeiri was hardly sure how to translate.

"Everybody is back. There's still an alert but everything's all right. It's still good." He changed to Ragi. "My father will see you have no trouble, Jico-ji, and I shall remind him. And I shall remind mani, too. I shall by no means let them send you away!"

"We would be honored," Veijico murmured with a little nod. "And your guests should not worry about this. We should not alarm them."

"Good people run the Guild now," Antaro said, little words their guests knew. "They are hunting the bad ones."

Irene had said nothing, just sat listening, hugging her robe close and shivering a little. "I don't think we ought to tell our parents everything," she said with a little laugh, and they all agreed.

"Are you cold?" Cajeiri asked. "We can order tea. Even at night, someone is on duty."

She shook her head. "Just scared," she said. "I'm always scared of things." Another little laugh. "I'm sorry."

"Not sorry," he said, and gave the old challenge. *"Who's* afraid?"

She held up two fingers, just apart. "This much. Just this much."

"We're safe," he said. *"Are* we safe, Jico-ji?"

"Safer," Veijico said. "Definitely safer."

"Good, then!" They had just a little light, sitting there around the table, in the dark. Human eyes were spooky, shadowy, and never taking the light. Veijico's and Lucasi's,

Antaro's and Jegari's, theirs all did, so you could see their eyes shimmery gold, honest and open. But with humans, one had to trust the shadows, and know their intentions were good. Irene shivered, she was so scared, sometimes. Irene had said—she just was that way.

But who had stood there facing his mother without a hint she was scared at all?

Irene.

He understood Irene, he thought. There were two kinds of fear. There was facing bullets, which meant you had to do something. And there was the long slow kind of fear that came of knowing there were problems and there was nothing you could do right away except try not to make things worse. His associates had seen both kinds in their short visit, and not shown anything but a little shiver after it was all over. Even Irene. She was very bright. She thought about things. She thought a lot. And she was certainly no coward.

He was proud of his little household, and he was increasingly sure he could count these three as his. He had attracted very good people. Mani had always said that was the best proof of character . . . that one could know a person by his associates. He felt very happy with himself and them, overall.

And when they all went back to bed—who was it who had to go to bed alone, with all this going on?

Him. And Irene.

"We can all sleep in this room," he said. It was a huge bed, and there was room enough, and they could just layer the bedding and make it all proper, the way folk did who had only one bed.

So they did that. His aishid got their proper beds for the rest of the night, and he and his associates tucked into various layers of satin comforters and settled down together, like countryfolk with visitors, in the machimi plays.

He had hardly ever felt so safe as then.

14

Getting up in the morning—was not easy. A splitting headache—did not describe the sensation.

Bren slid carefully out of bed, felt his way to the light, and rummaged in the drawer of the little chest for the pill bottles. The scalp wound had swollen. He had no desire at all to investigate it, for fear his head would come apart. He simply swallowed, dry, two capsules of the right color and crawled back into bed face down for a few more moments.

The rest of him was amazingly pain-free. Usually when he and his aishid had been in a situation, he emerged sore in amazing places. But the back of his head paid for all.

And he had to find out how Banichi was doing. That thought, once conceived, would not let him rest. He crawled backward off the high bed, felt after his robe, and padded barefoot down the hall toward the security station and his aishid's rooms.

The door was open, and there were servants about in the back halls, being relatively quiet. He heard nand' Siegi's voice, and Banichi's, which was reassuring. He reached the little inner corridor, nodded a good morning to Algini and Jago, who were there in half-uniform, and asked, as he stood in the doorway, "How is he?"

"Arguing," Jago said. "Nand' Siegi will not permit him to sit up until afternoon."

"Nor will we," Algini said, and cast him a look. "You are next, nandi. Nand' Siegi will deal with that."

He truly was not looking forward to that. "Cup of tea," he said, thinking hot tea might steady his stomach. The headache remedy was not sitting well.

He did not, however, get that far. Nand' Siegi turned in his direction, saw him, and came his way with business in mind.

And treating it *did* hurt. *God,* did it hurt! Nand' Siegi graciously informed him that it would scar somewhat, that he was very lucky it had not fractured his skull, that there were certain symptoms he was to report immediately should they occur, and that he *should* sleep on his face for several days. He was out of the mood for tea, after that, but by that time Jase was up, breakfast was about to be served, and Supani and Koharu were asking him whether he would dress for breakfast, or have it informally.

He was not sure he could keep toast down, his neck was stiff from tension and he did not want to tilt his head out of vertical. But he advised his valets that he would be paying a visit to Tabini-aiji as soon as the aiji wished. And he got up carefully, trying not to tilt his head, and made it to the little breakfast room, where Jase was having morning tea.

"How's the head?" Jase asked.

He sat down, staring blankly at the out of focus door, and took about a minute to say, "Sore. Damn sore."

"Tea?"

The door was still his vision of choice. It was uncomplicated. It didn't move. And he didn't have to turn his head to look at it. "Did Kaplan and Polano ever get any sleep?"

"You're white. Here." Jase reached across the little breakfast table. A cup of tea thumped down in front of him. "Drink."

He picked it up and tried, gingerly, without looking at it. It was strong, sugared, and spiced.

"Nand' Bren needs toast and eggs," he heard Jase say.

He was far from sure about that. He was not sure about the spice in the tea. He blinked several times, and brought the door completely into focus. That was a start.

"We're doing fine," Jase said. "The kids got some sleep, I understand. I did. Algini says he's been in touch with the Guild periodically during the night, and they've run down one of their fugitives. They have three others holed up in a town to the south."

"Trying to run for the Marid," Bren murmured, turning his head slightly, trying his focus on Jase's face, which was a shade blurry. "No surprise. But that won't be as ready a refuge now." Two more sips of tea. "Anything else?"

"Nothing that's reached me," Jase said.

He was sure there would be messages. The message bowl in the front hall was likely overflowing since dawn. He remembered the bundle of post-mortem letters he had put in Narani's hands. Retrieving *those* and destroying *those* was absolutely urgent.

He said, "Anything from Geigi?"

Jase shook his head. "Nothing. But I don't expect anything. We haven't advertised the problem. It's really been rather quiet until this morning."

"Last night," he said, "last night in your venue. How did it really go?"

"Amazingly well," Jase said, and the eggs and toast arrived. The youngest of the servants spooned eggs onto Bren's plate, scrambled, thank God, nothing requiring such focus as cracking a shell and eating a soft-boiled egg without spilling it. "Sauce, nandi?"

"Thank you, Beja, no. —The kids," he prompted Jase. "Damiri-daja. The dowager."

"Damiri-daja said very little," Jase said, "except at the last. Irene had a little speech, thanking the household. Damiri-daja asked Irene if her mother approved her being here, remarked how small she is, and told Cajeiri he'd done very well. It was an odd string of questions."

It *was* odd—on an evening when her son's guests were

sheltering with her because her husband's closest allies were out assassinating her elder cousin, who had probably just assassinated her father.

She was about to have a daughter of her own. Was it some maternal impulse?

Or had it been a political statement, intended to annoy her husband—from a woman very close to a politically-driven divorce?

Never forget, either, that her uncle Tatiseigi had been there as witness. God, he wished he'd been there to parse the undercurrents.

"Was Cajeiri upset?"

"Puzzled."

"Small wonder, that." He had a bite of toast, and the egg, and with the hot tea, his stomach began to feel warmer and a little steadier. It was awkward to eat, wearing the heavy ring, but he would not take it off. "At least it wasn't outright warfare."

"It wasn't that," Jase said, "I'm reasonably sure. Irene didn't seem upset at it. She's a shy kid. Timid. But she held her ground. We had to translate a question. She answered in very good Ragi, with all the forms I'd have used."

"Good for her," Bren said. "Good for Cajeiri. He's done all right." He shifted a glance up, as Narani appeared in the door, looking apologetic.

"The aiji wishes your presence, nandi," Narani said. "At your convenience, the message said. He is in conference with the aiji-dowager."

God. That meant—show up. Now. Possibly even—*rescue* me. Fast. He frowned, and those muscles hurt, right along with his neck. "Koharu and Supani," he said to Narani. "Immediately, nadi-ji, thank you. Tell Algini." He used the table for leverage to get up, *not* inclining his head in the process. "Best I get over there," he said. "He means now."

"Understood," Jase said. "If you need me—"

"I'm all right," he said. "Finish your breakfast."

There might be another breakfast. Or lunch. He had no

clear idea what time it was. He had to dress, get the damage to his scalp covered in a suitable queue, and look civilized, at least.

His valets met him in the hall, went with him into the bedroom—they dressed him, got his boots on without his having to bend over, and arranged his hair very gently so, they assured him, the wound hardly showed. He went out to the foyer, gathered up Algini and Jago—in a timing Narani arranged without any fuss at all, and went out and down the hall—a little dizzy: he was not sure whether that was the headache or the headache cure; but he made it the short distance down the hall and through Tabini's front door without wobbling.

He could hear the argument in the sitting room, something about Lord Aseida. It was the dowager's voice, and Tabini's, that was too quiet to hear. Cenedi was on duty, with Nawari, outside the sitting room door, and that was useful. Algini could have a word with them while he waited.

Jago, however, elected to come in with him.

He walked in, made the motions of a little bow, without putting his head too far out of vertical, and received the wave of Tabini's hand that meant sit down. "Aijiin-ma," he said inclusively, and carefully settled.

His late arrival meant a round of tea and, gratefully, a cessation of the argument for a moment.

"You have had a physician's attendance, surely, paidhi," Tabini said.

"This morning, aiji-ma. Thank you. And one thanks the aiji-dowager. Banichi and I are doing very well this morning."

"Your color is shocking," Ilisidi said.

"I would not risk the best tea service, aiji-ma," he said, and murmured, to the servant, "more sweet, nadi, if you will. Twice that." Ordinarily he preferred mildly sweet, but this morning he had an uncommon yen for the fruity taste. And salty eggs. Electrolytes, his conscious brain said. "And do stay near me, nadi. Please take the cup from my hand immediately if I seem to drift."

"You should not have come," Tabini said. "You might have declined, paidhi-ji."

"I could not keep this all morning," he said, regarding the ring on his hand. He drew down a sip of tea, which did taste good, and faced the quandary of courtesy versus prudence—tea delayed the necessity to get up and return Tabini's ring . . . he thought so, at least. He was just a little muddled about priorities. And about too many other things. And thoroughly light-headed, and not thinking well, since the exertion of coming here. "In just a moment, aiji-ma."

"Fool paidhi." Tabini set down his cup, got up, and came to him and held out his hand.

"Aiji-ma." Bren had set down his cup, eased the ring off and dropped it into Tabini's warm hand, which closed, momentarily on his.

"Cold," Tabini said.

"The tea helps, aiji-ma."

"Fool," Tabini said, crossing the little space to sit down again. "Fool. You shielded your own bodyguard last night. I have every suspicion of it."

"I truthfully cannot remember what I did, aiji-ma. We just sat against the wall, and there was a great deal of racket."

"Ha," Ilisidi said. "Racket, one can well imagine. We have had a lifelong curiosity to see the inside of that place. You have cheated us of the sight."

"I did not get beyond the Council chamber, aiji-ma. And this morning I am losing little details of what I did see there. Which likely will suit the Guild well. But one does understand we came out with everyone alive. Is that true?"

"True," Tabini said. "One is glad to say, it is true." Tabini set his cup down, and now conversation could shift. "We have the old Guildmaster back, we hear. The dead have risen up, the missing have returned, the retired have rescinded their retirement, and a handful of high officials installed this last year have proven difficult to find. We hoped that the Council meeting would have had all of them on the premises, but we missed five individuals, we understand. The restored leadership is interviewing members, starting with assignments to the Bujavid, ascertaining man'chi, kinship, past service, asking for references, and any other testimony that may apply. *Meanwhile* we have a matter arising which will regard the paidhi-aiji, and if you are able to hear it, paidhi, it would be good to set your staff on it this morning."

"One waits to hear, aiji-ma," he murmured—*hoping* it was a small problem.

"The matter of Lord Aseida," Tabini said, "is a storm blowing up quite rapidly, if predictably. The lords are all uneasy in what happened, and we are particularly concerned that the action may set your good name in question."

"That fool Topari," Ilisidi said, "is the one pushing this."

"Topari is irrelevant," Tabini said. "Of Tatiseigi's enemies, he is the very least."

"The man *thinks* in conspiracies," Ilisidi said. "He will argue against the television image if we provide it. He understands such things can be edited. I have it on good authority, *he* will be the problem. The others will let this fool put his head up and *see* what the answer is. He is exceedingly upset—the *arrest* of a lord is his issue—so he claims."

Topari. A lord of the Cismontane Association, south of the capital—a rural district even more conservative than the Padi Valley Association. It was a Ragi population, in the watershed *this* side of the Senjin Marid, and running up into the highlands.

That district, one readily recalled, detested humans on principle, did *not* support the space program, and Topari was part of that little knot of minor lords that, geographically speaking, sat between the Marid and the aishidi'tat. Regarding his relations with Tabini—Topari had not been signatory to Murini's coup—but likely only because that region rarely joined anything.

The brain was working. The head still hurt, but he felt the little adrenaline surge.

"You can do nothing with him, paidhi," Tabini said. "And we still say he will not be the principal problem."

"Leverage," Ilisidi said, "is his entire motive. Aseida could catch fire and he would care nothing for the man. But Topari sees a way to make a problem to *our* disadvantage and cause a problem."

A problem aimed at the aiji-dowager, Bren thought. And asked: "What, aijiin-ma, *is* his position?"

Right question. Tabini looked very annoyed, and Ilisidi had a quick answer.

"He is currently in a lather over *our* agreement with the Taisigin Marid," Ilisidi said. "That is the *entire* business."

"I am not about to take issue at a *Ragi* lord for objecting to the removal of a Ragi lord," Tabini said. "That is *not* the approach I can make to this situation, especially with my *grandmother* as one of the principals in this affair!"

"The paidhi asks the right question. What *is* his position? *Nothing* to do with Lord Aseida *or* lordly prerogatives. *We* are his *real* target. He objects to *our trade agreement* with the Taisigin Marid because he sees it as affecting the Senjin rail line which *his grandfather* built. He envisions the southern treaty as replacing his precious railroad—the only privately constructed rail still functioning in the aishidi'tat. Because of an imagined danger to his rail segment and *his* little slice of use-fees on shipments to Senji, he has made *me* his enemy—I believe *tyrant* was the precise wording when he discussed my character. And while a reasonable man might have retreated from his rhetoric of several decades past, *he* views the whole world as an absolute set of numbers. He views negotiation as a fault and a weakness. He calls *me* fickle, and changeable, but will apparently not believe I can back off from an inconvenient feud which never mattered greatly in the first place! That, Grandson of mine, is his *entire* concern with the fate of Lord Aseida, but I will wager you he *will* present a resolution calling for an investigation, and if *he* has his hand on it, it will be a resolution extravagant in its blame of *us* and Lord Tatiseigi for attacking that Kadagidi whelp who was trying to kill us!"

"You are *not* worried about your reputation," Tabini said.

"Of course not!"

"Well, his resolution will fail, when its own caucus fails to support it. And if the paidhi-aiji will simply supply Lord Tatiseigi with the record Jase-aiji has—you may have the satisfaction of publicly embarrassing Lord Topari."

"*And* creating a firestorm around *our* rail extension!"

God. Railroad politics. Trains were not only vital to the southern mountains, they were the *only* transport in the southern mountains, besides local trucks on roads that would daunt a mecheita. It was all going to start all over again. One saw it coming, everybody south of Shejidan wanting advantage to their own clan in the routing of the rail extension.

And Topari was the man to start it all sliding.

"Perhaps," Bren said quietly, "perhaps I can get ahead of the situation, before *anyone* proposes an investigation."

"You are wounded, paidhi!"

From Tabini, it was downright touching. Bren lifted a hand, a gesture to plead for a hearing of his point. "I recall the incident of the name-calling." The old man had, in a legislative session some years ago, called Tatiseigi ineffectual and Ilisidi an Eastern tyrant. Tatiseigi had, in turn, called him greedy, which, within the Conservative Caucus, had seen charges flying about graft and the siting of rail stations. Tatiseigi had emerged from the squabble with perfectly clean hands, since he had fought to keep rail *out* of his district, not to bring it in. "As I recall, his quarrel with Lord Tatiseigi also dates from the railroad dispute."

"Absolutely," Ilisidi said. "Absolutely that is behind his stirring this up."

"He is not the *only* one stirring this up," Tabini said.

"He is the one poised to be a cursed inconvenience," Ilisidi shot back.

"Tatiseigi can deal with him," Tabini said, "as deftly as he did the last time."

"Or I can deal with him," Bren said, and in the breath he had, with the room somewhat swimming in his vision: "Lord Tatiseigi has human guests at the moment. And Lord

Tatiseigi's complaint is our justification against the Kada-gidi, so he cannot take an impartial stance. I *have* actually exchanged civil words with Lord Topari in the past, unlikely as it may seem."

"Negotiation with the man?" Tabini asked. "It may only make him a worse problem. He is not accepting of humans."

"But *I* sit on the Transportation Committee," Bren said quietly. "I have not been active on it since our return—but in fact, I *will* have influence in the plan for the south, and I *am* the negotiator with the Taisigin Marid, all of which will directly affect his district. My intentions may greatly worry him."

"The bill on which you and my grandmother have staked an enormous risk—is still not voted on. The whole linked chain of the tribal peoples, Machigi's agreement, the whole southwest coast, gods less fortunate! is postponed, and may be postponed further, awaiting a resolution of this mess of the succession in *two clans*. If you make Lord Topari in any wise part of the Aseida stew, it may well spill into the west coast matter, and if those two become linked, *every* lord and village will take a personal invitation to argue their own modifications to the west coast compromise. We cannot res-cue you from that situation, if it goes awry. If you do lend this mountain lord *any* importance on these grounds or start negotiating with him before the west coast matter is voted on and untouchable, the Aseida matter can blow up into a storm that will take the west coast and the southern agreement with it."

"One absolutely concurs in your estimate, aiji-ma, and I take your warning. I shall not negotiate with him. But one can advise Lord Topari—privately, politely—with no audi-ence at all—that he is about to step into political quicksand. The Cismontane poses a nuisance to the southern agree-ment if he becomes a problem, but I may be able to do him a favor."

"By warning him off this."

"Warning him, exactly, aiji-ma. If he will talk to me—if he

is not a fool, and I have not had the impression that he is. He is a devout 'counter, yes, a traditionalist, yes. But if I warn him away from a political cliff edge, and he avoids a second embarrassing loss to Lord Tatiseigi, then he may even deign to talk to me on the railroad matter, when it comes at issue . . . so long as I am entirely discreet about the contact. He needs publicly to deplore human influence, true. But if I can prevent him taking Aseida's part in this, and if he warns certain other people off the idea—that will help us. One does recall that he lacks a Guild bodyguard. Several of his neighbors are in the same situation. They will not be getting the information that other lords have already gotten, quietly, from the changed leadership in the Guild. So he is in a position to make a public fuss and then to be embarrassed again, very painfully. But *I* propose to inform him—in a kindly way. Am I reasoning sanely in this, aijiin-ma? I think so, but a headache hardly improves my reasoning."

"Will he even speak to you?" Tabini asked. "You are in no condition to go to him. Nor should you!"

"My major domo is a remarkable and traditional gentleman. It would be the crassest rudeness to turn Narani away unheard. I can at least try such an approach and plead my injury to necessitate Lord Topari coming to me."

A deep breath. A sigh. "Well, well, do your best, paidhi. If you fail, then he may have to *have* his falling-out with Tatiseigi in public, and it *will* be untidy, and it *may* spill over into other debates, but I shall leave it in your hands, if you believe you can work with him. I have *two* vacant lordships to deal with, neither easy to fill, and I shall *not* be asking Topari for his opinion."

"Will you ask *Damiri?*" Ilisidi asked archly, lips pursed, and Tabini scowled in her direction.

"We are certain *you* will have advice."

"Who *is* her recommendation?"

"I have not asked her. Nor shall until she offers an opinion. Gods less fortunate, woman! She has a father to mourn!"

"Ah. We had hardly expected mourning on that score. But *she* will not take the lordship. *Nor will my great-grandson.* Let us agree on that, at least."

Tabini frowned. "To my certain recollection, *I* have that decision, alone, and I find no reason to forecast who it will be." He placed his hands on his thighs, preparatory to rising. "And we have kept the paidhi-aiji, who is distressingly pale, overlong, and made him work much too hard. Paidhi, you and your aishid will pursue the matter you wish to attempt. Cenedi will pursue business of his own. I have a meeting this afternoon with the Assassins' Guild, regarding ... business. And the aiji-consort will meanwhile make plans for the Festivity ... which we are now hopeful will come off without hindrance or extraordinary commotion. Paidhi-ji."

"Aiji-ma?"

"Rest. Care for your own household. And do *not* be talked into visiting Topari on his terms. We forbid it."

"One hears, aiji-ma."

Tabini rose, and offered his hand to his grandmother. She used his help, and her cane, and Bren rose and bowed as Jago moved close by him, in case the paidhi-aiji should unceremoniously fall on his face. Cenedi was now attending the dowager. Everything was back where it ought to be.

And he—he had to talk to Jase and send Narani on an errand into the city.

Preferably after a ten minute rest, with his eyes shut.

He was aware of his heartbeat in the wound on the back of his skull and tried to decide whether it matched the pounding in his temples. He just wanted to go home, lie down, preferably not on his back, and then maybe have another slice of buttered toast, to settle his stomach.

But he had to launch a campaign before he had that luxury ... and see if he could move a man who ruled mountains.

He was laying plans even as he walked home with Jago and Algini.

Tell Lord Topari, he would say to Narani, *that the paidhi-*

aiji wishes to forewarn him of evidence in the case of Lord Aseida, and that the paidhi-aiji wishes to meet with him discreetly and in confidence, preferring the honor of his company for tea in his residence— if he will be so accommodating. Say to him that the paidhi-aiji has been injured and is unable to walk any distance, but that the paidhi has heard of his concern and will not rest until he has spoken to him personally.

If there was one thing he had noted in the old lord, it was a sense of eternally frustrated entitlement, a sense that his mountainous district, though Ragi and part of the central lands, received everything last and least. Tea with a human might not be high on the list of honors Lord Topari craved— but Narani, country-bred himself, though coastal, might cajole the man into understanding at least *one* reason the conference was not taking place in an office.

Lord Topari, like other minor lords, lodged in town during the legislative session. The Cismontane, like many other small associations, seasonally held rooms for their representatives in the tashrid and hasdrawad in a moderately-priced hotel a few rows back from the esplanade at the foot of the Bujavid—off among the restaurants and office supply shops. Narani would take the tram down the lofty steps as far as the esplanade, and walk—it would not be far enough to necessitate local transport.

For the paidhi-aiji and his bodyguards to make the trek—the route would have involved the train station and a conspicuous Guild-supplied bus. He didn't think he had it in him. He knew he didn't. And he would, he thought, think better of Lord Topari forever, if Lord Topari would just come up the hill to disagree with him.

Son of mine, the letter went, that Madam Saidin had brought into the guest quarters, *be advised that the official celebration of your birthday will be on the day itself. Jase-aiji will come to your door to escort your guests to the paidhi-aiji's apartment, and to escort you and your aishid to our apartment for a private breakfast, at the usual time. There* will be a small luncheon, late, attended by family and by your personal guests. Appropriate wardrobe will be transferred by staff during breakfast. Kindly advise your young associates of that arrangement. The paidhi-aiji's staff will assist your guests.

Lord Tatiseigi has been requested, by separate letter, to escort your great-grandmother. He will, starting in late afternoon, lead a private museum tour for all official guests, ending at the supper hour in a buffet reception and formal Festivity for a larger number of guests, in the Audience Hall, to last about three hours.

Understand and explain to your guests that these arrangements in no wise reflect precedence, rank, or favor. The prime consideration is the capacity of the residency lift system and the need for the three of us to arrive at the appropriate time and together, as hosts of the event.

Understand too that for most of the day, your guests will be attached to the paidhi-aiji and Jase-aiji, not to you, nor should you signal or converse with them in public except for passing courtesy. You should direct your full attention to the various guests and officials.

My major domo has provided a list of ranks, titles, colors, and a brief history of the guests—a document which should by no means be carried to the hall. Kindly surrender the list to Madam Saidin once you have committed the necessary information to memory. She will destroy it.

It is also incumbent on you to make a brief speech to the reception guests stating the accomplishments since your last felicitous birthday and complimenting and thanking your guests for their attendance. I shall write it for you, and trust you will have no difficulty learning it. I shall send you that on the day.

Son of mine, your mother and I have every confidence you will carry off this felicitous event, the first state event in which you will stand beside us, with dignity and grace. We are confident you will conduct yourself in a manner that will solidly establish your good reputation before the court.

Bear in mind that your conduct in this event will follow you into adulthood, and that, while your eventual inheritance of the aijinate is presumed, it is an elective office, subject to the approval of the legislature.

Conduct your celebration with due respect to all your guests, old and young, and be aware that among them are individuals in various degrees disapproving of your human associates.

This event does not test your guests. It tests you, and your parents and great-grandmother. Opinions can be reversed, when they are held by honest and intelligent people, and, in your great-grandmother's words, it is easier to lead a mecheita uphill than to carry him. Keep that in mind, regarding any negative or unpleasant opinions, and be particularly courteous to difficult people.

Be gracious, be pleasant, and if you detect an opinion that seems too obscure to be understood, or should one seem too argumentative or hostile, refer that person to me.

Beyond this event, your personal guests and relations and the ship-aiji and the paidhi-aiji will all return to our apartment for a private reception and, we hope, a far more relaxed end to a successful evening.

Not have his birthday guests with him?

Three hours with lords and legislators and committee people?

A list of old people?

And make a *speech?*

It was going to be as gruesome as he had thought. Worse. His father had invited all the people *he* wanted and he had no say at all in it.

That made him *mad.* It made him *very* mad. But there was not a thing he could do about it. He had no way to arrange anything. Eisi and Liedi could get things from the kitchen. They could get a platter of teacakes. And they could all dress up and *pretend* they were having a festivity on the day after, maybe. But *he* would know it was not official. And his guests would find themselves left out of his real official festivity, and he was supposed to *ignore* them all evening?

There *was* a list of names attached, a long one. There must be a hundred of them.

He sank down on the couch and looked at it in despair. Boji, loose, on the chain the staff had found, and with Gene holding it, bounded over and sat on the arm of the couch.

The speech—was not that bad. It was about five lines. He could remember that. But—

"Is it bad news, Jeri-ji?" Artur asked.

What did he say? "My father. One expected something like it." He looked through the pages again, and there was nothing good to say. "I have to be with them all day. In the evening—a big public party."

"Then good news!" Irene said.

"Not so good," he said, holding up the paper with the list. "I have to talk to legislators, hundreds of them. All court dress, all formal court, all evening. You will have to stay with Jase-aiji and nand' Bren, and I have to stand by my parents and bow to stupid people all evening and smile." He put on his best court smile, mild, neither happy nor unhappy, just a motion. "I have to smile all evening. And we all have to be proper. All evening. One greatly regrets, nadiin-ji."

"Well, we can do that," Gene said. "With Jase-aiji and nand' Bren, we're fine, no problem."

"I shall not let stupid people talk to you," he said. "If anyone is stupid I will find it out and I shall throw them out of the hall."

"Are there going to *be* stupid people?" Irene asked.

He looked at the list, looking for certain names, but he particularly found some pleasant ones. Dur, for one. Young Dur, and his father. "Nobody from Ajuri or Kadagidi," he said, reassured by what he *did* see. "Calrunaidi will be there—my cousin on Great-grandmother's side. I can deal with him. Dur is good. The new lord of the Maschi is good. Lord Machigi's representative is good—I suppose." He kept reading, looking for problems. "Nobody really stupid."

"So we can do it," Gene said. "We stay with nand' Bren and stay out of trouble. Is there cake?"

"Cakes?" he asked.

"Birthday cake," Irene said. "It's a custom."

He did remember, from the ship. It was what humans did. Birthday cakes sounded good. "Like teacakes?"

"Big cake," Artur said, showing him with his hands. "In layers, with sweet stuff between. Fruit drink. We didn't ever have that at Reunion, not since I was little. But we do, on the station."

At the Festivity his father would give a speech. Probably the kabiuteri would give a speech. They had things to say on every formal occasion.

And he would give his speech. And stand and bow and probably sign cards.

A big cake sounded like a good idea. It would put everybody in a good mood.

Memorizing the list of guests was going to go faster than he first feared, too, because he already knew a lot of the people who were coming. He could just trust what he knew about them and study the handful he had never met.

Cake with sweet layers between, Artur said. Madam Saidin was handling things, with Great-uncle and Great-grandmother both being busy with the Lord Aseida problem, and nand' Bren had been involved with the really serious stuff going on with the Guild.

Icing with that delicate tangy-sweet flavor in the best teacakes. His favorite.

Great-uncle's cook could figure that out, he was sure.

He could ask. He should get *some* good things on his birthday.

And his guests were being very polite, the way they had been polite and good all the way through the visit, never taking things badly, never sulking—maybe somebody had told them not to. He had had hints they were under orders. But he knew he could not be that good that long if he was bored.

So maybe he had at least kept them from boredom. And maybe they would like seeing all the colors and the Audience Hall. There certainly would be plenty of fancy things and glitter. There was a museum tour beforehand. They would like that. And everything they saw down there would be new to them.

So maybe they would enjoy things more than he thought.

He would be talking to people and bowing and bowing and bowing until his neck ached, smiling just the right way for every rank—while they, he hoped, would be walking around with nand' Bren and Jase-aiji, looking at things that were new to them. The Audience Hall was fancier than most anything.

He only wished they were all back at Tirnamardi, and that they could go riding again, so they could *all* have a good time. That would make everything perfect.

Boji climbed up on his shoulder, reached down and tried to grab the papers from his hand. "No," he said. "Pest."

Boji climbed down his arm, and when he moved it, took a flying leap for the couch arm, and then back to his shoulder, with a screech that hurt his ear. He reached up and tugged the chain, shortening it considerably. Artur let it go, and he let it run to the end, still holding it, so Boji, who thought he was going to reach the desk, ran along the back of the couch in frustration, and made a dive for the bowl of fruit.

Which he did not reach. "Come here," Cajeiri said, and gave a series of clicks, mimicking Boji.

Boji came, approaching carefully on all fours, then sat up and stood up, and moved onto Cajeiri's knee.

"Look at that!" Irene exclaimed.

"He understands you," Gene said. "What did you say to him?"

"I have no idea," Cajeiri said, and laughed and scratched Boji on the side of his cheek, which he liked. Boji then climbed up his arm in a vaulting move and ended up on the couch back behind him.

Parid'ji could become attached—not man'chi, so Jegari

had said, but something like it. They were sociable among themselves, and with only atevi for a choice, some attached and learned to do clever things like retrieve a ball.

But they also stole things, Jegari had said. And it was true. Boji had made off with his treasured penknife and a brand new hair ribbon, which he had bitten through, freeing his little hands for a jump.

"Artur," Cajeiri said, and tossed him the end of Boji's chain. Boji went with it, clever creature, leaping for Artur, and grabbing at the chain in mid-air.

Artur was cleverer than that, and got the chain anyway. Boji had to be content with climbing up to Artur's shoulder and chittering at him—especially as Artur took him toward the cage. Artur clipped the chain to the grillwork, which gave Boji the freedom of the inside or the outside.

Boji was rather like them, Cajeiri thought, a short chain and a walk from this guarded place to that guarded place.

But they were all right, at least, and there would be a museum tour. His guests were safe. They *said* they were having a good time. They played with Boji—Boji liked it. They played cards, and he let them win at least half the time.

He sighed, which drew immediate stares from his guests, who were not stupid, so he could not even do that much— let alone throw a tantrum about it all. Being infelicitous eight had been hard. But right now it seemed safe and known. Nine was supposed to be a very felicitous year ... but Nine was unexplored territory, and he almost wished he could stay just eight.

Being nine, he had to stand there and look important and grown up, but having not one single thing *he* wanted, for three whole hours.

And give a speech.

That was not an auspicious start of being nine.

15

A little time lying down—that helped. Bren managed a nap very carefully, having shed his coat, and his vest, and lay carefully on his stomach, head on his hand, so as not to wrinkle the shirt.

A knock sounded at the door, and he turned a little and looked from the corner of his eye—it was Jago who had come in.

"Bren-ji. Narani reports Lord Topari is coming. Imminently."

Damn. And *good*. "How imminently?"

"Narani estimates half an hour."

Damn again. He didn't want to move. But he carefully slid off the bed—he and his valets had agreed that the helpful little stepping-stool should always be set precisely in the middle of the bedframe, so that he could find it infallibly with his foot. "My vest," he said, "Jago-ji. How is Banichi?"

"Sleeping," Jago said. "Tano is also sleeping."

"Good for both," he said. He straightened his sleeves, saw that Jago had taken not the vest he had just put off to lie down, but the bulletproof one, and considering Topari's opinion of humans, and his experience in the south, he didn't argue. He simply slipped his arms into it, and let Jago fasten it. "How did Narani report his disposition?"

"As unhappy."

"The brown coat." That was a day-coat that accommodated that vest, the *only* day-coat that would. Jago took it from the closet and held it for him, helped him settle the shoulders.

"A message from Tabini," Jago said, the sort of running report he usually got from his valets or his major d', "regarding the festivity schedule. A message from the aiji-dowager, which is actually Cenedi's report on security—Algini and I have heard it. There are no surprises."

"Good," he said. "Teacakes. Can we manage that?"

"Bindanda has anticipated the need," Jago said, "and arranged some small pastries, too, in the thought that such things, if unneeded for guests, never go begging."

"Excellent," he said. "We need to call Bujavid security."

"Better," Jago said. "I shall go downstairs and escort the lord up."

"Having him in the best mood possible," he said, "will be an asset. Thank you, Jago-ji."

"Look at me," she said, and gently angled his face to look him in the eyes and let him track her finger. "The pupils still match."

"Good," he said, wishing he dared take another painkiller. But he had an ill-disposed, rough-edged southerner headed for his apartment and he needed nothing to dull his senses. "The video from nand' Jase."

"The video and the viewer will be in the sitting room, should you wish."

"Excellent. One trusts Topari has a bodyguard."

"Yes," Jago said. "Algini just requested their records. If there should be any problem—shall we defer Guild objection to his escort, in the interests of the meeting, or shall we make one and bar them from entry?"

"Let them in," he said. "Let us be cordial to our guest . . .

and do not alarm him. Advise Jase and his aishid—no, I should advise him. His presence might be useful. Otherwise, just let Tano sleep. Surely you and Algini can deal with any problem."

"One suggests we ask two of the aiji's guards to fill in, to be sure."

Tabini's secondary bodyguards were the dowager's own, and their presence would brief Tabini *and* Ilisidi at once they returned to their posts. "Yes," he said. "Do that. Go."

She left, moving quickly. He took a slower pace to his office and left the door open, seeing to a little note-taking, while kitchen, serving staff, and Jago collectively saw to it they had a smooth welcome for a very problematic visitor, who must *not* get stopped and annoyed by the extraordinary security of the third floor.

Jase came in. "Visitor?" Jase asked, in the shorthand way of ship-folk. "I'm told he's a problem."

"He can be, easily. Conservative as hell, *and* he and his staff are probably the only citizens of his district that've ever met anybody who wasn't born in his district."

"We've seen that problem," Jase said. "Too long between station-calls."

"Only *his* district has never made a station-call, even on their own capital, not in the whole existence of the aishi-di'tat. The mountain folk only *heard* about the War of the Landing. They only *hear* about humans. This fellow's certainly the only one in his district who's ever met one of us, and that one is me, so it's a pretty small sample. Meeting you would double his entire experience. Kaplan and Polano in armor—and the technicalities of that recording from two angles—are going to be a bit much for him, I'm suspecting, but I'll try not to push matters."

"We're there if you need us," Jase said. "Kaplan and Polano are sleeping off last night. I can send them in if you want."

"We'll manage. We have reinforcement from next door."

He noted Narani's quiet appearance in the doorway. "Very well done, Rani-ji. How was he?"

Narani's little lift of the brows, the little hesitation, spoke volumes. "One believes, nandi, that the gentleman does not trust the invitation, but considers your position."

"And detests my filthy self being on this very exclusive floor?"

"That would be my estimation of his views, nandi."

"I almost want to stay and watch," Jase said, "but I urgently plan to read a book."

"I think we'll record this session, too," Bren said. "At least the audio. I won't review it myself, but the Guild will. The new Guild. The Guild that's not in the least happy with the amount of misinformation that's flown about in the last several years. I'm expecting them to ask for a copy of the Kadagidi video, too, since it's come into issue."

"We have absolutely no objection to that," Jase said.

The notion that one *could* rely on the Guild to take in such a tape, quietly disseminate just the information in it to the bodyguards of numerous lords, and that the lords and their bodyguards could have confidence in information under Guild seal being accurate—they had lost that confidence, in the last two years, when they had only feared that the Guild had a few serious *leaks*.

When they had begun to realize that the security problem was far worse than that—when they'd finally understood they were unable to trust the Guild's very integrity—that had been a nightmare. If *that* confidence had ever been undermined in the general public, the whole continent would have gone to hell on the fast track.

That problem was, they hoped, fixed. *Fixed,* to the point that if it were not that a certain minor lord was about to shipwreck himself and his association on an assumption— he could hope that the Guild would now function in the old way, that Guild experts would view the tape, the Council would review it, and then quietly pass the word through

Guild channels, so that they would not *have* to have a legislative investigation on the matter. Truth was truth, and truth, in this instance, truth had been filmed from two slightly different angles, simultaneously, and it was sworn to by one court official, a foreign head of state, two high lords of the aishidi'tat and a number of senior Guild who'd been there as witnesses. The Guild Council should fairly well accept it as it stood.

It would be a great relief if that happened and it all became quiet.

It would be a great relief if the Lord Aseida matter would drop like a stone and sink out of sight. In the old system, lords who were disposed to support Aseida, for whatever reason, ideally would simply get advice to the contrary, that the Guild, having deliberated, was going to rule against Aseida ... and life would go on, while Aseida would probably get a quiet retirement in a town where he could live reasonably and settle disputes about hunting rights or tannery fumes, granted he stayed out of trouble.

But the Guild couldn't straighten its internal business out fast enough in this instance. Tatiseigi could talk to others who would be disturbed by the incident, and persuade them on the strength of his own reputation. But Tatiseigi was *not* likely to make headway with the man he had publicly embarrassed, and as for the dowager meeting with him—

Not a good idea ... especially when the real thing at stake was *not* Lord Aseida's future, but the Cismontane Association and a few critical kilometers of privately-owned railroad that crossed a vital mountain pass.

So the best he could do was to try ... and *hope* that Topari would just let the Aseida matter drift off and talk to him about the thing he *really* wanted.

Algini eventually came in, saying that Topari was now in the lift system with Jago, and with his own bodyguard. The two Guildsmen from Tabini's staff had arrived, and were being briefed so far as they could be: they were simply to stand by the door in the event the rural bodyguard caused a problem.

There was no need for the paidhi-aiji to be waiting in the sitting room, looking anxious. Let Narani employ his skills and soothe the gentleman with attentions. Let Topari absorb the hospitality of the fairly traditional household, and be treated as a proper guest. It was *not* a bureaucratic office, or the legislative waiting room: it was a high court official's private home, and business *would* indeed wait while the traditional formalities were played out, and anger settled in the traditional way.

He heard the door open, and heard the arrival. Algini was out in the foyer, standing guard by the office, a convenient place to meet Jago and learn the gentleman's temper in a handful of discreet signals. The gentleman's attendants would politely split up, two to attend the gentleman and two to stand in the hall with the aiji's pair. Weapons? Oh, undoubtedly there would be weapons ... God only knew what sort—likely hunting pieces—but that was why Tabini's men were in the hall.

He gave it a little while more, until Narani would have time to see the gentleman seated, time enough to have the servants busy preparing tea, and time to for Narani to intone, in his best formal manner, "I shall inform the paidhi-aiji you are here, nandi."

He heard the door open and close. He waited.

Jago and Algini let Narani in, Narani said, as cheerfully as if he had not just dealt with an irate country lord, "Lord Topari, nandi, is in the sitting room."

"Thank you, Rani-ji." He got up, albeit gingerly, as he was doing things today, and walked into the hall and past the two Guildsmen and the two rural bodyguards, to enter the sitting room by the formal, proper door.

Lord Topari was as he remembered the man, a portly fellow, a little reminiscent of Lord Geigi, except he stood shorter and wider, and he entirely lacked Lord Geigi's genial manner. Lord Topari had one expression, set like concrete, and his eyes shifted hither and thither as if he expected ambush in this place of antique furnishings and delicate manners. He was dressed in a moderate fashion, a good green twill coat with leather trim, with a little lace at cuffs and collar, decidedly not in current fashion and decidedly not trying to be.

Jago was there already. So was Algini. And the viewer was set up.

"Nandi," Bren said, paying a painful and absolutely correct little bow as he reached his intended chair. "Thank you for coming on such short notice. Please, let us have a little tea." He signaled. Servants moved, and absolutely Narani, his master of kabiu, had thought of everything. It was not his most elaborate tea set, in case of breakage, but a very traditional one, about fifty years old; and immediately behind the tea service came a servant with a plate of teacakes and small pastries, the aroma of which complemented the tea. "The hour being such," Bren said, "one thought the cakes might be welcome." He took one himself, and took a little bite—should the gentleman have any notion there was any mischief about the cakes.

And if anyone could resist Bindanda's tea cakes he had no appetite for perfection. Topari did not have the look of a man who disdained fine food, and there *was*, indeed, a milder expression on that face once the orangelle sweetness reached Topari's senses.

That cake vanished, rather quickly, and two gulps of tea. The servant with the teacakes offered more.

"I have not been to Halrun," Bren remarked by way of small talk, naming Topari's house and village. "Is it high in the mountains?"

"The highest of all capitals," the man said immediately.

And the coldest, it was reputed.

"One is told it is quite beautiful in the southern mountains."

"We are not enthusiastic about strangers."

"Ah. Well, then to the loss of all the world, certainly. I

have always enjoyed the snow. And one understands winter never quite leaves Halrun."

"We do, indeed, keep snow on the peaks in midsummer."

"But Halrun itself is not at such a height."

"No," Topari said shortly, and took another teacake, which disappeared in two bites and a gulp of tea.

"Well, well," Bren said, seeing that the man was not settling, nor likely to if they wandered too far from the topic. He set his cup down, as host, the signal that business conversation was now in order.

The other cup, minus a last gulp, went down. Curious little gesture. Not quite city manners. The cup clicked onto the table.

"I do again thank you for coming, nandi," Bren said quietly. "And I shall not waste your time. Sources inform me that you are quite perturbed about the situation of Lord Aseida."

"I shall not argue it here."

"One entirely understands, nandi, but I have an utterly different motive in asking you here. I am no authority within the aishidi'tat, merely a voice, but I do know that your district has become very important, or will be so, in the future. Your strong leadership is important, and my principals have no wish to see political damage occur . . ."

"Is that a threat, nandi?"

"By no means, nandi. I have asked you here because I *have* consulted with others of the Conservative Caucus on the matter of the Kadagidi lord, and clearly you are part of that caucus, equally deserving of the information the others are being given, or may already have. Guild administration has changed. Information is being passed from the Assassins' Guild to various houses regarding that change and other matters. And realizing that your own bodyguard may not be tapped into that source, and that you have expressed concern about various events, I called you here to give you that information, for fairness' sake. Appearances will be preserved, I swear to you, and there will be no news of the topic of our meeting. That we two have business could involve a dozen things—the railway and the southern route, among others—perfectly logical for us to discuss." *There* was bait on a string. "But most urgently, nandi, let me state the real business, which you need to know—to have *proved* to your satisfaction: the action at the Kadagidi estate was entirely lawful. My bodyguard was fired upon and wounded. My Guild senior is at present lying abed injured, and as you see, *I* was not exempt from attack." He lifted a hand toward the cut on his cheek. "A minor scrape. There were, however, six holes in the bus in which I was standing."

"That is no proof. It says nothing as to who provoked the incident."

"I agree. It is no proof at all. But proof exists. First, a document delivered to the Guild last night contains the confession of two members from the Dojisigin Marid, who were coerced to lie in wait for Lord Tatiseigi, in an unFiled assassination which provoked our visit to the Kadagidi—since, at the time of the incident, Lord Tatiseigi had guests who were put at risk: the aiji-dowager, the aiji's son and heir, myself, one of the ship-aiji and three young folk from the space station."

"Humans!"

"Indeed, the three innocent human *children*, nandi, guests of the aishidi'tat, in a diplomatic maneuver *important* to the aishidi'tat. In the thought that perhaps Lord Aseida, who aided the two Dojisigi to gain access to the Atageini house, might not have *known* about the foreign guests, who were indeed under deep security at the time—I and a ship-aiji, a former paidhi-aiji—undertook to go personally over to the Kadagidi estate to advise Lord Aseida privately of the situation, and to ask for an apology, in the name of the dowager, and the heir, and Lord Tatiseigi. Had Lord Aseida appeared, heard me, and simply given a verbal apology, that would have settled the matter and relieved Lord Tatiseigi's honor and his of the burden in private, in such a way that would have ended the incident. The ship-aiji and his bodyguard were there to witness the Kadagidi response in the interests of *their* aijiin. And whenever a ship-aiji's guard deploys in a situation, they make a recording to prove what happened in the exchange. That is their custom. And that recording, which I am prepared to show you, shows our action and the Kadagidi response."

Expression touched Lord Topari's face, difficult to read: skepticism, one was certain.

"And this will be entered in evidence?"

"Nandi, it is to be filed with the Guild today. The confession of the two Assassins is already filed. And being informed that you *are* first to ask into the facts, as someone *should* ask—I have asked you here to *see* what happened, to see exactly what the Guild Council will see, should you wish to do so. I do not say you will be the last to see it—but you will be the first."

A suspicious look.

"It will be relatively brief, nandi."

"Television."

"Not precisely television, nandi," Jago said, moving forward, "but this viewer." She pushed a button and an image flashed up on the bare wall to the left, larger than life. Algini immediately dimmed the lights, and without Lord Topari precisely consenting—the images appeared.

Bren watched Lord Topari, whose face, in the reflected light, was grim and apprehensive, not pleased by what was simply a confusion of shadow at first, then the interior of the bus. It was the moment Jase's guards had put on their helmets.

"We are beginning," Bren said, "at the point at which the aiji's guard commenced recording."

On the wall, the view swung about, became the driveway, the still-distant house, the porch.

"Those are ship-folk notations superimposed on the image," Bren said, regarding the numbers at the edge.

That drew a sharp look from Topari.

"What do they say?"

"They are a signature, indicating the name of the guard, indicating the date and time. This is from a camera inside the armor of Jase-aiji's guard. Jase-aiji's bodyguards were on duty, as of this point, wearing protective armor."

Action proceeded. The bus stopped. Banichi got off and hailed the house.

The paidhi-aiji and the ship-aiji have come to call on Lord Aseida, Banichi's voice said distantly, addressing the Kadagidi guard. *They are guests of your next-door neighbor the Atageini lord, and they have been personally inconvenienced by actions confessed to have originated from these grounds. These are matters far above the Guild, nadi, and regarding your lord's status within the aishidi'tat. Advise your lord of it.*

"That is my Guild senior," Bren said quietly, "advising the Kadagidi of our approach and our request."

Kaplan and Polano got off, a confusion of images of the bus door and the side of the house, then a jolt resolving to a steady image of the house door, which had opened. A knot of armed Kadagidi Guild held the porch.

"This is the point at which I exited the bus," Bren said. "I descended behind the cover of the two ship-folk bodyguards and in the company of my own aishid, hoping to speak to Lord Aseida."

Banichi stepped again into camera view, rifle in the crook of his arm.

Are those alive? the other side called out; and now bright squares flicked here and there and showed shadow-figures within the walls, and one square flicked to the movement of a weapon, on the porch.

These are the ship-aiji's personal bodyguard, Banichi answered. *And the ship-aiji is present on the bus. Be warned. These two ship-folk understand very little Ragi. Make no move that they might misinterpret. The paidhi-aiji and the ship-aiji have come to talk to your lord, and request he come outdoors for the meeting.*

Our lord will protest this trespass!

"Your lord will be free to do that at his pleasure," Banichi retorted. *"But advise him that the paidhi-aiji is here on be-half of Tabini-aiji, speaking for his minor son and for the aiji-dowager, the ship-aiji, and his son's foreign guests, minor children, all of whom were disturbed last night by Guild As-sassins who have named your estate as their route into Lord Tatiseigi's house."*

"We will relay the matter to our lord," the Kadagidi said. *"Wait."*

A man left, through the door to the inside of the house. And thus far there was absolutely nothing wrong with the proceedings.

Except that targeting squares now flickered on shadows inside an apparently transparent building.

Another Guild unit came out onto the porch.

"Banichi!" that unit-senior shouted with no preface at all, swung his rifle up in a flicker of square brackets, and fired.

The scene froze. Stopped.

"I shall advance the image slowly at this point," Jago said.

It was hard to watch. Banichi fired, *clearly* the second to fire. In a series of images, Haikuti went backward as Banichi spun and went down, bullets simultaneously hit the bus, and a flash of fire and white cloud obscured their view for a few frames.

"Grenade," Jago said matter-of-factly. "Theirs." A fiercer blaze of light enveloped the porch, lit by green brackets.

"Jase-aiji's guard has fired," Jago said.

Bren had not seen that happen. He had been on the ground, trying to pull Banichi into cover. Then everybody had poured off the bus, through the smoke still lingering. What the camera showed was appalling.

Shadows ran past the camera—his bodyguard, and the dowager's men, headed for that porch, which was now a shattered, smoke-obscured ruin.

The image froze again, and went dark.

"This," Bren said, a little shaken himself, recalling the shock that made the ground shake, the smell, the stinging haze . . . "This is the point of law, nandi, that everything was proceeding in an ordinary way, and the Kadagidi guard had not panicked at the appearance of the ship-folk guards. Everything was proceeding quietly except that that second unit was moving to the door, which none of *my* guard knew. The Guild senior of the Kadagidi unit exited the building and opened fire on me and my guard. My Guild senior took the fire and fired back. Someone on that porch threw a grenade, and at that instant Jase-aiji's guard responded with their own weapons."

Topari sat silent.

"We also extracted, from that house, nandi, evidence of a connection between that Guild unit and the recent upheaval in the south. In the confession of the two Dojisigi Guild involved in the same incident, we have their routing from Murini's folk in the Marid *through* the Kadagidi house to attack the Atageini. We also recorded our interview with Lord Aseida, as we transported him to Lord Tatiseigi's house to give his account to the aiji-dowager. All these records are to go to the Guild, and will be available to Guild members, and ultimately to members of the legislature. The aiji wishes to find a suitable resolution of this matter, as quietly and expeditiously as possible."

"One sees," Topari said after a moment, and did not look happy. Then: "For whom are you speaking, nand' paidhi?"

Entirely civil question, entirely reasonable question.

"In this, I speak for the aiji, nandi. As for my own opinion, for what it matters, despite our differences, I deeply respect your leadership of the Cismontane, which has never acted except in reasonable protection of its natural interests. And, may I say, on the aiji's behalf, you never accepted Murini as aiji, either."

"We have not that enthusiastically accepted the aijinate," Topari muttered, blunt truth, and certainly not to the man's benefit. He *was* forthcoming with his opinions, one could say that. As to discretion—one was less sure.

"It is, alas, the old conflict," Bren said, "the old division between north and south, the guilds and the principle of out-clan assignment." One was very definitely conscious of the non-Guild status of Topari's two bodyguards, standing over to the right, opposite Jago and Algini. "But then, the aiji's maternal clan has only this month made peace with the Atageini after two hundred years of warfare—so the aiji does understand districts that, for some local reason, prefer local security and wish to settle their problems in their own way. Dissent from his administration will never be silenced. Likewise we have been assured that Assassins' Guild will make a fair investigation. That guild's former leadership, set aside by Murini, has returned, which is also not yet general knowledge, and you may now have at least as much confidence as you had in the Assassins' Guild prior to the coup." He shifted his hands to his knees, signifying an end to the interview. "I thank you for coming, nandi. You have been very courteous. And I shall not urge you to regard anything but what you have seen, which is the same as what others will see within a few hours. I know you have extreme reservations about me and my office, but you have met me courteously in the past and I hoped we could talk. You and I are bound to meet again in this Marid railroad affair—and I am encouraged to hope we can talk, then, too, and do so productively."

"When you will represent the dowager?"

"She has her views. I shall represent them at her request. But likewise if you have any message for her, I shall certainly carry it. Or to the aiji, either one."

"Then tell the *aiji-dowager* that the Cismontane is *not* pleased with her cursed self-serving agreement. The legislature never appointed her aiji, not in two tries!"

It was worth a diplomatic smile, a diplomatic nod. "I shall *not* remind her of *that,* nandi, but if you have observations on the railroad matter, I should be honored to represent you to her and her to you. That *is* my office."

Lengthy silence, this time. Then a gravelly: "I shall consider it." With which, Topari gave a parting style of bow. "Nandi."

"Nandi." Bren gave back the same, and Topari gathered his bodyguard and left ... with Jago both opening the way for them, and escorting them out, because otherwise Topari and his guards could not get downstairs through the lift system ... and *that* would tip the situation toward war.

Did we win or lose? Bren wondered, hearing the outer door open and shut. Did I accomplish anything—or open up a worse problem?

The adrenaline and the strength quite ebbed out of him with that thought, and the headache was—had been for several minutes, perhaps, ever since the lights had come back on—back in force. He thought about going to his bedroom, but the adrenaline of the interview wasn't going to leave him alone. He sank down in the nearest chair, light-headed. "Tea," he said. "The *strong* tea, nadiin-ji."

Servants moved, quickly. Hot water and tea met over at the buffet. He could smell it. His senses felt sandpapered raw, at the same time the room seemed a little blurry.

"You are quite pale, Bren-ji," Algini said.

"Tea will help. How did that go, Gini-ji? I have no good reading of him."

"He is a suspicious man," Algini said, "and verbally reckless. He went further than he expected to go. He *was* affected by what he saw—I was watching him. He saw your justification, and that, conversely, upset his resolve. He will likely try to reconstruct later *how* the railroad became involved in the discussion. But that mention has him thinking and wondering if it is a proposed trade. Now he will very likely want to test what you said and be sure he is not being led astray. He is a pessimist by reputation, never ready to assume he is being offered anything good. You have, one believes, made some headway with him."

"I felt I was bouncing words off a stone wall. But his district has legitimate concerns. I shall see if the dowager can be persuaded about his railroad."

"Dare you ever have the aiji-dowager and this man in one room?" Algini asked.

He opened his eyes and smiled—only slightly, because it hurt. Algini's humor was rare, and occasionally irreverent. "I think we should confine that exchange to letters," he said, and then had a clear thought. *"Cenedi* might be the logical point of approach."

"Cenedi would, indeed," Algini said wryly, "vote to keep those two apart."

The servant came, with the tea, which was not yet settled in the cup. He sipped it anyway, and found the dark brew a good taste. He heard a door open, down the main hall, heard footsteps not of the household, and knew it was Jase before Jase appeared cautiously at the door.

"Come in," he said. "Sit. Our visitor has left."

"So how did it go?" Jase asked.

"Not so bad, perhaps. Hard to say. —The teacakes are still available, are they not, nadiin-ji?" This to the servants standing by.

"Yes, nandi." One servant was preparing tea for Jase. Another hastened to offer teacakes. Bren declined. Jase didn't, but waited for his tea.

"The man's suspicious," Bren said, "no fool, which is usually good. We'll see if he finds a way to make trouble or if I offered him enough to intrigue him."

"Are you all right? You're pale."

"Just a little short of breath. It'll pass."

"You should be in bed."

"I'm considering it. But strong tea helps." He drew a deep breath. "And some things can't wait. If Topari decides not to raise a legislative fuss over Lord Aseida's fate, I've saved myself at least a week of work."

"At some cost. Bren, you *ought* to be in bed."

"I will. Soon." He wondered whether his queasy stomach

could possibly stand food. Teacake—no, he decided. Nothing of that flavor. Sweet was not sitting well on his stomach. "The Guild knows now exactly what we were dealing with it—and in the way of things, that information will go quietly to every house that has Guild protection, as to what happened, and what the truth was. We won't have to hold a showing for each and every one of them, I hope. Nasty moment, that."

Guild *would* be sending messages out. A lot of them.

The whole political landscape was under repair and revision—a vast improvement over the situation they'd had since they'd come back to the planet.

Damn, it was.

"Sandwich, I think," he said to Jase. "Then I'm just going to sit in a chair and relax for a while. I think I'll do that."

16

Jase-aiji had come to call—Cajeiri had heard the coming
and going, and Jegari's quiet spying had found out that
Jase-aiji was talking with Great-uncle, who had been having
visitors all morning—political visitors, Jegari said, because
of everything that was going on in the Guild.

It was the Conservative Caucus coming and going. Cajeiri knew what that was: Great-uncle was head of it, and
Great-grandmother was part of it, or at least—people in it
listened to Great-grandmother; but Great-grandmother
was busy and Great-uncle was doing all the talking, and
thus far his own aishid had kept trying to get information
with very little success—except to say that there had been
a very serious matter downtown, at Guild Headquarters,
and that there was another Ajuri dead—in this case, the old
man that had been so much trouble to everybody.

He was not sorry to hear that confirmed. He was worried
that Banichi and nand' Bren had come back wounded, he
was glad to hear that they were not in hospital, and he really, really wanted to go to nand' Bren's apartment and just
see them.

But Madam Saidin had said definitely they were all right,

and that nand' Bren was back at work and busy with business of his own.

But that the Guild might be straightening itself out, and that they had gotten rid of their problem—that was *good* news.

And if nand' Bren really was at work, he could not be too badly hurt. So he had sent a message by one of Great-uncle's staff, asking if everybody was all right and was Banichi hurt? And he had an answer back by the same servant, assuring him that Banichi had just had his original wound giving him trouble and that nand' Bren just had a headache and a little cut.

He felt a lot better, then.

And if it was not for the letter from his father, he would have been a great deal relieved.

But there was a good thing. Madam Saidin had said they could have the dining room all to themselves this evening, since Great-uncle was invited to mani's apartment for supper, and the staff would only have them to care for. They could have any dish they could describe. They could even have pizza if that was what they most wanted.

Meanwhile, Great-uncle kept up the meetings, having his bodyguard bring up this person and that person to take tea in the sitting room. One wondered how Great-uncle could drink any more . . . but it went on and on.

Politics. Politics. The Conservatives were the opposite of the liberals most of the time, and they constantly argued with his father.

Everybody *would* be there, he reminded himself, to wish him well.

No. They would be there to wish he would someday be *favorable* to what they represented. And if he would not be, they would wish he would never have been born. And still smile and bow to him.

Grown-ups were very good at that.

His father had said once, not so many days ago, something he remembered very keenly, "If you cannot please someone, at least make them believe you *might* please them."

"How does one do that with everybody?" he had asked.

"You ask them their opinion," his father had said, "you listen to it, and you nod and say something good about one thing in their idea."

"But what if there is *nothing* good?" he had asked, and for some reason his father had laughed and then said:

"If there is not, then offer them a doorway from their way to your way."

He had not understood. He had frowned. And his father had said:

"To do that, son of mine—you have to *understand* both sides."

That was a little different than Great-grandmother, who said, when he told her what his father had said, "Doorway, is it? Offer them tea, nod politely, charm them, make them think you might agree, and let *them* modify *their* position to persuade *you*. It usually comes to the same thing, but they think *they* devised the compromise."

He so *hoped* he could be that clever someday. But his father and mani had a long head start.

At least with Jase-aiji he had no such worries. Jase-aiji was on the side of the ship-humans getting along with atevi, and Jase-aiji knew atevi customs. Jase-aiji would help his guests put on a very good appearance for a whole roomful of people who had never seen young humans—more, some who had no desire to have humans on the continent at all.

And Madam Saidin was helping, too, to teach them the right phrases.

Even his mother seemed to have taken an interest in Irene—though he was still suspicious, and he especially remembered her pointed remark that it was a good thing *somebody* asked Irene's mother.

And he hoped they could all just continue to stay with Great-uncle. It actually seemed Great-uncle enjoyed having his guests in his premises, once Great-uncle had discovered his guests were in awe of his house and his porcelains and his collections. He had never imagined Great-uncle was that easy to charm.

Maybe it was that doorway his father had talked about . . .

So now Great-uncle and Jase-aiji were in the sitting room finding a lot to talk about, after all the others who had visited Great-uncle this morning. Jase-aiji stayed three times as long as most of the Conservatives had, and Veijico said they were talking very seriously about the space station and his guests' parents.

Well, *that* was a little scary. What did Great-uncle have to do with the space station at all?

But then Madam Saidin came into the guest suite and said Great-uncle wanted them *all* to come in the sitting room.

So everybody put on day-coats and made sure of their cuffs and collars, and they all filed out and up to join Great-uncle and nand' Jase in the sitting room.

One *so* hoped nothing bad had happened.

They sat, very properly while Great-uncle had them all served tea, and they sat and sipped and listened to Great-uncle make small talk with Jase-aiji.

Then Great-uncle asked casually, "Are you finding everything you need, nephew?" to which the only possible answer was yes.

Then Great-uncle asked, "Do your guests understand what we say?"

"Only about food and clothes, Great-uncle, and the things in your collection. And mecheiti, Great-uncle."

Great-uncle gave a little laugh, saying: "We hope they may need such words again, nephew." That set Cajeiri's heart to beating faster. Then Great-uncle immediately added, "but there are necessary gates to pass. You understand this."

"Yes, Great-uncle, one does understand. Father sent me a list. I have been studying all the guests. Father will send me a speech to make. It will not be hard. I shall do everything without a mistake."

"Wise lad," Great-uncle said.

And that seemed the only point of Great-uncle's having them there or talking to them at all, which seemed odd. Great-uncle left the apartment, going about his own grown-up business with Great-grandmother and the Conservatives, maybe down the hall in mani's apartment.

But Jase-aiji stayed behind and explained the arrangements to Gene and Artur and Irene in some detail, telling them that they were to stay very close to him, that they were to bow and thank anyone who wished them well, and be patient with people who might just stand and stare at them. They had already understood that, for the most part, but they listened very solemnly, and agreed that they would be ready for Jase-aiji and his bodyguard to gather them up and escort them down to the festivity.

So it was all just preparation for the festivity, and it was going to happen, and Great-uncle had just called them in for Jase-aiji to meet with them and explain procedures to be absolutely sure his guests understood. That was good.

Cajeiri stood by and listened to the explanation, reminding himself of ship-speak words, learning a few new ones, and meanwhile he kept thinking—

He kept thinking Great-uncle had hinted that there might—there *might* be a hope of going back to Tirnamardi before his guests had to leave. He was not sure his guests had understood that. He was not sure he ought to tell them, if Jase-aiji failed to mention it, for fear it was only an idle remark and would not happen. Great-uncle's hint was the sort of thing adults said when they were trying to get someone to behave—what was it his father had said to him?

Make them believe you *might* please them . . .

It was interesting how well that worked, even on him, even when it was clear as could be what the adults were doing to them.

He *had* to do everything well—to have even a chance of getting what he most wanted.

That was the way things always worked in politics.

Sleep, granted a settled stomach and a sense that things were moderately under control, was actually possible—finally, for the whole rest of the afternoon. Bren surfaced from time to time, listened for any noise in the household that might signal a problem, and drifted again, face down. Jase had taken word on the Topari meeting down the hall to Lord Tatiseigi, head of that caucus, and also to the dowager, who needed to know, and thirdly to Tabini himself—keeping everyone abreast of the little problem which one hoped would not blossom into a big problem before Lord Tatiseigi could talk to several of his most level-headed associates. The Conservative Caucus was briefed about the taped record of the Kadagidi encounter. They would have the chance to view it; and they would form a recommendation on the situation in Ajuri and the situation in the Kadagidi lordship.

The dowager would call in some of the Liberal Caucus and do her own damage control—Dur, in particular, would have some constructive opinions on the Ajuri situation, being part of the local landscape, and in a neighboring association. The Liberals would by no means object: the Liberals would all but hold a celebration at the notion the Kadagidi were being taken to task.

The aiji-consort, meanwhile, was bound to have a personal opinion about the future of Ajuri clan. He'd warned Jase to tread particularly carefully during his visit to Tabini's apartment, avoiding any contact with Damiri, and to be wary of any setup in the Festivity involving any contact of the children with Damiri. Damiri needed to be involved in planning the Festivity, and she was also well aware of the upheaval in her clan. That marriage had been under stress enough, and Damiri, who had a temper, did not do well with surprises. Whether the demise of Shishogi had made her situation easier or worse—had yet to be proved.

He shut his eyes. He slept the sleep of the moderately just.

And he waked finally with Narani's gentle presence in the room, turning on the lights.

"Nandi. An invitation from the dowager, for brandy after dinner, or for dinner, if you find yourself in sufficient health for such an event. Jase-aiji and nand' Tatiseigi are also invited."

"One hears," he murmured—there was time enough to get ready for a formal dinner, he was sure, or Narani would not have waked him; but there would not be all that much time, either, granted Narani would not have waked him any earlier than need be. He carefully levered himself up on his arms and put a foot over the edge of the mattress. Two feet—and he set himself upright very carefully.

The headache was indeed still there. More pills were in order.

Perhaps an appeal to Port Jackson for a gross of them.

"Banichi has waked," Narani informed him, "and he says he is feeling better."

"Is he following nand' Siegi's orders?"

"Somewhat, nandi."

Somewhat. He drew in a deep breath, set his feet on the ground, and said, "Thank you, Rani-ji."

He didn't wait for his valets. He put on his robe and headed down the hall barefoot, straight for the security station, where, indeed, Banichi sat—in uniform, shirtless, but having a heavy uniform jacket draped about his shoulders. The arm was, yes, still taped, Bren noticed critically. But boots were on, hair was in its queue, and Banichi was sitting there upright.

"Is this approved, nadiin?" Bren asked.

"It seemed we would do more harm stopping him," Tano said.

"Of the two of us," Banichi said, looking at him, "I seem to be faring better at the moment."

Barefoot, in his dressing robe, with his hair disheveled and with a brutal headache, Bren said, perhaps a bit shortly, "The dowager has invited me down the hall to dinner tonight. I shall need *two* attendants, amid all the others who will be present. One of them will *not* be you, Nichi-ji, and no amount of argument will convince me. You will not need your dress uniform."

Banichi nodded graciously. And was amused.

"He believes, however," Jago said, "that he *will* be in the escort at the young gentleman's Festivity."

"The young gentleman," Banichi said, "would be disappointed otherwise."

One entirely understood that point: the youngster had regarded Banichi as a second father, during the ship voyage—not to say Banichi had declined the attachment. Banichi would be sorely disappointed to be kept from that event.

"That will be a considerable time standing," Bren said, not happily; and looked to the others. It could not be the first time a Guild member had been on duty while injured. "Is there a way he can sit down?"

"The service hall," Algini said. "We can arrange a chair to be there . . . granted his sincere undertaking to use it from time to time."

"You *will* use it," Bren said to Banichi. "Are we agreed?"

"*Two* chairs," Banichi said.

He and Banichi were, in fact, a matched set; and an available chair during three hours of standing about, in the case the room started to go around, sounded more than sensible.

"One agrees," he said, wondering whether his entire aishid had just collectively put one over on him.

"We are," the dowager said after dinner, "hearing good things within the Guild. They are finding the things we fully expected them to find, and perhaps one or two things that surprise us. They are sifting records. They are interviewing reliable people and looking for other people they should be looking for. My grandson may complain about the individuals now in charge there, but they are setting things to rights."

It was good news.

"In the matter of Lord Aseida's future," Ilisidi continued, swirling brandy gently in her glass, "we have a reasonable situation in mind, a small house under the supervision of the very strong-willed lady of Corhenda, a subclan of Cie, a very practical-minded place. It has electricity, but phones are scarce. Its mills and tanneries are a blight, but then it always was barren. His artistic skills—we are told he paints—might enliven the house—perhaps the mills, who knows the limits of his talent? As for who should succeed him in the Kadagidi lordship, nand' Tatiseigi has a proposal."

"A modest one," Tatiseigi said. "He is a Kadagidi gentleman, a third cousin of mine, from the old union of our house with Kadagidi clan. He is ten years my senior, fifteen years retired—he ran the largest Kadagidi granary and the northern plains operations. He is a respectable fellow, never politically active, and what one might call a dedicated administrator. He has, besides, three daughters, and the eldest is a member of the Scholars' Guild. One believes he would only reluctantly undertake the burden of the lordship—but in order to put his eldest daughter in the line of that succession, he might; her husband is a quiet fellow, affable, whose skill is hunting management: he would not be a bad neighbor."

"If ever asked," Bren said with a little nod, "which one hardly expects to be—one would certainly support your opinion, nandi."

"Pish," the dowager said. "Nand' Siegi says we should not keep the paidhi too late tonight. You should go straight to bed, paidhi."

"Aiji-ma." Another careful nod.

"Go. You are entirely void of entertainment tonight, paidhi, and you need your sleep."

One had somewhat suspected it was not *his* somewhat cheerless and aching company the dowager had desired this evening, but that her aishid and his and Lord Tatiseigi's should all be in close contact for an hour or so.

And indeed, once he had left the sitting room and gathered up Jago and Algini, there was a somberness about his bodyguard that said he was right in that guess.

They left the apartment, the three of them. They walked down the main hall to their own door, and, once inside:

"Is there news, nadiin-ji?" he asked.

"There is news we should share with Banichi and Tano," Algini said. "Do not worry about it, Bren-ji."

"That is hardly going to allow me to rest," he protested. Narani had let them in; Narani waited to receive his coat, and he unbuttoned the coat and let it slip from his arms. "I shall worry all night."

"If we do tell you," Jago said, "you will not rest, either."

He looked at her. "Tell me, nadiin-ji. I *request* it."

"This is a security concern," Jago said, "but, Bren-ji, this is a *Guild* matter, and now we have Guild Headquarters operating as it has not, not even in our lifetimes. Have confidence in us."

He had not gotten that sort of answer from them, he thought, in some time—not since they had come back from space. It was a little off-putting—like the firm closing of a door. And then he thought—that was the way it was, before.

That's the way it's always supposed to be.

In that light—he felt perhaps he *could* oblige Jago and just let it go, as he had not, for some time, been able to let go anything in their realm. They hadn't known about the Guild's forty-year-old problem, simmering at a very low level, before the coup had changed things. The people they had just put in charge of the Guild hadn't known it was going on, either—or they'd have done something to prevent it.

But now the people who should be in charge *had* finally done something, and his aishid evidently thought the Guild was functioning again.

It wasn't the paidhi-aiji's job to second-guess that process. Maybe, knowing what he knew, he should still be alert, and a little on his guard, but even that—

No, if *anyone* could pick up a problem within the Guild as it reconstituted itself, figure it to be his aishid, and the dowager's aishid, and if they wanted to close that door on outsiders to their Guild and handle things by their rules, it was *not* the paidhi's job to put himself in the middle of it.

"Thank you," he said with a little bow. "*Thank* you very much, nadiin-ji. One actually understands. I think I *shall* be able to sleep, if *you* are confident."

"Rely on us," Jago said, and Algini just said, "Go to bed, Bren-ji."

Traffic in the city had suffered a major disruption with the blockage of the central city freight. Everyone's mail had been late yesterday.

But despite all confusion and difficulties, the crates from Tirnamardi had made it up to the Bujavid yesterday late, passed security, and finally poured forth wardrobe ... doubly welcome, Bren thought: he had been hard on his clothes this last few days, and court dress had borne the worst of it.

But nothing that came out of a shipping crate was fit to hang in the paidhi's closet, or their guest's, oh, no. The laundry backstairs had been in a frenzy of activity, receiving the contents of the crate and spilling forth freshly cleaned and pressed shirts and trousers and coats in rapid succession, filling two racks in the hall last evening. Now, this morning, when he returned from the bath, his valets opened his closet to show its racks filled with choices.

"One is extremely glad," he said to his valets, "and pleased, nadiin-ji. Have my casual *boots* possibly turned up?" He was down to his best and only pair, which had suffered bloodstains, and one lightweight pair of house boots he had never liked and hadn't packed for Tirnamardi in the first place.

"Indeed, nandi," Koharu said happily, and from the bottom of the closet, produced, indeed, the newly-returned boots.

But Supani, from the same source, and with a slyly expectant look, brought up a cardboard box done up in tape and string. Supani proffered the box, a wonderful box with a customs tag that said, even before he took it in his hands: *apparel: Bren Cameron, paidhi-aiji, the Bujavid, Shejidan.* The return address was a tag he well knew: his bootmaker's.

"It arrived with the crates, nandi."

His pocket-knife was in the tray atop the bureau. He opened the box in delight, expecting, since it was a largish box for one pair, perhaps two pairs of boots—that worthy gentleman maintained the special forms on a shelf in his workshop, and he had made several orders. But there were three pair, one gray dress, one black casual, and one stout brown pair of laced, high-topped and heavy boots with a note from his bootmaker: *If you can destroy these, Mr. Cameron, I'll replace them at no charge.*

He had to laugh, even if his head hurt. He sat down on the dressing bench and tried them on, with his valets' help. Even the pair with the reinforced tops fit beautifully, and the laces to the toe, not a common style on the mainland, made the heavy ones unexpectedly comfortable. "One is delighted," he said. "And relieved, considering tomorrow. But I shall prefer the old comfortable house pair today, baji-naji. One has no intention of stirring outside the apartment."

He went to the little breakfast room, had a lengthy and informal breakfast with Jase—who wanted to be kept abreast of events. He could not be briefed on all of it: there were details he could not divulge—but there were events in the Marid, the entire situation in the south, the situation that was sure to arise over the rail connections, the necessary cooperation of the station aloft where it came to shipping—and completely idle gossip from the station, and from the world—who was where, what the real story was on half a dozen topics, and what the inside story was on Toby's relationship with Barb.

"True love," he said with a shrug. "They're happy. Amazes me, but I'm far from objecting. If my brother ever does inherit this job—Barb's going to provide some interesting moments. She certainly puzzled Machigi, but we all survived it."

Jase laughed at the right places. And regaled him with a few Polano anecdotes. It was, all in all, a pleasant afternoon—and they spent an hour of it with his valets, putting Jase in all-out court dress. Jase had brought wardrobe down with him, but not in the newest mode, and the occasion demanded extravagance.

So with a little tuck here and there, and a good shirt, one of his newer coats would do. They settled from that to lunch, including Polano and Kaplan, on a day become remarkably sedate and restful. Algini came back and quietly reported his mission to the Guild accomplished. Measures were being taken. It was the one worrisome spot in the afternoon, the one thing that had him gazing down the hall at Algini's retreating back, and wondering, in this new resolve of no information, whether there was anything going on that *would* worry him if he knew. There had been something in Algini's face, a little tension that said business, but the paidhi-aiji was in the midst of outfitting and entertaining his guest, and Algini had only paid a passing courtesy.

Well, and the youngsters would, so one heard through the servant network, go back with a complete wardrobe of clothes—to model for parents and friends in private, perhaps, and the wardrobe would help them keep the memories—good memories, one hoped, in spite of all the goings-on. God, in spite of all their elders' machinations current and future, he hoped Cajeiri's guests could hold on to that bond.

They *would* get their private birthday party. He swore they would.

When they'd gone out to Tirnamardi, he'd envisioned a modest, low-key celebration, with just one preceding day for the youngsters to arrive from their retreat at Tirnamardi, tour the Bujavid, go to the museum, maybe an art gallery, or some other place the young gentleman and his guests could be assured of protection, then have a little human-style party after the family one. He'd been prepared to offer his dining room for such an event.

They'd come back under entirely different circumstances, and had more time here, and it *wasn't* a private party, far from it.

Well, whatever it had mutated into, Tabini willing, they might still go back to the relative privacy and security of Tirnamardi until the shuttle was prepared to fly.

But how that was going to work was becoming increasingly cloudy. The dowager and Lord Tatiseigi's presence was absolutely required in the day or so after, if the tribal peoples bill was going to be up for debate—not even to mention the succession question in Kadagidi and Ajuri.

He needed to be available for the legislature. *None* of them were likely to have time to deal with a handful of increasingly restive youngsters.

Jase, however—

Jase could escort the youngsters. Jase was still known onworld as the ship-paidhi. He wasn't fluent, but he could manage. It was a great deal to ask of Lord Tatiseigi, to turn his estate over to humans . . . so to speak.

But he could send them to his own estate of Najida, maybe. Or Taiben, Taiben, which detested roads, and distrusted outsiders . . .

Taiben would be safer . . . and it had mecheiti . . .

But the young gentleman's dearly treasured birthday present was resident with a herd in Tirnamardi's stables, and one did *not* put a child aboard a mecheita newly introduced to another herd.

Not to mention the politics of putting *Tatiseigi's gift* into a Taibeni herd.

He sighed. It was just *not* going to be easy.

They *couldn't* postpone the tribal peoples bill. Too much rode on it. He couldn't get free. They couldn't do without Tatiseigi. The dowager *had* to be there to push the bill.

"Deep thoughts," Jase said.

"How much ground time do you expect for the shuttle?"

"What? Do you need us out of here faster—or slower?"

"Is there *any* chance the kids could wait for the next shuttle?"

"No logistical problem with *Phoenix* or station authorities. We just load cargo instead. Next rotation we load the passenger module and leave six cans of dried fruit and fish paste. The parents, however . . . Shall I ask?"

"Tomorrow will tell," he said. "Let's just get the lad through the actual birthday."

"Not to mention your other operations."

"I haven't been a good host."

"I have no complaints. I really should leave you to your work. I came down here to assist, not to be entertained. And I can see you're up to your ears."

"You know, if *you* could delay the kids to another shuttle, we *could* actually get that fishing trip."

"You're threatening to take me out in a shell with no attitude controls to float on a hundred meter depth of turbulent water. This is the reward."

He laughed. "I wish I could absolutely promise it. But if you *could* shake yourself loose for another rotation, we'd have a better chance."

"This hasn't been the most opportune timing for us."

"It's no accident it hasn't. But you know that. Past tomorrow, things should be a lot less tense, and there'll be no public exposure. Can you manage it? These kids . . ."

"I know. Let me have a go at it. Gene's mother likely won't object. Irene's—" Jase shrugged. "Maybe. She'll run to ask her problematic friends, and *they* won't decline a chance that makes the kid more useful. Artur's parents— they'll want him back. They're just parents. But for the sake of an education—"

"He's certainly getting one."

"He is, that. Let me give it a try. Pending tomorrow."

"Yourself?"

"Oh, I'll be persuasive. If the kids stay, I can't leave them here alone, can I?" Jase made to get up. "I should leave you to your work, however. I've heard the staff coming and going. Things are in progress, and I'm in the way."

"Never," Bren said, but it was true, and he'd caught a sign from Narani in the hall that there was important mail in-house. "I had better cross-check with staff, however, and stay up on the details. Supper tonight if we're lucky."

"Formal?"

"Informal as hell, I hope. Are you running out of entertainment in there?"

Jase grinned. "We're amply supplied. My office doesn't let me alone. And Kaplan and Polano are on the longest leave of their lives, so I'm hearing no complaints. I don't know where their poker tab stands, but neither one gets more than twenty credits ahead of the other and it's been ongoing for days."

"Good." He laughed. "Good for them."

He saw Jase to the door, went to his office and settled to look through his mail—was not surprised when Narani arrived with the mail, and prominent in the batch was a message cylinder of the heraldic sort that usually circulated within the upper floors of the Bujavid.

Red and black.

The dowager, he thought, telling himself he needed to ask his staff how the preparations for the event were going.

"Thank you," he said. "Wait just a moment. There may be a reply." He opened the cylinder. The seal on the message itself was *not* the dowager's, however: it was Tabini's.

The numbers of the Festivity have officially come in as favorable for the event . . .

Rarely did official 'counters produce anything contrary, for something the aiji firmly decided to schedule. It was a bit of a non-announcement for most long-scheduled events, particularly those naturally containing fortunate numbers.

We have waited for these numbers, considering recent events. We are, as of a few moments ago, absolutely certain of them. Expect, at the Festivity, investment of my son as my heir.

Investment. Nine *was* a fortunate year, extraordinarily felicitous. But it was also extremely young to be officially set into a will. The traditional number for a child to be invested as heir was ... he recalled ... fifteen, the next entirely felicitous number after nine, and offering the greater maturity of that year as well as a fortunate numerology.

A formal investment, however, fended off inheritance disputes, or at least let them happen during the lifetime of the parent, when they could be quashed with authority.

Tabini's legacy wasn't a set of fishing or hunting rights.

But it *was* a little unexpected, this. For various reasons, Tabini himself hadn't had it. He was not sure it had actually been done for the aijinate since Tabini's grandfather's investment. Certainly it wasn't in Wilson's notes.

My wife is advised, and I am, in two other letters sent with this one, informing my grandmother and Lord Tatiseigi of my decision.

My decision. Not the plural. Not the imperial we. And *not* including Damiri in any implication whatever.

"Trouble, nandi?" Narani asked.

"Not trouble, exactly," he said. "The aiji is going to invest the young gentleman as his heir."

"Indeed." Narani hardly lifted a brow. Surprised? It was rare anything surprised Narani.

"It is, apparently, held secret until the event. Please keep it so." He had no doubts of Narani, who well knew how to keep secrets. "You look surprised, Rani-ji."

"One would say the last three years have certainly urged it."

An overthrow of the government and the whole world in upheaval. That, to say the least, was a reason to have intentions clear.

But one still had to wonder.

Had something significant gone on between Tabini and Damiri in the boy's absence—an understanding reached, or definitively *not* reached, since Tabini had taken initial steps to shift the birthday party from private celebration to national holiday—on the very day they had gone to the spaceport to pick up the boy's guests?

Tabini had evidently started that extreme move while they—including the dowager—were on their way out of the Bujavid, and dropping into a communications blackout. It was as if Tabini had waited for that.

He evidently hadn't mentioned his intentions to Ilisidi—who might have had definite advice about it.

Geigi had hastened the shuttle launch—so the boy had been able to pick up his guests a few days early and enjoy a little vacation before all hell had broken loose.

But had that been the only reason Geigi had moved things up? Had Geigi had a clue this was in the offing?

More, the dowager's servants were threaded all the way through Tabini's household. And yet—had she been surprised by it?

All Tabini needed do to arrange it was sit in his office, write a few orders, seal them and send them: Give me the numbers of the event. Give me the numbers if I do thus and such in addition.

Damn, he *hoped* this didn't mean Tabini had decided on divorce.

His headache threatened to come back in force.

What *had* Tabini discussed with Lord Geigi during their private conversations? And *did* Ilisidi know it was coming?

"Nandi. Will there be an answer?"

He blinked the room back into focus. "Rani-ji. One apologizes. No. No, there will not be an answer to this one. That will do. Thank you."

"Nandi," Narani said, and left the office.

God. If Geigi *had* gone up to the station with orders to get the kids down here . . .

Why? A distraction?

Maybe he was overthinking everything. Things too easily

ran in interlocking circles. That didn't help the headache, either.

But thinking often ran in circles, where Tabini was involved, circles that always ran right back to Tabini's tendency to keep his own counsel.

Tabini's quiet, even joking dismissal of his problems with his Ajuri wife?

Never believe Ajuri's move physically to reach his grandson would be dismissed. No. Tabini had been amazingly forgiving of Komaji's actions.

Damn.

Today was the day the birthday party *should* have returned from Tirnamardi, had everything gone as planned when they'd headed out there. Tabini had launched his own plan, ordered the numbers run—which meant he'd long since *had* to tell the 'counters what he was up to—and *then* having launched the inquiry about numbers—Tabini would also have had to tell the 'counters and kabiuteri what had happened at Tirnamardi and in the Guild. Keeping it from the arbiters of arrangement and felicity risked an infelicity in the goings-on that could turn into a political earthquake.

He'd had his moment of sheer terror pinned beside that shattered door in the Guild. Tabini had probably had his own moment in his sitting room the day after they'd returned, when Cenedi had told him they were going to go into the Guild and restore the old Guild leadership.

Well, if Tabini had surprised his grandmother with his plan to put the boy into his will—Ilisidi had certainly returned the favor with interest.

And God only knew what strings Tabini had just pulled with the College of Numerology to get a good outcome after the upheaval in the Guild.

He got up from his desk. Painkiller and pleasant company had thus far had kept the headache at bay. He backed it off with two deep breaths, then walked out and down the hall to the security station.

His aishid were all in their outer office, sitting in the arc of desks and consoles, apparently in conference.

"One would not wish to interrupt a discussion, nadiin-ji," he said quietly, "but one has just received an advisement from the aiji. He intends formally to name the young gentleman his heir tomorrow, in the Audience Hall."

Four faces showed rare surprise.

"An *investiture*," Algini said, rocking his chair back. It was an obscure word, a variation on the modern legal word he had read it to be. "The Guild does *not* know this. Has he run the numbers?"

"He says they have come back favorable."

Algini asked, warily: "Did you expect this, nandi?"

"In no wise did I."

"Sit with us, Bren-ji," Banichi said, and Bren sat down gingerly on the edge of the counter, closer to eye level. "It explains the aiji's intention in making this a public event. But did he give a reason, Bren-ji?"

"None. It was a very short letter. He has told Damiri-daja. He said he was writing to the dowager and Lord Tatiseigi."

"This was *not* anticipated," Algini said.

Banichi said dryly, "With encouragement, the best 'counters can find felicity in an earthquake. But it *is* useful, *considering* the changes in the Guild, that these 'counters will proclaim felicitous numbers. One trusts he *has* told them about the substantial changes in the Guild."

"It was not in the letter," Bren said, "but this information seems down to the moment."

"At nine years of age," Algini said. "This will surprise everyone."

"Investiture," Bren repeated. "Different from investment?"

"Only that it applies to the aijinate and to the highest rank of the College of Numerology," Algini said. "Tabini-aiji was never invested. Had the dowager strongly opposed his accession, that deficiency could have come into legal question. It has continued to be an issue with his detractors, who claim an infelicity in his accession. Murini of course was not given an investiture, and *he* was certainly an infelicity, with shocks still ongoing. Politically speaking—reviving the ceremony is a brilliant move. Doing it so young is a shock—but it will not be unpopular with the people."

"What does it do?" Bren said. "I know it in terms of a will. The aijinate is not technically inherited. Does it somehow *bind* the legislature?"

"It does not," Banichi said. "In ordinary inheritance, investiture sets business relationships for the future, makes the relationships public. And, especially with a family that has heirs through various contract marriages, it makes the future directorship of the business clear. To pass over an invested heir is only possible if the heir has disgraced the name or committed a crime. Investiture of an heir of the aishidi'tat establishes that the College of Numerology, the chief of which is the only other office that uses investiture, has set a stamp of good numbers on this heir being chosen on this date, and any change in those numbers thereafter has to go back to this point and demonstrate the origin and cause."

"It makes it far more difficult," Jago said, "to argue infelicity of origin."

Origin.

Damiri.

"Nine," Algini said, "carries the potency of an unbeatable number. And it will be six years," Algini said, "before another year almost as felicitous. Under present circumstances, with a second child coming, there is certainly motive."

"This," Bren said, "effectively disinherits the daughter."

"As regards the aishidi'tat, yes. It does. Having his son invested before this second child even exists—one sees, entirely, why he would decide on this course. The ninth year is indisputably fortunate; the next entirely felicitous year, the fifteenth—means six years in which speculation—and politics—might build around a second child. Considering the opposition to certain influences on the young gentleman—it is a statement, and a very timely one."

"It also makes clear," Banichi said, "that, given the history of the persons involved, the aiji-dowager, *not* the aiji-consort, could *instantly* be regent should anything untoward befall Tabini-aiji in the next twelve years. The executor of the inheritance would be, legally, of the aiji's bloodline."

"*That* would cool the opposition," Jago said, "since the persons most likely to plot against Tabini-aiji have no desire to see the dowager in power."

"*And* removing rights of succession for the daughter," Banichi said, "leaves no argument that could make Damiri-daja regent if he leaves the daughter in her care—as he has promised to do. Damiri-daja may have title to her daughter. But that daughter will not have the aishidi'tat. And there has been some speculation about that, should something happen to Cajeiri."

"The city will be wild tomorrow night," Jago said, "once that news is run out."

"An excitement that would tax resources at the best of times," Banichi said. "Bren-ji, we have kept this as quiet as possible—but the Guild had a choice last night, when the new leadership seized control of communications. We could continue the old communication system—which could expose our operations to the remnant we are hunting. We could shut the system down entirely. We could continue to use it but redefine the signals for a given few, which could create dangerous confusion. Or we could go ahead with technical changes, which would lock everybody but a chosen few out of the system entirely. The Council opted for the latter, which will deny access to any units not specifically cleared, until they can be approved into the system."

"We cannot reach the Guild?"

"*We* can. *We*, that is to say we four, the dowager's units, those assigned to the aiji, and those assigned to Lord Tatiseigi, will all be cleared into the system from the beginning. This includes the aiji's under-classified personal guard;

Guild Headquarters, and units that it puts in place in and out of the Bujavid. We have argued to have the young gentleman's bodyguard put onto the system, but thus far we have not moved the Council on that matter, since the Council is still reviewing records and has not cleared them. It is solely on our recommendation and Cenedi's that the Council has not removed that unit from the young gentleman's premises because of the date of their assignment. We will be able to use our equipment through the change, but we *are* noticing small interruptions. We were warned of this. We are assured there will be no interruptions from tomorrow afternoon, but we count that an optimistic assurance. Reliable Guild assets are moving into position right now, but, in the same security considerations, *we* are not informed in all cases where, or in protection of what."

The paidhi-aiji was supposed to stay out of Guild affairs. The resolution of his non-involvement had held, what? Less than a day.

"The Guild, however, does not yet know the aiji's intention for the event," Bren said.

"No," Algini said. "They do not. And this is not information I would gladly commit to the network at the moment."

"One of us," Banichi said, "needs to make another journey down to headquarters, before the crowds make van traffic impossible."

"One hopes they have the headquarters doors back up," Algini said. "They will have to reduce building security and reactivate numerous units to take duty in the streets, one assumes, without full communications resources."

"Will you go?" Banichi asked him.

"Surely you will *not*," Algini said. "And Cenedi has already made one such trip today." Algini rose from his chair and reached for his uniform jacket. "Baji-naji, I should be back in an hour or so. I shall inform Cenedi on my way."

"Take four from Cenedi," Banichi said. "Better this floor be short five guards than have you approaching Headquarters alone. And ask them again to put the young gentleman's bodyguard into the network. Name them again those of the Bujavid guard in whom we have confidence. Tell them— I leave it to you what to tell them. Convince them if you can."

"Yes," Algini said, agreeing, buckled on his sidearm, zipped his jacket, and left.

At least, Bren thought, the kabiuteri and the 'counters had been discreet enough that the dowager's network hadn't picked it up—a testament to the historic integrity of those individuals.

The Bujavid printing office, too, which also prided itself on discretion, had to have gotten its orders now, at least as far as the director, who at least would have cleared the presses to run. The cards to be handed out to the public, as well as the special run for the attendees at the event, would likely be in process within the hour, boxed, and kept in tight security until the official release ... in the Audience Hall, and on the steps. Such public distributions were limited usually to thirty thousand of the first issue, and while atevi crowds understood the principle of keeping an orderly line, the distribution of cards could not be without Guild presence in force.

Unfortunately, at the moment, Guild presence in force had some problems.

"I had best leave you to your concerns," Bren said quietly. "I have no needs at the moment. Jase-aiji is in his room and I am answering correspondence. I shall need nothing today that I foresee, unless the dowager sends for me. I shall ask Jase-aiji to check on the children."

He went back to his office, hoping Algini managed a quick passage, and hoping Algini *had* picked up a unit from the dowager's household.

Traffic would be picking up down at the foot of the hill. The long-awaited Festivity being tomorrow, the streets down in the hotel district would be filling up with booths. By evening, as the crowds grew, anticipating tomorrow, the smaller streets would become absolutely impassable to van traffic. That meant those wealthy sorts accustomed to the luxury of the finer hotels and their ready transportation were going to have to use the common rail or go on foot to their destinations.

It would not likely be as crowded as at the seasonal celebrations, but short notice or not, people rarely lost the chance for a holiday, and would go to the largest town or city they could manage—to Shejidan itself if they were near enough. Certainly the whole city population would be involved in the event. Little eateries and open-air pubs would be busy around the clock. The usual number of individuals would imbibe too much, perhaps spend too much, and definitely eat too much, having a splendid time along the way. Musicians would have country dances chaining through amiable crowds—

Or at least that was the sort of atmosphere one hoped would prevail, given the recent goings-on. Number-readers and 'counters real or self-proclaimed would solicit coins at one-legged wandering booths shaded by the black and gold umbrellas of their trade—apt to be a brisker business than usual, given the rumors bound to be circulating in the drinking establishments. Entertainers were not so formal— they'd take the coins that came their way either in a bowl or a bag, as they circulated through the prospective audience. There'd be drink, food, excess before the small hours of the morning . . . likely a little broken pottery, a few canopies knocked askew . . .

He had never, himself, ventured down into the press. He had the security of the Bujavid. In a year when he had felt competent to navigate the events—security had become far too precarious. But he had been as far as the Bujavid's upper steps, and seen the banners and the press below.

And the colors. Festival clothing observed heraldic colors only for the lords and their households. For everybody else it was a display of only occasional political significance. The lords of provinces and associations would have their

tents going up out on the northeastern shoulder of the Bujavid hill, and outward, in an ancient precedence of place.
Clans major and minor would be flying their flags there and
representing their clan, offering services to any of their own
who might need them—impromptu Contract marriages
were not unknown, sometimes repented with sobriety.

And the tents offered shelter to clan lords, lost children,
and others who might want to take a break from the noisy
goings-on in the streets without braving the crowds on the
way to the hotels.

Najida was entitled to a tent. He had not provided one—
and he should. He was resolved to do it, and to provide
transport for Najida folk who wanted to come so far, and
for staff of his who wanted to go down: they so deserved
that benefit—granted security improved. In a public Festivity, the lords actually resident in the Bujavid would not
likely be braving the press of bodies down in the hotel district; but those seasonally resident in the hotel district might
well take a night in the tents—the noise on the esplanade
was not conducive to sleep. It was ordinarily one night of
moderate rowdiness, a second of mild madness and a great
deal of food and drink . . . utterly, utterly out of the question, but he conceived the oddest longing to go down there
himself—granted his bodyguard ever approved.

Tabini-aiji hadn't had to organize the city event: city officials, guilds, vendors and licensed purveyors of this and
that knew exactly what to do, since they did it several times
a year. The aiji only needed issue one phrase in his decree:
a day of public Festivity . . . and the restaurants would be
preparing to fire up their mobile carts, the vendors would
pick their wares, the district officials would prepare banners
to be hung, and the whole nation would start looking for
train and plane tickets before the echoes died . . .

That would have begun on the very morning they'd been
out riding at Tirnamardi, enjoying life.

Well, it was positive politics, this time, a happy event, a
chance for people to enjoy themselves.

The numbers had turned out, and the aiji was ready to state that there would be *no* consideration of a second child as heir. Whatever numbers had prevailed in Cajeiri's life were taken into account, accepted as favorable, apparently with no more argument.

With human guests to witness it.

With the whole nation to witness it.

Tabini had made his move, one could guess, in some apprehension his own existence was at risk.

Tabini had had no advisement the aiji-dowager was going to make hers in her own fashion, double or nothing, and take on the Guild. They'd surprised each other.

He was not too surprised when a message arrived from the dowager's apartment, under the dowager's personal seal.

It said: *We trust you have heard from our grandson. Of course the numbers are felicitous. We have seen to that.*

Jase-aiji and the young guests will not forget this event. And their attendance will stamp them forever, if they are wise.

Jase-aiji often speaks to the ship and to Lord Geigi. They should not, in decency, be informed yet. Advise him.

The aiji-consort may have her child. We can now be sure of ours.

We are very pleased.

Damn, he thought. But there was nothing in the letter or the conclusion his aishid did not know. It only remained to slip the hint to Jase—without himself being certain quite what the dowager meant by *stamp them forever.*

"I have a notion," he said in that conversation with Jase alone in the sitting room, "that the ship-captains and the human authorities are getting a strong signal from Tabini-aiji and the dowager. One only wishes one understood it." He spoke in Ragi, naturally as breathing, and switched languages, to enter another referent. "A signal about the status of those kids."

"Does she know about the pressure—to send the Reunioners off to Maudit?"

"She may," he said. "Between you and me, it's at least a signal her personal plans don't include Maudit."

"I'm not sure I get the nuance. Am *I* included in this idea?"

"Three kids. One of you. It's an infelicity if combined. The verb governs all preceding."

"So I'm included."

"I think definitely. She's handed you responsibility for those kids. *And* they're not going to Maudit."

Jase had a troubled look in his eyes. "I had both figured on different grounds, actually, before the message. Tell her, since I figure you're the designated channel, and I shouldn't write to her unless she writes to me—"

"That would be true."

"Tell her I'll protect the kids. Personally. And officially. And no, if she asks, I'll keep this from the ship until she agrees I can say something. I answer to Sabin on this, but her word to me was—you make the judgment call."

Sabin, senior captain, was no fool. Let the one of the four fluent in the language and adept in the culture assess what was going on on the planet. And with the four captains in agreement, and with Lord Geigi, head of the atevi space authority, backing them—the Mospheiran station authorities would be fools to back the emigration of the Reunioner refugees, badly as the Mospheirans wanted to shed the Reunioners . . . who *were*, never to forget it, actually under the four captains, *not* the Mospheiran government.

Politics, politics. The aiji-dowager had just, in the atevi proverb, taken hold of the strongest stick to stir the stew, not attempting to use her fingers.

"So the kids aren't going to Maudit," Bren said.

"No," Jase said, a breath of an answer. "Given how things have turned out down here, not any time this century, if I have anything to say about it."

17

It was the day. It was finally the day. Cajeiri was out of bed at the very first urging, dressed in the better-than-usual shirt and trousers his valets presented, and was slipping on a day-coat when Gene and Artur came rolling out to say, somewhat confusingly, "Please enjoy the day you are born!" And then in ship-speak: "Happy birthday, Jeri-ji!"

He grinned. It was impolite, but he was so happy he could hardly help it. He bowed and said, "Thank you, nadiin-ji," just as the other lump in the bed sat up and became Irene, with her pale hair every which way. "Oh!" she said, and grabbed her nightrobe in embarrassment, with Eisi and Liedi standing there, and herself where it was not quite proper for her to be.

"We layered the bedclothes, nadiin-ji," Cajeiri said with a calm little bow, "and we are all very proper, all of us."

"Indeed, nandi," Eisi said, unperturbed, and about that time Veijico and Antaro turned up out of their room, in proper dress uniform.

"Happy birthday," Irene said, from her seat deep in bedclothes. "Happy birthday, Jeri-ji!"

"A felicitous ninth!" Antaro called out. "Our young gentleman has reached his fortunate year!"

The other door opened. Lucasi and Jegari were there, half in uniform. "Felicitations, Jeri-ji!"

"Felicitations, nandi," Eisi said with a solemn bow, and "Felicitations!" Liedi said.

Boji just shrieked and rattled his cage in excitement.

"Your honored uncle bids you and your guests to breakfast," Eisi said. "As you please, nandi."

It was the best morning ever. It truly was.

It was the best breakfast ever, because Uncle's cook had been asking him ever since they arrived what his favorite things were for every meal, and it was everything he liked in one huge breakfast, just himself and his guests, because staff said Great-uncle was having breakfast with Great-grandmother, and they would all meet for a state lunch at his father's apartment. Nand' Jase was to come for him half an hour before noon, but the state lunch was for mid-afternoon because there would be no supper, only the Festivity buffet in the Audience Hall.

That was the gruesome part. He could not have his aishid with him at the moment—Jegari had told him before he and the others had left—because *they* had to go ahead to nand' Bren's apartment and talk to Tano and Algini about codes, which was why they were missing breakfast, and they would meet him there when Jase-aiji brought them all there.

That was one thing he wished somebody had asked him. He would have had cook send a special breakfast for everybody.

Then Madam Saidin stopped him as he left the breakfast room and handed him a rolled paper.

"This is from your father the aiji, young gentleman, your speech to memorize for the Festivity tonight."

"A long one?" he asked anxiously.

"Only a few lines," she assured him. "Very short."

Well, that was not too bad. And Madam would not lie to him. So they all trooped back to the guest quarters, his guests all in good humor, to sit and let breakfast settle for two hours. *He* got to change to court dress, at least all of the suit except the coat, and his guests got to sit about in comfortable clothes. He was envious of that.

He had to suffer a scratchy flood of lace and memorize a stupid speech.

He unrolled the paper to find out what he had to deal with. And it was not three lines, it was three whole paragraphs.

It started:

I thank all my family, all my associates, all my allies, all my family's allies, all you good people. I am fortunate nine, today, and I thank you for coming. I thank my mother, who has done her best to guide me, and my great-grandmother . . .

And it went on to say things like:

. . . lords of the associations, lords of the districts, lords of the provinces, thank you.

. . . urging cooperation toward a prosperous and felicitous year . . .

He dropped into a chair and went on staring at it. It was a horrid lot of categories to remember in order, and his mind was every which way today.

But he could do it. He had memorized all the districts and the capitals and the imports and exports and the lords and their heirs and their families. He had memorized the names of the treaties, in order, that had built the aishidi'tat. He saw them, and he kept thinking of heraldry and emblems and imports and treaties, when he needed to be thinking about the words.

He had memorized the descent of his family from the War of the Landing.

He had memorized . . .

With a prodigious shriek, Boji streaked to the chair, seized the paper and, trailing his chain, carried it off to the top of the bureau.

"One is extremely *sorry,* nandi!" Liedi exclaimed.

"Let us not startle him," he said calmly. "Close all the doors."

They would not make *that* mistake.

But all of them stalking Boji made Boji nervous, and with the paper in his teeth, Boji leapt for a tapestry railing, then for the crystal chandelier, setting it rocking and jingling, but trailing the chain.

Eisi snagged it, and tugged. Boji jumped for Eisi's shoulder, sending the chandelier swinging wildly. Snagged, Boji threw a screaming tantrum and bared his teeth, crumpling the paper in his bony little fist when Eisi tried to get it away from him.

"Boji!" Cajeiri said sharply, and Boji looked his way, wide-eyed above the mangled paper in his paws. "Come here! Come!"

Boji fixed on him. That was a good sign. He held out his hand, and Boji nipped the paper in his teeth and took a flying leap for his arm, where he wrapped himself with all four limbs, Eisi still holding the chain.

"Give it to me, Boji," Cajeiri said. "Give it to me." To his surprise, a little tug freed the mangled paper from Boji's hands. He took the chain from Eisi and, since he was still in vest and shirt, he let Boji run up to his shoulder and perch there, even if his feet hurt. He had the chain. He had the paper. His guests were all amazed and amused and impressed.

He gave the paper a little snap and casually handed Boji off to Liedi, feeling very grown-up, very dignified. Even Great-grandmother could not have called Boji to good behavior. But *he* had.

"That's pretty good!" Gene said.

"He's adding it up," Irene said. "He knows who to salute, doesn't he?"

"Smart," Artur agreed.

He tried not to seem surprised at all. He uncrumpled Father's letter, which had gotten chewed a bit, and had holes here and there, but it was good enough. He glanced at it enough to know all the words were there.

"Are parid'ji relatives to atevi?" Artur asked, which was

a question that upset some people, mani said, but Cenedi had said probably, and his tutor had said . . .

"Maybe," he said. "There were bigger. There still could be in the mountains on the Southern Island, maybe even this far north. The parid'ji used to live as far south as Shejidan, but all that forest went away. There used to be forest all the way across the Atageini ridge and clear on to the mountains, a long, long time ago. And there was forest all over the Southern Island, except the coast. But that was before the three islands blew up."

"Volcanoes?" Artur asked in ship-speak. "Mountains and fire?"

"Big explosion!" he said. "Volcanoes." He wanted to remember that word. "The big map in my office." That sounded so important. "I can show you where."

Their eyes lit up. They were excited.

So had he been excited when his new tutor had told him one of the isles was reportedly reappearing above the waves and smoking—and he had immediately had a wicked thought that nand' Bren's boat might be able to go to the Southern Island and even down to the Southern Ocean . . .

But then his tutor had talked about the weather in the Southern Ocean, which was why ships did not sail any further south than from the Marid up the west coast, and why the seas between Mospheira and the mainland were far calmer than the open seas where the winds blew all the way around the world without any land to stop them. When the three islands had blown up, that had been the barrier to the Southern Island's east coast, so even going there now was dangerous.

Lord Machigi's ships, big metal ships, were going to sail all the way around the teeth of the southern shore, and clear up to mani's territory in the East. That was part of the new agreement between mani and Lord Machigi. And nand' Bren said they thought they could do it, if the space folk helped them. He should ask nand' Jase how they could do that . . .

But the question at hand was about parid'ji and their ancestors, and how the forests had used to be. So with a grand flourish of his cuff lace, he took a stylus and pointed out the continental divide on his beautiful wall map, and told his guests about the white-faced parid'ji which people had used to think were dead people come back to visit them ...

"Ghosts!" Irene reminded him of the word.

"Ghosts!" he said. And he knew a lot about the superstitions of the East, which he had told them on the ship, in the tunnels, where he had told them about the visiting dead near Malguri and all sorts of scary things they had liked.

They were excited, and with the map he could show them all sorts of things, and every location of every ghost story he knew about ...

Right until Madam knocked at the outer door and brought Uncle's staff to gather up his guests' wardrobe on racks to take to nand' Bren's apartment. He had lost track of the time he had. It was almost time for nand' Jase to come get them.

Well, that was all right. He memorized fast. He pulled the mangled paper from his coat pocket and he would be very careful, when staff wanted him to change to his Festival best, to be sure that paper went with him. He was sure he would get plenty of time to memorize the speech once he reached his father's apartment. He always had to do a lot of waiting about: everybody *said* they needed him, but it usually amounted to him sitting in a corner bored and waiting while his father attended some business that had come up.

The rack of court clothes rolled out a back servant's passage, disappearing into the hidden corridors to reappear, one was certain, in the back halls of nand' Bren's apartment, part of the mysteries of servants.

And it had no sooner rattled off out of the bedroom than Madam reported Jase-aiji had arrived to escort them.

"Here we go," Gene said, as if they were about to take off and fly.

"Here we go," he echoed. He had yet to be presented his court dress coat. He had on only its vest, a very elegant black and gold. He carried the paper in his hand, and let Madam show them out into the corridor and as far as the front door.

Nand' Jase waited outside, with his bodyguard in their scary, noisy white armor—but with the faceplates up, so it was just Kaplan and Polano, familiar and lively, in all that strange skin. Mani's guard, Casimi, had come along, too, perhaps for the numbers. Eisi and Liedi were going to go along to nand' Bren's to help his guests dress—but also because nand' Jase was not as good with Ragi as nand' Bren, and Kaplan and Polano could hardly put words together.

His valets helped him put on the beautiful court coat Uncle's tailor had made him—he liked the lapels and wide cuffs, especially, which were inky black, and the rest was all gold and black brocade, the black shiny and the gold sparkly. He slipped the paper into the broad right pocket, patted it flat as he went out, and gave a little bow to Madam Saidin, concerned that his parents might not let him come back this evening, or maybe not even tomorrow, once his parents got their hands on him.

"Thank you, Saidin-daja," he said. "One hopes one is coming back. Thank cook and thank my great-uncle."

Great-uncle had not shown up to see them off. But he would see Uncle at lunch, he was quite certain.

And maybe if mani could not get him free of his parents' apartment, nand' Bren could invite him, and make everything work out.

The youngsters' wardrobe preceded them, a rattling arrival in the middle hall—there was no missing it. Bren straightened his cuffs, done up in his own court dress, there being no sense dressing twice in the day for an appointment at lunch.

Not so with the youngsters, who arrived in the foyer all shyness and anxiety, with nervous little bows.

"You're doing fine," he said in ship-speak, at which there were deep breaths of relief. "Do you understand the schedule? Captain Graham will be back in a moment. He'll be with you through all the events and you'll need to stay close to him at all times. Make yourselves comfortable in the sitting room. Is there any problem?"

"No, sir," Irene said. "We're all right."

"Don't be nervous. Come." He showed them into the sitting room, where young staff had laid out tea and very small sandwiches. "There will likely be a very fancy lunch, but you *daren't* spill anything, and not everything will be safe to eat. My advice is eat all the sandwiches you want before you go, so you're not that hungry, and when it comes to the buffet tonight—this is very important—stay to the desserts."

"Neat!"

He had to grin. "I know. Not a hard idea. The desserts are safe—if I spot one that isn't, I'll advise Jase. The rolls are safe. Staff is supposed to be careful of you. But if you want to try anything, ask Captain Graham and don't experiment, not even a taste, no matter how good it looks: we don't want you to spend tonight in hospital. There's one tea you absolutely shouldn't have. He'll warn you. Fill up here where you know the food is safe, eat very carefully at table and don't risk spilling anything on your clothes. It's going to be a long, long day. You've been excellent guests. Keep it going just another few hours. It's very, very important to Cajeiri that you not make a mistake."

"Yes, sir." Heads bobbed. Looks were very earnest.

"Anything we can do, anything you need, or if you're in distress, Jase first, then me, or any of my staff. Got it?"

"Yessir."

Excellent kids, he thought. Kids who'd been warned within an inch of their lives—but kids who'd borne up in good humor through a hell of a lot that hadn't been in anyone's planning.

"You've been good beyond any expectation. Carry this evening off for him and there's an outside chance we can send you somewhere you can have some fun, maybe with the Taibeni."

"The mecheita-riders?" Eyes went large.

"They're completely loyal to Cajeiri. A very safe place. And I'll do everything I can to arrange it, if you just do everything you're asked, be patient with delays, and don't mess it up. Twelve more hours, and if the aiji's enemies don't create a problem, you're out of it and clear. Jase will be here in a moment, and he'll fill in the rest for you."

God, he *hoped* he was telling the kids the truth. The combined force of staring, believing eyes went right to the nerves, while his *if* was still a very big word.

"Nandi," the major domo said, welcoming Cajeiri and his bodyguard into the foyer. Jase-aiji paid courteous nods and immediately left, going back up the hall. "Welcome home, young gentleman."

"Nadi," Cajeiri said with the requisite little bow. Servants were close about them—until the ones near the inner hall folded backward in startlement, ducking heads, as his *father* arrived, his father likewise in court dress, and solemn, and accompanied by two of his bodyguard. All the servants backed up, clearing room, and Cajeiri gave a deeper bow.

"Son of mine," his father said solemnly. "You look very fine."

"One is gratified, honored Father."

"And everything is going smoothly?" his father asked, coming very close to him.

"Yes, honored Father."

His father took him by the arm very lightly and maneuvered him so that he could speak close to his ear. "Son of mine, you look particularly elegant, and so does your aishid—a credit to your great-uncle's household, but one needs to forewarn you. Your mother is already having a difficult day, and so is the staff. Your mother had secretly ordered a coat and vest from your regular tailor, and she was not willing to deliver it to your great-uncle's house, but your tailor is greatly out of sorts about this, and this being her present to you—it has set her out of sorts. If you wish to please your mother—and one advises you this would be very desirable today—send staff to your suite and have them bring the black and red brocade instead."

He *liked* his black and gold brocade coat, which his mother would call too old for him, but he was *nine* today, and he had three red and black ones, besides. He said quietly: "Uncle had Master Kusha come in because of my guests, honored Father. They had nothing suitable, and Master Kusha and his staff worked very hard."

"One will do everything to honor master Kusha's efforts, but you would not be politic to ignore your mother's gift, son of mine. And besides, the 'counters have figured red into the numbers."

He was not happy. But he understood. "Yes," he said, and to Jegari: "You know my coats. Can you recognize the new one?"

"Assuredly, nandi," Jegari said, and with a bow to his father, hurried off through the servants and down the inner hall toward their suite. Cajeiri began sadly unbuttoning the elegant black and gold coat, and his father helped him, with that and with the vest, right there in the foyer in front of everybody. He was sure he blushed, and he was angry about it, but his father was on *his* side, which was the important thing. And he knew how much politics with his mother mattered, for everybody's good.

Next time the 'counters did the numbers, however, he swore he was going to have his say in it. And wear black and gold if he wanted to.

But it would be his thirteenth birthday before he ever got another festivity, and his fifteenth before another big one, which he swore was not going to be *public,* either. He was verging on a bad mood. And could not afford to sulk.

"Very well done," his father said, handing off his favorite new coat and vest to the major domo, who gave it to the servants to deal with. "Be agreeable, do not frown at your mother, and thank her nicely for the new coat and vest, if you can possibly manage it. Count it training."

"Yes," he said. By then Jegari was back, with the new coat and vest, which at least went well with the black trousers and boots, the new vest being shiny black with glittering red woven in, and the coat being nearly all black with a little red—the vest at least fit well, as it should, and the coat fit, and his father with his own hands helped him do all the buttons, in front of all the servants and their bodyguards.

"One is very impressed," his father said. "You have grown in more than height this year, son of mine. One is *very* proud."

That was twice for blushing, but this was for a different reason. He gave a little bow as his father finished the last adjustment of his lace cuffs. "Thank you, honored Father. One will try very hard today."

"Come to the sitting room," his father said, and showed him the way as if he were an adult guest in his own home.

His mother was there, in black and green, Ragi and Atageini colors combined. She looked pleased as he came in, and mani had taught him how the game was played. He bowed to his mother, who did not get up—getting up was increasingly hard for her—and bowed a second and a third time, and said, without any sulking,

"Thank you for your gift, honored Mother. One was quite surprised."

"You look very fine," she said, looking extremely pleased. "How grown-up you look."

"One is happy to be a fortunate age," he said. *"Thank* you, honored Mother."

There was, of course, tea. There were very fancy teacakes, one of a flavor he did not like, but his mother did, and he got it by accident. He took one bite, and nerved himself and swallowed the rest of it, smiling and washing it down with tea, thinking it was rather like the change of coats. One could get through anything, if there was a reason.

"The numbers of the day are fortunate," she said. "And

the whole country has turned out to celebrate the day, son of mine. The banners are out and the whole city will be in festival. You may see them from my windows."

"I shall look," he said. He truly had no desire even to go into the nursery, which had all the windows, but he thought perhaps he should, at least once, so when he had had his tea, he did go, and stood with his mother looking out past the filmy lace of the nursery windows. Very small and distant, there were colorful banners, and the tops of the tents, and the main street, even farther, crowded with people.

"The city is happy," she said, with her hand on his shoulder, "and so should you be."

"One is indeed happy," he said dutifully, already wishing to be back in the sitting room. "One is very happy."

"Your father favors you," she said, and her fingers pressed his shoulder hard. "He favors you so extremely your sister will rely on you for the least scrap of his favor. *Say* to me that she will not go wanting."

He did not look at her until one fast, wary glance, and she was gazing out the windows, into the hazy distance.

"I shall take care of my sister," he said, and her hand pressed once, then relaxed. "Have I not told you I shall? If she relies on me, I shall be her older brother."

"As you should be," she said. "Always remember that."

An uneasy thought struck him. "*You* will be here, will you not?"

"That is always at your father's pleasure. But someday it will be at yours."

"You are my mother," he said with complete determination. "I only have one."

"That is good to know," she said. "Shall we return to the sitting room?"

He was only too glad to do that.

Getting three kids into unfamiliar garments and giving them a meaningful lesson on *how* to keep the cuff lace out of the soup and the soup from landing on one's collar lace was no small undertaking. Turn your wrist to the outside covered the first; and Keep your chin up was the other. They practiced with water, as less damaging than soup.

"Very well done," Jase said. "I shall try not to be the one to have soup go astray. You all have your speeches, if you need them."

"Yes, nandi," Gene said, with a very proper bow. "And one will pay very close aggravation to persons."

"Attention," Bren corrected quietly. It was a very easy mistake. "Elegantly done, Gene-nadi."

"Attention," Gene repeated, a little chagrined. "Yes, sir."

Bren set his hand on Gene's shoulder. "You three are extraordinary. Keep up the manners just until midnight, and don't panic if you make a mistake. You're all three very small, people won't possibly mistake you for adults, and while children have all kinds of leeway . . . everyone's *very* impressed when they get things right. So just bow and apologize, and if you really have an accident, you have several spare shirts in my apartment. We *can* rescue you if we must, but we'd so much rather not. And the farther we get from the apartment the harder it becomes. Security's extremely tight."

"Yes, sir," Gene said in ship-speak. "We won't mess things up. We really won't."

"Good. Good." Bren let the boy go and cast a look at Jase. "We're about due. Dur's just made it up to the floor. I need to go. If you can follow with the youngsters, we'll expect you in about ten minutes. Kaplan and Polano are ready?"

"Suited up and ready," Jase said. "We'll be right over."

"See you," Bren said, and went out to the hall. Staff told staff, and his bodyguard showed up a moment later, Banichi with them, *without* his sling, at first glance, but then one noted the black, slim support for the injured arm.

Good for that, he thought. He had his hair arranged to hide the stitches, had a little paper of pills, not for atevi consumption, in his right pocket, and a second number of pills, not for human consumption, in the inside pocket of his dress coat, nicely done up, not to mention the discreet little pistol he had in his right-hand coat pocket ... he had not carried it to the Guild. It did not mean he could not carry it to Tabini's apartment.

"Nichi-ji," he said as his aishid joined him. "We are agreed, are we not, each to take a rest as appropriate?"

"We are agreed," Banichi said.

"Do we have a promise, Nichi-ji?"

"We have an agreement, Bren-ji."

It was as good as he was getting. Narani opened the door for them, and they walked out and down the short distance to the aiji's door—which, as it chanced, was still open, Lord Tatiseigi having just arrived with, as it proved, the aiji-dowager.

One simply stood a bit back and let that party sort itself out. There was some little hushed and prolonged to-do involving a coat, about which neither was pleased. But Ilisidi said, "It is the boy's event, Tati-ji. He will wish not to affront his mother."

"His mother," Tatiseigi muttered, but said no more of it.

One didn't ask. One was simply glad to get through the door, past the foyer, and into the enforced civilization of the dining room, where, indeed, the younger and the elder Dur were already present, and the formalities were a welcome relief.

The dining table was at full extent, with places for thirty-three persons, including Jase and the three youngsters, and an assortment of lords and spouses. It was diplomacy at full stretch. Even Lord Keimi had come in from Taiben—very, very rare that he put in a court appearance; but it was a pleasant arrival. Haijden and Maidin were there. And Jase and Cajeiri's guests arrived, Jase resplendent in the borrowed coat and the youngsters in immaculate and proper court dress—shy, and a little hesitant about getting to seats, but Jase, who could read the name tags, settled them properly, and sat down in a seat of high rank next to Tatiseigi, who was family—with the youngsters at his left, as Cajeiri's guests. As minors in Jase's care, they were seated far higher than their rank would have allowed.

But good-natured Maidin was next to them, and Dur was across the table, which was a very deft bit of diplomacy. The servants brought a cushion for Irene—the boys being just the little degree taller that made a cushion a bit too much; and the youngsters sat with their hands tucked and their eyes darting about the glittering table and the glittering guests—very, very quiet, the three, on best behavior.

Other lords arrived, the Calrunaidi, strangers to the aiji's inner circle, but on the rise; the Brusini and the Drusi, with current spouses. The company stretched to the end of the table with other arrivals, and the noise level even of quiet conversation became significant.

The youngsters sat staunchly silent, already stuffed with little sandwiches and teacakes, and shyly responding to servants' questions or deferring them to Jase, who ordered them small glasses of fruit drink ... which they very judiciously sipped without much tilting.

The table was full. Conversation remained polite. Bren and Jase had followed their own prescription of sandwiches and teacakes to assure they had enough to eat *before* they had to deal with a full-blown state affair of thirteen courses, three or four involving gravy.

The doors to the hall opened, and Tabini, Damiri, and Cajeiri joined them, the boy in a black and red brocade he had not been wearing when he had stopped by the apartment to drop his guests off. No. He had definitely changed coats. *That* had been the controversy.

Bren rose, as they all did except Ilisidi. He seated himself when everyone sat down, and the servants began moving about, supplying more wine, or a change of drinks as the kitchen readied the first plates.

There were introductions all around, Calrunaidi being new to the aiji's table, and Jase not having been at such an event in years. Cajeiri was experienced in state functions—

he sat primly proper, kept a pleasant face, accepted the appetizer and didn't touch it . . . the proper fate of that appetizer in Bren's own opinion, but Ilisidi relished it.

They had twelve more courses to survive. He ate a very little of very mild things, he was careful about the wine, no matter how tempted, and he listened far more than he spoke. He had the edge of a headache already, and dared not take another pill. The youngsters pushed food about on their plates and only ventured a taste now and again of something which would not drip.

Typical of very large gatherings in Tabini's apartment, only Tabini's bodyguards and Cenedi were in evidence: Jago and Tano had sworn to him that Banichi was going to commandeer a chair in the security station and stay there—at very least.

He wished the paidhi-aiji had that option. But he sincerely hoped Banichi was doing exactly that.

They served the seventh course, pickled eggs—one thought of Kaplan and Polano, and Bren wished they had the ones he was served.

Artur made the mistake of moving a dish to accommodate a servant's reach, and a water goblet nearly went over. Conversation stopped, Artur turned bright red and apologized very quietly. The servant bowed profoundly, embarrassed, and Jase quietly reassured the boy. More, Lord Maidin engaged the youngsters in a kindly way, and the conversation continued, a welcome distraction.

Near the head of the table, Cajeiri relaxed, let go a pent breath, and the dowager kept Tabini and Damiri engaged without missing a beat, while Tatiseigi listened.

Artur remained nervous and quiet, but disaster, thank God, had not happened. Down the table, meanwhile, one of the adult guests had a red wine droplet slowly inching its way down the side of the glass, which Bren watched in dazed, edge-of-headache fascination—until a watchful servant, during service, deftly blotted it with a folded napkin.

Luncheon continued, relentless, to the very last sweet

and elaborate confection, a sort of fruity cookie with icing, which the youngsters did not resist; but crumbs were no great calamity.

They had lived through it. And no one had gotten into an argument. The dowager and the aiji-consort had sat across the table from one another without so much as frowning. Lord Tatiseigi had managed a much better mood than he had in the foyer, and he was about to become the center of attention as they moved on to the next event of the day.

It was a great relief.

"We are due in the lower hall," Tabini said from the head of the table. "We are gratified by the attendance of our intimate guests—and by the unexpected grace of our great ally, one of the ship-aijiin, who has visited our table for the first time in years, and by the attendance of our son's guests, who have braved the journey itself and behaved very sensibly under extremely trying circumstances. Let us welcome them."

"Indeed," most said, while the youngsters looked bewildered—until Jase cued them to bow in place and accept the compliment.

"Now we shall go downstairs," Tabini said, rising, "and we ask our guests to observe security and keep themselves and staff within the secure area."

That was the standard request for a formal affair in the lower hall. Events were—one surmised, without looking at a watch—proceeding exactly on schedule. He rose as the others did. Irene slid off her chair with a thump and tried not to look responsible. Bren smiled at her—it was far less racket than most of the heavy chairs made. Over all it was a good show they had made, and he wanted to tell the youngsters so, but there was Lord Calrunaidi looking to renew acquaintance and to comment on the delicacy and manners of the human youngsters—"They are the young gentleman's age? So very small, so nicely mannered."

"I shall relay it to them, nandi. Thank you on their behalf.

They have worked very hard to acquire court manners to honor the young gentleman."

"Excellently done," Calrunaidi said, and nodded to the youngsters across the table. "Excellently done," he repeated, a little more loudly, as if volume would help understanding.

"Thank you, nandi," Irene managed to say, and everyone bowed.

"So grown-up!" Lord Calrunaidi said. "Excellently, excellently done!" One thought distractedly that if he could have come by young humans as guests for his own remote household he would have ordered a handful of them. It was one conquest made, and of a rising star at court.

Jase simply and efficiently marshaled the youngsters into a close knot and had them following him as they headed for the door and the outer hall. Jase's guards were standing by; and they would take the service elevator down—one of the aiji's guard would get them to the lower hall with a minimum of fuss and back through the servant passages to reach their station.

Impeccable in timing, Banichi and the rest of Bren's aishid fell right in with him as he reached the foyer, right behind Lord Tatiseigi's guard. Banichi was, he was glad to see, looking perfectly fine, perfectly in order, and he *hoped* Banichi had had a chance to lie down for the interval.

They exited to the hall, walked at a leisurely pace toward the lift that would take them downstairs, and stood about the lift door awaiting their own turn, just behind Jase and the youngsters, who were trying to wait quietly and politely.

The lift came back: they made it in, with only his aishid, the youngsters and Jase.

"Well done," Bren found the chance to say. "Just do as you've been doing."

"Sir," Gene said; and, "I almost ruined everything," Artur said.

"Not nearly," Bren said. "You did well. Perfectly well. Relax. Everyone relax."

Deep breaths. And the lift reached bottom and let them out into the ornate lower hall, which instantly drew looks from the youngsters, who had never yet seen the most ornate hall in the entire Bujavid. There were plinths and pedestals, vases and statues, every door carved and no few gilded, not to mention the sculpted arches of the high ceilings and the carved jade screens and the jeweled live-fire lamps and the milling crowd of not-quite-intimate guests in full court finery in the intersection with the main hall.

"Oh, my God," he heard Irene say, the youngsters quite frozen in the path of his bodyguard, and the lift needing to return for more guests.

"The Bujavid at full stretch," Jase said, deftly steering Irene aside and catching Gene by the shoulder. "Just stay with me. I'll be staying close with nand' Bren. We're relying on his security. Don't stray."

Tano and Algini were staying with Jase to assist him. Banichi and Jago were at Bren's back. The main hall was a moving kaleidoscope of people—a good number of them in Guild black, the one element of the Guild presence that a Guild sifting of their membership couldn't ask to stand down. The lords of clans, districts, and provinces—and in many cases the managers of regional businesses and civil offices *had* their own security presence, and in all but a few instances it was Guild. It was a security exposure which, given the nature of the event, there was no preventing, and now came the truly worrisome part of the evening. They had tens of thousands of people down on the esplanade and coming partway up the steps to the Bujavid because of the card distributions. The Nine Doors were shut, but they also had reliable guards both out on the landing and inside, between the long steps and this lower, usually public, hall—

Presumably, since Algini's advisement to the Guild, the Guild had positioned as many units as possible out into the streets to keep order.

But nobody could ever guarantee the streets against fools, and with the best intention in the world, the Guild could not guarantee the man'chi of every member of every unit and every servant in the lower hall. The Shadow Guild had never had any hesitation about civilian casualties—or any other sort. They only hoped that the Shadow Guild was without orders at the moment.

Bren's heartbeat kicked up as they moved through the crowd—pressing forward, not letting themselves be cut off, on the general path toward the museum—the fivefold doors near the main public entry. Display cases stood as pillars in the middle of the hall, the very first displays of state treasures an ordinary citizen would meet as he came into the lower hall—the emphasis this season was on porcelains.

All five museum doors were open, the space beyond lit with spots of electric light on particular glass cases. Into that central doorway Tabini and Damiri went, with the dowager, and Cajeiri, and Lord Tatiseigi, and the paidhi-aiji had to keep up, maintaining the set order as, within the crowd, other lords began to seek their own assigned order of entry.

It was Lord Tatiseigi's event, a part of his priceless porcelain collection having been shipped in for public exhibit. Now the opening of the exhibit would be associated, in national memory, with the investiture of his nephew as future aiji of the aishidi'tat. Lord Tatiseigi could hardly be happier . . . that face was not accustomed to smiles, and he clearly had one as he passed the doors.

Bren passed the doors himself, under the scrutiny of the museum's assigned security, into a vast hall of spotlighted cases containing small tea services and porcelain vases, ancient cloisonné armor—he was himself pleased to have a chance to see it, knowing it was an unprecedented appearance of the treasures. So many exhibits came and went in the Bujavid, as convenient as a venture downstairs—but he often enough found himself missing the very ones he most wanted to see. This was a very welcome exception.

And the youngsters, who had known only the featureless, identical panels and muted tones of the ship's passenger section and the stations—they were in awe of living trees and ordinary rocks, convolute porcelains and glittering metalwork and any other texture the world offered them.

More, they had begun to recognize things. One case stood central, centerpiece of the armor exhibits, and they went right for it: a mecheita-rider's cloisonné armor, on a model mecheita gleaming in gold accents and war-capped tusks.

From that extraordinary figure, their attention flitted to the tapestry backdrop of mountains and woods, and a company of riders worked in the muted colors of paeshi silk. And they pointed out the fortress on the hill. Would earth-born youngsters even notice the details of a tapestry like that?

He wasn't sure. He might have, having the interests he did. But he had never been the average youngster. That was how he had landed here, tonight.

"Come in, nandiin, nadiin," Lord Tatiseigi said, over a provided microphone. "You see pieces which have never traveled outside the Padi Valley, some of which have never entered the national registry until now. Please take your time, and please accept a card for the exhibit itself."

There was a little murmur of pleased surprise. Signed and ribboned cards were always welcome. And the crowd, cleared bit by bit through the guarded doors, began to disperse through the various aisles of the main exhibit area, and through archways that led to exhibits that were also open this evening—related items, one noted, which placed the Atageini treasures in historical context.

The museum director took the microphone, and began a formal address, thanking the aiji, the aiji-consort, the aiji-dowager, the heir, and Lord Tatiseigi, and then managing a neat segue to future exhibits of ancient blackware and brownware.

And back again, as all but one of the five doors shut, greatly reducing the ventilation in the room, and not helping the general noise level.

The Director segued neatly back again to the exhibit, naming the major eras and regions of porcelain production in terms of glazes and clays subdivided and categorized in a history that went far back before the aishidi'tat.

". . . you will note, in the fourth row, the legendary Southern blues of the pre-disaster period . . ."

Bren actually understood Southern blues: the beautiful glassy aqua color that could no longer be made in the old way, since the Great Wave had wiped out the Southern Island culture. Tatiseigi did indeed have a collection that rivaled that in Lord Machigi's district, and one could only surmise what had been lost in that long-ago cataclysm.

". . . in the peripheral cases, and beyond the western archway, you will discover an interesting sequence of massive figured ware, then the freestanding figures of the Age of the First Northern Rulers, which followed the collapse of the Southern Island . . ."

That was suddenly interesting. The theory that the elaborate figured porcelains of the current age were an outgrowth of the pillar-like Reverence Statues of the northern lands, as the north met porcelain techniques from the survivors of the Southern Island culture . . . that was a notion he had heard, and he was familiar, too, with the theory that there was possibly a relationship to the Grandmother Stones of the tribal peoples, with which every museum-goer on Mospheira was familiar. Those were all but unknown on the mainland . . . except where the Edi and the Gan had settled.

But that theory, their guide said, was mired in controversy involving the origin of the tribal peoples themselves, who refused to accept the notion that they were part of the northern culture. They maintained they were descended from former lords of the Southern Island, and that the Grandmother Stones of the Southern Island had been swept away in the flood.

There was some support for the southern origin: they were a matriarchal people, unlike the patriarchal north.

But there was political heat behind the question, and the Director immediately veered off the topic, beginning to acknowledge the various notables present, a long, long list that was going to take the next quarter hour at least.

Bren bowed a little as his name was mentioned, fairly early in the list. The youngsters, who had showed a very human tendency to flit this way and that, took Jase's cue to stand respectfully and bow, as Jase and the three of them were mentioned . . .

Then, inevitably drawn by what glittered, and by objects they readily recognized—they were off to peer through the glass at a tall vase covered in parid'ja figures.

The youngsters had drawn attention of their own, admirers of the artworks glancing aside and moving back from the children and whispering discreetly behind hands or printed exhibit guides.

But the fact that the children bowed properly when cued amazed and mollified the onlookers, much as if a trio of parid'ji had shown evidence of civilization. And despite their somewhat excessive energy, they were not misbehaving. Algini and Tano and Jase together availed to keep three youngsters under relatively close management. And onlookers began to relax and smile, even laughing, watching them as much as the exhibit.

Cajeiri likely ached to go through the exhibit with just as much energy—but of course he didn't leave his parents' side. Nor could the youngsters go to him or even so much as wave at him, no. It was just not done.

That was the sad part of the affair, one he would mend if he possibly could . . . but there was no help for it. Tabini, and therefore Cajeiri and Damiri, were constantly engaged with important guests this evening, constantly besieged with introductions and well-wishes—a state affair in full spate, and leading to an announcement that would set the boy further apart from ordinary life. What could one say against it? It was the boy's rank. It was what he did. It was what he was born for and would always have to do.

Maybe, Bren thought, it was the boy's years on the starship that had sharply defined him—years like his father's at Malguri, in the dowager's care. Tabini had *sent* the boy up to the station *with* the dowager—and now Tabini had brought three human kids down here, for reasons that a human fenced off very carefully, saying he still didn't understand the motive. He had to be careful of *thinking* he understood the motive ... it was a potentially dangerous step across the interface, the very thing he had been supposed to prevent.

But maybe the motive wasn't alien from atevi politics. Damiri hadn't been happy with the dowager from before her son had been taken up to the space station and put in the dowager's care—while Tabini had drawn the dowager closer and closer, from far back.

He should know. *He'd* been the initial lure, to get Ilisidi out of Malguri.

He'd had no idea, at that point, how very deeply Ilisidi had detested his predecessor in the paidhi's office.

Tabini had given him a gun, taken him target-shooting quite illegally, in terms of treaty law—and sent him off to visit his grandmother.

How did a sane man interpret *that* move? Did the elements add as straightforwardly as they might in a human situation?

Maybe was the same with Tabini's inviting the kids down now. Experience us. Know us. Make up your own minds. Show us who you are.

They were so damned *young*.

But could a boy brought up in the heart of court intrigue be that young, or that innocent?

The boy stood, elegant and conspicuous, in a light that made that black coat spark red fire, his darkness and that brightness as ornate as the exhibits, beside a father of which he was the smaller image, beside a smiling mother who, despite her condition, looked as perfect, as iconic, as any cloisonné image in the cases.

What do I do, he asked himself, *to protect this boy? What can I do?*

Keep those kids out of trouble. That's one.

The museum was crowded with the elite—typical of such events, Guild presence had diminished down to two bodyguards for the lesser guests, in the interest of saving space, and the other half of those units would be occupying the hall outside, reinforcing Guild presence on the lower floor. The echoing buzz of voices took on a surreal quality, and he began to realize his thinking had grown just a bit distracted. It was too warm in the room. There were very few benches, and he longed for one . . . but there were none vacant.

"How are you?" he asked Banichi.

"I am not in difficulty," Banichi said. "Are you?"

"No," he said, an outright lie. Then, on a breath: "I have a painkiller. Do you need it?"

"No, Bren-ji. Do you?"

"I have had one." He cast a meaningful glance at Jago—watch him, he wanted to say. Don't let him push it. But Jago said, "You are quite pale, Bren-ji."

"Am I?" He drew several deep breaths. "It seems warm in here."

"It is," Jago said. "Bren-ji, you *will* sit down."

There was a bench, as a lady rose to talk to an associate. Jago deftly moved to the area, the lady moved off, and what could one do?

Bren walked over and quietly sat down, exhaled, did *not* rest his head against the wall. It was near an air vent. That was a considerable help. The bulletproof vest was hot, and stiff, and a very good idea, he was sure. But he wished he could shed it.

It was dull. It was very dull, with the museum committee head making yet another speech.

And Cajeiri remembered the speech he had to give.

One had a chance certainly, with all the other speeches going on, to memorize it.

Except—

Except he had changed coats.

There was still time. There was plenty of time. He was good at memorizing.

"Taro-ji," Cajeiri whispered, leaning close to his aishid. "The paper. My speech. I left it upstairs, in the other coat. Can you possibly go up and get it, nadi?"

"I shall try," Antaro promised him, and backed out of the group and left quickly, down the side of the room.

The others had heard. "I should have realized it," Jegari said. "This is my fault, nandi."

"I am the one who changed coats," Cajeiri said and drew a careful, quiet breath, not wishing to have his parents notice the exchange.

"It will not be easy for Taro to get up there," Veijico said. "They have refused us clearance. They are being very stubborn on that."

"They." If it was any of his father's guard, or his great-grandmother's, he could deal with that.

"The Guild itself," Veijico said. "Even Cenedi tried. But they will not clear us to have the codes."

"Well, but Antaro is clever," he said. Antaro could very often talk her way through things none of the rest of his aishid could manage.

And it was, after all, *his* room, *his* residence she was asking access for. If she could just get upstairs, even if his father's major domo had sworn on his life not to unlock the apartment door, surely he could just get the paper from his pocket in the closet and slide it out to her.

Surely the rules were not that tight.

Once the major d' talked to his father, he might have to admit to his father he had lost the paper, but his father would at least have to admit that he and his aishid had solved the problem.

And he would be perfect in his speech. So his father could not fault him.

*　　*　　*

Sitting helped. Bren drew far easier breaths. The cool air from the vent helped even more. Banichi, however, would not take his seat and sit down. And he himself could not stay there. He nerved himself for a rise to his feet.

"Nandi," Jago warned him just as he came upright, on his feet, and he saw, edging up on him—

Topari and two of his guard.

"Nand' paidhi," Topari said, reaching him, and sketched a bow.

How did *he* get an invitation? was Bren's initial thought, but he put a smile on his face.

"Nandi. One hopes the evening finds you well."

"Well enough," Topari said without a bow. "Nand' paidhi, you said there would be a meeting. Your office has not answered my letter."

He had not instructed his secretarial office, not expecting Topari would take that route, and a single day did not put any ordinary message to the top of the stack in his secretarial office. He gave a small, automatic bow, not needing to feign mild surprise. "One rather expected you would simply send to *me,* nandi, directly, as indeed I invited you to do. What did this letter regard?"

"A meeting," Topari said—the man had the manners of a mecheita in a mob run. "A meeting with the aiji-dowager."

"Regarding?"

"I have exchanged messages with several of my neighbors. We have questions. We need to be consulted, more than that—*considered*—in this rail matter. We *insist.*"

"Indeed, nandi, there will certainly be a consideration of your interests."

"Freight is one thing. Passengers are another. We maintain our sovereignty. We shall have *no outsiders* setting up business in our station."

"I think it extremely likely we can do business, nandi." Bren said to him, and thank God young Dur, out of nowhere, moved in with, "May one be introduced, nand' paidhi?"

It was a rescue, an absolute, self-sacrificing rescue. "Ah! Nandi, nand' Topari of Hasurjan, up in the southern mountains. His district maintains a rail station which could be quite important in the southern route, and he has concerns that Transport will certainly want to consider. —Nand' Topari, nand' Reijiri, whose father is lord of Dur, in the Coastal Association, and who *is* on the Transport Committee."

"The father, that is."

"Indeed, nandi," young Dur said, and Bren took the practiced shift of balance and step backward and away, disengagement, with deep gratitude, and without his bodyguard having to remind him of a fictitious other meeting. He extricated himself from the little cul-de-sac and made it all the way to the next aisle of displays. No telling to whom Reijiri might pass the man next, someone worthy, he hoped. He worked his way closer to the front of the hall, and out of convenient view.

There was, one was grateful to see, another air vent.

Then there was a massive waft of cooler air, as two of the four shut doors opened—security had had *all* the doors shut—and now evidently had relented. No few of the crowd murmured relief.

Antaro arrived inside, one noted, by one of those doors. One had no idea where she had been.

"One cannot get through," Antaro reported, in a tone under the general buzz of conversation in the hall. "I have tried the lifts, the stairs, and the servant passages, and they are all shut down. No one is allowed to operate the lifts and communications are not working. I succeeded in phoning your father's apartment, and Eisi has retrieved the paper, but he cannot leave the apartment. Even the major domo cannot get clearance to come downstairs, and the guards on the stairs will not even talk to me, nandi. Veijico might. She has more seniority on the books. Or one could go to Cenedi."

"He would tell mani," Cajeiri said. "No. No, Taro-ji. It is

almost too late as is. They have opened all the doors. Likely we will be going to the Audience Hall almost any moment."

"One regrets, nandi, one greatly regrets this!"

"By no means," he said. "I am the one who left the paper. I remember enough of it. I have almost all the pieces. My father will hardly notice. Certainly no one else will. It is by no means your fault."

"One is very certain," Antaro said, still breathing hard, "one is very certain it was composed to be felicitous. Be careful of numbers, nandi. Think through the numbers. Your father will have been very careful of that."

"I shall. I can. It will be all right, Taro-ji. No one will notice it at all."

"One earnestly hopes," Antaro said. She had never seemed to be that distressed, even when people were shooting at them.

"It is stupid anyway," he said, "that they do not recognize us. It is certainly not your fault. And I have it memorized. I just need to recall it."

He did remember a lot of the speech. There was one line in the first statement he was not sure of, but he could get it back, if only people would let him alone for just a few moments, and if his aishid could protect him from more people wanting to congratulate him on his birthday. There was *no* way to get off in a corner for quiet. His father insisted he stand nearby, and most of the people who congratulated him he was sure just wanted an excuse to talk to his father.

He gained a few moments of quiet, however. He stood and tried to think of the missing words. He tried—

Then his father called him to meet an elderly lady from the northern coast, up where the world froze, and she asked him questions, and all the while the minutes were ticking down toward their shift to the Audience Hall.

A nine-year-old's birthday party, Bren thought. And the majority of attendees were over sixty. The three young guests flitted fairly sedately under Jase's control, in quest of interesting things in the cases and trying very properly to keep their hands off the glass. The honoree of the day, meanwhile, remained bravely proper, still meeting and talking with elder guests, while his parents and great-grandmother did the same, while his great-uncle sat signing ribboned cards and likely discussing pottery glazes.

There were all these wonderful things to explore and Cajeiri could not even come near his own three guests, who did not rank high enough to stand by him, nor even *see* the exhibit. He'd *become* one, along with the rest of his family.

Poor kid.

"And these guests," one elderly lady asked of Bren. "What will *they* report in the heavens? What will the ship-aiji say, with all these terrible goings-on at Tirnamardi?"

"Jase-aiji is a strong ally of the aiji, and he and his body-guards have reassured the children—not forgetting at all that these children are very strongly loyal to the young gentleman."

"To the young gentleman himself, more than the ship-aiji?" another lady objected.

"To the ship-aiji, yes, they are obedient; but the young gentleman has their loyalty."

"Yet humans do not, do they," an old man objected, "truly *have* man'chi. How can they feel?"

"Yet *I* feel, nandi," Bren said patiently, finding himself back in an old, old role. "And one hopes my loyalty to the aiji is not in doubt."

"By no means, nand' paidhi. One hardly meant—but they are so *young!*"

"Indeed, nandi, one takes no offense at all: you are right to question. For us, a childhood association is not a trifle. These children are part of a population rescued from great danger, taken from their home and moved to the station above us. On that voyage, they met the young gentleman. He was their only comfort in a strange and harsh existence, and they attached to him in the strongest possible way. His generosity, his curiosity, and his kindness attached them to him, clearly in a way a year's absence has not dimmed, and though they are all, despite their size, older than he is, *he* leads. He always has. Do accept my assurance that these three have, just as atevi youngsters do, many caretakers, atevi and human, all of whom have the strongest possible concern for their good character."

"Wise," an old lord said, nodding. "Wise proceedings."

Flattery? Politics? The old man had six grandchildren. There was a warmth about his expression.

"They seem interested in the exhibits," a woman said.

"Nandi, they are. The color, the images, the representations are all very exciting to them."

"Commendable," the old man said. The conversation dwindled to courtesies, and the old gentleman meandered off among the lighted displays, talking to his bodyguard.

"Well done," young Dur said, who had turned up by his elbow.

"One hopes so," he said. Adrenaline was absolutely on the ebb. He had put out too many fires this evening, already, in what was supposed to be a relaxed social event, and had three hours of a far more important court function yet to go.

Two of the Liberal Caucus lay in wait near a red figured vase, with questions about the tribal bill. "Your vote will secure the west," Bren assured them, "and *prevent* another dispute with the Marid. That will remove the need for a strong naval presence, and direct the funding toward merchant shipping."

"It *will* work," he assured another such inquirer, at the next turn. "The Southern Ocean is *not* impassable. We have vastly improved weather reports, vastly improved technology, vastly improved navigation *and* stabilization in heavy weather. I have a report upcoming in the Transportation Committee this session, on the ship technology."

"Assistance from the ship humans. What, nandi, can ships in the great ether understand of ships at sea?"

"Ah. It is not the ship technology we are borrowing,

nandi, but their vantage point. They can see the storms coming. They can declare a safe route."

"Even through the Southern Ocean?"

"They have an excellent view, nandi, and are learning from us, as well. They can steer ships around hazards. But first the tribal bill. The tribal bill is key to everything."

Another lord, a Conservative, approached and asked: "One has heard a rumor, nand' paidhi. What is the truth on the upheaval in the Guild? And why this damnable malfunction in Guild equipment tonight?"

He was intensely conscious of Banichi and Jago, right at his shoulders, and of the lord's own aishid, considerably lower in Guild rank, right behind him.

"It is a technical matter," he said, "about which one has very little information. But the Guild has promised extensive reform of the system, which has created confusion, especially in recent weeks. The aiji is extremely optimistic."

"Indeed, nand' paidhi?"

"Very much so. He entirely supports this change, and I do not doubt he will say so in coming days."

"You are still backing the tribal bill, one hears."

"Definitely, nandi, with complete enthusiasm."

He escaped, half a step, when another accosted him with: "Nand' paidhi. You *are* backing the bill."

"As is Lord Tatiseigi, nandi, as is the aiji-dowager."

"That *she* will is no news. But Lord Tatiseigi—"

"He stands with the aiji-dowager."

"One imagines there might be agreement," the second said dryly. And the first:

"What of the removal of Lord Kadagidi? One would hesitate to believe the rumor, that this attack was arranged by the Liberals, and that this concession is the price of the tribal bill."

"One would call that removal not a concession, but a correction long overdue, nandi," he said firmly, then lowered his voice conspiratorially. "One vital to the security of the aishidi'tat. Lord Aseida, nandiin, was not ignorant of circumstances behind the coup. The Guild will be investigating."

"Indeed, nandi!"

He knew these two. He knew their tactics . . . the two worst gossips in the midlands. "There will be abundant proof of the entire exchange at Asien'dalun, nandi. The aiji is in possession of evidence, and I shall be pleased to show you and anyone else who asks all the proof they could wish, both of what happened and what almost happened, which is far worse; it involves the arrest of several hidden agents. You are unaware, no doubt, that Lord Aseida in recent days threatened the aiji-dowager, the young gentleman and his guests. Lord Aseida claims ignorance of the plot, but the intention behind it was clearly to harm the administration."

"That can be *proven,* nand' paidhi?"

"To the satisfaction of any who wish to see the photographic evidence. *Minor children,* nandiin. *Foreigners* who, as *guests,* have now witnessed an illegal act on the part of a lord of the aishidi'tat. This was assuredly *not* the way the young gentleman hoped to impress his guests."

"So the young gentleman was *not* at Malguri," a newcomer observed.

"No. He was not. He was at no time at Malguri. For security reasons, he was a guest of his great-uncle at Tirnamardi." Again he lowered his voice, so the second lord had to lean forward to hear. "The Kadagidi lord's own bodyguard received orders from a remnant of the Murini faction to help Assassins from the south eliminate Lord Tatiseigi. Possibly they neglected to tell their lord about their illegal actions, or the purpose of southern Guild arriving in the household. There is a *little* doubt. That is *why* Lord Aseida will likely be asked to resign the lordship. As the aiji inquires more deeply, there may be more evidence tying Lord Aseida himself to some of these decisions—and he would be very wise to take that offer while it is available, especially since this all unfolded to the annoyance of the aiji-dowager, whose patience is very short, and whose influence

is considerable. The Guild will be going through papers re-
covered from Lord Aseida's own office."

"Indeed," that lord said quietly. And that ended that line
of questioning.

"One regrets," Banichi said with a deep sigh, "that that
problem reached you."

"We are neither one as agile as we might be. How are
you faring, Nichi-ji?"

"Not too badly," Banichi said.

The doors were all open, now, and some attendees had
found their way back out into the cool hallway. Lord Tatiseigi had passed out all the cards, and joined Ilisidi in a walk
about the cases, Lord Tatiseigi personally commenting on
his treasures to a number of interested attendees. Tabini,
Damiri, and Cajeiri were still conversing with elderly guests,
while Jase and the youngsters were off in a side hall, with
the Reverence Statues.

It was almost time. Tabini was, at the moment, a bit apart
from Damiri, who was listening to an older woman who was
casting disapproving glances back at Cajeiri's guests—who
were doing absolutely nothing amiss at the moment. Cajeiri
was not frowning—Cajeiri was too well-brought-up for
that; but Cajeiri's shoulders were stiff and his hands were
mangling a program sheet behind him.

Tabini cast one of those glances that was as good as a
summons.

Bren moved closer, gave a little bow. "My wife," Tabini
said in a low voice, "is pursuing her own course this evening,
pressing her own notions of the Kadagidi succession. She
will *not* have her way."

Damiri trying to interfere in politics could not please
Tatiseigi. And had he heard right? What had *Damiri* to do
with the *Kadagidi* succession? The Ajuri one made perfect
sense. But had she notions about both?

"I have advised my grandmother not to vex my wife on
this occasion," Tabini said curtly. "Stay with the family.

Please attend my grandmother in the assembly, and assist Lord Tatiseigi to keep those two apart."

"Yes," he said, wondering how, precisely, he was going to do that.

A soft horn sounded, out in the hall, a strange rising and falling note, audible from the open doors. The kabiuteri had cleared and opened the ceremonial hall, and the premises were arranged for the start of the evening. The Audience Hall was opening: non-participant guests and the public— of which there were none, this evening—were to take their place behind either of two red satin ropes in the main hall.

The red ropes ordinarily marshaled the attendees into a small stream entering an event. In this case, it would let the aiji and his guests enter the premises through the central door of the five, walk along a clear aisle between the ropes, and take their places in the Audience Hall ahead of the crowd. One had not *planned* to be in that elite group—one had planned to join Jase and the youngsters and reunite his aishid.

Tabini, Damiri and Cajeiri passed him at a sedate pace, with their bodyguards; Ilisidi and Lord Tatiseigi followed, with theirs; and Bren dutifully fell in after, with Banichi and Jago, leaving Tano and Algini to assist Jase getting into the hall.

His job was, he gathered, to engage the aiji-dowager and keep her apart from Damiri; and possibly to try to divert Damiri, if it came to that.

Four of the museum's doors were open, and people were exiting, a brisk movement into the two areas roped off. The central door remained shut until Tabini's approach, at which point it opened, affording the family that easy crossing past the observing crowd toward the center door of the Audience Hall.

All but one of its doors were shut. The centermost, between the ropes, was open, welcoming the family into what, compared to the hall, was lamplit darkness.

They reached the doorway, their eyes just beginning to

adjust—and suddenly a bank of lights blazed at them, painting them all in white glare, as much as one could see at the moment.

Television cameras. The lights were near the dais, cameras focused, at the moment, toward the open doors and the incoming notables. They blinded security: *that* was a problem. But Kaplan and Polano were somewhere in this room, and after the initial rush of adrenaline, Bren reassured himself with that thought.

They were safer than usual in the Audience Hall: they had not the general public, just the museum event attendees lined up at the red ropes outside, and they went at a sedate pace, with knots of Guild black separating the glitter of the notables, and there was a gracious atmosphere about their progress, nods from the family—excepting Damiri, who walked in her own world—to the family's particular supporters and associates the other side of the rope.

There was a buffet set up—the smells were in the air; there was Bujavid staff, shadows over on the right. There was a long table, likely for the cards.

There was, at the end of the room, the dais, and the chair Tabini used for audiences in this room. The cameras were set up right at the corner of those steps.

And that was where everybody stopped *except* Tabini and his bodyguard, who kept going up the steps. Bren stopped. So had the dowager, and Lord Tatiseigi, and Damiri, and their bodyguards. The doors behind them were opening—he heard the thump, and the muted noise of the crowd suddenly louder, and when he turned to look he saw someone—likely Tano and Algini—had gotten Jase and the children to the fore, so they were first through those doors, at a sensible pace: it was *not* the inclination of atevi lords to push and shove. The cameras were on them, all the doors were open, and a great number of notables and their bodyguards came into the hall from all four doors ... more, he realized, than had been at the museum event: they had acquired a larger crowd, a much larger crowd.

Security was wound tight . . . and only a few of the Guild were getting much in the way of communication—he had no idea what kind of information had passed: information that the system would be down, perhaps, perhaps an urging to report anything worrisome, perhaps the assurance a few of the senior Guild *were* getting information steadily, and that more would be brought online as the evening progressed.

Hell of a situation they had. In this case—it wasn't the lords' rank that determined when that would happen—it was the seniority and reputation of their bodyguards, a team at a time, and it would, one guessed, be ongoing.

Out in the city, in crowds, most of the Guild keeping order out there were running dark, with no communication even with each other.

The crowds wouldn't know it. The news service wouldn't know it.

The young gentleman's bodyguard was among those not informed. The boy was being very quiet, very proper—standing with a frowning Damiri at the foot of the steps; and Lord Tatiseigi was, one was glad to see, between them and the dowager's part.

Tano and Algini arrived, with Jase and the youngsters, and by now Jase and the youngsters had other guards—Bren had seen them, too, as he turned, right by the doors, one on a side, two white-armored figures that had attracted a little curiosity from the attendees at the back of the room. They might be statues. They intended to be. They had gotten into position before anybody, even the news crew. And they were not going to move, not a light, not a twitch, until the room was deserted again.

"Kaplan and Polano are back there," Bren said to Jase—the atevi crowd cut off all view of the back of the hall. And to the children: "Quite the show, isn't it?"

"What's next, sir?" Gene asked.

"Quite a lot of speeches, likely. Be patient."

"They will be," Jase said, his hand on Gene's shoulder.

Atevi etiquette was the order of the evening, however, and Jase let his hand fall. "Are we all right to be where we are?"

The youngsters were the only children in the hall: at the front was the only place they could stand, and be able to see.

"You're fine," Bren said. "They're with you. There's a service door right over to the left. If I disappear for a while, that's where I'll be. If there should be any problem—that's where to go."

"Understood," Jase said, and that was one problem he could put from his mind.

Damiri was clearly *not* in good sorts this evening, arms crossed and locked, face set in a scowl. God only knew what sort of exchange she had had with Tabini to prompt Tabini to ask *him* to intervene—but it could not be good. The crowd in the museum had not been the sort of crowd to cause problems of a rowdy sort in a place like that. But in the Audience Hall, after a certain time, with alcohol involved . . .

With the political surprise the aiji intended . . .

With the Guild running dark and most of the members unable to communicate . . .

God, he wanted this evening over with.

Mother was *not* happy. She gave Great-uncle a sharp answer when he asked her if anything was the matter, and Cajeiri had said, very quietly, "Honored Uncle, I shall stay with her." It was not what he wanted to do. He had far rather get a moment to go over to his guests, but he was on best manners, and he was afraid even to look at them right now, because they would likely wave, and he could not answer them, and then they would think they had done something wrong.

Maybe it was the television cameras his mother disapproved. His mother had sworn when the lights had gone on in their faces. She had said a word he had never heard her say. And she had had words with his father in the museum, too—he had not heard what they had said, but his mother had been upset about something.

Nobody had told *him* there would be television cameras, either, or if someone had—he had not been paying enough attention. But he was more worried than angry.

He had gotten through meeting people in the museum. He had leaned heavily on the system of clan colors—which were also the relationships and the history, the way new clans built off old ones.

But sometime before midnight he was supposed to make that speech.

He had to remember that missing line, that was what. And there were television cameras, and he had to get it right. It was one word. One *word*, and if he could remember that, he could remember the whole rest of it.

He thought he could, at least.

They were using the old-fashioned oil lamps, besides the electrics, the way they did for evening parties, and probably once everybody was in place they might dim the lights again and leave only spots of light. The place smelled of food: there was a buffet set up, and his stomach noticed that, too. He had only pretended to eat lunch. If they did dim the lights, he thought wildly, if nobody was paying attention, he might get away for a few moments to find Gene and Artur and Irene at the buffet. Usually buffets were not that formal. But—

With television cameras on them—how could they? If he so much as moved, television cameras were likely to go right to him.

He could not think about those things. He just had to concentrate on remembering the speech. If he embarrassed his father by being a fool with the speech, it was not just his mother who was going to be in a bad mood.

The first line was—

The first line started, all speeches did, with *Nandiin, nadiin . . .*

No. It did *not* start that way. That was what confused him. It started with *I thank my family . . .*

He could just not get beyond that.

Why did it have to start differently? Why did he have to forget one word right in the middle of the beginning? He could remember everything after that, if he could just remember the first part.

He would not say anything infelicitous. That was the main thing. He would say something polite, and he would avoid infelicity. There were seven kabiuteri on the landing of the dais, just a little below where his father was sitting. You could never mistake them, with their square, brimless white hats and their white robes. And they were there to keep the felicitous gods happy and the infelicitous ones out of the hall. Even if his father called it nonsense.

The lights dimmed down, and one of his father's bodyguards came down the steps, a moving shadow, coming for him, he began to realize. The camera swung toward that man, and that man came down to the third step and bowed to *him*.

The television lights were on him, white, like giant eyes.

"Young gentleman," his father's bodyguard said, and wanted him to come up. He started that way. His bodyguard did, on either side of him.

Then the lights left him and swung up to where his father was coming down the steps. He could hardly see in the sudden dark. He could *not* stumble. He took the steps very carefully, felt Antaro's hand at his elbow, ready to help him, but he managed on his own, and climbed to the place where his father stopped, up in the light, where his father's black brocade glistened like Guild leather; his own coat blazed with metallic red.

Drummers and string-players started up from somewhere in the dark edge of the buffet, and the kabiuteri banged their staffs.

At the foot of the dais, where the light barely reached, his mother stood watching; and he saw Great-grandmother,

Lord Tatiseigi, and nand' Bren. They were right at the steps, his mother and Lord Tatiseigi and nand' Bren all a spot of brightness, and mani's black lace drinking up the light.

There were far more people than had been in the museum. The whole hall was full, and just people moving created a noise.

A horn sounded. One was not supposed to gawk, but every head turned. He supposed he was permitted.

A kabiutera's assistant on the steps had the horn, and blew it three times in all, until the voices and the echoes died away.

Then the senior kabiutera lifted his hands and intoned something in a language that hardly even seemed Ragi. He had heard it before, he very dimly recalled, when he was very small, maybe five. Maybe six. It was spooky-sounding, the whole thing. But when he looked past the kabiutera, in the television lights, he finally spotted nand' Jase, and where nand' Jase was, Gene and Irene and Artur would be—just there, right beside nand' Bren.

He saw something else, too, far, far back near the doors—two hazy whitish shadows, like massive marble statues in the reflection of the floodlights: Kaplan and Polano were on guard, as tall as Banichi when they were in armor, and he was amazed. Ordinarily there were little flashing lights and sometimes light inside the masks so you could see their faces, but nothing showed right now. They could really *be* statues. People might think they *were* statues.

But they were safe, were they not? Everybody had to be safer since nand' Bren and Banichi had straightened out the Guild.

He wondered whether his mother had refused to come up here with them. Or what his parents had been fighting about.

His mind was going in every direction, with the noise, and the people, and the sights. He needed to be thinking. He needed to remember . . . because he was sure his father was going to make *his* speech, and then he would have to.

He was out of time. The missing words might come back to him if he was less scared. He had not planned on being scared. But right now his mouth was dry and his heart was pounding faster than the drums.

The boy looked, somehow, taller tonight—shining black and red brocade, which as the light hit it, blazed glints of fire, the smaller image to Tabini's own solemn, shining black. Bren took in a breath, watching the boy become what he had always been intended to be—about to watch the boy he knew become . . . something he hadn't expected him to become yet.

A heavy load was about to land on very young shoulders. It was going to be one more burden on a boy who already had had his childhood curtailed . . . whose dearest possessions had been, oddly enough, a world map and a little notebook of drawings of a spaceship, a boy who had wanted to be a musketeer, and hoped to see dinosaurs.

Cajeiri had grown tall, for nine. His shoulders were getting broader, a fact that coat made evident. He would look a lot like his father when he was grown, Bren thought, and that would be no bad thing at all.

Their Cajeiri.

His. His aishid's. They *had* helped get him here. He felt more than a little possessive, though he was very far from saying so.

Ilisidi would not hesitate to state her claim, not in the least. But she had not said a word tonight. She had been uncharacteristically quiet, apparently content to watch, with a certain—was it a smile?—on her countenance at the moment. He had rarely seen her in such a sustained good mood.

The vacancy of the dais, instead of all the family together, the appearance of father and son together, alone, on the most fortunate of birthdays, with the television focused on them—

People throughout the hall took in the sight, and there was an undertone of comment—how the boy had grown;

how much like his father he looked; and then the horn blew again, and kabiuteri moved out to various posts in the room, clashing their staffs on the floor, a racket echoing throughout the still assembly.

The steady drums and the music of the strings—stopped, leaving an embarrassed mutter of comment that quickly died away.

"Be you still!" the senior kabiutera shouted out from the dais, banging his staff on the floor. "Be you still! Be you still!"

They were going ahead with it.

With the whole city, the whole nation following it on television.

Cajeiri's father laid a hand on his shoulder. "Son of mine."

Cajeiri looked up. "Honored Father."

His father maintained that grip. A staff hit the floor another three times, louder than mani's cane, impossible as that seemed, and a silence descended on the hall, in which the stir of a single foot seemed apt to echo.

"The numbers have been counted," the oldest kabiutera proclaimed, "and this gathering is felicitous. This time is the right time."

"Nandiin, nadiin," his father said, his voice ringing out over the shadowy hall. "This is my son. With you as witnesses, I pronounce him my heir, grandson of my father and mother, great-grandson of my grandfather and grandmother. I call on the tashrid and the hasdrawad, at the appropriate time, to proclaim Cajeiri son of Tabini as aiji of the aishidi'tat, heir of all my titles and rights. I call on my kin and my associates to support my heir's claim and to give him their man'chi."

There was a murmur, then the ripple of a shout, so loud it made Cajeiri's heart jump. He did not flinch. His father's hand kept him from that.

The staff struck the floor three more times, restoring silence so deep he could hear himself breathing.

His father's heir. That was odd. He already knew he was that.

But the man'chi of all these people? His mind started scrambling after names, colors, relationships.

He really wanted to give his speech later. After he had remembered the missing line.

"Son of mine," his father said aloud, and touched his elbow. "Speak loudly," his father said under his breath, "and keep your head up."

Keep his head up. He could do that much. But he was not certain he could get enough breath to his lungs to make anybody hear him.

He had the first part. If he just plunged ahead, the connecting word might pop into his head.

"*Thank you, all my family, all my associates, all my allies, all my family's allies . . .*"

And there it stalled. The missing bit did not come to him.

The quiet persisted. Someone down in the gathering cleared his throat and it sounded like thunder.

". . . I am fortunate nine, today, and I thank you for coming."

The back part was just gone. Not just the back of the sentence. *Everything* after that. He was facing all these important people and they were going to think he was a fool. Worse, the kabiuteri would be upset with him and they could call the whole evening, his whole *year,* infelicitous.

He could not just stand there. Keen in memory, his right ear stung as if mani had thwacked him for forgetting. Keep going! she would say as he sat at her feet, aboard the starship. Think, boy! Think *faster!*

Banichi would say, Practice until your *body* remembers.

He was supposed to tell people what he had learned since he was infelicitous eight, and he was supposed to talk about his family and thank people, that was what.

And his great-grandmother and his mother and nand' Tatiseigi and nand' Bren were all at the foot of the steps waiting for him to get his wits about him and do that. He had to say good things about everybody, especially his mother. He could not make her mad, especially in front of everybody.

He had to say something. He had to do it his way.

"I thank my father, who is not afraid of anybody. I thank my mother, who has done her best to guide me. I thank my great-grandmother, who has defended me. I thank nand' Bren—" He realized he should have said *the paidhi-aiji*, and he should have put Great-uncle after his great-grandmother, and worse, it was infelicitous four: he plunged ahead to find five. " —who saved my life. And I thank Great-uncle Tatiseigi who taught me the traditions." He could not stop there. He could not leave out semi-felicitous six and seven. "I thank Lord Geigi and Jase-aiji, who taught me about things in space." Unlucky eight. "I thank the Guilds for the things they do." And nine: nine was the felicity he had to reach to match his years. "And I thank my tutor for teaching me why things work. I know the geography of the world and I know every clan and their colors by heart. I know why it rains and how airplanes fly and I know where comets come from and I know why tides and storms happen. I am learning kabiu." He said that for the row of kabiuteri, in their patterned robes, who were standing there looking worried. Promise everybody something, his father had told him. And he remembered something mani had once said. ". . . Because the traditions and the harmony make art, and art makes things beautiful, and we all are better and kinder and wiser when we live with beautiful things. We become better when we know *why* things are beautiful. I want to know everything I can and learn as much as I can and do as much as I can and meet as many people as I can. I shall try very hard in my fortunate ninth year." He had to get in everybody else, and talk about the aishidi'tat, and not take too much time about it, because people had a right to get restless in long speeches. He wanted to end with a felicity. "I want my father to be aiji for a long, long time. And I wish everybody to have a good time, whether you came for my father or if you came for me or if you came for the aishidi'tat. Most of all the aishidi'tat is important, because the aishidi'tat is our home, and we have to make our home the most beautiful place there is. Thank you, nandiin, nadiin."

He gave a little bow. It all had sounded good to him when he was saying it, but increasingly toward the end, he had realized he was letting his ideas run over each other, the way mani had told him never to do.

Now there was just silence. He thought he had sounded stupid and his father was going to be upset that he had not given the right speech at all. The kabiuteri were going to find an infelicity. He truly hoped that he had not just done something really, really terrible to his father in that regard.

Then he heard Great-grandmother's cane strike the floor. Once—twice—three times. "Long life and good fortune!" she shouted out. And then everybody shouted out, almost together. "Long life and good fortune!"

He drew in a whole breath. And felt his father's hand on his shoulder.

"Did your grandmother write that speech?" his father asked him ominously.

"No, honored Father. I—lost the paper. I had it memorized. Almost. And then I forgot it."

His father's fingers tightened. His father looked at him long and hard and seriously, and then laughed a little. "The kabiuteri passed the speech I sent you. Yours will pose them at least a three-candle question. They will be at it all night."

"Did I do wrong, honored Father?"

"You had the Recorder scrambling, the poor old fellow— he all but overset his ink pot. He will at least have it down in shorthand. And if he fails, there *is* a recording. *There* we have innovated. And there can be no future debate of what was said and done."

The television. He had not even thought about the television once he was talking. But now the lights for the cameras began to wink out, one at a time, so that the room was going darker and darker and their eyes by lamplight could make out people, rows and rows of people.

"The city will have the news now," his father said quietly. "But nowadays it will not travel by rail to the outer provinces. The whole aishidi'tat will know it at once. You are legally, formally, as of now, and forever, my heir." His father began to walk him down the steps, carefully, since they had just been in brighter light and everything still looked dim. "Mind your step. Feel your way and make no mistakes. A runner will be going down the Bujavid steps in the traditional way, by torchlight, carrying the proclamation on parchment, with its seals. I signed that this afternoon He will go all the way to the Guilds, ending at the Archives, where he will file the declaration of Investiture."

"Nobody told me!"

"This was done for your benefit, son of mine. It is now done for the first time since your great-grandfather's Investiture, from before the East joined the aishidi'tat. The ka-biuteri are extremely pleased to have the custom renewed—ecstatic, to put it plainly—and they will find felicity in every syllable of your speech. Between us, the longer the speech, the more adorned with fortunate words and well-wishes, the more easily kabiuteri can find good omens in it. We have just resurrected a tradition one hopes you will maintain in your own day. And you may be quite proud of the distinction. Your great-grandmother is delighted."

He supposed it was a great honor. He was glad if he had done well: he had tried to name nine people and give something good to everybody, the way his father had advised him, but he could hardly remember anything he had said except in generalities. Ever since Assassins had turned up at Great-uncle's house, he had felt as if he was being shoved from every side in turn, scattering every thought he had—

Mani would not have forgotten everything she had just said. Mani never grew scattered. Mani always knew what mani wanted. She never forgot a thing.

So what had he said? He mostly wanted everybody to live

for a long time, he wanted no more wars, and he wanted the world to be beautiful and peaceful . . . it was stupid that some people wanted the world neither beautiful nor peaceful.

He thought it was likely the same people his father and his great-grandmother wanted to be rid of.

So he supposed his mother was right, that he really was his great-grandmother's, more than anybody's.

"There will be cards to sign," his father said, steering him off the last step and, yes, toward a long table set with flowers, where there were candles, one of which belonged to a waxjack: it was now lit; and there were rolls of ribbon and stacks of cards, and they were not going to get to eat.

"Shall *I* be signing, honored Father?"

"That you shall, a card for every person here. The ones given out in the city, some twenty-seven thousand of them, will lack a signature, but they will have a stamp and ribbon . . . you may sit beside me and sign your name first."

He wished he had practiced his signature. He was still not satisfied with his signature and he was not used to doing it. He wanted a chance to change it someday. And maybe now he never could. And he had no seal ring, nothing like his father's, which could make a seal official: he always used just a little wi'itikin stamp he had gotten, but it was a trinket, not a real seal, and he did not even have it with him. His pockets were empty. Just empty. It was a condition he was not at all used to.

He reached the table, where secretaries and officials bowed to him and his father, and their bodyguards took up position without being asked.

The oldest secretary, a man whose hair was all gray, arranged a little stack of cards to start with . . . in front of the black-draped chair at the end of the table.

"You need only sign here, young aiji, and pass the card to your father. He will sign it. Then we shall apply the seal and ribbons."

His father said: "Take your time. *Speak* to the people."

"Yes, honored Father." He sat down on the edge of the

seat. He tested the inkwell and the pen on a piece of blotting paper, and was glad the table was covered in black, so if he spilled ink, nobody would know.

And the first person in line was mani herself.

"We do not, as a rule, collect cards," she said solemnly. "But we shall be very glad to display this one. Well done, Great-grandson."

"Mani," he said, and ducked his head: he hardly knew what to say. He signed his name and passed the card carefully to his father, who said, "Honored Grandmother," and likewise signed it, passing it on to the secretaries, who would sand it and finish it with an official seal and red and black ribbons.

The next in line was Lord Tatiseigi. And the third was nand' Bren. It was all very strange.

It was even stranger, when he signed a card for Jase-aiji, and a card apiece for Gene and Artur and Irene. "These are to keep," he explained to Gene. "To remember."

"We shall remember," Gene said, and very shyly said, when his father signed the card next. "Thank you very much, nand' aiji."

It was the same with Artur and Irene. And then young Dur, Reijiri, came to the table.

"One is very glad you could come," Cajeiri said, and meant it.

And to the elder Lord Dur: "It is a great honor you could come, nandi."

"You are a credit, young aiji, you are a great credit."

They were calling him not young gentleman, but young aiji. Were they supposed to call him that? His father had always said he was his heir. But was that somehow truer than it had ever been? Was that what his ninth birthday festivity meant, just because it was the fortunate ninth? Or was it because of that paper a messenger was carrying through the city?

Nobody had told him his ninth birthday would change everything.

Was he going to have to be like his father, now, and be serious all day, and sign papers and talk business to people? He wanted to go back to Great-uncle's house and ride with his guests. That was what he *wanted*, more than anything . . .

But he was supposed to be thinking about people right now, being polite to lords his father needed him to impress, all these people in the hall, as many as he had ever seen in this hall at once.

And he smiled at those he knew and those he knew only by their colors. He was careful not to miss anybody. He thanked them for their good wishes, and meanwhile he could smell the food and knew everybody who left with a card was now free to go over to the buffet and have something to eat. He had not really eaten since breakfast, and a very little at the formal lunch.

But neither had his father. That was the way things were, if you were aiji.

It meant looking good, even if your stomach was empty.

Was one justified in being personally just a little proud of the boy? Bren thought so.

Lord Tatiseigi was walking about with a glass of wine in hand and a smile on his face, and Ilisidi—Ilisidi was talking to the head of the Merchants' Guild, very likely getting in a word or two about the Marid situation, doing politics as always, but looking extraordinarily relaxed and pleased.

Jase and the youngsters had been through the buffet, with small, safe cups of tea and a few safe sweets—the buffet would hold out for hours, and the alcohol had started to flow. Bren took sugared tea and a very manageable little half sandwich roll, stationing himself where he could watch the individuals he needed to watch.

Damiri had a cup of tea, and a congratulatory line of people—that could go on, and presumably it was going well. She had no part in her husband's or her son's card-signing, no formal part in the ceremony, but that was the way of things—the aiji-consort was *not* necessary in the inheritance. She was, legally speaking, not involved in the question.

One noted Tabini had mentioned his own mother in his address, and that was a first—a Taibeni woman, never acknowledged, never mentioned, *not* in Ilisidi's favor, and for what he knew, no longer living. But if Ilisidi had taken any offense at that one mention, it was not in her expression at the moment.

Politics. Tabini had *mentioned* his Taibeni kinship tonight. The Guild, which had so obdurately found every excuse to ignore his Taibeni bodyguards . . . had just undergone a profound revision. Lord Keimi of Taiben was in attendance tonight: Cajeiri's *other* great-grand-uncle had just, after two hundred years of war, signed a peace with Lord Tatiseigi.

The aiji-consort's clan was as absent as the Kadagidi, the proven traitors. *Cajeiri* had been the one to acknowledge his own mother—Tabini had not mentioned her; but then, by the lines of inheritance he was reciting, no, he not only had not, he *could* not have mentioned her. It just was not the way things were done. It was up to her son to acknowledge her.

And he had. Thank God he had. Had Tabini urged him to it?

Likely. Tabini was trying hard to keep Damiri by him, no matter the increasing problems of that relationship. Tatiseigi likewise was doing his best by that relationship, ignoring Damiri's flirtation with Ajuri.

The Ajuri banner had been prominent at the side of the hall tonight, for anyone who looked for it. The Kadagidi banner was *not* present. And there was only one person who could have made the decision to allow the Ajuri banner, given Lord Komaji's banishment.

Tabini.

The banner had been here; but Damiri had not worn its brilliant red and gold this evening, just a pale green pleated satin that accommodated her condition, a color not quite saying Atageini, but suggesting it. Her choice?

Perhaps it had been her choice, on an evening where she had no official part. It was at least — political. Damiri stood in a circle of lamplight, attended by Ilisidi's guards, wished well by her husband's associates, on the evening her son received sole title to her husband's inheritance. And nowhere in Ragi culture did a lord's consort, male or female, have *any* part, where it came to clan rights and inheritable privilege — it was just the way of things.

Tell that to Ilisidi, who had stepped forward twice to claim the regency, and to sue before the legislature simply to take the Ragi inheritance as her own. He had never quite appreciated the audacity of that move.

But then — Damiri had not been running half the continent before her marriage, and was not in charge of the spoiled, immature boy Valasi had reputedly been at his father's death, a boy who had never, moreover, had an Investiture ... nor allowed one for Tabini.

One could see ... a decided difference in situations: Ilisidi, already ruler of half the sole continent, versus Damiri, the inconvenient offspring of a peacemaking interclan marriage gone very wrong — in a marriage some were saying, now, was becoming inconvenient.

Damiri, carrying an inconvenient surplus child, with her father's clan very close to being dissolved for Shishogi's treason, was not in an enviable situation, should Tabini divorce her. The only thing that prevented a public furor about another of Ajuri's misdeeds was the Guild's deep secrecy: it would swallow the person and the name of Shishogi so very deeply not even Ajuri clan might ever know the extent of his crimes — or even that he had died in disgrace.

Just a very few people inside Ajuri had to be asking themselves what they were to do with what they knew, and where on earth they would be safe.

Tabini didn't want her taking on that lordship, for very good reasons. And there went her one chance of becoming a lord in her own right, setting herself in any remote sense on an equal footing with Ilisidi.

"Bren-ji," Jago said, and nodded toward the east corner.

There was the service corridor. And Tatiseigi was positioned nicely by the dowager's side, not likely to leave her now, and Damiri was fully occupied with well-wishers. The major ceremony was past. It *was* a good time to go aside and take a break—most of all to let Banichi take a rest, he thought. He yielded and went in that direction: the door was open, the hallway only dimly lit, letting people supplying the buffet and bringing back dishes get in and out of the hall without a disturbing flare of light.

The promised chairs were there. It was, indeed, a relief. He sat down. Banichi dutifully did the same.

"How are you faring?" he asked Banichi.

"Well enough," Banichi said. "There is, indeed, no need."

"Of course not," Jago said.

Bren let go a long, slow breath. "He did very well, did he not?"

"He did excellently well," Tano said.

"How is the city faring?" he asked, wondering if information was indeed getting through channels.

"Very well," Tano said. "Very well indeed . . . a little damage here and there, simply the press of people. A bar set a television in a window, and attempted to serve drink on the walkway, and there was a complaint of disorderly conduct—it was nothing. The cards are still being distributed, from several points, and those lines are orderly."

It was nothing. That was so much better a report than they could have feared. Algini scoured up a carafe of tea, and they kept themselves out of the way of serving staff coming and going.

"The runner has reached the Archive," Jago remarked, listening to communications. And then: "Attendees in the hall have become curious about Jase's bodyguard. They have stayed quite still. Cenedi has sent guards to protect them."

One could only imagine, should Kaplan or Polano grow restless and switch on a light or two. Or move. "Jase says they can rest in there fairly comfortably," Bren said, "with the armor locked. One cannot imagine it is that comfortable over time." He drew a deep breath. "And I should get back to the hall, nadiin-ji. Banichi, can you not sit here with Jago a while? There is absolutely no problem out there."

Banichi drew a deep breath. "Best I move, Bren-ji." He shoved himself to his feet and drew a second breath.

"We may find an opportunity to quit the hall early," Bren said, "all the same. We have done what we need to do."

He walked out into the hall, and indeed, Tabini-aiji and Cajeiri had finished their card-signing and finally had leisure to talk and visit with well-wishers.

"Bren." Jase overtook them, and Bren turned slightly, nodded a hello to Jase and Cajeiri's young guests.

"So," he said in ship-speak, "are you three managing to enjoy yourselves?"

"Really, yes, sir," Gene said.

"We love the clothes," Irene said. "And we got our own cards."

"Treasure them," he said. "You won't find their like again in a lifetime. Onworld, they're quite valuable."

"Do we call him Cajeiri-aiji now, sir?" Artur asked.

"That *is* a question," Bren said, and glanced at Banichi. "What *does* one call our young gentleman now?"

"'Young gentleman' is still appropriate," Banichi said, "but Cajeiri-aiji, on formal occasions; or nand' aiji, the same address as to his father."

"Can we still call him Jeri?" Gene asked.

"Not in public," Bren said. "Never in public. Never speaking *about* him. He'll always be Cajeiri-aiji when you're talking about him. Or the young aiji. Or the young gentleman. But what he is in private—he'll define that."

"Yes, sir," Gene said. And bowed and changed back to Ragi. "Nandi."

"Jase-aiji." Bren gave a little nod and walked on toward the dowager, who had gotten a chair, likely from the other service passage, and who was quite successfully holding court over near the dais, with a cup of tea in her hands and a semicircle of attendance, including Lord Dur and Lord Tatiseigi.

Protected, still. He was satisfied. He turned the other direction, to let that gathering take its course, and to let that pair pursue necessary politics, and saw, at a little remove, Lord Topari.

That was not a meeting he wanted at the moment. He veered further right.

And found himself facing, at a little remove, the aiji-consort and her borrowed bodyguard.

She was looking right at him. Eyes had met. Courtesy dictated that he bow, then turn aside, but when he lifted his head, she was headed right toward him with intent, and etiquette demanded he stand there, bow a bit more deeply as she arrived, and offer a polite greeting.

"Daja-ma," he said pleasantly.

"Are you pleased?" she asked outright.

"One is pleased that your son is so honored, daja-ma. One hopes you are enjoying the evening."

"Is that a concern?"

She was set on an argument, and he was equally determined to avoid it. He bowed a third time, not meeting her eyes, not accepting a confrontation.

"My question was sincere, daja-ma. One apologizes if it gave offense."

"Who killed my father?"

He did look at her, with a sharp intake of breath. "I did not, daja-ma, nor did the aiji-dowager, nor did Lord Tatiseigi, who would have received your father had he reached Tirnamardi. It is my unsupported opinion, daja-ma, that Tirnamardi is exactly where your father was going, and that the most likely person to have prevented him getting there was his uncle—your own great-uncle. Shishogi."

Her eyes flashed, twice, luminous as they caught the light. "What do *you* know?"

"A question for us both, daja-ma: what do you know of him?"

"That you killed him."

"I never met him. Nor did my aishid, in that context." He saw her breathing very rapidly. "Daja-ma, are you well? There is a chair in the servant passage."

"Why would he kill my father?"

"Do you know, daja-ma, *who* your uncle was?"

"That is a very strange question."

He was acutely conscious of his own aishid, of the dowager's men at Damiri's back, of a crowded hall, though they were in a clear area. "There are things that I cannot discuss here, daja-ma, but that your husband surely knows."

"Did *he* assassinate my father?"

"Daja-ma, your husband believed he protected you in dismissing your father, who was under pressures we do not accurately know. But to my knowledge the aiji did *not* wish his death. Your father may have discovered things he may have finally decided to pass to Lord Tatiseigi, as the closest to the aiji he could reach."

"I am weary of riddles and suppositions! Tell me what you *know,* not what you *guess!"*

"Daja-ma." He lowered his voice as much as possible. "We are not in a safe place. If you will discuss this with some person of close connection to you, one suggests Lord Tatiseigi."

"The dowager's closest ally!"

"But a man of impeccable honesty, daja-ma."

"No! No, I insist on the truth from *you.* You advise my husband. And I am set at distance. I am told I shall *not* be permitted to leave the Bujavid. I cannot claim the Ajuri lordship. I cannot go to my own home!"

"Daja-ma, there are reasons."

"Reasons!"

"Your great-uncle, daja-ma." He kept his voice as low as possible. "I believe he did order your father's assassination. If you wish my opinion of events, daja-ma, your great-uncle plotted a coup from the hour of your son's birth. When the aiji sent him to the space station, out of reach, and in the dowager's keeping, it so upset your great-uncle's plans he launched the coup to remove the aiji, and possibly to appoint you to a regency until the succession could be worked out. But you fled *with* your husband."

Her look was at first indignant, then entirely shocked.

"You had no idea, did you not, daja-ma?"

"This is insane! My great-uncle. My great-uncle is in the Guild."

"He *was* in the Guild. Exactly so. And not of minor rank."

"Ajuri is a minor clan!"

"That is no impediment. What would you have done, daja-ma, if the Guild had separated you from your husband and asked you to govern for a few months—or to marry—in a few months, for the good of the aishidi'tat."

"You are quite out of your mind!"

"Did anyone approach you with such an idea, daja-ma?"

"Never!"

"Perhaps I am mistaken. But I am *not* mistaken about your great-uncle's support—with others—of a Kadagidi with southern ties, to take the aijinate. And one is not mistaken in the subsequent actions of your great-uncle, whose subversion of the Guild created chaos and upset in the aishidi'tat, setting region against region, constantly hunting your husband, and then trying to seize your son. A great deal of what went on out on the west coast was aimed at removing me, and the aiji-dowager—and, again, in laying hands on your son. We had *no* idea at the time. Your husband declined to bring his son back to the Bujavid, preferring to confront these people in the field rather than in the halls of the Bujavid. What he feared in the Bujavid—I do not know. But it was substantial."

She stared at him in shock, a hand to her heart. And he was sorry. He was intensely sorry for pressing, but it was, there in a quiet nook of her son's Investiture, surrounded by his aishid and the dowager's men, the same question that had hung over her marriage, her acceptance in her husband's household.

"Your father had just become lord of Ajuri," he said, unrelenting, "in the death of your uncle. There were, one fears, questions about that replacement which I had not heard—about which your husband may have been aware. The Guild was even then systematically withholding information from your husband's bodyguard, on the excuse that he had appointed them outside the Guild system. The heads of the Guild knowingly put your household at risk with *their* politics, of which, at that time, your great-uncle was definitely part. The Guild also withheld information from *my* aishid—more than policy, I now suspect, in a deliberate act which put my life in danger and almost killed your son. There was a great deal amiss on the west coast . . . but the threads of it have run back to the Guild in Shejidan. Realizing that, the aiji-dowager's aishid and mine began to ask questions, and to investigate matters inside the Guild, which, indeed, involved your great-uncle. *He* is now dead. Unfortunately we do not believe all his agents in the field are dead. So there is a reason, daja-ma, that the aiji has forbidden you to take the Ajuri lordship. There is a reason he, yes, *questioned* your clan's man'chi and wanted your father and his bodyguard out of the Bujavid, and you safe within it. And you should also know, daja-ma, that the aiji has since then strongly *rejected* all suggestions that your marriage should be dissolved for political convenience, insisting that you were not complicit in your great-uncle's actions. More, by retaining you as his wife, he has now placed you in a position which, until now, only the aiji-dowager has held. The aiji-dowager has questioned your motives. And I have begun to incline toward the aiji-dowager's opinion—that you *are* independent of your late great-uncle, independent also of your father, your aunt, and your cousin, and also of your great-uncle Tatiseigi. You never courted power. But power may someday land in your hands. And at very least, throughout your life, you will find not only your son, but your daughter besieged by ambitious clans. You have strongly resisted the aiji-dowager's influence. But, baji-naji, you could one day *become* her. Do not reject her *or* her allies. *Learn* from her. That is my unsolicited advice, aiji-ma. Now you have heard it."

She was breathing hard as any runner. She stared at him wide-eyed in shock, saying nothing, and now he wished he had not thrown so much information at her, not all at once, not here, not—tonight.

"One apologizes, daja-ma. One truly does."

"You are telling me the truth," she said, as if it were some surprise. "You are telling me the *truth,* are you not, nandi?"

"I have told you the truth, daja-ma. Perhaps too much of it."

"No," she said, eyes flashing. "No, nandi, not too much. *Finally,* someone makes sense!"

"One at least apologizes for doing so here, daja-ma. Understand, too, your husband held these matters only in bits and pieces. None of us knew until a handful of days ago."

"Paidhi," she said, winced, breathing hard, and suddenly caught at his arm.

"Daja-ma!" He lent support, he held on, not knowing where or how to take hold of her, and Jago intervened, flinging an arm about her, holding her up.

"I think—" Damiri said, still somewhat bent. "I think I am having the baby."

"The service passage," Banichi said. "Gini-ji, advise security; advise the aiji."

"What shall we do?" Bren asked, his own heart racing. "Is nand' Siegi here?"

"Call *my* physician," Damiri said, and managed to straighten. "I shall walk. There will be time. First tell my husband. Then call my physician."

"Two of you stay with her," Algini said to Damiri's security: "The other go privately advise the aiji and stand by for his orders. Bren-ji, stay with us."

Never complicate security's job. He understood. They walked at a sedate pace, Damiri walking on her own, quietly taking Algini's direction toward the service passage, past a number of people who gave their passage a mildly curious stare.

No one delayed them. They reached the doorway of the service passage, met servants exiting with food service, who ducked out of the way, startled.

"There is a chair, daja-ma," Bren said, "should you wish. You might sit down and let us call help."

"No," Damiri said shortly. "No! We shall not stop. Call my maid. Call my physician!"

"Security is doing that, nandi," Jago said quietly. Banichi continued to talk to someone on com, and Algini had eased ahead of them—he was up at an intersection of the corridor, giving orders to a uniformed Bujavid staffer, probably part of the kitchen crew.

"We have a lift car on hold," Tano said.

"I am perfectly well, now," Damiri said. "I shall be perfectly fine."

One hoped. One sincerely hoped.

They had finished the cards. Cajeiri's fingers ached, he had signed so many, and toward the end he had begun simplifying his signature, because his hand forgot where it was supposed to be going.

He *wanted* to go find his guests and at least talk to them, and ask how they were doing; and he *wanted* to go over to the buffet and get at least one of the teacakes he had seen on people's plates, and a drink. He very much wanted a drink of something, be it tea or just cold water. His throat was dry from saying, over and over again, "Thank you, nandi. One is very appreciative of the sentiment, nandi. One has never visited there, but one would very much enjoy it . . ." And those were the easy ones. The several who had wanted to impress him with their district's export were worse. He had acquired a few small gifts, too, which his bodyguard said he should not open, but which would go through security.

Mostly he just wanted to get a drink of water, but the last

person in line had engaged his father, now, and wanted to talk. He stood near the table and waited. And when his father's bodyguard did nothing to break his father free of the person, he turned to Antaro and said, very quietly, "Taro-ji, please bring me a drink of something, tea, juice, water, one hardly cares."

"Yes," she said, and started to slip away; but then senior Guild arrived, two men so brusque and sudden Antaro moved her hand to her gun and froze where she stood, in front of him; the other three closed about him.

It was his father the two aimed at; but his father's guard opened up and let them through, and then he realized, past the near glare of an oil lamp, that they were his *mother's* bodyguard.

"They are Mother's," he said, which was to say, Great-grandmother's. And they were upset. "Taro-ji, they are Mother's guard. Something is wrong."

"We are not receiving," Veijico reminded him, staying close with him as he followed Antaro into his father's vicinity.

"Son of mine," his father said, "your mother is going upstairs. It may be the baby. She has called for her physician. We are obliged to go, quickly."

"Is she all right?" he blurted out.

"Most probably. She has chosen not to go to the Bujavid clinic. She is giving directions. Nand' Bren is with her. Your great-grandmother has heard. She will make the announcement in the hall." His father set a hand on his shoulder. "Do not be distressed, son of mine. Likely everything is all right. We must just leave the hall and go upstairs."

"My guests," he said.

His father drew in a breath and spoke to his more senior bodyguard. "Go to Jase-aiji. Assist him and the young guests to get to Lord Tatiseigi's apartment. Advise my grandmother to take my place in the hall. She may give the excuse of the consort's condition. —Son of mine?"

"Honored Father."

"Will you wish to go with nand' Jase, or to go with us?"

He had never been handed such a choice. He had no idea which was right. Then he did know. "I should go where my mother is," he said. "Jase-aiji will take care of my guests."

"Indeed," his father said, and gave a little nod. "Indeed. Come with me. Quickly."

He snagged Jegari by the arm. "Go apologize to my guests. Tell them all of this, Gari-ji."

"Yes," Jegari said, and headed off through the crowd as quickly as he could.

Only then he thought . . . *What about Kaplan and Polano?*

The Bujavid staffer guided them through a succession of three service corridors, to a door that let out across from the lifts, in an area of hall cordoned off by red rope, and Guild were waiting beside a lift with the doors held open. Recent events still urged caution—but, "Clear," Banichi said, and they went, at Damiri's pace, which was brisk enough.

"We are in contact with the physician," Tano said in a low voice, "but he is down in the hotel district, attempting to get to the steps through the crowd. Guild is escorting him. They will activate the tramway to bring him up."

It was moderately good news. "Should we," Bren ventured to ask Damiri, as they entered the lift, "call nand' Siegi in the interim, daja-ma?"

She drew in a deep breath. They were all in. The door of the car shut, and Tano used his key and punched buttons. The car moved in express mode.

Damiri gasped and reached out, seizing Bren's arm, and Algini's, and they reached to hold her up.

"I think," she said, "I think—"

"Daja-ma?"

"Get my husband!"

"We have sent word," Bren said. "He is coming, daja-ma."

"Are you sure?" she asked, and gasped as the car stopped. "Paidhi, he is not going to be in time."

"Just a little further," Banichi said. "We can carry you if you wish, nandi."

"No," she said, and took a step, and two. They exited the car into the hall, with a long, long walk ahead.

"Tano-ji, go to nand' Tatiseigi's apartment," Bren said, still supporting Damiri on his arm. "Tell Madam Saidin to come. And nand' Siegi if you can find him."

Damiri opened her mouth to say something. And kept walking, but with difficulty. One truly, truly had no idea what to do, except to help her do what she had determined to do.

Banichi, who did not have use of one arm, moved to assist on the side he could, and Algini gave place to him. He said, quietly, "We are in contact with your staff, nandi, and Madam Saidin is on her way. So is your physician, at all speed. Here is nand' Bren's apartment. We could stop here, should you need. He has an excellent guest room."

"No," she said, but quietly, in the tenor of Banichi's calm, low voice. "I shall make it. I can make it."

"How long has this been going on?" Banichi asked, and after a deep series of breaths, Damiri said,

"Since yesterday."

"I would not spoil my son's festivity." Deep breath, and in a tone of distress. "With him, I had two days."

"It can be sooner."

"I think, nadi, it could be before I get to the doors."

Halfway to her apartment. "We are approaching," Bren heard Algini say. And his ears told him, too, that someone was coming behind them, likely Madam Saidin. "The hall is secure. You are clear to unlock the doors."

The doors ahead did open, wide, and the major domo and Damiri's personal maid came hurrying out in great distress, ran to them and paced along beside as, behind them, indeed, Madam Saidin came hurrying into their company.

"One can assist her, nandi," Madam Saidin said, easing

herself into Bren's place, while Damiri's maid took her arm on Banichi's side.

"I am no great assistance in this," Jago said, "but I can at least provide communications."

"Go," Bren said. "Stay with her as long as need be."

Tano arrived at a near run, from behind them. "Nand' Siegi says he has not done this in thirty years, but he is coming, Bren-ji."

"Well done," he said. He thought perhaps he should go back to his apartment and wait there for news, but he was one person who *could* give orders if something had to be decided, and someone who could at least answer questions and explain to Tabini, when *he* got here—*if* protocol would let him get here—and he was determined to stay. He followed, stopped in the foyer with the major domo as Madam Saidin and Damiri's maid assisted Damiri down the inner hall, toward her own suite, with Damiri's two bodyguards and Jago following. Servants were hurrying about, everyone hushed and trying not to make a commotion.

Bren just stood there, with his aishid—with Banichi, who by the sound of his questions knew more than the rest of them put together regarding Damiri's situation.

"One had no idea what to do," he said to his aishid, a little out of breath.

"One cannot say Jago has," Banichi said. "But she will tell us what she can learn, and the dowager's men will not go past the sitting room."

"Do *you* need to rest?" he asked. "Nichi-ji, do not hesitate."

"One has no desire to add to the commotion," Banichi said. There was a small bench built into the foyer wall by the major domo's office, not an uncommon arrangement, and he quietly took it. "You might sit, Bren-ji."

"I am too worried to sit," he said, but he did sit down, for fear Banichi would get up again. "I precipitated this. I was too harsh with my answers. I was far too blunt. I upset her."

"You gave her answers, Bren-ji. They were not pleasant

answers, but they were answers. And she seemed to have wanted them."

"Still . . ." he said, and saw by the sudden doorward look of everyone in the foyer that someone was coming. Human ears picked up nothing yet; but Algini took it on himself to open the door, hand on his pistol as he did so.

"Nand' Siegi," he said, and held the door open until the old man arrived, with an assistant carrying two cases of, one supposed, medical equipment and supplies.

"Where?" the old man asked, out of breath, and Tano showed him and his assistant down the inner hall and into the direction of the major domo, before Algini even began to shut the outer door.

But Algini stopped, and held the door open. "The aiji is coming," he said.

Banichi used the bench edge to put himself back on his feet. Bren stood up, and the major domo arrived back in the foyer, from down the hall, agitated and worried. Algini ceded him the control of the door as numerous footsteps approached.

Tabini arrived, with Cajeiri, with his double bodyguard, and Cajeiri's, too many people even to get into the foyer conveniently.

"How is she?" Tabini asked at once.

The major domo said: "Well, aiji-ma. She seems well. Nand' Siegi is here."

"Paidhi!" Tabini said, shedding his coat into the major domo's hands, and there was no assistant to provide another. "Take care of my son."

"Aiji-ma," Bren said, and Tabini, in his shirt sleeves, and with only his junior bodyguard, headed down the long inner hall, toward his wife's suite.

Cajeiri cast a worried look after him, then looked Bren's direction. Worried. Scared, likely, and trying not to show it.

"Your mother walked to the apartment," Bren said, "and she seems well enough. Nand' Siegi just arrived."

Nobody had taken the boy's coat. The major domo had

gone back down the hall in a hurry, following Tabini. Guild was talking to Guild, meanwhile, exchanging information partly verbally, partly in handsigns, and there was a general relaxation.

"I think we could do with a cup of tea," Bren said quietly. "Can we arrange that?"

"Yes," the Guild senior of Tabini's guard said, and headed down the same hall, while Bren steered Cajeiri, Cajeiri's bodyguard, and his own three toward the sitting room, the civilized place to wait.

"Sit," he said to them, in consideration of Banichi. "Everybody sit. We are not in an emergency now."

"Is she really all right, nandi?" Cajeiri asked.

"She seemed quite in command," Bren said. "Madam Saidin is there; Jago is, and now nand' Siegi." There was another small commotion in the foyer, even as he spoke. "That may be her own physician—he had to come up from the hotel district."

"Jago reports your father is with her, young aiji," Tano said, "and she knows you are here."

"My father says I should not go back there," Cajeiri said unhappily.

"There are so many people," Bren said. Two of the kitchen help were making their tea, over at the side of the room: there was not a senior servant nor a woman to be seen, when ordinarily a handful would have flitted through, checking on things, being sure the fire was lit, the chairs were set. "I think that *is* your mother's physician who just arrived." He could see an older woman and a younger pass the door. "Everyone who needs to be here is here."

"My father sent word to nand' Jase," Cajeiri said, "and he is going up to Great-uncle's apartment. I think my great-grandmother has taken charge of the party."

"That was well-thought," Bren said.

"But Kaplan and Polano . . ." Cajeiri said. "How do they get upstairs?"

That was a question. The poor lads were down there for

security. "One believes Jase will give them orders; and they were prepared to be there until the party ended. They will be there for your great-grandmother, and, one supposes, Lord Tatiseigi's safety, as well. And your guests will be upstairs, able to get out of these fancy clothes, so one supposes they are more comfortable than we are."

"Is she going to be all right, nandi?"

"There is nothing that indicated anything to the contrary, young gentleman. She simply knew it was time, and she had us all escort her upstairs. Apparently," he added, because the boy and his mother were too often at odds, "she has been having pains since yesterday, but she wanted you to have your festivity without the disruption of her taking to her bed. She thought she could get through the evening."

"She did?"

"She is quite brave, your mother is, and she knew it was a very important evening."

Cajeiri just stared at him a moment. "I wish she had said something."

"But your father would have worried. And you would have worried."

"She *is* going to be all right?"

"Baji-naji, young gentleman, but your mother is too determined a woman to do other than very well."

"I am glad you call me young gentleman. I am not ready to be young aiji."

"You had no idea your father would do that?"

"None at all, nandi!"

The boys were standing by, awaiting a nod before setting the cups down. Bren gave it, and took the teacup gladly enough.

Cajeiri put sugar into his. And drank it half down at one try.

"Did you ever get to eat?" Bren asked him.

"No, but—" Cajeiri began, when there was a sudden noise of footsteps from down the hall, and the major domo came hurrying in, to bow deeply in Cajeiri's direction.

"Young gentleman, your father sends for you."

Cajeiri set the cup aside, looking scared.

"Is it good news?" Bren asked sharply, startling the man, who bowed again.

"The aiji-consort is very well, nandi. The young gentleman has a—"

Cajeiri bounced to his feet and headed out the door at a run, taking a sharp right at the door, his young aishid rising in complete confusion.

"—sister," the major domo finished, and bowed in consternation. "Please excuse me, nand' paidhi!"

The major domo hurried after. Cajeiri's bodyguard stood by their chairs, confused.

"As well sit and wait, nadiin," Banichi said, as Tano and Algini looked amused. "There is no use for us back there."

Bren let out a slow breath, and took a sip of tea, affording himself a little smile as Cajeiri's young bodyguard settled back into their chairs, deciding there probably was no further use for their presence, either.

But they might as well finish the tea.

Mother was propped with pillows, and her hair was done up with a ribbon. Father was in a chair at her bedside. And there was a white blanket in Mother's arms, just the way it was in the machimi. It all seemed like a play, like it was somebody else's family, somebody else's mother and father, on stage.

But he came closer, and Mother smiled at him, and moved the blanket and showed him a little screwed-up face that hadn't been in the world before.

"This is Seimiro," Mother said. "This is your sister."

He looked at his father, who looked at him; he looked at his mother. He looked at the screwed-up little face. He had never seen a really young baby.

"Is she asleep?" he whispered.

"She hears you," his father said. "But she cannot see you yet."

"Can I touch her?"

"Yes," his mother said.

He put out his hand, touched her tiny fist with just one finger. She was unexpectedly soft, and warm. "Hello, Seimiro," he said. "Hello. This is your brother."

"Do you want to hold her?" his father asked.

She was so tiny. He knew he could. But she was so delicate. And his mother would be really upset if he made a mistake. "No," he said. "I might do it wrong."

"Here." His father stood up, and carefully took the baby, and carefully put it in his arms. She was no weight at all. She made a face at him. He could hold her in one arm and touch her on her nose, which made her make another face, and made him smile. But it was a risk, all the same: he very carefully gave her back to his mother, who took her back and smiled, not at him, for doing it right; but at her.

Well, that was the way things were going to be. But she was new, and he could hardly blame people for being interested.

He just said to himself that he had a long, long head start on Seimiro, and she would have a lot of work to catch him.

There were a lot of things he could show her.

Even if they had sealed up some of the servant passages. There were still ways to sneak around the Bujavid.

Jase made it back: Madam Saidin had gotten home, and taken over, and Jase was willing to trade news over a glass of brandy.

Kaplan and Polano were still stuck in the hall, being statues, but they were comfortable enough, and there were atevi guards standing near them who knew what they were, and who had orders to get them back upstairs once the festivity had broken up.

Everybody was in the sitting room. Everybody was sitting, Bren, Banichi and Jago, Tano and Algini, even Narani and Jeladi, all indulging in a modest brandy, and everybody debriefing, in safe privacy. Even Bindanda came in, their other plain-clothes Guildsman, to get the news straight from those who were there.

"The baby's name is Seimiro," Jago said. And: "Damiri-daja had no trouble at all. And well we hurried. The baby was there before nand' Siegi was."

Jase said, "The youngsters were a little worried when they saw everybody leaving—so were the guests. But the dowager took over and explained the situation, and I took the youngsters right on up to Lord Tatiseigi's apartment: the guests were headed for the wine and brandy, very happy."

"One wishes the youngsters could have had a better time," Bren said.

"Oh," Jase said, "they had fancy dress, they had the museum, they had all the lords and ladies, and seeing Cajeiri and the ceremony—they were very excited. They asked me more questions than I could answer. Then the baby coming—they knew why they had to go upstairs, and then with Madam Saidin helping deliver the baby—they were very excited."

"One hears the city is going wild," he said. That was, at least, what his bodyguard reported, and he had no doubt of it.

"The printing office is calling in staff," Algini said, "and they are preparing another release of cards for tomorrow: the birth announcement."

"And no trouble?" Bren asked.

"None," Algini said. "One hopes our remaining problems are busy relocating, and where they *have* been, we may be interested to learn. For tonight, at least, we can relax."

Relax. With a glass of brandy, good company, and everybody safe and well. It was a special occasion.

"Will you want to stay here tonight?" Father asked, in the hallway. Mother and the baby were asleep, though Father said they would probably have restless nights for quite a while.

Cajeiri gave a little bow. "One has guests waiting, honored Father, and if I may, I should go to nand' Tatiseigi's apartment and explain everything. If I may."

"Yes."

The enormity of everything struck him then, and maybe, he thought, he should have said something special—about the inheritance and all that. And the ceremony. And the surprise. He gave a deep, deep bow.

"Thank you, honored Father. Thank you very much. And one is very sorry for forgetting the speech."

"You did very well this evening. One was quite proud of you."

He straightened up, heat rushing to his face. He could not remember his father saying that. "I shall not be a fool. I shall study. But I do not want to be aiji for a long, long time."

"You are a good son. A very good son. One is twice proud. Go. Behave yourself. *Enjoy* the day."

He did, instantly about infelicitous four paces down the hall before he remembered, then, to make a grown-up exit, and turned and bowed deeply. "Thank you, Father."

"Indeed," his father said, and nodded, and Cajeiri walked sedately all the way down the hall, collected his aishid, and walked a little more briskly outside and up the hall past nand' Bren's apartment.

"Her name is Seimiro," he said, thinking of it.

"Is she pretty?" Lucasi asked.

"Wrinkled," he said, making a face, and laughed.

"Babies are like that," Antaro said. "I saw my cousin after he was born."

They were in the hall with no other escort, no guards at the end. They came up on Great-uncle's door, and it opened, Madam already having gotten a signal from Antaro, and in they came, Madam very happy to have them back.

"Come right on in," Madam said, "into the sitting room."

He had a little suspicion when Madam did not take his coat, and when Madam showed him straight to the sitting room, that his guests had not gone to bed.

Indeed, they were all three waiting, in their court dress, with, in the midst of the side table, a very large—cake. It was iced like a teacake. But it was large enough for everybody and the staff. And there was a candelabra beside it and beside that, three boxes wrapped up in brocade fabric.

"Happy birthday!" they all said at once.

He laughed, he was so surprised. And they insisted he open the boxes, one after another: there was a little handwritten notebook from Irene—"A lot of words you could use," she said; and he saw words he had never seen before, with the rules for pronouncing them. And from Artur there was a little clear shiny marble that lit up. "Just set it in any light," Artur said, "and it recharges."

And from Gene there was what looked like a pocketknife, but it unfolded in screwdrivers and picks and a magnifying glass.

They were wonderful gifts. And then Madam lit the candles and they cut the cake, and all had some—Madam said they had made another cake for staff, and his guests had told them how such a cake had to be—it was iced like one piece, but inside it was in layers and pieces, and Greatuncle's cook had made the icing orangelle-flavored, his favorite, in clever patterns.

They had fruit drink, and cake, and told stories until it was past midnight and Great-uncle came home, asking whether he had seen his sister, and how his mother was.

"My sister is fine and my mother is, Great-uncle. My father is very happy."

"Excellent," Great-uncle said. "Excellent. Such a day this has been! Congratulations, young aiji."

"Nandi."

"A fortunate day, indeed. Your ninth year and your sister's first—all on one day."

He stood there a moment, realizing . . .

He had a sister. And she was born on *his* birthday.

His birthday was *her* birthday. Forever.

Nobody had asked him about that. Worse—his next fortunate birthday would be his eleventh. And from zero, which was today, the very same day would be *her* infelicitous second: they were always going to be out of rhythm, and nothing could ever fix it.

Except if they celebrated each other's fortunate day with a festivity.

He had to make a deal with his sister about birthdays. There could be a sort of a festivity every year.

"Is there a problem, Jeri-ji?" Gene asked.

He saw Great-uncle venturing a taste of his extraordinary cake, and very definitely approving.

"No," he said, and felt mischief coming on. There were *so* many things his sister needed to learn, not to turn out as stiff and proper as people could want her to be. "No. Not a one."

**Lord Geigi, Lord Regent in the Heavens:
His History of the Aishidi'tat
with commentary by Lord Bren of Najida,
paidhi-aiji**

Before the Foreign Star appeared in the Heavens, we, on our own, had reached the age of steam.

We had philosophically and politically begun to transcend the clan structure that had led to so many ruinous wars.

We had eleven regional associations which agreed to build a railroad from Shejidan to the west without going to war about it.

Within the associations, there had been artisan guilds for many years. But during the building of the first railroad, many guilds, starting with the Transportation Guild and the Builders, had not only transcended the limits of clan structure, Transport and the Builders ended by transcending the regional associations. They were the first political entities to do so.

Clans had long formed temporary associations of regional alliance and trade interest. These were associations of convenience that often broke up in bitter conflict.

That was the state of things when, three hundred years ago, the Foreign Star arrived in the heavens.

It appeared suddenly. It grew. Telescopes of the day could make out a white shape that seemed to reflect light instead of shining like a star. The Astronomers offered no one theory to account for it. Earliest observers said it was a congealing of the ether that conveyed the heat of the sun to the Earth. But as it grew and showed structure and shadow, the official thought came to be that it was a rip in the sky dome and a view of the clockwork mechanism beyond.

The number-counters agreed it was an omen of change in the heavens, and most said it was not a good one. Some tried to attach the omen to the railroad, for good or for ill, and for a whole year it occupied the attention of the lords and clans.

But it produced nothing.

And under all the furor, and with a certain sense of something ominous hanging above the world, the railroad from Shejidan to the coast continued. Aijiin, once warleaders elected for a purpose, were elected to manage the project, holding power not over armies, but over the necessary architecture of guilds, clans, and sub-clans, for the sole purpose of getting the project through certain districts and upholding the promises to which the individual clan lords had set their seals.

Empowering them was a small group which itself began to transcend clans and regions: this was the beginning of the Assassins' Guild, and their job was to protect the aijin against attack by others of their profession serving individual lords.

The Foreign Star harmed nothing. The railroad succeeded. If the Star portended anything, many said, it seemed to be good fortune.

The success of the first railroad project led to others. Associations became larger, overlapped each other as clans and kinships do. And significantly, in the midst of a dispute that might have led to the dissolution of these new associations, the Assassins' Guild backed the aiji against three powerful clan lords who wanted to change the agreement and break up the railroad into administrative districts.

We atevi have never understood boundaries. Everything is shades of here and there, this side and that. It had not been our separations and our regions that had brought us this age of relative peace. It was associations of common purpose, and their combination into larger and larger associations, until the whole world knew someone who knew someone who could make things right.

And now this one aiji, backed by the Assassins' Guild, had made three powerful lords keep their agreements for what turned out to benefit everyone—even these three clans, who collected no tolls, but whose people benefited by trade.

That aiji was the first to rule the entire west. The first railroad and the power of the aiji in Shejidan joined associations together in a way simple trade never had. Now the lords and trades and guilds were obliged to meet in Shejidan and come to agreement with the aiji who served and ruled them all. This was the true beginning of the legislature and the aishidi'tat, although it did not yet bear that name.

And without lords in constant war, and with the Assassins enforcing an impartial law, townships sprang up without walls, not clustered around a great house, but developing in places of convenience, with improved health and new goods. Commerce grew. Where conflicts sprang up, the aiji in Shejidan, with the legislature and the guilds, found a way to settle them without resort to war.

Shejidan itself grew rapidly, a town with no lord but the aiji himself. It attracted the smaller and weaker clans, particularly those engaging in crafts and trades. And those little clans, prospering as never before because of the railway, backed the aiji with street cobbles and dyers' poles when anyone threatened that order. The guilds also broke from the clan structure and settled in Shejidan, backing the aiji's authority, so that the lords who wanted the services of the Scholars, the Merchants, the Treasurers, the Physicians, or the Assassins, had to accept individuals whose primary man'chi was to their guilds and the aiji in Shejidan.

The Foreign Star had become a curiosity. Some studied it as a hobby. Then as a village lord in Dur wrote, who lived in that simpler time . . .

One day a petal sail floated down to Dur from the heavens, and more and more of them followed— bringing to the world a people not speaking in any way people of the Earth could understand. Some were pale, some were brown, and some were as dark as we are. Most landed on the island of Mospheira, among the Edi and the Gan peoples. Some landed on the mainland, near Dur. And some sadly fell in the sea, and were lost.

For three years the Foreign Star poured humans down to the Earth, sometimes whole clouds of them. Their small size and fragile bones and especially their manner of reaching the Earth excited curiosity, and won a certain admiration for their bravery. Poets immortalized the petal sails.

These humans brought very little with them. Their dress was plain and scant. They seemed poor. Wherever they landed, they took apart the containers that had sheltered them, and used the pieces and spread the petal sails and tied them to trees for shelter from the elements. They tried our food, but they sometimes died of it, and it was soon clear they could eat only the plainest, simplest things. They were a great curiosity, and one district and another was anxious to find these curious people and see them for themselves. Some believed that they had fallen from the moon, but the humans insisted they had come from inside the Foreign Star, and that they were glad to be on the Earth because of the poverty where they had been.

There was no fear of them by then. They spoke, and we learned a few words. We spoke, and we first fed them and helped them build better shelter. We helped them find each other across the land, and gather their scattered associates. We were amazed, even shocked, at their manners with each other. But they seemed equally distressed by ours.

—Lord Paseni of Tor Musa in Dur

The Foreign Star, as the man from Dur wrote, had for

years been a fixture in the heavens. The Astronomers had long ago proclaimed that it had ceased growing, and that, whatever it was, it did not seem to threaten anything.

Then humans rode their petal sails down to the west coast of the continent and the island of Mospheira. They were small and fragile people and threatened no one. With childlike directness they offered trade—not of goods, but of technological knowledge, even mechanical designs.

The unease of the man from Dur might have warned us all. But some humans learned the children's language, which allowed them mistakes in numbers without offense.

The petal sails kept falling down, hundreds and hundreds and hundreds of them, until there were human villages. They brought their knowledge. They built in concrete. They built dams and generators: they built radios and other such things which we adopted . . .

And finally they stopped coming down.

The last to come were not as peaceful as the first.

We had no idea why.

But the ship that had brought the humans and built the Foreign Star had left. It was of course the space station they had built in orbit above our Earth.

And the last to come down were the station aijiin and their bodyguards, armed, and dropping pods of weapons onto the world.

ii

<<Bren>> The origin of the Foreign Star was a human starship, *Phoenix,* which had as its original purpose the establishment of a station at a star far removed from this world. They held all the knowledge, all the machines, and all the seeds and plans that would let the ship orbit some moon or planet as a temporary base for four thousand colonists to live aboard. The colonists would build a station core and outer structure and set it in full operation.

Another ship would follow *Phoenix,* with more colonists.

That second ship would bring equipment which would let the orbiting station eventually set down people and build a habitat on a world far less hospitable than the Earth of the atevi.

But something happened. The ship-folk believe that the ship met some accident and was shifted somewhere far off its intended course. The ship tried to find some navigational reference that would tell it where it was. The fact that reference stars were not visible where they should be indicated to them that something very drastic had happened.

Phoenix gathered resources such as it could and aimed toward the closest promising star. It saw, among its several choices, a blue world much like humans' own ancestral Earth. The world had the signature of life—which meant they would indeed find resources there. The world had no artificial satellites. They picked up no transmissions. This informed them there was no space-faring civilization there.

They ended up in orbit about the Earth of the atevi.

They saw, below them, towns and villages. They saw technology of a certain level—but not high enough to come up to them, and their law, remote as they were then from any law but their own conscience, ruled against disturbing the world, even if they had had an easy means to land and ask help . . . which they did not.

The colonists had come prepared and trained to build an orbiting station. They gathered resources from asteroids, manufactured panels and parts and framework, enclosing themselves from the inside out and housing more and more workers. This became the core of the station. They built tethers, and began the construction of the station ring, to gain a place to stand. Barracks moved into the beginnings of the ring. The first children were born. Spirits rose. They were going to survive.

Phoenix crew was supposed to have supported the colonists this far and then move on. The ship-folk were space-farers by trade and nature and had no desire to live on a colonial station. But now that the colonists were safe, and now that the ship was resupplied and able to leave—it troubled the ship-aijiin that the ship now had no use and nowhere to go next. They had only one port, and clearly the station was not where they wanted their port to be. The blue planet had exactly the right conditions and everything they needed . . . but it was owned, and the ship-folk's law said they should not disturb it.

The ship had long argued against the building of any elaborate station in orbit about the planet. They wanted the colonists to leave off any further development of the station they had, use it as an observation point and a refuge should anything go wrong, and build another, larger station out at Maudit. They should, the ship-aijiin said, leave the inhabited world alone until, perhaps, they might make contact in space some time in the future.

The colonists, born aboard this station, and with all the hardship of the prior generations, had no desire to give up their safety and build again—least of all to build a station above a desolate, airless world. They wanted the world they saw under their feet. They wanted it desperately.

The station aijiin also argued against building at Maudit. They needed their population. They needed their workers—and they wanted no rival station. They absolutely refused the ship's solution.

The argument between station authorities and ship-aijiin grew bitter. *Phoenix,* now hearing these same officials claiming authority over the mission and the ship itself—decided to pull out of the colonial dispute altogether. They considered going to Maudit with a handful of willing souls and building there, then trying to draw colonists out to join them in defiance of the station aijiin—but that idea was voted down, since the colonists even at Maudit would still be in reach of that living planet, and the crew was vastly outnumbered if it came to a confrontation on the matter. By now the ship-folk did not entirely trust even the colonists they considered allies, with the green planet at issue.

The ship's crew voted to take aboard those colonists who

wanted to leave, and go. They went a year out into deep space, to a star with resources of metal and ice. There they set up a station they called, optimistically, Reunion.

From Reunion, the ship continued its exploration, through optics, and by closer inspection. The crew no longer hoped to find their own Earth, but they did hope that by increasing the human population at Reunion, then, from Reunion, establishing other colonies at planets or moons of some attraction—they could then revisit the population they'd left at the Earth of the atevi and convince them there was an alternative to landing.

Alternatives, however, did not immediately present themselves. The station at Reunion grew. But there was no suitable world. More troubling still, in one direction, they found the signature of another technological presence.

Back at the first station, from the week of *Phoenix*'s departure, the authorities had begun losing control. All that had stopped the colonists from going down to the Earth in the first place was the simple fact that, among the colonists or on the ship, there was nobody who knew how to land in a gravity well, or fly in an atmosphere, with weather and winds. *Phoenix* itself had been fairly confident that the colonists would, without the ship's crew, have to agree among themselves to survive, and that the solution would not involve experimental manned landings on the planet.

But the colonists had a considerable library. And in those files they found a means within their capability to build, to aim, and to operate.

They pointed it out to the station aijiin.

They demanded action.

The station aijiin gave in. They built machines that would land in undeveloped land, and explore. If those reported well, they would build a craft to land by parachute, that would carry a scientific team, such as they could muster.

Those would go first.

All went well down to the second stage. The team, composed of names still honored by place names on Mospheira, met the tribal peoples . . . and after a brief period of good report and apparent progress—they vanished, with no clue, even to later generations.

The program was shut down, and remained shut down, for a long time. But dissatisfaction grew, in claims the station aijiin had been too timid. There were other places. There was empty land, even on the island. There was a whole other shore. There were extensive forests. There were vast plains where no one at all lived. There was a very large island south of the main continent.

Station authorities tried to silence the idea. The population had increased, but the space station had not. The ship had taken away the machinery that might have let them add more room easily. And then supplies began to disappear.

Small conspiracies assembled simple life-support for small capsules, shielded against the friction of the atmosphere, and provided with only one button, which would blow the shield off the parachute in the event the sensors that should do that automatically—failed.

By twos and threes they launched these fragile capsules toward the gravity well, and parachuted down.

When colonists learned the first capsules had come down safely—and more, that they were welcomed—more and more groups fled the station. The station-aijiin attempted to find and destroy these efforts, and the desperation of the colonists only increased. Workers refused to work. Groups stole materials in plain sight, and threatened anyone who tried to stop them. And the station grew more empty, and shut down, section by section. Those manufacturing materials said openly what they were for, and a small group exercised discipline enough to keep the effort going despite the objections of station aijiin.

Their technicians deserted. Station maintenance suffered. At the very last there was no choice for the administrative and systems managers but to join the movement. They mothballed the station, set the systems to maintain stable orbit so long as they could, and parachuted their armed bodyguards and themselves to the planet.

The last sudden band of humans, who emphatically resented being there and did not want to adapt to the planet in any way, changed everything.

Atevi suddenly attacked, for no reason humans understood.

In fact atevi had long since been pushed past the limit, and when they met the managers and the large load of weapons, they had finally pushed back.

iii

<<Geigi>> Characteristically, we reacted to this threat in our clans, our guilds, and our associations. Offense to one of us triggered others, to the dismay of the humans.

Coastal associations responded. Then the aiji in Shejidan moved to assert control, and took over leadership in the War of the Landing: this absorbed the last western clans still holding apart from the aishidi'tat, and eventually brought the Marid in as well.

The aiji formed a strategy to contain the problem reasonably rapidly: to push the humans off the continent and onto Mospheira, where the greatest number of humans were already living. Mospheira was the home of the Edi and Gan peoples, who had first met the humans, and who were part of the bloodiest action, but they were not part of the aishidi'tat, and were not Ragi, nor of the same customs. They persisted in attacking the humans on their own, with disastrous results.

The aiji offered the tribal peoples refuge from the fighting, in two small areas of the west coast where they could pursue their traditional ways and their livelihood of fishing. Without attacks coming at them on the island, humans found it a place of safe retreat, and centered their non-combatants there—which left only the most aggressive humans on the continent, exactly the situation the aiji wanted. The humans on the mainland could now be attacked and maneuvered into small pockets that could be cut off.

The War of the Landing ended with the humans on the mainland cut off from supplies, with no way back to the space station, and with no prospect of rescue from the island, or even of retreat to it, since the forces from the Marid held the strait. The aiji in Shejidan offered these groups a choice: extermination, or a way out. Humans might have ownership of the large and rich island of Mospheira, the conditions being first, total disarmament—the weapons they had were to be taken out to sea and sunk.

Secondly, and this was why the aiji was so generous: surrender of the technology. In return for an untroubled sanctuary, the humans were to send a paidhi to Shejidan to live, to translate, and to supervise the gradual turnover of all their technology to the aishidi'tat—namely to the aiji ... and they were not to build or use any technology that was not approved by the paidhi.

The desperate humans had a very limited understanding of what a paidhi was. They understood that he was to mediate, translate, and that he would be their official in the aiji's court, so they picked the most fluent Ragi speaker they had, hoping to stall off any demand for their weapons technology.

That was very well, the aiji said to them, through the paidhi they sent. There would surely be areas of agreement, and very useful things would serve.

That *any* knowledge could be turned to other purposes, and that atevi scientists were already finding out the secrets of foreign machines they had captured, was something the aiji failed to mention.

That there was still a starship the humans hoped would someday return was a matter humans had failed to mention, on their side.

But that agreement brought sufficient peace: this was the Treaty of the Landing, on which all our dealings with humans have been based. The Foreign Star, empty, continued to orbit the world.

Humans, vastly outnumbered, set about transforming Mospheira to suit themselves.

The aiji in Shejidan argued convincingly that the association atevi had formed to defend themselves should not be dissolved, since who knew if there were more humans to arrive from the heavens?

The allied association of the Marid had joined the aishidi'tat at the last moment, and would not accept the guilds: it maintained its own. Likewise the East was not yet part of the aishidi'tat in any permanent way.

But in the same way atevi had built the railroads, they had found pragmatic ways to work together—and the number-counters found fortunate numbers in the suggestions of an extension of the association—so it was felicitous that the Western Association, which was no longer just western, should stay together to respond quickly to any further difficulty from the humans on Mospheira.

The lords of the outlying clans and the regions, the aiji said, all should sit equally in the legislature in Shejidan, and they should all have a say in the laws of the aishidi'tat, the same as those born to the cental region.

The aiji further divided the entire continent into defensive districts, and these became provinces, with their own lords, also seated in the legislature. This added a few extra votes to critical regional associations, to balance the dominance of Shejidan: this pleased the lords.

The aiji then went to the guilds with another proposal: that, as they had all worked across regional lines during the War, they should continue after the war, adding a special privilege and formal principle. The guilds of the expanded aishidi'tat should have no respect for clan origin in candidacy for membership or in assignment: in fact, the guilds of *every* sort, like the Assassins, like Transport, should become their own authority, assigning members to posts only based on qualification, officially now without regard to kinship, regional association, or clan. This placed all power over membership into the hands of the guild masters.

The heads of the various guilds, interested in maintaining the power they held under war conditions, saw nothing but advantage in the aiji's proposal. The idea was less popular with some of the regional associations, who still held apart from the guild system—but in the main, it became the rule, not by statue, but by internal guild rules, and there was nothing the regional associations *or* the newly created provinces *or* the clan lords could do about that—if they wanted guild services.

The Assassins' Guild, in private conference and at the aiji's request, agreed to one additional rule, that no one of their guild could seek or hold a political office or a lordship. They received a concession in exchange: that, as they were barred from politics, they would have certain statutory immunities from political pressure. Their records could not be summoned by any lord, their members would testify only before their own guild council, and the disappearance or death of any member of that guild, granted the unusual nature of their work and the extreme discipline imposed on the membership, could only be investigated by that guild and dealt with by that guild, by its own rules.

There were other, more detailed, provisions in that Assassins' Guild charter, and there were peculiar ones, too, in the regulation of other guilds, and also in privileges granted the residents of Shejidan, to have their own officials, independent of any clan.

It was a tremendous amount of power the aiji let flow out of his hands.

But it also meant the aiji in Shejidan gained the support of the city and all the guilds, and now outvoted any several regional lords.

And from that time, the Assassins, freed of political pressure, became not only the law enforcement of the aishidi'tat, but the check and balance on every legal system, the unassailable integrity at the heart of any aiji's rule.

The new principle of guild recruitment across clan and regional lines had an unintended consequence. It brought ideas into contact with other ideas, and fostered a flowering of arts and skills, invention and innovation—a cross-pollination that within a few years ended one major cause of wars. Even the domestic staffs that served a clan lord might be from different clans, different regions, and different philosophies, all working together.

It was, in that sense, an idyllic era of growth, discovery, and change—with occasional breaches and dissonances, true—but the clan feuds grew fewer, and more often bloodless, to the wonder of those who thought in the old ways, and distrusted the new.

There were two exceptions.

There had once been a great power in the southern ocean, which had conquered and colonized the Marid before the Great Wave had destroyed all the seaboard cities on the Southern Island. The Marid, of a culture separate from the north, had been reaching for the west coast before the petal sails had begun to fall . . . and while it had cooperated with the aishidi'tat during the War of the Landing and remained officially a member after the Treaty was signed, it refused to allow what it called the Shejidani guilds to make any assignments in the Marid—and it did not have all the guilds. It maintained its own recruitment and training centers for the Assassins, the Treasurers, the Merchants, the Artisans, the Kabiuteri, and the Builders, as well as some unique to their region. The five clans of the Marid united only infrequently, maintained their seats in the legislature of the aishidi'tat, and their disputes frequently resorted to warfare among themselves.

The Eastern Association, headed by Malguri from the time of the War of the Landing, was the second isolate entity, a vast territory walled off from the west by the continental divide, and by the storms of the Eastern Ocean. Its small clans and its three cultures had united with the West for the first time in the face of the threat from the heavens.

But after the Treaty, as before, Easterners hunted, fished, and worked crafts, never having formed the guilds that were so important in the rest of the world.

They were, however, fierce fighters, and one guild had gotten a toehold in the East during the War of the Landing—the Assassins. They had organized their own training, their own guild hall, and ran their own operation in the East during the War. The Eastern Assassins' Guild affiliated itself with the Guild in Shejidan. It allowed certain of their members to be *assigned* by the Guild in Shejidan— but allowed no outsiders to come in. They were good, they were impeccably honest, they were in high demand because of their reputation, and recruitment was easy because of the general poverty of the East. But the East was otherwise separate from the guild system of the aishidi'tat ... until Ilisidi, aiji in Malguri, was courted by the aiji in Shejidan.

Ilisidi-aiji brought a great deal to the marriage. She joined the vast territory of the East to the aishidi'tat. She had her own opinions, and voiced them, and being widowed, she continued to voice them in support of a list of causes including opposition to human presence, opposition to industrial encroachment, support for the environment, and concern for the unresolved west coast situation in the regions facing Mospheira. She maintained a considerable and independent bodyguard, larger than any other lord in the East or the west, and when widowed, she refused to give up her young son to the aiji's maternal grandfather.

She maintained control of the Bujavid, made herself aiji-regent, since she did not succeed in having the aishidi'tat accept her as aiji in fact—and she simultaneously refused to leave Shejidan—while she kept an iron control of Malguri. She continued well into her son's majority to have her own agenda, and her own very large bodyguard, which by now had extended her authority over the entire East, and which maintained her safety, even in annoying a number of the powers of the aishidi'tat in Shejidan.

Her son, Valasi, finally succeeded in establishing his own

authority as aiji in Shejidan, with the help of the Taibeni clan of the Padi Valley, his grandmother's clan, and others of the north and mountain regions. He was twenty-seven by the time he made his bid for power, and Ilisidi conceded to him, finally, as he gained sufficient votes in the legislature.

Valasi made a contract marriage with a woman of the Taibeni, quickly produced an heir as insurance, and found it convenient to follow that contract marriage with several others, of whatever region he needed to draw more firmly into his hands. This bedroom diplomacy solved several petty wars.

He also gained several important technological advances through his partnership with Wilson-paidhi, including aviation and early television, and in all, had a strong grip on power, while he avoided having his eldest son in the hands of his various wives by putting young Tabini into Ilisidi's hands and urging the aiji-dowager to keep Tabini safe in her own estate at Malguri.

This kept his minor son and Ilisidi both separate from the center of politics. It kept the center of the aishidi'tat very happy, in the absence of their chief irritant, the aiji-dowager, but Valasi's concentration on trying to keep power out of Ilisidi's hands had left the west coast of the aishidi'tat embittered: they viewed Ilisidi as their ally, and her departure to Malguri as Valasi's definitive refusal to deal with their problems.

The west coast clans, notably the Maschi at Targai and Tirnamardi, had been forced to play a cautious kind of politics, balanced between the Edi tribal people, who supplemented their traditional fishing with piracy and wrecking, and the Marid clans, who saw the west coast as naturally theirs. Marid shipping was the principle target of the piracy. The Marid at times pursued their aims with contract marriages in the west, but all the same, given the resentments of the Edi people, unwilling settlers on that coast, and clan wars inside the Marid, all these moves came to was a generally unsettled condition on the west coast. The north coast fared somewhat better, in the happy relationship of the Gan tribal people with their nearest neighbors, also mariners, on the island of Dur—

But the adjacent Northern Association, while not in the same ferment as the south, and somewhat inland, had its own ambitions. The head of the Northern Association, within the aishidi'tat, was the lord of Ajuri clan . . . and he, pressed by a struggle inside his own clan, arranged the marriage of a young relative, Komaji, to an older lady of the ancient Atageini clan—the Atageini lord being one of the closest allies of the aiji-dowager, and at the moment engaged in politics with Valasi-aiji, in a dispute with their nearest neighbors, the Kadagidi.

It was a marriage of great potential value for Ajuri. It proved, however, unfortunate, in the death of the Atageini lady soon after the birth of a daughter, Damiri, under circumstances some called suspicious. Lord Tatiseigi of the Atageini, in a heated confrontation with Komaji, handed over the baby to Komaji, thus breaking the association with Ajuri and terminating the Ajuri hope of having a relative in an influential position within the great Atageini house.

Valasi-aiji managed to patch the quarrel between the Atageini and the Kadagidi, and simultaneously prevented the Atageini lord from Filing Intent on Komaji. He also kept the southwest coast out of the hands of the Marid, and had got control of the aishidi'tat back into western hands and out of the hands of the aiji-dowager.

Valasi was accounted a great aiji.

He died unexpectedly, however, with his heir still short of the twenty-three years of age required to be elected aiji.

The aiji-dowager returned to Shejidan with her grandson Tabini and applied to be elected aiji herself, citing the complex business of the aishidi'tat, particularly in view of increasing traffic with the Mospheirans, who were beginning to colonize neighboring Crescent Island, and who were developing industry without restraint—a matter which left the northwest coast of the continent on the receiving end of the smoke and the effluent.

She repeated her argument that several areas of the aishidi'tat remained a problem, since they had been stopgap arrangements following the War of the Landing; and she also proposed tough new negotiations with Mospheira about the protection of the environment.

The legislature balked ... on all points. Regional interests did not want pieces of the post-War treaty reopened, for fear of having *their* pieces of it reopened. The Marid certainly did not want *her* solution to the west coast problems, and nobody but Dur cared about smoke that was mostly landing on the Gan peoples, since they had never signed on to the aishidi'tat.

Ilisidi ruled as aiji-regent through the last of Tabini's minority and through the last years of Wilson-paidhi's service, aided by a Conservative coalition headed by Lord Tatiseigi of the Atageini.

Meanwhile Damiri, now a young woman, disaffected from her Ajuri father and angry, deserted a family outing during the Winter Festivity in Shejidan and presented herself to her influential Atageini uncle, asking to be taken in by Atageini clan. Lord Tatiseigi, who had not sought this, and in fact had only resumed relations with Ajuri at all to further the aiji-dowager's cause, saw in the young woman her mother in her youth. Being himself childless, and the holder of a great political power which teetered constantly on the edge of disaster because of that—he sent a conciliatory letter to the Ajuri lord, saying that he had found the missing young lady, that she was, typical for the child of a contract marriage, having a crisis of man'chi, and that he would be willing to entertain his young niece until she grew equally dissatisfied with the fantasy of life in her mother's clan.

In point of fact—the observation was not a lie. But Lord Tatiseigi likely had no intention of letting the young lady grow dissatisfied with her Atageini heritage. She was indisputably of his bloodline, she was pretty, she was intelligent, certainly enterprising, and he needed an heir, which, bajinaji, he had not produced. The Ajuri marriage originally had had that consideration. If she came still with an unfortunate attachment to Komaji of the Ajuri, he judged that a surmountable difficulty. The Atageini were richer, more powerful, had a stronger influence in government, and if the young lady attached man'chi to him rather than to Komaji, he might have what he greatly needed.

So things ran for that year. Tabini passed his twenty-third year.

And finally, mustering an unlikely but temporary coalition of the Taibeni, the Kadagidi, the Marid, the mountain clans, and the Northern Association—Ajuri was all too ready to support anybody but the aiji-dowager, who was Tatiseigi's political patron—Tabini was elected aiji in his own right.

People feared there might be a confrontation—extending even to armed conflict and the breakup of the aishidi'tat if the aiji-dowager would not relinquish power. Some even feared humans would take advantage of such a conflict and attack the mainland. People were storing food in their houses and the requests to the Assassins' Guild for hired protection in such an event were reportedly unprecedented.

The aiji-dowager and Tabini-aiji, however, appeared together on that new and still-rare medium, television, as well as radio, and the aiji-dowager congratulated her grandson on his election and wished him well.

The aishidi'tat, and indeed, the human population on Mospheira, breathed a sigh of relief. Wilson-paidhi, notorious for granting Valasi whatever he wanted, to the extent the aiji-dowager feared a human plot to undermine atevi morals, withdrew from public life entirely, in deep disfavor with, now, the new aiji, and wanting only to get off the continent alive.

The aiji-dowager retired to Malguri, with occasional visits to her apartment in the Bujavid, visits notable for their tension and difficulty.

Tabini, as aiji, did as he had said he would do: he dropped the environmental matters—telling his grandmother he would revive that negotiation once Wilson-paidhi finally retired, a decision he was trying to hasten. Tabini also conducted several actions designed to protect the west coast from the Marid's ambition, including a promise to the Marid to protect their shipping from piracy—and he used that as a pretext for an order increasing the size and armament of the Mospheiran navy, incidentally strengthening his position regarding Mospheira.

He needed the Conservatives on board, and found his opportunity to gain the man'chi of the aiji-dowager's chief ally, Lord Tatiseigi—when he met Tatiseigi's niece, Damiri.

Wilson-paidhi retired. Tabini-aiji was far from a technophobe, and had always a deep interest in technology of every sort, different from Valasi-aiji, who had primarily pressed Wilson-paidhi for things his advisors thought might lead to better armaments—wires were one such development. And in this he differed from Ilisidi, who deeply distrusted and despised everything human, and who had mostly treated Wilson-paidhi as an adversary—one she had to force to carry her ecological concerns to human authorities, and whom she considered utterly and foundationally unreliable.

There was a crisis looming in the Marid, and a report of a suspected fracture in human politics—possibly worse if fed by what Wilson-paidhi could say, once he began to talk to his superiors and possibly to persons less discreet. Nobody had ever trusted Wilson-paidhi. No one could tell whether Wilson-paidhi was having a good day or not. After Wilson-paidhi's decades on the continent—as a translator—nobody on this side of the straits could tell what Wilson-paidhi thought, what he felt, what he was reporting to his government, whether it was accurate or whether Wilson-paidhi even knew whether it was. No one had been able to tell, especially lately, whether Wilson-paidhi was, in fact, an enemy or outright unbalanced. Some of his actions had given the latter impression . . . and in fact there had been some suggestion that the wisest course for Tabini-aiji to take on Wilson-paidhi's retirement was to have Wilson-paidhi meet an accident while he was still in reach, and before a madman reached the island enclave and began to report imaginary wrongs and insane plots.

He might be served the wrong sauce at dinner, perhaps, or tread on a waxed marble step. The man was fragile as porcelain, and moved like it. He had no bodyguard. He was entirely undefended, and Tabini-aiji personally doubted the humans on Mospheira would raise too great a fuss about losing a man who was, after all, on his way out and more than a little strange.

Tabini-aiji made up his mind, however, to send Wilson-paidhi home unscathed, and not to begin his new relationship with humans, about whom he was intensely curious, with an assassination—or to initiate a crisis which might have the humans *declining* to send a paidhi without certain assurances. That could lead to a serious crisis in international affairs, and if he ever granted any assurances, it would set a very bad precedent. A diplomatic standoff would not be a good beginning at all . . . not for an aiji who wanted concessions from humans.

Tabini-aiji even assigned two of his personal bodyguards to get Wilson-paidhi safely onto a plane, against the not-too-unlikely chance that some other power—such as the aiji-dowager—might decide Wilson should not report all the details of his dealings with her.

Tabini-aiji could not be sure what humans would send him: another old stick of a man like Wilson-paidhi. A determined ideologue. A person with an agenda of his own.

He was absolutely delighted to have a paidhi his own age. And one who *spoke,* more to the point, without writing things down and consulting his dictionary.

Before, however, any sort of relationship could develop,

given the situation Tabini-aiji was hearing about on Mospheira, and the situation in the Marid, and his own contemplated relationship with Lord Tatiseigi's niece—he needed to enlist Ilisidi, who had reared him, not as his potential adversary, but as an ally.

She had retired to Malguri, that ancient fortress, holding occasional meetings with her Eastern neighbors, meetings regarding him, he was sure.

Someone made an attempt on the new paidhi's life.

Tabini-aiji was far from surprised that would happen. He had assigned the new paidhi bodyguards. He had given the new paidhi a very illegal firearm and seen to it the new paidhi had at least rudimentary instruction in using it and hitting a target.

Tabini-aiji had made himself look as innocent of any harm to the paidhi as he could possibly look, inviting the paidhi to a retreat at the Taibeni lodge he favored for brief holidays, making him a personal guest—which would signal *most* people inclined to make a move against the paidhi that they would have him to deal with.

His grandmother had, however, said she would like to talk to the new paidhi. His grandmother was undoubtedly expecting Tabini to keep his word and open a discussion with Mospheira about the smoke.

And if there was one person who could breach his grandmother's private fortress at Malguri—and convince his grandmother that they were dealing with somebody very different from Wilson-paidhi—it was the person about whom she was most curious.

He attached bodyguards—and sent the new paidhi to the aiji-dowager.

He knew his grandmother very well. He had gained her attention.

She knew what her grandson was up to. And she came back to Shejidan of her own will, intensely engaged— suspicious, but engaged. And Bren-paidhi was, for his part, likewise engaged.

That engagement completely changed the political landscape. It drew Lord Tatiseigi, however reluctantly, into Tabini's camp—which was doubly convenient. The match with Damiri became possible . . . and that was a more than political matter, which could be done with a contract marriage with or without an heir produced. Tabini-aiji wanted Damiri-daja, not as a contract marriage, but in a way lords rarely arranged their relationships, as a lasting marriage and a lifelong ally.

It complicated matters that Damiri had, predictably, had her differences with her uncle Tatiseigi and gone off to her father now and again. Ajuri was a minor clan, and it was the matter of a little unfortunate public attention. He sent Damiri-daja a letter. He sent one to her father *and* to her uncle. He wanted her to take up residence in Shejidan, with him, he wanted a reconciliation of Ajuri clan with her uncle, and he wanted a formal marriage—

Unwise, his advisors said, pointing out that the Northern Association was not the best bargain on its own, being small and frequently divided into factions, and that Lord Tatiseigi had enemies among the aiji's strong supporters, some of whom had perfectly eligible daughters for perfectly sensible contract marriages.

Besides, such a strong affiliation with Lord Tatiseigi would smell strongly of his giving in to the aiji-dowager and falling under her control. Damiri-daja's youthful actions had gained notoriety, and painted her as a creature of flightiness, shallowness, and hot temper.

Tabini-aiji ignored all of the advisors and married her. The quarrels with his wife matched, in reputation, his quarrels with the aiji-dowager—a fact which leaked out by the ancient sources—servants—and not, thankfully, the news services on the television the Conservatives so despised.

As aiji, he did request restrictions on emissions on Mospheira and Crescent Island. He also instituted air traffic control, greatly antagonizing the number-counters, who were powerful especially in certain regions of the aishidi'tat, and powerful among the Conservatives. He clamped down on the Messengers' Guild, which had developed some internal problems and was under accusation of graft and other misdeeds. He supported regional lords against encroachments by neighbors, stating that land questions had been settled definitively by the charter of the aishidi'tat and he was taking that as the final answer.

He attempted to exert Shejidan's authority over the Marid, which remained a problem. He established a peaceful relationship with the East, under Ilisidi's governance of Malguri.

He gained all sorts of minor concessions from the new paidhi and greatly annoyed the Conservatives by sending blueprints of numerous trivial machines to the Scholars' Guild.

He refused to allow Filing on any monetary matter, until he had had testimony from officials of the Treasurers' Guild. The Assassins' Guild protested its own prerogative. He maintained his position, and the rule held.

And he gained Bren-paidhi's cooperation in increasing his communication with the Mospheiran government, despite the rise of anti-atevi sentiment by certain groups in the island enclave.

iv

<<Bren>> One reason for the stir among the radical groups on Mospheira was precisely the improved relations between the mainland and Mospheira. The radicals wanted separation, not cooperation—and they were increasingly upset by the paidhi's actions. They always made their greatest political gains by alarming the public, and elements of that party took to the airwaves with a campaign of rumor mixed with sufficient facts to make people uneasy. The paidhi at times ran a certain risk in his visits to Mospheira, but Mospheiran tradition forbade any overt display of protection.

v

<<Geigi>> Things were going fairly well, however . . . until without any warning the starship *Phoenix* arrived at the space station. The Mospheirans suddenly found the authority of the ship over their heads and the *Phoenix* captains found that all the humans that should be on the station were down on the planet.

Tabini-aiji suddenly doubted every assurance the Mospheiran government had given him.

vi

<<Bren>> *Phoenix* made radio contact with Mospheira. Liberals were extremely anxious—having no wish to have another argument with a ship authority which had no understanding of them or the atevi.

Radical groups on Mospheira were literally dancing in the streets. They wanted instant access to space—they called it rescue—and they wanted *Phoenix* to threaten the aishidi'tat and remove the Mospheiran government.

The *Phoenix* captains, being no fools, took a look at the cities on both sides of the strait. Their prosperity surpassed any expectation, but their cultural difference was clear, even from space. *Phoenix* received a rational though cautious response from the Mospheiran government, asking who was in command and what their condition was and whether they needed help.

The ship-aijiin overheard the demands of the radicals in their monitoring. They saw nothing on the planet to indicate hostilities except in the radicals themselves.

The government of Mospheira was certainly deeply perturbed at the entry of a new power into their affairs, but they were reassured that *Phoenix* accepted the situation, was not in imminent distress, and was anxious not to involve itself in local politics.

Phoenix was upset that the station was in serious decay—the captains were very anxious to see it operating again. Their interests, they assured Mospheira, were only in their ship and its safety. *Phoenix* wanted a port.

The Mospheiran public, and in fact the government, remained a little fearful that the ship might try to become their government.

That was what the radicals wanted to happen. They saw a return to space as everything they wanted ... including access to advanced weaponry.

The Mospheiran government was equally determined that the people it should send to space, if it could send anyone, would be those most worried about the ship's intentions, the most determined to secure Mospheiran control of the station.

By no means did they want to let the radical groups get into direct association with the *Phoenix* crew.

vii

<<Geigi>> We were highly upset with the sudden turn of events, and suspicion still ran deep. Bren-paidhi assured Tabini-aiji and the aiji-dowager that the Mospheiran government had not expected the return of the ship, and that Mospheira was determined to gain control of the station, preventing the ship from doing so. Mospheira, he said, was determined to prevent the radicals getting to space or laying hands on advanced technology.

He said further that the only way to preserve atevi rights in this situation was for atevi to speak to the ship-folk directly, invite them to negotiate, and make it clear that the local authority was the aishidi'tat, not Mospheira. They should in fact offer to ally with the Mospheirans in their demands for complete control of the station, and be prepared to share that authority with them.

There was one drawback to everybody's plans, of course, and it was an old one. None of the starship pilots knew how to fly in an atmosphere. None of the atevi or Mospheiran pilots, who well knew how to fly in atmosphere and gravity, knew how to fly in space.

There were no ship-construction facilities at the mothballed station, which had no population and no workers.

And critical natural resources necessary to build a spacecraft were available *only* on the mainland. Mospheira had been trading for them—but the mainland could cut that off cold at any time.

Phoenix had the blueprints—the complete library in the data storage of the starship. But atevi had the mines, the factories, and the resources.

Negotiation and unprecedented cooperation between Mospheira and the mainland built a small fleet of shuttles.

Negotiation with the Mospheirans and *Phoenix* gave half the station to atevi, half to humans.

Tabini would ultimately set an atevi lord, myself, Lord Geigi of Maschi clan, to be in charge of the half of the station.

But before that day came a great upheaval.

The technology that came with the shuttle plans brought massive change to the economy of both Mospheira and the mainland. It required new materials, computers, new plants—it brought all manner of things that poured new goods into the hands of Mospheirans. Of course denial of access agitated the radicals of Mospheira, who most wanted to be lords of space—a situation neither the liberal Mospheirans nor any ateva ever wanted to have happen.

But on the mainland, among us, the shock was as much cultural as economic. For two hundred years the paidhiin had carefully brought technology onto the mainland—items like telephones, and, lately, airplanes, plastics, and transistors. These were benign in most ways—beneficial, unless one asked the older folk.

Then the space program poured new materials and new concepts down from the sky, advice telling us where to mine, with new ways of doing so, telling us how to manufacture, and offering us modern ceramics, and even dropping down certain materials from space.

All this challenged us philosophically. Traditional numbers-causality and the mediaeval concept of astronomy met starfaring equations and a universe that clearly did not consist of a clockwork sky dome and an ether that surrounded the sun and planets. That realization upset the Conservatives . . . and the paidhi-aiji had to open a clerical office simply to answer the letters from people asking, for instance, if a shuttle taking off would let the atmosphere escape.

And there was the politics of it all, which fell on Tabini-aiji. Some districts where the ecological impact would be minimal or which had transportation advantages were awarded manufacturing facilities, rousing resentments from those equally deserving who did not get such facilities—and of course there were areas that wanted none of it, and bitterly resented the economic advantage to those who had such industry.

The fractures in atevi society began to multiply.

On both sides of the straits, people found the whole world changing.

Then the ship-captains admitted the existence of another colony out in deep space, their Reunion Station, which they had never mentioned. This was especially disturbing to the Mospheirans. *Phoenix* next confessed that their reason for coming back to the Earth now was a need to put the Reunion population somewhere.

Why? the world asked.

Then *Phoenix* made a third and terrible admission: they had, they said, met hostile strangers in space, who might attack Reunion.

Some on both sides of the strait were inclined to tell *Phoenix* that they regretted the distress of these people very much, but they were not going to give permission to bring the Reunioners to *this* world.

Then *Phoenix* made yet another admission, the infelicitous fourth—that, in its own library, Reunion Station had the location of the atevi sun, and if Reunion fell—the Earth of the atevi might see these hostile strangers arrive here.

viii

<<Bren>> In the urgency of building the shuttle fleet, the mainland had seen change after change, wealth had poured into places of poor land that had not had wealth, and society had become increasingly unstable, but the alternative— having decisions taken in the heavens without atevi participation—was insupportable.

Tabini-aiji had already pushed the citizenry to the limits of their patience when he found out what the ship-folk had confessed. He was angry. And now he was suspicious that neither atevi nor Mospheirans had been given the truth. He decided to take strong action to find out the situation in space, and be sure that things were as the *Phoenix* captains said they were. He charged Bren-paidhi, who knew humans, and the aiji-dowager, who would not be put off with lies, to go find out the truth. And because he now knew that the news of the ship's deception would bring his household increasingly under threat, he sent his son, both to learn the new knowledge, to understand humans, and to be taught by the woman who had taught him.

It was a desperate dice-throw, with no knowledge of the scale of the universe, or the fact that the ship could not communicate across that distance, or how hard and dangerous it would be.

ix

<<Geigi>> Tabini-aiji made a decision that shocked the aishidi'tat and revised all calculations. He set all his scattered household out of reach of his enemies: his son, the

aiji-dowager, who had ruled the aishidid'tat more than once, and the paidhi-aiji, who could understand humans.

He had also set a technologically adept atevi population in the heavens, governed by Lord Geigi, who *had* the ability to reach the Earth if he were given a target and an order.

If he himself were to die, Tabini-aiji reasoned—his grandmother and his son would gain power in the heavens, come back, and take back the aishidi'tat. If they failed to return, then Geigi and the atevi in the heavens would declare an aijinate, contact reliable lords on the Earth, and reshape the aishidi'tat in whatever way it had to be shaped to preserve atevi control of the world.

Tabini-aiji did not, however, intend to die. He had reduced his household by two. He became more cautious, was far less frequently in transit, far less exposed to threats from unstable persons. He had not been advised of any Filings against his supporters, nothing of the sort, even though he daily expected it. He had begun to suspect something was being organized, but if it was, it was not behaving in any legitimate way. It had the flavor of the Marid—but the Marid was troubled by none of the issues that troubled the rest of the aishidi'tat.

He asked the Guild to investigate, and they reported only the usual persons, the usual statements, the usual activities, none of which reached to Shejidan. He relied on the information he was getting from the Guild—and from the ship-paidhi Yolande Mercheson—who may have failed to understand one quiet warning, from a source who did not sign the letter.

The ship left the station. The aiji-dowager, the heir, and the paidhi-aiji went with it, not to return for two years.

But—perhaps it was the note given the ship-paidhi that had alarmed the conspirators, or perhaps the indications that the aiji was taking precautions and might discover who they were: rumors grew more frequent than fact. Some believed humans had kidnapped the dowager and the heir. Some said the ship had never left and they all were dead.

Within the year, the conspirators moved. They intended to assassinate Tabini-aiji in his residence. They discovered he was not there. They correctly guessed he might have gone to Taiben, and they attempted to strengthen their assault there—but that entailed some confusion. Murini of the Kadagidi had already proclaimed himself aiji, and Tabini was not dead. The attacks were simultaneous, to control all means to reach the heavens: the shuttles, the airport at Shejidan, the dish at Mogari-nai. The conspirators seized the shuttles being serviced. And they seized the radio station. They believed that Lord Geigi had thus been removed as a threat, with no means to replace the shuttles or to threaten the world, because they believed there were no mines in the heavens and that there would be no communication with the heavens because they held Mogari-nai.

Tabini and Damiri narrowly escaped from Taiben, but their bodyguards did not.

Rather than go to the neighboring Atageini estate and bring Lord Tatiseigi into danger, too—they crossed the Kadagidi's own territory and used the skills Tabini-aiji had learned in Malguri to hunt and survive, making no contacts at all for a year.

The conspirators were hunting them everywhere they could think of. The last place the Kadagidi expected Tabini-aiji to be was on their own borders.

The atevi on the space station meanwhile began to plot what they could do with only one shuttle, and there was a question of whether to land it on Mospheira and send a mission to contact Tabini-aiji.

But Lord Geigi received repeated assurances from the humans that the aiji-dowager, the heir, and Bren Cameron were going to come back on a certain date, or close to it ... and he argued against risking the one shuttle still in their control. He instead communicated with Mospheira, and with the assistance of Shugart-nadi and other humans, began to build communications and to position certain relay stations, made fearsome and self-defending, to unsettle the regime.

X

<<Bren>> *Phoenix* had reached the Reunioners—and
ended up facing an alien species, the kyo, bent on destruction of the human station which they viewed as an invasion.
Nobody on Reunion had a clue how to open communication with foreigners of any sort. Neither, as happened, had
the kyo themselves any concept of negotiation with outsiders. But having aboard *Phoenix* two species in cooperation,
a skilled translator and diplomat, as well as a revered elder—the aiji-dowager; a child—the aiji's heir; and ship's
personnel who had been living with atevi for a year—all
this was persuasive. Two species working together as we did
completely amazed the kyo. The kyo were willing to ask
questions, particularly by the cooperation of a kyo who had
come to communicate with the aiji's young son. From this
small beginning, each side found out what the other wanted.

It was agreed the Reunioners would be removed and
transported out of kyo territory.

Phoenix did this, partly by force, partly by agreement of
the Reunion population. The library was stripped, the population was removed, and *Phoenix* set out for the Earth of
the atevi. The young gentleman, the aiji's heir, achieved an
education far beyond what the aiji envisioned in sending
him: he dealt with the kyo authorities, became acquainted
with the ship-aijiin, and also with several young Reunioner-
folk, while pursuing his other studies under the personal
supervision of the aiji-dowager—a teaching both traditional and thorough.

xi

<<Geigi>> *Phoenix* returned to the world, and in the same
hour the aiji-dowager learned what had happened in her
absence, that Tabini-aiji had been overthrown.

She did not delay. Lord Geigi urged her to all possible
speed, fearing that Earth-based telescopes would show the

ship docked at the station, and that once their enemies on the planet knew that the ship was back, they would expect the shuttle and know who might be on it.

The aiji-dowager, the aiji's son, and Bren-paidhi took the shuttle which Lord Geigi had kept ready for their return. They landed on Mospheira, then with Mospheiran assistance, crossed onto the continent and went to Taiben and with Taibeni help, went on to Atageini territory.

Lord Tatiseigi opened his doors to them. Murini-aiji had instilled terror in the citizenry, but Lord Tatiseigi aided them with all his resources as the news of their return spread.

Tabini-aiji and Damiri-daja were not far away. They received word and arrived at Lord Tatiseigi's estate.

Terror might have aided Murini at the first, but it had gained nothing but resentment from the citizenry. Once word spread that the aiji and his household were alive, that the humans had kept their word, and that the station aloft and the humans on Mospheira *were* indeed their allies, the people gained the courage to rise up in their hundreds of thousands and support Tabini-aiji and the aiji-dowager.

Unfortunately it was easier to restore the aijinate than to undo the damage Murini had done.